Of Silk and Fang

A Sullivan Chronicles
Adventure

By B. Jeffrey

<u>Sullivan Chronicles</u>
The Hollowing
Of Silk and Fang
Clockwork Clowns (2024)

Of Silk and Fang

A Sullivan Chronicles Adventure

Book 2

B. Jeffrey

Published by B. Jeffrey

www.sullivanchronicles.com

Cover art by Thea Magerand (https://www.ikaruna.eu)

ISBN: 979-8-9856364-4-4

Library of Congress Control Number: 2022922155

Dedications

For my parents who instilled in me the importance of education, of continual learning, continual reading, continual self-reflection; of hard work and never saying the word *can't*, and that a failure is just another opportunity; of knowing when to speak up and speak out, and knowing when to stay quiet and not just listen, but really hear. I may not always succeed, but my parents gave me the tools to realize that the fun is in the journey, and that the journey should never end.

And for all my girls. They're the reason for everything I do.

Prologue

Spot quivered in the dark. He had long since abandoned trying to reach his master. They had been overwhelmed and separated by the hairy horde that stampeded over walls, ceiling, and floor. The creatures had emerged in a deluge from every black tunnel, every tiny hole, every escape route.

The Master had quickly and decisively cleaved a path through the dark caves, retracing their steps to the exit home. His hundreds of whip-like roots had cleared even the largest of monsters—which bulked nearly five times Spot in size—faster than they could attach their sticky anchors. Their jaws and fangs were of no use on the Master's bark, and his sheer mass bowled over their delicate bodies like a boulder through a field of puffwort. He had left a gooey, hairy mess in his wake, and felt no remorse as he progressed along the tunnels to the egress.

For the Master, the creatures were not deadly. They might capture and immobilize him, but they could do no real damage. Eventually, they would tire of chewing on his bark, realize he was of no nutritional value, and forget about him in their insatiable search for sustenance. Once left alone, he could free himself from almost any predicament and be on his way, none the worse for wear. Albeit somewhat irritated at being delayed.

Spot, however, would quickly be recognized as edible; wrapped up, tenderized, stored away until he was nothing but a flimsy bag of juices to be drunk at leisure. And although the Master steamrolled over the endless waves of chittering monsters, he had in no way spared a thought for his trusted pet trailing along in his wake.

His only focus had been the eggs.

Those milky-white orbs, gathered so delicately in a chiffon sack, were cradled tenderly in the Master's limbs, sheltered from the claws, and fangs, and sticky webs that their attackers had employed in attempts to retrieve their unborn offspring—whether to eat or to liberate remained to be seen in this den of cannibals.

Once Spot had helped sniff out the clutch, the Master's attention had turned elsewhere. It was not that he did not care for Spot, in his own way; rather, the Master became extremely focused on his projects, to the detriment of everything else. And his current project involved finding the eggs of these hairy, many-legged nightmares, liberating them from their world to be hatched in a strategic location where they could wreak the most havoc.

That agenda had begun many hours ago with a quest through the magic doorway, directly into the depths of the warren...

...The immediate area around the door was a large cavern with half a dozen surrounding passages. All deserted, dark and silent. It was the suffocating silence that set Spot's nerves on edge. He felt the wrongness of it. No echoes, no wind, no sense of distance. The minute sounds of his padded feet, the Master's roots scraping on the stone floor, every vibration was absorbed immediately, like they were walking through a furry blanket that hovered just inches from their bodies. It gave Spot the feeling of being watched by unseen specters hovering just to the left, or right, or behind, but close enough to reach out and smother him.

The Master grumbled in a resonant rumbling mumble about wisps sticking to his branches and fouling his leaves as he walked. So much so that he ultimately cursed and paused to pull out a bouquet of luminescent saluna leaves from somewhere hidden in his boughs. Their soft green glow shed an eerie light on their surroundings, and Spot was not entirely certain he found the increased visibility reassuring. The light revealed their dire condition, and the reason that echoes died: webs. The passages were plastered in many and varied patterns of silky filaments, ranging in thickness from a strand of fur, to one of Master's smaller roots. They draped the walls, dripped from the ceiling, even bridged their way to the floor. Spot's smaller size, and the fact that he was following the Master, had been the only reasons he was not completely entangled. But the Master looked like a decomposing old tree, turned weather-beaten-gray from age and disease, branches drooping and already a home for the bark beetles and other infestations of dead wood. It was an illusion, of course. He was merely covered in layers of webs dragged from the passageway. Master would live on for many hundreds of seasons.

The webs in the tunnels nearest the doorway were ancient; unused and undisturbed by any creature for decades; caked with eons of dust, fallen rocks and tunnel shards. Spot knew they had to branch out further into the warren to find Master's prize, and so did the Master. He pushed Spot into the lead, encouraging his pet to sniff out the creatures, while he used his roots to keep the webs away from his hound.

It took some time for them to make their way to an area with fresh cables. The instant they did, the smallest of the creatures converged. No bigger than a single pad on one of Spot's flexible toes, they scampered over the floors, dangled above their heads, and frolicked in the layered silk curtains that adorned the walls. The passages had gone from forsaken desolation to uncomfortable overpopulation at the turn of a corner. Thankfully, the Master's light made them skittish. As did, of course, Master's size, plus his numerous and constantly moving appendages.

Even though most creatures ran for cover, Master squashed the slower in droves. Spot, ever mindful of keeping his feet as clean as possible, had hopped and tiptoed around the fuzzy animals. The few he stepped on burst like ripe berries, but with a sickening crunch, and a sticky pale goo, rather than sweet juice. Spot took to sweeping his feet across the ground in a swaying dance, knocking any stragglers from his path, thus sparing not only their lives, but his sensibilities. He also hoped that this small act of kindness might afford him some consideration should the fates turn unkind in this den of horror.

As they traveled deeper into the warren, the creatures became larger. Spot had been uncomfortable with the throng of toe-sized animals, but when those were replaced by the plum-sized, he wanted nothing more than to retreat. The Master, however, was undaunted and pushed on. Plums were replaced by squash; squash supplanted by pumpkins; pumpkins pushed out by those equal to Spot in size.

Distressed was an understatement for Spot's state of mind in the presence of the massive ones, especially since they seemed to grow more aggressive the larger they became, with the bigger eating their smaller kin. There was ample evidence of cannibalism; smaller denizens wrapped in the cocoons of their brethren, hanging in various forms of decomposition, from freshly caught and still twitching, to long since emptied of insides; only a dessicated, crumbling shell left to decompose in their silken prisons.

The Master moved forward without hesitation, encouraging Spot to continue sniffing out the eggs. His only acknowledgement of their situation was to become louder with his roots. He flicked them about, stretched them, wiggled them, swatted them at the creatures. He slapped them on the rocky floor with a noise that even Spot shied away from. The hairy creatures sprang several feet on the diagonal each time the thunder cracked in their vicinity.

Spot's primal instincts told him, in no uncertain terms, that he was in extreme danger, as these creatures could leap three times as far as he could. The Master's size still offered protection, so Spot stayed close, tightly surrounded by Master's ambulatory roots. He was sure it would only be a matter of time before these predators realized that the largest intruder was outnumbered by the hundreds, and could be quickly overwhelmed. It took every ounce of courage Spot could muster to focus on the faint smell of eggs and not the overwhelming aroma of death, decay, monster excretion, and the sickly sweet body odor of these enormous arthropods.

The local denizens grew to twice Spot's size before Spot located the pods. They no longer directly attacked the Master. Neither did they flee in terror and leave the Master in peace. They lurked just out of reach, waiting and watching to see what these intruders would do, wondering how they could capture what clearly must be food enough to sustain them for some time.

The Master wasted no time once he saw the egg pods hanging from the ceiling. He whipped forward a root, yanked the sack of unhatched creatures from its perch, then turned and fled back the way they had come with an undulating gate, uncommonly graceful and fast for one of such immense proportions. Spot quickly fell outside Master's protective limbs, surprised by the unexpected retreat. He immediately bounded after the Master; the monstrous inhabitants immediately pursued. Spot was unsure whether they were upset about their young being stolen, or their food escaping. Either way, he did not want to be left behind.

The jumpers converged first. Large bodies scampered along every surface, black shadows against the pale gray silk surroundings. They were faster than Master, whose bulk blocked Spot from racing ahead. They brought their assault like hyenas in a pack, pouncing onto his back, attacking his trunk, working hard to get their fangs through his branches and into his bark, still not understanding that it would do them no good. Even if they could penetrate his outer shell—it was very dense and unyielding—their venom would likely have no effect on his metabolism. But they did not know that, so they continued to cling and climb, claw and bite.

The Master barely slowed with their added weight. He set a few limbs and roots to the task of swatting, plucking, knocking, even stabbing at the attackers, and they fell away as fast as they had attached.

Spot was forced into acts of acrobatics in order to remain free. He jumped over falling bodies, dodged attackers that sprang for him, and used the Master's bulk and defensive actions to block approach from other angles. He called on every instinct, used every bit of skill and reflex to just stay alive and keep moving. He did not think. He just moved.

They fought their way down several tunnels in this manner, probably made it at least halfway back to their exit before Spot was overwhelmed. At an intersection of passages, Spot was knocked sideways by an attacker; an anonymous brown blob of fur and legs that careened into him, bowled him over, and pushed him down a smaller side passage. On a positive note, the marauding hordes continued following the Master, unaware or uncaring that Spot had disappeared from the melee. He was left with only one attacker, which proved difficult enough to deal with. Its front legs worked hard to clamp onto him, while its jaws tried to stab, and its hind legs were busy pulling silk from its spinnerets to gum up Spot's hind quarters.

But Spot was just as agile, and his feet more nimble. He used his unique paws and the strong digits of his rear feet to grasp those hind legs and turn them back on their owner. The creature found itself in a web of its own making, rear appendages quickly trussed like a calf in a rodeo. Still dealing with the deadly front end of the monster, Spot pulled no punches. Free to use his hind legs for leverage, he flipped himself and his enemy over. He then had the high ground, and the anchorage. He kept a firm grip on two of the arthropod's front legs, lept and twisted over the rotund abdomen to land on the opposite side, and with a downward force, snapped the weaker bones in the creature's legs. It let out a squeal of pain while its remaining limbs flailed about, losing any interest in grasping prey.

Spot immediately fled, not wasting another second standing still, waiting for another attacker to find him. He shot down the smaller tunnel, away from the larger creatures, knowing he was already woefully lost to his Master.

One last look behind revealed that his foe, in its incapacitated state, was quickly being overwhelmed by its smaller cousins. Dozens of the squash-sized creatures were descending from holes and tiny tunnels to take advantage of what would probably be the best meal in their lifetimes. The larger creature was being quickly shrink-wrapped, immobilized and dragged off for slow tenderization in some deep, dark hole. Spot would have felt bad for the creature if it had not been trying to do the same thing to him only moments before.

Spot remained free of pursuit from that point on. At least free from the larger, more threatening beasts. The smaller ones were still everywhere, but they fled at Spot's presence, albeit only to a distance safe from being trampled. Spot was sure they followed, keeping tabs, hoping he was injured enough that they could eventually feast on his weakened carcass. No matter. He was still uninjured, and was making his way closer to the level where the doorway home should be. He followed his nose to the smell of fresher air, free from the petrifying stench of fresh webbing, numbing toxins, and recent scat. His sniffer faithfully led him through the zone of the tiniest of the horrible creatures, back to the tunnels full of dust, and void of activity, back to the area he knew he had traveled only hours before.

However, it was no longer deserted. Spot kept to the smaller tunnels, quietly prowling along, using his ears and nose to their full abilities. He could hear, and smell the larger creatures scrambling around in the big tunnels. They seemed agitated and full of anxious energy. But Spot did not hear sounds of them subduing prey. He heard nothing that sounded like Master thrashing or fighting, or being captured, so he risked a peek from his hidden tunnel, and his excellent predatory night vision enabled him to see the doorway he had been searching for, closed and locked, surrounded by the largest creatures who had clearly followed the Master here, then lost him as he had escaped through the portal. Fortunately for the Master, his hunters were not intelligent enough to open the door themselves. Master was free, and probably not giving a single thought more for this world, or for his lost pet.

Spot slunk quietly back down his side tunnel until he found a nice cubby where he could remain hidden, but see in all directions. He decided to rest and wait. Surely the creatures would tire and return to their own level, where food was more plentiful. When they did, he would slip back to the doorway and make his way home. He *would* make it. He just had to be patient.

He settled in and did his best to stay quiet, remain alert, and stave off panic. As it turned out, he had a long time to wait.

—1—

Planning

"Calliope, have you seen the lantern flashlight," Ben called up the stairs to his daughter, who was still pouting in her room.

"I have no idea what you're talking about," came the sing-song snarky reply, muffled by her closed door.

"Of course not," Ben sighed to himself and ran a half-frustrated hand across his clean-shaven head.

He understood Calliope's frustration. He knew that if the roles were reversed—she the parent and Ben was her son—there was no way he would be left behind while she went on another adventure to Quilium, the sprite homeworld. And Calliope was for sure her father's daughter. At least in respect to her sense of adventure and confidence in her abilities. That apple had not fallen far from the tree. Fortunately, even ironically, now that Ben analyzed the situation, her actual capabilities—both physical and mental—had proven to surpass even her own imaginings, while Ben's track record was less than stellar. On three separate occasions, he had traveled through the City of Doors to another world, and each journey, while exciting, and adventurous, and illuminating, had also been harrowing, and dangerous, and had landed him in very hot water.

His trek to the first world (when he had no concept of what the doors in The City were capable of, or the feat he had accomplished upon crossing the threshold), had dropped him into a mountain greenhouse resplendent with views of a lush land, incredible plants, and unbelievable animals. Unfortunately, it was also home to formidable, inhospitable creatures called Tree Lords; one of which had immediately captured and imprisoned Ben.

While he managed to escape his prison cell with relative ease (he was rather proud of his lassoing and knife throwing demonstrations during that event), upon sneaking away, he had almost immediately crawled into a toxic shrub, poisoning himself to incapacitation. A bit of good fortune saw him saved by a much friendlier otherworldly creature; an animal that, from a distance, Ben had mistakenly thought was a cross between a small lion and a bird. He had assigned it an informal classification of blinx (bird-lynx), before a closer inspection revealed it was more lemur than bird. Its "feathers" had actually been a mane of strangely-shaped, forest-green strands of fur. In that field of green, however, had been a single speck of brown, which had enticed Ben to name his new friend Spot.

After Spot had saved him from the poisoning, more calamity had ensued, which Ben was still trying hard to purge from memory. Ultimately, it led to him fleeing for his life from that planet, with the Tree Lord in hot pursuit. His only salvation had been hiding for a short time on a second world, which had turned out to be home to another tree-like species: the sprites.

Unfortunately, for them, the Tree Lord had followed Ben to their planet, and while Ben had eluded his hunter and managed to return home with no further damage to himself, the Tree Lord had taken an interest in Quilium, and brought with it a deadly fungus that had quickly decimated the sprite population.

The ramifications of that second, albeit brief, adventure had been for the sprites to seek justice, or atonement, or maybe revenge, for their saddening losses. They had come to Earth, kidnapped Ben's daughter and her friend Stephanie, originally to force his return to stand trial of some sort, but later to fulfill his promise of bringing a cure for their plague.

That third trip to another world began as a mission to rescue the girls. However, an unexpected invasion by a new foe—the mountain cave-dwelling, leech-like Slizeg creatures—had put the kibosh on that plan. Ben, and Stephanie's mother Emily, had been swept up in that new war, quickly captured and dropped into a disgusting pit deep under the enemy's mountain.

It had been Calliope and Stephanie that had turned the tables and rescued the adults. They had befriended a more-than-capable amalgam of friends from various sprite communities; colorful characters with complimenting talents and a curious blend of personalities. They had orchestrated not only an escape for Ben and Emily, but set in motion the means of rescuing almost all the sprites, and defeating their slimy enemy in record time. It was another blow to Ben's success record, but a solid gold medal and resounding win for Calliope and Stephanie.

This, of course, was Calliope's most powerful argument for why she should be allowed to go with Ben when he returned to the sprite world to deliver more "medicine" and visit with their new sprite friends. But no self-respecting parent would take their child, willingly, into the same life-threatening situation they had just barely escaped only a few weeks ago. Ben continually explained to Calliope that this trip back would allow him to assess the situation, to see how the sprites were coping with their slimy foe, and whether their infections were under control.

Ben had kept his promise to his sprite friend, Garran, and returned after a two week hiatus. Garran had met him just outside the huge copper doorway on their planet, and given Ben an update. The Slizeg were still sending out nightly raiding parties. It turned out, they had more than just the one tunnel from their underground lair, and had been wreaking havoc on the other side of the mountain range, as well as to the north. Tormad and clan Darroch had sent emissaries to sprite villages in the north and east of the mountains, spreading word of both tactics to use against the Slizeg, and cures for their deadly fungus. It was slow going, and spreading sprite resources thin.

Garran admitted that it was still not safe to travel without a large security detail, and suggested that Ben return home and check back. They set up a recurring, two week meeting for information swap, and for Ben to bring samples of different fungicides, and even a few fertilizers to augment their recovery process. The Dangjong sprites—a monk-like healing community from the mountain regions—latched onto these curatives with gusto and an intellectual interest that bespoke their ever curious and studious natures. They took meticulous notes of how much to use for what symptoms, effects, side-effects, timing, dosage, and much more. They had already been world renowned healers, but now their reputations catapulted to miracle workers. And for the bringing of these remedies, Ben had gone from destructor to honored ally.

Ben's next trip was quickly approaching, so he was prepping his gear with the normal ritual. It was his packing which had triggered Calliope's current mood. Her opinion was that if this was just a check-in meeting, there was no danger, and no reason she should not be allowed to come. Ben's reasoning was that there *was* still a dangerous element on Quilium, which was why this was only a check-in meeting, and he would not put her in danger. Parental logic and child logic were often at loggerheads.

The plan was for Ben to leave in two days, but first, he had Calliope's birthday party to orchestrate. He would have a house full of twelve-year-old girls, plus a few parents, eating pizza, cake, and ice-cream by this time tomorrow, and he had a lot of cooking to do.

Of course, Ben was no stranger to a kitchen. He had earned money during and after college by working his way through every position in a restaurant; from busboy, to short order cook, to manager. Somewhere along the way, he had picked up the baking bug. He loved the fact that he could feed Calliope meals created from scratch, no preservatives, simple ingredients, and very healthy. Many a Sunday morning had started with silver dollar buckwheat pancakes, mini omelets loaded with veggies, and a bowl of fresh fruit.

Thanks to a fancy bread machine that had been a gift from his wife, years ago, they tried a new bread recipe every week. But one staple the bread machine cranked out regularly was pizza dough. Once Ben had figured out that magical recipe, they had never ordered another pizza. Everyone enjoyed customizing their own, from thin crust to deep dish, and the smell as they baked in the oven was amazing. So, for Calliope's birthday party, he had three large pizzas to make, fresh fruit to clean and cut, and a very special cake to bake. That was going to be his pièce de résistance. It was a cake that Calliope and her friend Stephanie would instantly recognize and appreciate, but everyone else would probably see as a bit strange.

Ben set the bread machine to working on the first batch of pizza dough, then ambled to the basement to finish packing his gear. Maybe he had left that flashlight in the wine cellar. There was also a chance he had left it on Quilium. That was the last place he remembered using it. He still had his headlamp, but he liked the lantern-style flashlight when camping. No matter. There was an old clunky one gathering dust in the basement. If he couldn't find his favorite, he would snatch the spare. It was just another quick information swap with Garran. He probably wouldn't need a camp light, anyway.

****

Calliope stuffed the flashlight into her backpack, and once again tucked a blonde ringlet lock of hair behind her ear in a frustrated maneuver. She was not sure why she was prepping her gear for a trip. She knew her dad was not going to give in and let her come. Not this time, anyway. She just felt like she needed to do something, to move towards going back, even if the gesture was only a token.

The doorbell sounded its flatly mechanical gong and pulled Calliope from her discontented musings. The first of her party guests had arrived one day early. It had to be Grandpa Chicken—so nicknamed because he had a small flock of chickens to give him fresh eggs every day. When Calliope was little, that was how she differentiated her two sets of grandparents; Grandpa Chicken was Ben's dad, Samantha's dad was Grandpa Fish, since he was always fishing. It was way more fun and descriptive than using their real names: Nigel and Noah, respectively. Plus, for a toddler, it was less confusing than two names that alliterated.

Samantha's parents lived in Northern Minnesota. They usually drove over for Calliope's birthday, too, but this year they couldn't make it. That worked out well for Ben. With all the strange happenings of a doorway to another world being in his basement, fewer house guests would be much less stressful. Out of necessity, Ben had to let his own dad in on the basement secret, but he did not want the circle of trust to get any bigger.

Calliope heard the front door open, and her dad greeted her grandpa. She finished tucking and organizing the contents of her backpack, cinched it closed, and jammed it deep into the back of her closet. It was well camouflaged behind hanging clothes, a bin full of too-small outfits headed for charity, and an overflowing shoe rack.

With covert preparations on track, she headed downstairs to say hello. She expertly hopped over a stack of clean laundry waiting on step four, then leapt from step three and stuck the landing with a thud.

"Grandpa!" Calliope rushed into the kitchen and gave her grandfather a hug. "What did you bring me?"

"Happy birthday, Calliope Anne." Her grandfather was a bear of a man. An inch or two shorter than Ben's six-feet, but broader across the chest and shoulders, and still working the sinew and muscle of a man constantly doing physical labor, even into retirement. Adding to his vigorous appearance, he had also held onto his thick, dark hair, now salted in spots with white. A marked contrast to Ben's shaven pate.

Nigel returned his granddaughter's hug. "Your birthday's not until tomorrow, so you'll have to wait for me to pre*sent* your *pres*ent." He accentuated the phonetic differences on the two words, causing an obliging groan from his granddaughter.

"Good one, grandpa," she flowed through the stereotypical eye roll, disengaged from the hug, snagged an orange from the ever-full bowl on the table, and said, "Well, then, since I cannot have my *pres*ent at pre*sent*, I'm off to my room. I'm sure you two have lots to talk about." She turned a snooty, clearly affected aloof tone to them both, gave a regal, chin-up farewell, "Father. Grandfather," then left for her pre-teen sanctuary.

"Nicely done, granddaughter!" Nigel called to her retreating back. Then he turned to his son. "What was that all about?"

"It's a long story, Dad, and why I asked you to come down a day early. How about we grab a cup of coffee and I'll tell you everything."

"It's *that* serious that it needs coffee?" Nigel quipped.

"It's that serious that it needs a good Scotch," Ben stated with seriousness, "but it's way too early in the day for that, so..."

Ben started his tale the same way he had recounted it to Calliope and Stephanie, what seemed like a year ago, before the sprites had kidnapped them. He told his dad about the original fishing trip, following Spot the Blinx to the hidden cave and its giant portal to the City of Doors, then of all the adventures that followed. And just like Emily, Stephanie's mother, Nigel was understandably skeptical.

"It's all true, grandpa!" came Calliope's muffled yell from her room. Ben shook his head in fatherly exasperation as he was reminded of how well sound traveled through the air ducts from the kitchen to Calliope's room directly above. He should have known she would be listening in.

"And don't forget to tell him how Stephanie and I saved you and Emily, dad!"

"I was getting to that part, smarty-pants," Ben shot back. He resumed his tale, making sure to accurately, and proudly, relay the heroics of Calliope and Stephanie.

"So, that's it, dad. That's why I wanted you down here early. I'm going back in a few days, just for a check-in, but pretty soon I'll be going to Quilium for a week, and I'd sure appreciate it if Calliope could stay with you while I'm gone. She can help with the chickens, chop firewood, play in the woods, and keep her mind off not being able to travel back with me."

"Well, of course she can stay with me. I'd love the time with my granddaughter. But, criminy, Ben! This is a lot to take in. I mean... It's in your basement?! Right now? Down there?" He pointed to the basement door.

"Down there." Ben nodded. "You want to see it? I can take you into the City of Doors and show you a few, but we won't travel anywhere. It's still too dangerous."

"Yes." Nigel said with fervor. "Hell yes!"

"Hey eavesdropper!" Ben directed his yell at the air duct. "You want to take your grandfather to meet Poppie?"

There was a banging of doors, a rumble of young feet on the stairs, and mere seconds before Calliope sprang into the kitchen, fully clothed in her travel pants, hiking boots, t-shirt, and small backpack. She snatched three oranges from the bowl, dropped them in the pack, grabbed a water bottle from the fridge, added a few granola bars, then zipped the pack closed.

"Ready," she said, with her most business-like face and relaxed stance, one finger hooked on the backpack strap, the other in her pants pocket.

Ben and Nigel stood frozen in identical poses, eyebrows raised, mouths open in incredulity.

"What?" Calliope asked in response to their look.

"Well, I do wish you would prepare a bit more for traveling," Ben quipped, as he shook off his surprise.

"Ha, ha," Calliope mocked. "You know as well as I, that anything can, and does, happen when we walk through those doors, dad. I'm not going in there again without a little preparation. At the very least, I'm wearing good shoes this time." She wriggled her toes in her Merrell hiking boots.

"Uh, should I gear up as well?" asked her grandfather.

"Well," Ben contemplated, "she has a point. As do the Boy Scouts. 'Be prepared.' We should probably all grab a small pack and some provisions. If anything were to happen, and we got separated, a pack with some food and water would be a comfort."

Ben popped into the basement store room, grabbed two day-trip backpacks and returned to the kitchen, adding snacks and water to each, as Calliope had done.

"I think that oughta do it for food. I don't plan on going in far. Just a look-see to show grandpa that we're not crazy."

"Too late," said Nigel. "I already know you're both nuts. But that's what makes you so interesting." He smiled and patted his granddaughter on the shoulder.

Ben led the way to the basement, making one final stop in the storage room. A plastic, triple drawer unit—one of those inexpensive, all-purpose, flimsy units ubiquitously found in college apartment bathrooms, garages, and under sinks—held collections of useful gadgets. The first he opened held various sizes of flashlights and headlamps. Calliope's was noticeably absent. Ben's was already in his pack, so he just grabbed one for Nigel.

The next drawer held an assortment of compasses, braided paracord wristbands, and whistles. The purposes of the compass and whistle were obvious, and the wristbands could be unbraided to get nine feet of strong cord that had a thousand uses. It could even be pulled apart in layers to tease out finer threads, useful for fishing line, sewing, binding branches, the list went on. Nigel, having been a Marine for a dozen years, had taught his son, and then his granddaughter, many of those tricks. It was amazing how many ways a three dollar bracelet could save your life.

Ben's pack and Calliope's always had these essentials, but he grabbed one of each for Nigel's pack.

"One can never be too careful," he told his dad.

The third drawer held different fire starters: flint and steel, tins with stormproof matches, even a fancy fire piston made of aircraft aluminum, complete with tinder and carrying case.

"Just in case," he added, handing a flint and steel to his dad. "It weighs little enough. No reason not to take it."

"Right," Nigel drawled, sardonically. "Just an ordinary trip through a magical door to another planet. What more could we possibly need? I mean, we have a whistle!" He held up his dollar store plastic prize. "And it's yellow!"

"Don't worry, grandpa," Calliope patted him on the arm and gave him a comforting smile. "I'll protect you."

"I know you will, kiddo." Nigel winked at his granddaughter.

"Ok, let's do this," Ben said, leading them to the wine cellar at the back of the basement.

Ben had made some improvements to his basement wine room. He had replaced the old, light, wooden door with a custom safe door, just like one would find in a jewelry store or a bank vault in an old western. It was slightly wider than a normal door, coated in glossy black paint with a single gold pinstripe near the edge, which flowed into a decorative flourish at the corners. From the center sprouted a five prong handle, and above that was a round faceplate with keypad and small display screen.

Around the door, the once stick-frame and gypsum board walls had been replaced by poured concrete, faced with large, tan travertine tiles. The whole effect was one of a Tuscan vault for an Italian wine collector. And it did still hold wine, though nothing requiring such elevated security.

Ben avoided the door at first, and walked over to a small workstation in the corner. There sat a narrow desk, something Ben had built with rustic design out of reclaimed barnwood, in keeping with the Old-World feel, that held a large monitor and keyboard. He quickly typed in a password and the screen split itself into eight separate camera angles. The first two showed the inside of the wine vault, a view from opposing corners. The next five displayed different sections of a strange and irregular looking hallway wrapped in almond-colored rattan wicker-work—this being the tunnel Ben had described to his father. The final rectangle spotlighted a heavy steel door with all of its gears and locking bars immobile and engaged.

"Wow," said Nigel, "you've been busy."

"After we returned, I didn't waste any time securing the entrance. I tore down my old wine room, concealed the hole in my foundation, then had a crew come in and build my new wine vault. I put the security cameras in myself and hooked it all up so I can remotely view the inside from this station, my laptop, or even my cell phone. There's another, lighter steel door that blocks the entrance to the tunnel, but if anything were to make it through that, it should never make it out of the vault. Of course, I don't have any way to force it back down the tunnel, but I'm working on that. Maybe a fire suppression system that sucks out oxygen, but some creatures, like sprites, don't necessarily need to breathe. I don't want to set things on fire, but maybe I could turn the heat up to uncomfortable levels. Most likely, I'll have to come up with a combination of systems for different scenarios. Until then, I'm trusting that the City of Doors stays deserted, and nothing ever comes our way."

"Sounds to me like the best security would be to destroy the portal, collapse the tunnel and seal up your basement," said Nigel.

"The thought has crossed my mind, dad," said Ben. "But, I have to admit, the place is amazing, and the prospects of visiting other worlds, meeting other creatures, like the sprites, is too compelling. You'll see."

"You really will," Calliope assured her grandfather. "You'll meet Poppie and that'll be enough to make you want to keep coming back."

"Well, then," said Nigel, "let's get this show on the road."

Ben gave his daughter a wink, then moved to the vault door. A few quick taps on the keypad, a spin of the handle, a light tug, and the eight inch thick door swung open. Nigel gave a low "whoa" as he scanned the eighteen impressive locking bolts that had retracted into the door.

In the room, Ben had restored his wine racks on all sides, had included a small tasting station in the right hand wall, and even placed a small cafe table with two wrought iron and wood chairs, in the corner. The room itself looked like a typical wine room, nothing out of the ordinary.

"There's a tablet over here, in case the sprites come through and need to contact us. I showed Garran how to use it, but since their fingers are wood, they have to use the stylus I clipped to the side. They can tap a button to ring a doorbell, or use voice commands to dictate an email in case we're not home when they come. It's all pretty well automated. They're catching on to our tech pretty fast."

Ben quickly made his way to the back wall, and tugged a fake bottle near the bottom row. There was a click, and the entire center section of the wine rack moved, just a bit. Ben pulled on the right side, to swing the rack open on silent hinges. Behind that, was another, unadorned, steel door, painted flat black. This one had a recessed hand grip, and several flat slide mechanisms—two at the top, two at the bottom—that secured the door with steel bolts into the concrete. Ben flipped them all open, and pulled.

The other side was pretty much how Calliope remembered it; like walking inside a living, woven wood basket. The only additions were the cleverly hidden cameras and very tiny LED lights at the ceiling. Ben touched a sensor pad in the wall, and a soft white light illuminated the tunnel.

"Voila!" Ben said. "The living tunnel."

"Holy cats," breathed Nigel. "This is some amazing construction. Look at the weaving of the wood. That's going to be incredibly strong. And you say this was grown?"

"Completely grown," said Ben. "And still growing, as far as I know. These are roots from still-living plants. The sprites just...'asked' them to grow in this way."

"Man, what our world would look like if we had the ability to do that," said Nigel.

"It would certainly give new meaning to the term 'Eco-friendly building'," said Ben.

They continued down the tunnel, under the arching canopy of the walnut tree's roots, which elicited another gasp from Ben's father. The once blonde of new-growth roots had since deepened closer to chocolate with caramel swirls, and their size had grown as well. Above the humans' heads were dozens of supports as large as Ben's thighs, looking far more graceful than any log cabin's truss system. Ben suspected that being still alive, those roots would also prove to be much stronger than conventional lumber. Maybe, once Quilium's hazards had been eliminated, Ben would ask the sprites to grow a cabin for Calliope and him in the woods near a good fly fishing river. Maybe someday.

The group continued through the lengthy section that cut diagonally under the school soccer field, and finally emerged into the portal chamber. The walls still held their artwork of strange flowering ferns growing without light, filtering the air, and perfuming it with an aroma of fresh jasmine.

"Here it is," said Ben, pointing to the door. Calliope looked at her grandfather and waited.

Nigel studied the door from a distance, taking in the decorative elements: the large florette at the base, the heavy metal studs along the edges, triangular vine designs at the corners, and gears and screws along the top. He noted the surrounding frame, all matching, mottled, silvery metal. No rust or pits, but perfectly smooth in cloudy tones of steely-gray. He wondered how far it really extended, as it disappeared unevenly into the clay after only a yard or so on either side of the door.

"It looks like you stumbled across a World War II bomb shelter," said Nigel.

"That it does," agreed Ben.

"Well," said Calliope, "are we going through, or what?" She had that impish grin that told Ben she was ready to take over this tour and show her grandfather who was the real adventurer in the family.

Ben walked over and spun the handle. "There's no camera for the other side. I tried, but there was no way to get a cable through, and—not surprisingly, really—wireless signals don't come back. Cell phones don't work once you walk through, either."

"I guess that's to be expected, if you really are traveling to another planet. You would have to have one heck of a long distance calling plan," joked Nigel.

Ben pulled the door open and stepped through. Once he was completely inside, the familiar amber lighting began to glow around the ceiling edges. On his last trip, Ben had collected his own steampunk pin from one of the many dispensers architected into the walls of this strange underground city. They still theorized it was underground due to the lack of windows, plus the assumption that the whole building had been "grown" like the doorway they had just traversed.

Calliope was on his heels and already calling for her mechanical friend. "Poppie! We're back! Poppie, can you give us some help?" she called into the air.

"Give her a few minutes, and she'll be here," she told the men. "She usually goes back to her chamber, much deeper in. That seems to be her main home, although she did wait for us up in that corner perch, once." She indicated the fleur-de-lis decorated cube at the ceiling.

Nigel poked around the room while they waited. He peered down the hallways, inspected the spiral staircase leading up, appraised the embossed design of Calliope's school on the back of the doorway home. All the details of Ben's unbelievable story were unfolding in incredible reality for him. Ben knew how overwhelming this could be, but his dad was taking it all in stride, as Ben knew he would. Ever the stoic.

It was not long before they heard Poppie's whirring and clicking echoing down from the spiral staircase. Calliope skipped over and greeted her at the railing.

"Poppie!"

"Pop, pop, pop, pop" came her strange friend's excited reply. The tiny flying fairy executed her usual greeting of a few happy pirouettes above their heads, then relaxed into a flutter in front of Calliope's face. Calliope copied her friend's dance, and ended with a giggle.

"I missed you, Poppie. And we brought someone for you to meet." She pointed at Nigel. "This is my grandfather. He is my dad's dad. If that makes sense to you?"

"Pop."

The fairy's gears spun up and she fluttered over to Nigel. She gave him a robotic bow and head nod in greeting.

Nigel marveled at the flying animatron, her numerous tiny gears, sprockets, pistons and pulleys, all spinning and whirring and working at this function or that. Her softly-glowing amber wings were a blur behind her. He noted the exquisite detail and realism of her head, with pixie haircut and tiny ears, almond eyes and button nose, and that shy smile that garnered instant affability.

"It's a pleasure to meet you, Miss Poppie. Thank you very much for befriending my granddaughter and leading her out of this maze."

"Pop," the fairy replied.

"Well, what should we show your grandfather?" Ben asked Calliope.

"Hmmm. Let me think." Calliope took a few seconds to muse, then, "I know! Let's take him to *Intersection Spring*. He'll get to see some rotundas, a bunch of doors, and the basics of this place."

"Good idea. And it's not too far in, so we can go and return in a little over an hour," Ben said. He turned to his dad and explained, "It's one of the few places where rock is exposed—which is why we're guessing we're underground—and clean spring water cascades down to fill tiny basins before disappearing into cracks in the floor. And it's at an intersection of hallways; hence the name."

"Not very creative," joked Nigel.

Ben shrugged. "Lead the way, kiddo."

Calliope confidently headed up the spiral staircase, Poppie hovering above her, Nigel and Ben following behind. Her controller pin was doing its job of turning the lights off and on, so the next level came to life as the lower died. The glow from the chandelier illuminated the dusty stone staircase, which was devoid of any sprites on this trip. Not for the first time, Ben considered bringing a mop and bucket of soapy water with him to rescue the inky granite from its shroud of dust. And the cobwebs were getting worse, too. He didn't remember them being this bad on his last trip. In fact, he couldn't remember if he had ever seen cobwebs in here. Maybe some furry little creatures were creeping in on his visits. It wouldn't take long for those little guys to make themselves at home. However, Ben had never seen other insects in here, either, so he wasn't sure how long spiders would survive without food.

Calliope bounded up the regal staircase, not allowing her grandfather much time to explore the second level. She found the third level, with its ornate, silver inlay map and guiding street signs, to be much more interesting. Ben was inclined to agree. With the grand staircase lead-in, the wide open rotunda and its many connecting hallways, Ben likened it to the stately vestibule of some 1930's opera house. Any minute, he expected to hear the warning tones signaling everyone to take their seats before the show commenced.

"This is a key feature of this place, grandpa." Calliope was standing on the base of the inlaid flower map. She swept her arms wide, indicating the silvery lines flowing from the tips of the petals to the many branching halls. "We think of them as street signs that name each hallway and give direction. We can't really read the symbols, but they're different enough that we can remember which is which. To get to the sprite homeworld, we follow 'Quilium Way.'" She pointed to the line traveling right of the staircase.

She pirouetted off the flower and along the long, thin, silvery line. Youth always found time to dance. Poppie imitated her revolutions in the air. Apparently, mechanical pixies found time to dance as well. They carried their movement all the way to the pilaster at the edge of their target hallway.

"And here, grandpa," she paused for dramatic effect, gesturing to the flowery relief with its camouflaged button, "is another bit of magic."

She pushed the button, and out popped a circular object the size of a silver dollar. It was a thing of delicate copper and nickel gears, miniature pivots, levers, and springs. It was intricate, obviously mechanical, and quite beautiful. Its construction reminded Calliope of Poppie with her whirring and clicking machinations.

"Whoa!" exclaimed Calliope. "This is new."

Her father and grandfather hurried over to inspect her new prize.

"I wonder what this one does," said Ben.

He took his own pin off his shirt and held it next to the new model. The cylindrical pin, made of gold with silver detailing, had no moving parts, and, from all outward appearances, seemed non-mechanical. Perhaps everything was hidden inside the pin, enclosed and protected. Something had to be triggering the lighting. Ben had never fully believed it was magic, just some technology they did not understand yet. But the new object—more of a pendant or brooch than a pin—laid its secrets bare for all to see. Its tiny gears moved with a rhythm slower than a watch; instead of one click per second, there was a series of clicks in succession, once every few seconds: *click, click, clickity-click*—pause—*click, click, clickity-click*. Each click came from a separate section, a separate grouping of gears and pivots. One grouping had a lever see-sawing in and out of the gear's teeth. They could not see the purpose of the gears—what they were driving, or counting, or managing—but they were working away at something.

"Look at the edge," Ben ran his finger along the outer edge of the brooch. "There's a very thin line of crystal trimming the rim."

"What does that mean?" asked Calliope.

"I'm not sure," said her dad.

"Maybe it's some sort of display, or light," said Nigel, peering over Ben's shoulder.

"Awfully narrow for a display," said Ben. "Maybe an indicator light. But an indicator for what?"

They all shrugged. No one had any other ideas, and Poppie didn't offer any hints.

"Well, it's very fancy," said Calliope. "I guess you get this one, Grandpa." She held out the brooch.

"Excellent. I'll be the guinea pig."

"We've all been there, dad," said Ben.

The brooch had a sort of alligator clip on the back, so Nigel used that to clip it on his shirt placket. He gave a thumbs up to the others, indicating he was ready for the next surprise.

"Ok, Poppie, let's take 'em to the waterfall."

They headed down the hallway, the lights following them like a perpetual halo. They passed doors on the left and right. Nigel took them all in, and Ben could see the wonder and interest on his face as he absorbed the relief features on each one. He especially liked the mountain worlds. Like Ben and Calliope, he enjoyed hiking and climbing. Although, his climbs were limited to scrambles over rocky terrain; he had never picked up the full-out climbing bug.

Before long, they reached their target: the exposed rock wall with its mineral rich curtain of water cascading from several natural looking cracks in the ceiling. All streams coalesced and eddied in a shallow pool at the bottom before working their way through fissures in the floor.

"This is as far as we should go today, dad," said Ben. "But this water is clean and delicious." He filled his cupped hands under a flow, then drank deeply. "Ahh."

Nigel and Calliope followed suit. They drank their fill, looked around, examined a few doors, poked about in the branching hallway, then decided to head back. Nigel was speechless, impressed, and above all, more curious than he had been before entering. He said as much to his son, as they made their return journey. Ben offered to show him the map of the City that he had been putting together, disclosing that they had only scratched the surface of this wondrous place. Nigel was excited to see it, and offered to help fill in any missing pieces with future expeditions.

But those explorations would have to wait. They all had a very busy weekend ahead, with a very important birthday party.

—2—

A Birthday Party

The house was fully decorated. Ben had three large pizzas ready to pop in the oven, and the cake was hidden in the basement, ready for its surprise unveiling. The guests were just starting to arrive, and soon the party would be in full swing.

Ben was unsure if their otherworldly adventures had been the catalyst, or if Calliope was just naturally maturing with a sense of social responsibility and caring, but while planning her party, Calliope declared that she did not need any more toys, or games, or knick-knacks. Her invitation had asked that anyone wanting to bring a gift, please choose an unwrapped toy, suitable for a boy or girl ages five to ten, and she would deliver them to the Pediatric Oncology department at the nearby cancer center. There was a program set up to get toys to sick children who needed little moments of fun and joy wherever they could get it. So far, five girls had arrived, but Calliope's gift table had ten gifts. Everyone had brought two—one for a girl, one for a boy. None of them could make up their minds, and all the parents had been thrilled to support the cause. Ben was delighted with the generosity of her friends, and he beamed with pride for the amazing young lady his daughter was becoming.

The last to arrive were Stephanie and her mother, Emily. While Stephanie had been over numerous times since their return, Ben hadn't had much of a chance, or a good excuse, to see Emily. She had evidently been busy with a large project at work and putting in overtime hours. Ben's only chance to talk to her had been when she would drop Steph off to hang out; and those play dates were only allowed after Ben had installed his vault door and security system. Emily had come in to inspect them, briefly, then grudgingly agreed to let her daughter stay. Sleepovers, however, were still off the table.

Ben could hardly blame her. The last slumber party had resulted in the girls being kidnapped and put into some very dangerous situations. The fact that Calliope and Stephanie had not only saved themselves, but also their parents and an entire race on another planet, still did not mollify Emily's concerns for her daughter's safety at the Sullivan household. Several thick steel doors, and eight cameras, however, were a good start.

"Sullivan," Emily greeted Ben. "Steph tells me you've seen the twig a few times, and they're still having problems?"

"They are," said Ben, ignoring her usual derogatory nickname for the sprite, Garran.

"And you're going back again, tomorrow?"

"I am."

"What about Calliope?"

"My dad is going to look after her here. I could just go for a few hours and come back, but since my dad was here for Calliope's birthday, I figured I'd stay a little longer and not rush the visit. We told him everything and even took him into the City, just to that first waterfall. He's up to speed." Ben waved his dad over.

"Dad, this is Emily LaPointe, she and her daughter Stephanie were our companions on our little adventure."

"Ha, adventure, he calls it." She extended her hand to greet Nigel. "Nice to meet you, Mr. Sullivan. You can call me Emily."

"And I'm Nigel," he took her proffered hand and shook.

"So, what's your take on our little secret?" she asked.

"Incredible. Unbelievable. All those worlds, just a short walk away."

"Yes," countered Emily, "just a short walk for any nightmare that wants to come through Ben's basement."

"Good point," said Nigel. "And from the security he has installed, I think Ben knows this as well."

"Let's hope it's enough. Personally, I would have caved in that whole tunnel and moved. But that's just me."

A hubbub from the living room made the adults move in to investigate. The girls had fired up an old classic video game and pulled out the peripherals: plastic drums, a microphone, and mock guitar with buttons instead of strings. They picked an oldy, but a goody: The Beatles, *Here Comes the Sun*. Stephanie crooned the lyrics, while Taylor pounded the drums, and Megan did her best to tap out the beat on guitar. Calliope, Sophi, and Melina sang backup and danced like no one was watching. Their progression was off, the refrain had some mumbling and jumbling of lyrics, and the tone was flat in areas, but the giggling and the dancing were spot-on.

"Oh, my," Emily winced as her daughter completely missed a note.

"Yes, this is perhaps best left to the kids," said Ben. "Anyone want coffee?"

"I'm in," said Nigel.

"You know I'm in," said Emily.

They left the burgeoning rock stars to continue practicing their trade and retired to the kitchen.

****

The pizzas had been a hit. Only a few scraps remained, and the girls were anxiously awaiting cake and ice cream. Ben went to the basement where his masterpiece sat on the coffee table, encased in a plastic cake container. Ben grabbed the two-foot sheet pan and lugged it up to the kitchen. Everyone gathered around the island for the unveiling.

"Is anyone ready for cake?" Ben asked.

He was greeted with enthusiastic affirmations, so with the appropriate fanfare, he pulled the cover and revealed the confection. There was, as Ben had anticipated, a long silence as everyone puzzled out what it was. Those who had been to Quilium knew instantly. And their first reactions were what Ben had predicted. Each of the ladies, including Emily, were wide-eyed with mouths dropped open, because the cake was a miniature replica of one of the slimy slug-monsters they had battled on another world, only too recently. Lumpy arms and legs, bloated belly, and fiendish head were all decorated with pale-gray icing, overlaid with moss-green in certain areas to provide definition and shadow, and to represent the lichen which grew on the beasts. But the face was the true reflection; from tarry eyes to blood-red, circular mouth with rings of jagged white teeth, it brought back bad memories for Emily.

"Oh, you must be kidding, Sullivan," whispered Emily. "That's disgusting. And creepy. And disgusting."

"Not to kids," Ben replied. "And the best way to conquer your fears is head on."

"And head on to you means turning those fears into cake and eating them?"

"Yep. I love cake. And pie. More pie than cake, but who has pie for a birthday? Candles don't work as well. Unless it's pumpkin. Mmmmm. Pumpkin."

"You have issues, Sullivan," said Emily, shaking her head to herself.

"I love it, dad," said Calliope, laughing.

"What is it?" asked Megan.

"It's a character from one of her dad's stories," supplied Stephanie. "It's called a Slizeg. Part slug, part moss-monster, all disgusting. And now it's yummy cake."

Ben had arranged the twelve birthday candles in various spots around the creature's body. Some were angled or cockeyed; reminiscent of arrows sticking out from a brutal attack. He quickly lit the candles and gave Calliope a wink.

"Happy birthday to you...." Ben began the refrain, and everyone else joined in. The song finished and Calliope took a deep, deep breath, knowing the candle layout was going to make a single blowout tricky, but she wanted that lucky wish. She was economic with her exhalation, quick with her cranial maneuvers, and even spun the cake platter to reach the last one and achieve victory. All twelve candles extinguished with a single, drawn-out puff. She made her silent wish while everyone applauded.

Ben handed Calliope the cake knife.

"Carve it up, sweetheart."

Calliope dug in with a piratical "Argh!" She quartered the effigy with surgical precision, and served up arm parts, hands, legs and feet to her friends. Ben doled out ice cream, and the girls retreated to the kitchen table with full plates.

"Yum, lemon!" Ben heard one of the girls say.

Calliope had saved the face for those "in the know." She gave an eye each to her dad and Emily, a moss-covered piece of snout to her grandfather, while she and Stephanie spit the serrated mouth and licorice rope, toxic tongue.

"Well, you sure did capture the likeness, Sullivan," said Emily. "Let's hope the flavor isn't reminiscent of the real thing. Thankfully, the smell is much better."

She took a taste, and Ben was happy to notice the lines on her face change from hesitant disgust to pleasant surprise.

"Wow, Sullivan! You made this yourself?"

"Yep."

"Not bad."

"Thanks. The lemon cake recipe is from the internet, but the buttercream frosting is my grandma's. It's always a hit. Even when I add gray food coloring."

With bellies full of sugar, and being twelve year old girls, the level of energy and noise shot through the roof. Calliope corralled them back into the living room for several rounds of *Dance-Dance Revolution*. Soon, the music was blaring, the girls were cheering and sweating, and laughter abounded.

The adults remained in the relative quiet of the kitchen and took advantage of the empty table.

"So, Sullivan," Emily began, "did you take a watch to the Twig, so he doesn't have to tell time with his hands any more?" She mimed stacking her hands from the sun to the horizon to estimate hours until sundown. Ben noticed the soft-pink polish on her freshly manicured nails. A subtle, not ostentatious color. It suited her.

"I did, as a matter of fact," said Ben. "And we soon figured out that their world rotates around their sun in just under twenty-three hours, so our time system really doesn't work for them. Ideally, if they were to create their own system of time, I would recommend they move to a base-10 system—like the metric system for weights and measures. Swatch, the Swiss watch company, tried to introduce this concept in the late 1990's, but it never caught on. The twenty-four hour, sixty-minute system is just too well-ingrained in our world. It would be too expensive and too difficult for everyone to change over. But, if we were starting from scratch, it seems like it would make more sense."

"You're just full of fun facts, aren't you," teased Emily. She turned her attention to Ben's father. "And how about you, Nigel? What's your story?"

"Not much of one, really," Nigel said. "I was in the Marines for a few years, in my youth. Graduated from the school of hard knocks and went to work for one of the Big Three car manufacturers in their hayday, before they outsourced all the jobs to Mexico and Korea. I built up a decent pension, before they got rid of those, too, and I retired to a sizable piece of property in the country with most of my faculties intact and good enough health to still enjoy life. Some years back I "inherited" three chickens from a neighbor who went into foreclosure and set them free in the woods. Now I have twenty-four chickens, two coops, a goat, and a tractor. Between my small hobby-farm and chopping wood to heat my house through the winter, I keep pretty busy from sunup to sundown."

"I'll bet you do," laughed Emily. "And by the looks of things, I'm guessing Ben inherited his hairline from his mother's father?" She motioned to Nigel's mane of thick walnut hair.

Nigel laughed. "That he did. Good guess."

"Hey, I don't miss my hair one bit," said Ben. "A few flicks with the razor in the morning and my look is perfect all day. Nice and cool in the summer, and I can wear any hat, any time, and not worry about having hat-head. Works for me."

They continued the rest of the afternoon with idle chit-chat while the girls burned through their supply of video games and snacks. When evening arrived, Calliope's friends said their goodbyes and quiet returned. Stephanie and her mother remained a bit longer, much to Ben's delight. He was glad Emily had stuck around, and had not just dropped Stephanie off and left. This was the most time he had spent with her since their return from Quilium, and he was glad to see that he still enjoyed her company.

It seemed his father did, as well. While Ben cleaned up the birthday remnants of frosting-smeared paper plates, glassware and silverware, Nigel regaled her with tales of Ben's childhood. More than once, Ben had to reign his father in from revealing embarrassing history. It grew worse once the rest of the girls departed. That's when Calliope and Stephanie joined them and egged Nigel on to share even more stories. Suddenly, Ben was reconsidering the success of the evening.

"So, Ben," Nigel addressed his son, "when are you taking off for your camping trip?"

Everyone's attention immediately switched to Ben, waiting for his answer. They all knew that the "camping trip" was his planned visit to Quilium.

"Tomorrow morning. I'll be leaving bright and early, right after a good breakfast."

"How long are you staying this time?" asked Emily.

"Just an overnight. I don't think I'll be leaving the clearing around the doorway, so I'm taking my tent to just camp in the woods. I'll stick to that area you girls found with higher levels of salt in the soil, just in case we get a stray visitor."

"So the Slizeg are still a problem?" asked Stephanie.

"They've been pushed back into their den under the mountain, for the most part," said Ben. "But, better safe than sorry. I'm not ending up in one of their pits again."

"You say that like you have a choice. If they come en-masse with their blowguns, you're going to find yourself a guest of their hospitality again," said Emily.

"Funny you should mention their blowguns," said Ben. "Turns out, that's quite the useful design. It's not only good for delivering their neurotoxin, but also salt pellets. The sprites have designed some nice darts to deliver a salt payload. It's not as deadly as salt-tipped arrows, but they can carry a hundred darts in a bag on their hip compared to a dozen or so arrows in a quiver. When they encounter large parties of Slizeg, it ends up being about the numbers. And Sprites are not killers, no matter how horrible their enemy. They say the salt darts are just enough of a deterrent to drive the slugs back into their hidey-holes."

"They're nicer than I'd ever be," said Emily.

"Speaking of being nice," interjected Stephanie, "do you think we could take a quick trip in and just say hi to Poppie? I haven't been back in there in weeks."

Emily thought for a minute, then looked at Ben and cocked an eyebrow as the unasked question of his opinion.

"Well, we visited The City and Poppie yesterday, and everything was quiet and normal. I think it's safe."

She considered Ben's opinion of 'safe' to be quite a bit less than a mother's. Begrudgingly, she reassessed the safety precautions he had installed, how carefully and slowly he had made his return trips to evaluate the situation on Quilium before letting his daughter accompany him. He did seem to be applying appropriate caution. And, truth be told, she was more than a little curious about the City of Doors and its secrets.

"Ok. We can go. But just for a quick visit, and then we need to go home, Steph. You may be on summer break, but I have work in the morning."

"Yay!" both girls exclaimed. They jumped up and headed for the basement.

"Not without us!" Emily yelled after them.

"Don't worry," said Ben, "I'm the only one that can unlock the door to the tunnel. No one is going anywhere without me in the lead."

As before, they all geared up with minimal survival packs stuffed with necessities. Nigel pinned the clockwork brooch to his backpack strap, and the others followed suit with their steampunk pins. With jewelry added to everyone's gear, Ben led the way through the tunnel, to the bomb shelter door, then across the threshold into another world.

First to enter, Ben's pin awoke the room's amber lighting. The girls followed, with Nigel bringing up the rear. Calliope immediately set about calling for her mechanical friend, with Stephanie adding her welcoming call as well. They did not spend long in the first chamber, but climbed quickly to the upper level, assuming Poppie would be coming from that direction anyway, and meet them in the more interesting room.

They kept their train in order; Ben in the lead, Nigel at the caboose. Calliope looked back to see if Grandpa Chicken had retained his excitement, or if the novelty had worn off. To her amazement, a thin ring of yellow light pulsed from her grandfather's new badge.

"Whoa! Grandpa, your pin is glowing," she exclaimed.

Everyone turned to gather around Nigel as he crested the landing. The pendant's gears were spinning as before, but Calliope was right, a yellow light was indeed emanating from the crystal bezel.

"Aha! I was right. The crystal *is* a light," Nigel said.

"A light for what?" asked Ben

"Yellow is traditionally a color for caution," chimed-in Emily.

"That was my thinking, too," added Nigel.

"Let's hope not," said Ben. "I was just beginning to think this place was safe."

"Well, maybe that explains why it gave you a different pin," suggested Emily. "Maybe The City has decided you need to be more cautious."

"Can't say as I wouldn't like more of a heads up than I've had in the past. I've run into my share of surprises in here."

There was a collective pause as everyone processed the new development. Nigel was wondering how the mechanism worked. Ben was wondering what The City could consider a warning. Emily was wondering if they should all make a run for the exit and leave this place for good. The girls were wondering what the adults were wondering.

"So, do we keep going, or turn back?" asked Stephanie.

"Keep going," asserted Calliope. "We don't know if that's really what the light means. It could just mean that it's on and working."

"It wasn't on yesterday," said Nigel.

"Maybe it just needed to get reset. You know, like restarting your laptop. We left and came back. That was a reboot."

"Hmm. Maybe," said Ben. "Either way, I'd like to see if it does anything else. I say we keep going, but be alert and cautious. Assume it's a gentle warning."

He looked at Emily to get her opinion. Her brows furrowed in concern and thought, but she did not immediately object. With a look around the room, and a considering gaze at the girls, she nodded her agreement.

"Extreme caution." She aimed her remark at her daughter and Calliope. "We stick together. Close together. No wandering off or touching anything new."

"Deal!" both girls agreed together.

Ben looked at his father to gauge his temperament and saw the same querying look reflected back.

"This is your operation, Ben. I'll follow your lead. However, I'm noticing your mechanical pixie friend still hasn't arrived. Is it normal for her to take this long?"

"No. She's usually here before we hit the top of the stairs. Then again, we've really only been in here a handful of times..."

"If Poppie's in trouble, then we have to help her, dad!" Calliope's concern was evident. Stephanie reflected her friend's worry.

"Sweetheart, I hate to say it, but if Poppie's in trouble, in here, I think we're all in trouble. We definitely aren't going looking for it."

"But dad, she saved Stephanie and me!"

"I know. I'm sorry Calliope. Look, we don't even know if she is in trouble. Let's just give her more time to get here, ok."

With all eyes on Ben, he made his decision. "Let's follow the same path we did yesterday, to *Intersection Spring*, and assess the state of the place. If all looks normal, maybe we go a bit deeper and hit *The Garden*. Grab some plums and then head home."

No one argued the point, although Emily scowled a bit about

continuing to *The Garden*. However, she kept any objections to herself. For the moment.

The grand staircase at this level was just as barren as the day before, still untidy with spiderwebs. In contrast to his opinion yesterday, Ben found some comfort in this today. If there were a dangerous creature in here, the spiderwebs would be disturbed. Maybe. If anything, they were more prolific. Ben took that to mean nothing was scaring the spiders. And if spiders were not scared, he certainly would not be.

The group entered the third level rotunda and found everything normal. The lights came up, the silver lines in the floor sparkled, the hallways exiting around the room were quiet and dark. But still no Poppie. Ben had been hoping she would be waiting for them here.

They followed *Quilium Way* to its hallway and continued on to *Intersection Spring* with no incident. The group was quiet; each lost in his or her own thoughts, with senses on high alert. They all felt the tension, the hoping, the apprehension, the various emotions playing off the myriad imagined scenarios. Ben found the usual quiet, unchanging nature of The City oppressive today, rather than reassuring.

"Well, so far, it's business as usual in here," said Ben with what he hoped was a reassuring smile. "Shall we continue on?"

"Poppie's still not here," said Calliope. "Should we call her again?"

"I don't think so, Calli," said Ben. "We're going to pass by her home port on the way to *The Garden*. Why don't we maintain caution until we can see if she's there."

He looked at Emily. "What do you think? Keep going?"

"Honestly, maybe it's just my womanly intuition, or maybe I'm just nervous being back here for the first time since our last misadventure, but something feels off." She paused, considering the pleading looks on the girl's faces. "It's been quiet so far, so I'm willing to keep going, but after we check in on Poppie, I think we should call it a day and head back."

Nigel nodded his agreement and rested his hand on the belt knife he had borrowed from Ben's stores. It was already loose in its sheath.

Ben led the way and the others fell in line. They were no more talkative than the last leg of their journey, and they still encountered nothing out of the ordinary. Ordinary being a relative term in a city full of magical doors and flying clockwork pixies.

After another thirty minutes, many twists and turns, up a few staircases and down several halls, they reached the rotunda where Calliope and Stephanie had first met Poppie. They emerged into the large room along the silver filigree Calliope had named *Poppie's Path* all those weeks ago.

As the lights around the room awoke, Stephanie called out quietly to the ceiling. "Poppie? Poppie, are you home? We need your help, Poppie." There was no response.

"It seems she isn't home," said Nigel. "Maybe she has work she needs to do in other parts of this place. Ben, didn't you say this place is immense? I'm sure it requires maintenance. Perhaps she's just changing a light bulb or something."

"Whatever the reason," said Emily, "I think we've pressed our luck enough for today. I say we go home. Ben can check back again tomorrow on his way to meet the sprites."

"That's a good idea," Nigel agreed. While he was increasingly curious about this place, he was uncomfortable having the girls in an unknown situation, especially given the wild stories he had been told.

It was a hasty retreat back the way they had come, with lots of peering down darkened side halls, and many a paranoid glance behind. They were all feeling it now, that intuition, an itch at the back of their brains, the suggestion that someone was watching. Or something. And yet, nothing materialized. No strange sounds collided with their own footfalls, no shining eyes peered back from the shadows, and no ghostly specters caught the corners of their eyes. They returned to the iron alloy door, with it's gears and familiar embossed molding of Parkview Middle School, and gave a sigh of relief.

Once back in the Sullivans' basement, all doors closed and locked, packs stowed, it all seemed a bit paranoid. Besides Poppie's mysterious disappearance, The City of Doors had been quieter than ever. Ben remained resolute that his trip would continue as planned the next morning. He assured the girls he would conduct a thorough search for Poppie on his return trip home.

The Lapointes took their leave, but only once Emily had pulled Ben aside and urged him to be extremely careful. She did not want to worry Calliope, but she believed it was more than their imaginations at play. Something was not right in The City. Ben assured her he would travel with caution, then walked them to their car.

It had been a long day, with a successful birthday dance party, and a stressful adventure. Calliope retired to her room. Ben and Nigel cleaned a bit, but then followed suit. Tomorrow would be another day. Ben wanted to be well-rested for whatever came his way.

—3—

A Meeting Gone Awry

Everyone was up bright and early for a big breakfast of eggs straight from grandpa chicken's chickens, homemade multigrain toast, fresh fruit, and the requisite quota of morning coffee. All-in-all, Ben had a good feeling about this trip. Yesterday's worries seemed like pure imagination. He was not advocating recklessness, but a good night's sleep always did wonders to clear the mind.

He had several presents for his sprite friends, including two, one-pound bricks of dark roast coffee for Tormad, as well as a seed starter kit for growing their own coffee trees. The gruff, bristlecone sprite had developed an obsession with the drink that rivaled Ben's own. And he was quickly gaining a following of true believers amongst other sprites, from every clan. With their talent for growing plants, Ben would not be surprised to find the Quilium version of Starbucks in every village within a few years.

For Ima, he was bringing three wispy, silk scarves, picked out by Calliope. One each in pastels of yellow, green, and pink. They were just big enough for the Temizan warrior to wear wrapped around her waist and hang along one side, in a sort of kimono-style belt. Sprites still had no use for clothing as protection, but it seemed decoration was a different matter.

"Ok, dad," said Calliope, "last chance to have me come along and watch your back. You know how sneaky those Slizeg can be."

"Nice try, kiddo," said her father, "but it's just me this trip. Don't worry. According to Garran, they are making good progress on containing the Slizeg. It won't be long before it's safe for you to join me."

"Safe is boring."

"Well, we won't be that safe, Calliope," said Nigel, "we're going to have some fun of our own. We'll hit *The Summit* and do some climbing." He knew a day at the indoor climbing gym would improve her mood.

"Can we take Stephanie, too?"

"Absolutely!" said her grandfather.

"Cool. Thanks, grandpa."

"Anytime, peanut."

"Thanks dad," said Ben. "And now that your day is planned, it's time for me to get a move on. Anyone coming to see me off?" He looked at his daughter hopefully.

"Sure, dad. And you can help me check my climbing gear."

The extended family descended to the basement storage room. Ben gathered his already prepped gear by the vault door, then returned to forage through their stocks and get Calliope's climbing gear ready. She had an old backpack always full of the basics: shoes, chalk bag, tape for fingers, carabiners, belay device, and harness. She would not need more than that.

"Looks like you're all set, kiddo." Ben looked over his daughter's gear, checking for wear. "Might be time for both of us to get some new shoes. I'm bettin' yours are cramping your toes up pretty good now. It's your own fault, though," he smiled at his daughter. "I keep telling you to stop growing."

"Yeah, dad. I'll get right on that." Her tone indicated she didn't understand a parent's fear of their children growing up.

"All right. Enough dawdling. Time for me to head out."

Ben donned his pack—bedroll bouncing at the bottom, machete

dangling from the side—and stalked to the vault where a few musical taps on the keypad and a spin of the ship's wheel saw them back in the wine room. He pulled the secret bottle-lever on the back wall and the hidden charcoal door was revealed. Once the bolts were slid open, Ben gained access to the tunnel, and flipped on the string of lights which twinkled merrily along the basket-weave passage. To Ben, it had the ambience of a comfortable café. All that was missing was a little soft jazz humming through hidden speakers.

"Ok. This is where I should leave you." He hugged his daughter and shook his dad's hand. "See you both tomorrow afternoon. Have fun while I'm gone."

They both said they would and wished him a safe trip. Calliope reminded him to say hello to Poppie and all their sprite friends. Ben gave his assurances, then pulled the door shut behind himself, and paused to drink in the atmosphere of the umber, almond, and sepia-toned, root-encompassed passage. A deep breath supplied the soft aromas of jasmine and earth, relaxing him and putting his mind into a peaceful state.

There was something to be said about the start of a journey. Both he and his gear were clean and dry, he was well fed, fully stocked, and fully rested. The possibilities and expectations of the coming adventure fueled an excitement that made him feel half his age. Usually, by the end of his camping adventures he was tired, hungry, sore, and filthy from head to toe. And his gear was in need of a hose-down. But there was something to be said about that stage of the journey as well. Sure, he was exhausted and dirty, and feeling every one of his years, but it was the exhaustion born of accomplishment, of being in nature, of exercise, of fresh air and adventure. It was the exhaustion of building great memories. Which is why, no matter how sore his joints became, or how tired he felt, he couldn't wait to do it all over again.

Ben reached the end of the tunnel and wasted no time cranking the portal open. The darkness on the other side was pushed back softly by the unobtrusive glow of the LED lights; the last in the strand hung a few feet behind his head. He stepped over the threshold and felt the tiny ping in his brain that somehow changed how he heard and understood language. Slowly, the amber glow of The City grew in intensity, warming the dark steel of the room. Not for the first time, Ben wondered at the quiet of this place. How could it be all hard surfaces—steel and iron and wood—and not feel oppressive, cold, and echoing. It was always a pleasant temperature, and sounds seemed to be absorbed as if the walls were adorned with tapestries and the floors covered in carpet. It was, in a word, cozy.

"Hi Poppie!" Ben called out to the pixie. "I could use a little help, and a little company on the way to Quilium."

There was no response. He hoped his dad was right, and their mechanical friend was off in other parts of The City, busy doing whatever she normally did when the Sullivans were not around. If so, she would catch up when she could. Either way, Ben knew his way well enough.

He trudged up the spiral staircase, then stopped at the base of the dusty stone steps. There were definitely more cobwebs adorning the ornate ironwork railings. In some spots, it was hard to tell the difference between iron work and spider work. The state of this level was now reminiscent of some haunted movie mansion. He would not be surprised if a spooky breeze were to suddenly ripple through the silvery webbing to complete the image.

Maybe Ben was feeling spooked from Emily's dire warning the night before, or maybe his own sixth-sense was kicking in, but something definitely did not feel right. According to the sprites, they had never seen any other living thing down here, and they worked for years spying on Ben. Why would there be so many spiders in here now? There could not be that many sneaking in from Earth, or following the sprites from Quilium. For that matter, he was not even sure there *were* spiders on Quilium.

He gave another shout for Poppie. "Poppie? If you can hear me, I'd really like your help. I have some questions. Poppie? I'm headed for the Sprites' doorway. Meet me on the way, if you can."

He stood quietly, listening for any sound. Nothing. Instead of the relaxing calm Ben usually experienced in The City's tranquility, today's silence brought unease, and the feeling of being watched. Grains of trepidation were building in the back of his mind. Something was not right.

Immediate stealth seemed like a prudent option. Ben decided to stop calling out to Poppie, become as quiet as possible to hear anything coming his way, and keep his head on a swivel. He contemplated removing his pin to deactivate the city's lights. He would be a heck of a lot more stealthy without the amber glow projecting his every move by fifty yards. He could navigate just fine with the small flashlight in his pack. Much more covert. But then he remembered his last misadventures in the dark. The first time, the Tree Lord he had nicknamed Oakenpuss had found him with no trouble in the pitch black of the unlit hallways. On his next, chasing after his kidnapped daughter, Garran and his sprite cohorts had easily lain in wait for him in the dark. He had not known they were there until they were nose-to-nose on the stairs. No, he clearly was at a disadvantage in the dark. The risk of discovery was far outweighed by the extra fifty yards of advance notice. Not to mention the same fifty-yard buffer behind.

With his imagination on overload, he took a second to cinch his straps tighter and unsheathe his machete. Better safe than sorry. He patted his left thigh pocket, reassuring himself that his throwing knives were within reach. He took a deep, calming breath, then started up the stairs, oblivious to the many multifaceted eyes watching him from the darkness of the side passageways.

****

"Oh crud," Ben thought to himself. He felt the hairs on his neck stand up like an angry cat's, and fight-or-flight adrenaline began pumping at the same pace as his racing heartbeat. "This is not good. Not good."

He had reached *Intersection Spring*, and it had changed dramatically since his previous day's visit. Thick spider webs draped the edges of the spring, like sheets of white silk stretched out to dry at any crazy angle. What looked to be an egg sack the size of a laundry bag clung to the crease between wall and ceiling, filled to bursting with spheres the size of light bulbs.

A definitive conclusion struck Ben: there was no way that these spiders were from Earth. If, in fact, spiders were what were making these webs. Ben had his doubts that they were from Quilium, either. He could not stop his mind from conjuring up images of the door he had seen on his first journey, all those years ago; the door he had instinctively avoided like the plague; the door adorned with carvings of some very aggressive, very large-looking eight-legged monsters.

But where they had come from was of secondary concern right now. What he really needed to concentrate on, was the fact that he was apparently standing in its nest. Or their nest. What if there was more than one? There very well could be. He turned slowly around, scanned up and down, along the ceiling and down the hall as far as the hall light would illuminate. It was quiet, no sign of movement, no creatures of any kind. He pulled out his large flashlight, the one with a cutting LED beam of light that could go beyond the 50 yards. He shone it down the hallway to the left of the spring, along the wall under the egg sack. To his horror, he saw what was clearly trapped and dessicated prey, ensconced in a cocoon of silk. And it was, itself, a massive spider. Its legs had to stretch over two feet in diameter, and its body was as big as Ben's face. He had to assume that whatever had trapped and eaten this creature had to be bigger, faster, stronger.

Ben's mind conjured up giant nightmares. He envisioned the doorway to that spider world being propped open, the creatures from the other side roaming through at will. He imagined hundreds, maybe thousands, with the hallways leading to their doorway becoming more and more adorned with the delicate horror of spider spinnings.

Spiders were never one of Ben's favorite creatures. Any spider larger than a penny was to be avoided. These dead ones were larger than dinner plates, so he wanted to do more than avoid them. He wanted to run away, as fast as he could. But which way? He really wanted to go home, but if he did that, Garran would wonder why he missed the rendezvous and come looking for him. Then again, sprites were wood. Maybe they didn't need to worry about toxic venom, or becoming food. Maybe they were used to creepy-crawly things and didn't mind the numerous, unblinking, jeweled eyes, or the twitchy movement of long, furry, multi-jointed legs.

Ben turned to look down the hallway leading home. It still seemed quiet. Where was Poppie? He could really use that pixie's help right about now. He pointed his flashlight to the edges of the amber lighting. There was a glint, and fast movement to the other side of the hall still in darkness. He followed with his light. Several silvery circles flashed back at him, and more fuzzy dark shapes leapt back. They were there, behind him. And there were at least half a dozen, cutting him off from the way home. His nerves made the choice for him, he would head to Quilium. Fast.

It seemed these things were keeping to the darkness for now. Maybe the lights were keeping him safe, but he wanted more guarantees. He did not know if spiders had a sense of smell, but he thought he remembered something about them tasting with their feet. He fumbled around in his pack pockets. He had a can of pepper spray in there for discouraging forest creatures. Maybe it would do the same for spiders. He found it, but held it in check. It was probably best to first check for spiders down the corridor to the sprite's homeworld. He would be in a world of hurt if he set off the pepper spray behind, then found himself blocked from moving forward. If that were the case, he would save the gas for direct engagements.

He whipped the flashlight to the west, scanning the far walls, ceiling, and floor. It looked clear. That was his best bet, then. He moved down that hallway, stopped just the other side of the threshold, and stowed his flashlight. He took a deep breath and held it, then shot the pepper spray in a giant circle; from floor to wall to ceiling to wall back to floor. He walked backwards, then, and sprayed another blast in mid-air, to really give the hallway a pungent odor. Then, he turned and ran, pepper spray still in one hand, machete in the other. Every few minutes, he slowed to look behind. The City's lighting revealed nothing behind, but Ben's skin crawled with dread. He could feel them back there. He knew they were coming. Maybe they were stalled behind the cloud of gas, but more than likely, they just hopped through and continued on their hunt. Still, the light seemed to be keeping them at bay. He turned and continued to run. He still had a good thirty minutes of travel ahead.

****

Ben's mad dash for Quilium had him winded and covered in sweat. He had passed several intersecting tunnels that had clearly seen spider activity. Fresh-looking webs upholstered the passages, turning the ninety degree angles of wall and ceiling into rounded arches of silk. After passing each, he sprayed another circle of pepper gas, like some ancient mystic burning sage to ward off evil spirits. And after each sighting, his adrenaline spiked again, and he was off at a run, his breathing coming in ragged, wheezing gulps for air, the pack on his back feeling like half a tonne of bricks to his pumping legs.

It was the spiral staircases he dreaded most, though. As he traveled up, he felt exposed from all angles. It gave the spiders so much time to gain ground. He hoped the light really did keep them away, but that left him with another problem: his pin did not activate the lights on the next level until he was practically poking his nose through the ceiling. He had no idea if he was sticking his head into the mouth of some ginormous arachnid, or walking into a web the size of a Volkswagen. Then, once the lighting above started to come on, the lighting below started to fade, leaving his legs exposed to the creatures he could sense hunting behind, just waiting for their chance to pounce.

His mouth was dry, but he dared not take time to drink from his water bladder. His hands were sweaty, but he dared not release his grip on the can, nor his machete, to wipe them on his pants. His lungs ached, but he dared not slow down, even for a minute. He could feel a trap closing in from all sides. So, like any frightened prey would, he just kept running.

Finally, protractedly, Ben reached the hallway for the door to Quilium. The lights yawned to life. The passage was thankfully clear of spider signs: no webs, no silvery eyes, no furry legs. Ben scrambled down the hall to the alcove and doorway emblazoned with tiny little creatures living amongst the trees. He reached it and threw back the lever, releasing the six locking bolts, then pulled open the door. To his surprise, the chamber on the other side—usually dark and quiet—was fully lit, the sand-colored granite and quartz reflecting the light from dozens of soluna leaves. The stone echoed with the voices from many sprites, the most obvious one being Garran himself.

"Ben Sullivan!" the sprite greeted him. "We were hoping you would still come. There have been strange things happening in Chathair Doras." He called The City of Doors by its sprite name.

"You're telling me," panted Ben. "I've been hunted the entire way. I didn't think I was going to make it. It's spid---aaaaaaaaaah!"

Ben was suddenly sucked backwards, away from the alcove, back down the hall and out of Garran's view.

"Ben Sullivan!" Garran screamed. But only the faint yelling of his human friend traveled back, quickly growing fainter, until all sounds ceased with an ominous finality.

Garran turned to a burly oaken sprite and said, "Go to the Temizan and find Ima, tell her Ben Sullivan has been taken in Chathair Doras. Tell her to bring her team. Then travel to clan Darroch to find Tormad. Tell him the same. Tell them I have already gone in, and to find us. We are going to save our friend."

—4—

A Rescue Party

Calliope took a deep breath to steady her nerves. She closed her eyes against the fear, the frustration, and the disappointment she felt building. This could not be happening, not again. How could she let herself be trapped over and over? How could she have made all the right choices, all the right moves, and still end up in this position?

The journey to this point had been hard won and fraught with pain. Her hands were scraped and blistered. Blood ran in a single rivulet down her shin. Her toes felt like they had been smashed in a vise, and her arms were shaking with fatigue from her shoulders to her fingers. But, she would get through this. She would claim victory.

"Come on, Calli," called Stephanie from her position on solid ground. "You just need to stretch a little further."

"I *am* stretching," Calliope's frustration grunted out.

She knew she did not have much time. Her strength was failing. This was it. One last lurch forward was all she had left. It was now or never. She inhaled deeply, dug her cramped toes firmly into the rock and pushed off. Her left shoulder hit the rim of the overhang as she floundered for the handhold she knew was hiding above her. But as her right arm swept the blind side of the wall, her left arm could no longer hold her weight. Gravity's relentless pull sucked her body down. There was no stopping physics. Grasping, clawing at the rough surface, she let out a bitter wail, edged with a touch of primeval panic.

"Nooooo!"

She hung in mid-air for the briefest of heartbeats. The world slowed and her senses guzzled the details of her surroundings. Electric lighting washed the wall in antiseptic-white. Only the weakest of shadows grew in the odd nook or cranny behind man-made handholds that blossomed in a putty gray field. The cool air slipped through her swimming fingers, and raised the tiny hairs on her arms as they stretched and waived. There was a smell of closed-in space, of wood and concrete, of chalk, and a bit of stale sweat. Her eyes focused on the handhold she had just lost, and she willed herself to retake it, to reach further and defy her circumstance, to latch onto that vivid pink rock shaped like a goofy banana, bolted to the underside of her nemesis: *The Burgundy Roof.* So named because some climber, months ago, had marked their path up this impossible slope with burgundy colored tape, as they conquered it, all the way to the top; a feat Calliope had tried to accomplish a dozen times, and failed. Make that a dozen and one.

She snapped to a halt as the rope caught her harness and arrested her fall. Grandpa was on belay, always ready. This was their second day of climbing, having come late the day before, and early this morning, and it was her third attempt at this route today, so Nigel knew the drill. He brought Calliope back to the ground in a slow descent.

"You just need one more inch, kiddo," he told her. "Keep eating your Wheaties and you'll get there. Probably by Christmas at the rate you're growing."

Calliope sat dejected in her cornflower blue harness, swinging with the toes of her strangely shaped, multicolored climbing shoes dragging along the floor. Nigel had the finger-thick red rope locked down in his belay device, so he felt no strain. He let her swing for a bit while she chewed on her defeat.

Calliope's arms burned, and the rivulet of blood on her shin tickled and itched as it made its way to her shoe. It stemmed from a dime-sized scrape that was already coagulating. "You know, Wheaties aren't really that healthy, grandpa. Dad says some egg whites, whole grain toast and a little Greek yogurt are a good breakfast for bone and muscle growth."

"It's just an expression from the old days, Calli."

"Yeah, dad has a lot of those expressions. I tell him, sometimes those expressions from the old days should stay in the old days." Calliope grinned at her grandfather and wiggled her eyebrows. Stephanie snickered in the background.

"Well, I'll take that into consideration, you cheeky little monkey. Now, hop off. It's Stephanie's turn to climb. Why don't you take a break, clean up that cut on your shin, and have a snack," said Nigel. "That was a tough climb. You'll need to build your strength back up before you go again."

She nodded, stood up, and untied her harness. "Ok. I guess I'll take a break from that route for today, too. Maybe I'll do that turquoise splitter over there." She gestured to a narrow crack that ran floor-to-ceiling, bordered by very few bolted-in handholds, and those so small that they were useful only as pinch holds or toe crimps. She had clawed halfway up that one in the past, but it always took a measure of skin from her fingers. She was not as excited to beat that one, as it was really more about how thick your calluses were. And not many girls wanted rough, callused fingers.

Stephanie, although taller than Calliope by a few inches, was not about to attempt *The Burgundy Roof*. She was content to tackle *Misty Blue*; an intermediate route marked by summer-sky-colored pieces of tape. Midway up the wall, there were two large holds that Stephanie was adept at wedging her feet into, allowing her to stand snug to the wall, and not use her arms at all. She enjoyed the view as she chalked up for the second half of her climb.

While Nigel and Stephanie moved to a rope close to *Misty Blue*,

Calliope kicked off her slightly too small climbing shoes, then rummaged in her backpack for a protein bar and water bottle. She also grabbed a single packet alcohol wipe to scrub the crusty blood from her shin and sanitize the scrape. The bleeding had stopped, and the wound was not deep, so she did not bother with a Band-Aid.

A small smear of now cinnamon-colored blood had made it onto the rolled up leg of her most comfortable, often-worn, stretchy hiking pants. Just another decoration amongst the sewn up tears and patched holes that uniquely branded her attire. She had worked hard to earn every one of those badges, and she wore them with pride. But this newest stain was only a reminder of defeat. Maybe the wash would wipe it clean, and take with it the memory of failure.

Snack in hand, wound all clean, Calliope used her pack as a backrest and stretched out on the floor. She plucked her cell phone from a pocket to peruse her social media while her friend scaled the wall. It did not look like she and Stephanie were missing much in the way of pre-teen activities today. Mostly, their friends were settling into summer vacation with a lazy day of television, or sunbathing around Marion Phillips' pool.

After a morning of climbing (and maybe spending a nice lunch with grandpa, if they could talk him into Tripp's Gourmet Burger and Shake Emporium), lazing about a pool sounded like a good idea. Grandpa wouldn't mind if they ditched him after lunch. He would probably be ready for an afternoon nap on the back patio, anyway. They had a hammock out there with the supernatural power to lull anyone to sleep, at any time of day. Add to that a full burger-belly, and you were guaranteed a meat coma. Calliope had half a mind to call dibs on it herself, but the day was too beautiful to waste napping.

She checked her email next, and was surprised to see a message from Garran in her inbox. She sat up and tapped the little envelope icon to open the sprite's missive.

Calliope, your father is in danger. Strange things are afoot in Chathair Doras. He was taken. Sucked back into the city by a creature. I did not see what took him, but he knew he was being hunted. I have called for Ima, Tomar, and their teams to join me. We are going after him. Do not fear. We will get him back. It will take time.

Do not enter Chathair Doras in search of him. It is too dangerous. I will bring you updates when I can.
Stay safe!

-- Garran

Calliope read the email twice. "Grandpa, Steph, we have to go!" she called. Stuffing her gear in her pack, she ran over to her grandfather and showed him the email while Stephanie held her place on the wall.

"That's from the sprite he was going to meet?" Nigel asked. Calliope nodded. "Stephanie, rappel down," he called up, "Calliope's right. We have to leave immediately. Her dad's in trouble."

Stephanie knew what that meant. She called back "On rappel!"

"Rappel on!" came Nigel's reply and he readied himself to lower the young climber. Stephanie stepped off the wall and sank into her harness. She swung into the wall and used her feet to gently kick off. Nigel let out slack to give her a slow descent. Seconds later, she was on the ground, clambering out of her gear.

"What's going on," she asked in a hushed tone. Calliope showed her Garran's message while they gathered up the last of their gear, donned their street shoes and headed for the car.

"That means your dad's been missing for a whole day and night," said Stephanie when they made it to the privacy of the car. "What are we going to do?"

"We're going to gear up and go in after him," Calliope said, determination locked into her features.

"Whoa, whoa, whoa, young lady," interjected Nigel. "The sprite's email said The City is too dangerous for you right now. Your dad told him something was hunting him and it grabbed him! The sprite himself is going in with an army. We are not going in there as two girls and an old Marine."

"Come one, grandpa!" pleaded Calliope. "You're not that old, and Stephanie and I already proved we can handle ourselves. We fought the Slizeg and won!"

"Well, technically, we hid behind a rock and threw salt. It was the sprites who did most of the fighting and winning."

"Not helping, Stephanie!" Calliope hissed at her friend.

"No, Calliope. Your dad would never forgive me if I put you in harm's way. Heck, I would never forgive myself." Nigel shook his head and gave his granddaughter his *"this conversation is over"* look. He started the car and they drove home in silence; each deep in thought, contriving and discarding strategies in desperation.

Calliope was so lost in imagining rescue scenarios that she did not even realize their car was in her driveway, and her grandfather had switched off the ignition.

"Calliope, your father is tough. Whatever happened, I'm sure he's already figuring a way to get himself out of it."

"I know, grandpa," she said, "but he even admitted that when the Slizeg put him in that pit, he had no idea how to get out. If we hadn't come to rescue him, he'd still be down there." With an expression of seriousness more mature than her young years, she said, "Sometimes we all need a little help. And sometimes, just a little help is all we need to tip the balance. Dad might be in need of just a little of our help. You know?"

Nigel sighed. He never was good at denying his granddaughter. She could break his will at age two, just by giving him a pouty face.

This glimpse into the mature, logical woman she was becoming didn't just play on his heartstrings, it sparked familial pride.

"Let's get inside and check for any more communications from that sprite. Also, let's check the cameras in the cellar. I want to make sure nothing has made it through to our side." Before he could exit the car, however, it hit Nigel that Stephanie was not another granddaughter.

"Oh, Stephanie! I'm sorry. We should probably take you home first. We're going to be occupied for a while, so this is the best opportunity to drive you home."

"What?! No way, Mr. Sullivan. I want to come in, too. I want to help."

"That's very kind of you, Stephanie, but I don't think your mom would approve." He said the last not just for Stephanie's benefit, but his granddaughter's as well, as Calliope was nodding her head in excited agreement with her friend. She obviously wanted the company. But, while Nigel could appreciate her wanting a friend—and deep down, he realized it would be helpful, emotionally, for Calliope—he also knew that Stephanie was not family, and it was not his place to decide what level of danger to put her in. Best to drop her at home and take no chances.

"I'll tell you what," Stephanie slipped into the negotiation mode all young girls have perfected by age five, "let's go inside, and I'll call my mom immediately and let her know what's going on. She can come and pick me up if she thinks it's not safe. I know she wouldn't want you wasting time driving me home when Calliope's dad is in trouble. You have more important things to do. My mom will understand what's at stake. Deal?"

Nigel thought about that for a minute. He really did want to get in the house and check the monitors.

"All right, young lady. You have a deal. But I want to talk to your mom after you're done explaining."

"Works for me," she said.

With a deal struck, they exited the car and hustled into the house, Stephanie was already on the house phone talking to Emily. Nigel listened to her divulge all the details they had so far, plus their current deal. Then, she handed the phone to Nigel.

"Here you go. I told her you wanted to talk to her, but she's already getting in her car and heading over."

Nigel accepted the phone. After a quick hello and verification that she was on her way, he hung up and put the phone back in its cradle. "Ok. She should be here in about five minutes. Let's check the basement and make sure we don't have unexpected guests."

Calliope led the way down and was first to the monitors. They quickly determined that the tunnel was empty and all doors were securely shut. Everything looked peaceful and quiet. Calliope felt some anxiousness lift, but she was not totally relieved. Part of her had hoped some creature had made it through. It would have answered the question of what had taken her dad, plus forced her grandfather's hand to take action. Now, they were back to waiting, and not knowing.

"Grandpa, I know you said we can't go after dad, but can we at least get our gear ready in case we *have* to act?"

Nigel considered her request. He realized allowing her to prepare was one more step towards letting her go in, but he was also chomping at the bit to take action. He could understand her desire to be *doing*.

"Alright, kiddo. Let's see what kind of gear we think we might need if we 'hypothetically' went after your dad."

In the storage room, Calliope grabbed her spearmint green seventy-liter pack, then her mom's blue seventy-liter for her grandfather to use. As she started going over the packs checking for wear and tear, Stephanie surprised her by slapping the muted-purple twenty-four-liter daypack onto the prep table.

"Hey, as long as we're just 'hypothetically' packing for a rescue mission, there's no reason I can't 'hypothetically' come along." Stephanie preemptively responded to the opposition brewing from both Calliope and her grandfather. Any further discussion was cut off as the doorbell rang.

"That's my mom. I'll get it while you keep packing." She trundled back upstairs.

Nigel and Calliope heard the door open, and the Lapointes greet each other. Then two sets of footsteps came back down to the prep room.

"Nigel, I'm sorry about Ben," Emily said as she entered the room. "What can I do to help?"

"Thanks, Emily. I'm afraid right now, all we can do is wait to hear back from those sprites." His voice held conviction, but Emily saw the wily Marine flash across his face.

"I see you're packing, though?"

"It's just in case something changes and we have to go in and help my dad fast," Calliope answered. She rummaged through the first aid kit, making note of missing or low supplies.

"We need to beef this up," she declared to the group. "We have stuff upstairs in the linen closet."

She abandoned her spot at the bench and ran upstairs. Moments later, she was back with a handful of bandaids, a roll of gauze, a small bottle of rubbing alcohol, and packets of various painkillers: aspirin, ibuprofen, naproxen sodium. She organized the supplies in the plastic case, then set it aside to be one of the last items packed.

There was an order to packing a backpack. A carefully considered arrangement based on weight and need. Bulky items that you did not need often, like a sleeping bag, or ground pad, went on the bottom. Heavy, hard gear that you did not need until you set up camp, like a cook kit and stove, went in the core of the pack, usually wrapped in soft items, such as the tent body, or extra clothes. The top of the pack was reserved for things you needed often, or in an emergency. First-aid kit, rain gear or jacket, and toilet supplies were good choices. Snacks, compass, knife, flashlights and other tools went in various pockets or clipped to loops for frequent, convenient access on the trail.

Calliope and Nigel packed in a coordinated assault. Calliope took the cook kit and tent, Nigel took the heavier, bulkier climbing rope and gear. Each had packets of dried meals, but Nigel packed the water purifier. Stephanie worked the third pack with lighter stuff: emergency tube tent, dried meal kits, hydration bladder, and camp cleaning kit containing essentials for washing the body, and clothes. She stuffed the pockets and straps with tools, lights, lip balm, and protein bars. This did not escape Emily's notice.

"Uh, Stephanie, my dear, what exactly are you doing?" she addressed her daughter in a motherly tone.

"I'm just prepping an extra pack. It doesn't hurt to have something ready on the off chance it's needed. By someone. Anyone really. You never know."

"Oh, I *know*," said Emily. "I *know* it won't be you."

"Unless those sprites come back and tell us it's all clear, and Ben's fine," said Nigel, "none of us are going in there."

They finished their packing with no news developing from the cellar. The cameras showed empty, quiet passages. No one was quite sure what to do next. Calliope felt a sense of anticlimax. From the receipt of the email, to the rush home, and the hurried packing, Calliope had anticipated that events would carry them forward; draw them into The City.

"Nigel," Emily said, "I could use a cup of coffee. How about we go upstairs, get the girls something to eat and I'll raid Ben's private coffee stash. I know he has some good stuff."

"Sure. I could use a cup myself."

The group retreated upstairs. Calliope went reluctantly, not wanting to leave the monitors, but she was assuaged by the reality that she was only upstairs. She could return in seconds to check the monitors, plus the sprites would probably be gone for some time tracking her dad. They would ring the cellar's doorbell, or email again when they returned. She would not be out of touch.

Once in the kitchen, Emily pulled open Ben's coffee drawer. There were several brands of coffee pods ready to be dropped into the single-serve machine, but she knew she liked the eco-friendly, compostable brand Ben stored in the hermetically sealed glass jar. It was a roast called "Bold of Body, Bold of Mind," a deep, dark coffee that filled the kitchen with its warm, roasted aroma, and it had the added bonus of an extra kick of caffeine.

"How long will you wait before going in?" Emily spoke to Nigel softly as the coffee maker steamed, spurted and squelched through its brew cycle. The girls were in their own discussion at the table on the other side of the room, unable to listen in.

"What do you mean?" asked Nigel.

"I mean, I haven't known you very long, Nigel, but I know Ben. I can see from where he gets his overdeveloped sense of responsibility— and the heroic. Your eyes give it away. You're trying to figure out the best way to go after Ben. If you weren't responsible for Calliope, you'd be in those tunnels right now." Nigel didn't respond, but Emily recognized the sheepish grin of someone caught doing something they shouldn't. "Aha! I knew it."

"You're a parent. Tell me you wouldn't do the same thing if it were Stephanie. No, you don't have to tell me, because you already *did* do it! When Stephanie disappeared into that tunnel in the basement, you followed right after, with less knowledge about the dangers you were facing than I have right now."

"I'm not arguing with you," Emily proclaimed. "In fact, I'm offering to help. I can take Calliope home with me. I'll take care of her, no matter how long it takes for you to find Ben and bring him home."

Nigel thought for a minute. "If I know my granddaughter—and I do—she's not going to be very happy about being left behind."

"You're right about that. But just present it to her this way," Emily said, "By staying with Stephanie and me, we're in the loop. We can come back here every day to check for messages or progress. I'll make sure she stays close, but stays safe. I assume the other scenario is that she gets shipped off to her grandmother in Florida?"

"That was the option I was considering, yes," said Nigel.

They passed the next hour discussing topics designed to keep everyone's mind off of the cellar and Ben's predicament. It was not working. Inevitably, eyes wandered to the basement door. When anyone's cell phone bleeped an alert, Calliope jumped to check hers for a message. Even the house creaking in the wind set everyone on edge, ready for an attack, as their imaginations conjured up a myriad of nightmares emerging from below.

But just when Nigel was about to suggest that they all take a break and leave the house for a bit, the doorbell rang. Not the front doorbell, but the one Ben had set up inside the wine room. The one behind the vault door. It could only mean that the sprites had returned. And if they were ringing the bell, they had returned without Ben.

Calliope was first to descend, the others a breath behind. At the monitor, they could see Garran standing nervously inside the wine cellar, his head swiveling from the tablet he was tapping, to the closed door behind him that hid the tunnel beyond. Nigel reached over Calliope's shoulder and switched the monitor from two screens to eight, giving them a view from the cellar to the iron gears of the doorway for The City. They were surprised to see that the door was still ajar. Nothing seemed to move in the tunnel, however. Only Garran poking frantically at the tablet.

"Garran, we're here." Calliope spoke into the microphone on the camera clipped to the monitor. They watched Garran jump backwards as her voice startled him. He punched at another icon on the tablet, allowing him to speak back.

"Calliope, thank The Spirits! We were unable to reach your father. We were overrun. I have lost several of my people. I do not know what these creatures are, but they are quickly taking over Chathair Doras. One chased me through, preventing me from closing the door behind. I do not know how long I have, but I had to warn you, and you must find a way to close the doorway."

"Ahhh!" Emily exclaimed. "Something just moved over camera six! It flew right in front, blocking out the whole picture. I couldn't see what it was."

"Not flew," said Garran. "Crawled. They crawl along the walls and ceiling as easily as the floors. But it is the filmy mesh they fling that must be avoided. It is sticky. It can wrap you up. The more you struggle, the more it clings. It can immobilize you enough that the creatures pounce with their many legs."

"Many legs?" Stephanie interjected. "How many?"

"Six. No, eight," Garran replied. "I believe they have eight legs, covered in light fur. And their eyes reflect light like a multifaceted jewel. That can give away their position in the dark, if you catch them with your electric soluna sticks."

"Eight furry legs. Jeweled eyes. Throw sticky mesh. We all know what these are, right?" Calliope wanted to put a name to what she was sure they were all thinking. "Spiders!"

"Garran, how big are these creatures?" Nigel was eager to get as much information as he could, as fast as he could in case whatever creature actually was in there, came and grabbed the sprite.

"Some are no bigger than my fist. Some are as large as three sprites. Almost as large as Ben Sullivan."

The girls gasped at Garran's description. Emily let out a censored parental curse. Nigel ignored their shock and continued. "And how many? Do you have an idea of their count and how much of The City they occupy? Which hallways are safe?"

"We were overrun, surrounded, then hunted by several tens of creatures. I would guess there are even more; perhaps several hundred occupy the hallways. As for which hallways are safe? None can be safe for sure, but any tunnel that they occupy in numbers is adorned with that silvery mesh they secrete. Avoid those at all costs."

Garran jumped and spun to face the door at the back of the cellar. "It's here, on the other side of the door." He brought up one of the Temizu's ebony blades, held it high and steady, point forward, in the attack stance Calliope and Stephanie had seen many Temizu warriors use when fighting and sparring. Garran had clearly been studying with his graceful neighbors.

"Hold on, Garran," Nigel called. "I have something that may help." He turned to the ladies who were already looking at him. Shock from the realization of what lurked on the other side of those doors combined with Nigel's statement of help, and the realization that he intended to open the heavy vault door. Their one sure defense.

"Keep your eyes on the cameras. That back door should hold until I get back. I need to get something in the garage. I'll only be gone a minute or two."

Without waiting for a response, he bolted for the stairs. They stood in mute shock, listening to Calliope's grandfather thumping up the stairs, across the kitchen and out the door to the garage. He must have left the door open, because they could hear what sounded like cans and tools hitting the ground, then something heavy scraped across the concrete pad. A minute later, they heard him retrace his steps back through the house. He appeared around the corner holding a long metal pipe with what looked to be a soup can on one end, and a hose extending from the other. Attached to the hose, and pulling heavily on his left hand, was an off-gray twenty pound propane tank, assumingly snatched from the Sullivan family grill.

"Good God, Nigel!" exclaimed Emily. Her sharp mind had quickly put the pieces together. "You are not going in there with a homemade flamethrower!"

"Not homemade," said Nigel. "Ben bought it at the home improvement store." He pointed to the sticker on the tube which proclaimed it to be a "Weed Dragon."

"It's his garden torch for burning weeds and stuff. Works great. Perfectly safe."

He hoisted the tank to the prep table, then upended the large backpack Stephanie had just packed.

"Sorry, Steph. I can't carry this thing in there. I need to get it on my back somehow."

With that, he proceeded to unzip the backpack's full access panel and set the tank inside. Zipping it up was impossible—it was much larger than the pack could hold—but a few bungee cords through the pack's lash points and the tank's handle bundled the package. He spun it around, so he could slide into the straps, buckle it up, and stand.

"Not too bad," he told his audience. "A little bulky and off-center, but much better than carrying it, and I have my hands free." With that, he pulled a heavy duty pair of gloves from his back pocket and jammed his hands in.

"Calliope, can you open the vault door please?" He walked over to the Victorian portal with its modern access panel, and Calliope followed. She paused to look up at her grandfather.

"Are you sure about this, grandpa?"

"Damn straight, kiddo." He was calmly confident, standing there with flamethrower barrel draped along his right arm, spark striker ready to go in his left hand.

"Wait, wait," Calliope jumped back into gear storage and returned with her dad's climbing helmet and a long, narrow cardboard box. She jammed the helmet on her grandfather's head and cinched the strap. Then, she popped open the box and displayed a new machete with sheath, still wrapped in plastic. "Dad just got this. After our last adventure, he figured I should have my own. He special-ordered it."

Only the handle was visible, but Nigel could tell it was a quality tool; full tang extended through a hardwood handle, with brass pins and a decorative brass wire wrap near the top of the grip. With Nigel's nod of approval, she unwrapped it and clipped it to his backpack over his right shoulder, ready for an easy draw.

"Time to go. Calliope, open the door for me, please."

Nigel readied the striker. Stephanie monitored the monitors. Calliope tapped out the combination to open the door, spun the wheel to release the bolts, and pulled.

"Good luck, Nigel," said Emily.

With an acknowledging nod, Nigel turned the knob to start the gas, struck a spark, and with a not so subtle "poof," a soup can sized flutter of orange flame awoke from the end of the pipe. Nigel opened the control knob a bit more and the orange flutter morphed into a cobalt jet a foot long.

"Whoa!" the girls all exclaimed at once.

"Make sure you keep that away from Garran," Stephanie said. "He's wood, remember."

Nigel gave her a nod, then turned to his granddaughter. "Shut this door as soon as I walk through, and lock it. I don't want that thing getting past me and into the house." Not waiting for a reply, he stepped through to find Garret still poised and ready in front of the back door. A quick glance backwards affirmed his granddaughter had followed directions.

"Garran, I had hoped to meet you under less dire circumstances, but I'm Ben's father. I'd like to thank you for attempting to go after him, then coming here to warn us about the spiders."

"Spiders?" Garran glanced sideways at his new comrade.

"Well, that's what it sounds like. Hairy creatures with eight legs and able to spin, or throw webs: sticky, silvery, thread-like stuff. We have many, many different varieties of spiders on Earth, but nothing near as big as seems to be waiting on the other side of this door. The biggest we have here is about the size of a dinner plate. And let me tell you, any spider bigger than my thumb is enough to give me the heebie-jeebies."

"Yes," said Garran, "I would say I have the...heebie-jeebies myself, right now. But I am glad you are standing with me to help, Nigel Sullivan, father of Ben. And I, too, wish circumstances were less dire." He gave the flamethrower a nervous, sideways glance. "I must also admit that your fire stick is giving me a bit more than heebie-jeebies. In truth, my instincts are telling me to run as far away from that as I can."

Nigel gave Garren a sympathetic nod. "I can surely understand that. But don't worry. I will be extremely careful." He turned his attention back to the tunnel door, where they could still hear the thumping and scratching from the other side.

"I think we had better see what we can do with our unwanted guest on the other side, Garran. Especially since the other door into The City is still open. We don't want any of his friends to join him. I'm afraid more than one or two of these things will be more than we can handle."

"On that, you are correct, Nigel."

"Plus, it's already getting warm in here from this flamethrower. It's going to be an oven before much longer." He spied a rubber door wedge resting near the jamb. Maneuvering it with his foot, he positioned the point a few inches from the bottom of the rear black door, planted his boot firmly behind it, then made ready to throw the latches.

"Here's what I think we should do," he addressed Garran. "I'm going to open the door, but only an inch or so. We'll see if it tries to squeeze through. If it does, I'll hit it with the flame and either catch it on fire, or wound it enough to force it back. If none of that works, and it keeps coming, you stick it. If we force it back, we keep up the chase all the way down the tunnel, through the door to The City. If we get that last door shut, we take a minute to regroup and think about next steps."

"I concur with your plan. Let us proceed," said Garran.

Nigel took a deep breath, then reached up to throw the latch.

—5—

Spiders and Spot

Ben was dragged along at a galloping pace. He could not move his arms, and his legs scrabbled just to keep his body from careening into walls. His captors had bound his torso in the thickest silken thread Ben had ever felt, which was par for the course, since they were the biggest spiders Ben had ever seen. From everything he knew about spiders—which was not much, and was probably overinflated nonsense from bad science-fiction movies—Ben had expected to be bitten into submission, drugged with neurotoxins, then hung up in a silken cocoon until his insides gelatinized into a drinkable goo suitable for spiders to slurp up. The reality, so far, was a twisted version of a Western where the villains tether the local sheriff behind a horse and drag him at a breakneck pace until he is so battered, bruised, and bloodied, he might as well be dead. The differences here being: first - he was not being dragged by a horse; second - he was not a sheriff; third - they had wrapped him in so much strong, soft silk, he was not actually being battered and bruised. Sure, he was a little worried about his head banging around, but since the tow web connected from his back, past his head, momentum kept his noggin relatively clear of collisions.

As they charged along, Ben's control pin was turning lights on and off around them. This was both a blessing, and a curse. On the positive side, Ben was able to somewhat track where they were headed; counting the twists and turns, the ups and downs. They had jounced uncomfortably down a few flights of stairs, and Ben was not eager to traverse another level.

On the negative side, the lights allowed Ben to see the numerous furry-legged followers that seemed to find his mad journey fascinating. It seemed every new hallway, and every intersection increased the train. Creatures of all sizes scrambled along walls, clung to the ceiling, even clambered over each other. It was maddening. Ben wanted nothing more than to be freed, but to escape now meant being overwhelmed by the oncoming horde of terrifying, gigantic arachnids. He did not relish that scenario.

On and on they went, until Ben thought he might recognize the area they were traveling. He caught glimpses of designs on doorways that looked familiar. Not familiar like he had passed them many times on his way to Quilium, but identified enough for him to guess he had seen them on his first trip into The City, five years ago. And that made terrifying sense, because that was also when he had seen the door with the symbols of gigantic, angry-looking spiders. He was more and more suspecting that that was his final destination.

Final, like where the spiders would stop, he clarified to himself. Not final, as in final resting place. There was no way he was accepting the fate of the fly in the web. If he could just move one of his hands to a pocket, any pocket, he was sure he could find something to cut himself loose. Problem was, one hand was stuck tight to his belly, and the other to his upper thigh. He could not get to his pockets.

Abruptly, Ben's sled-run came to a halt. The followers, however, did not. A wave of black legs enveloped Ben's surroundings, but thankfully, did not descend upon him. They came to a restless stop, boiling in anticipating waves, all jittery legs, gleaming eyes, and scary fangs. To be fair, only some had fangs, and those teeth were on the small side, but Ben reasoned that any tooth large enough to protrude from a closed mouth was definitely a fang. And anything that could be considered a fang could be considered to have venom. And anything that had venom was definitely something to be wary of.

Just as one or two curious, or brave, or hungry followers seemed to lose their patience, Ben was hoisted upward. His torso left the ground, then his legs, setting him to dangling and spinning as he rose in the air. At half a rotation, he saw the winding staircase just in time to jerk his head to the side, avoiding a collision with the bottom corner of an ornate iron step. His shoulder was not so lucky.

The spider hauling him upwards had no regard for spatial navigation of cargo. Ben considered its thinking to be somewhat less than a caveman's: *Go through hole. Pull food through hole. Eat food.*

After two unsuccessful tugs and the accompanying clashes of shoulder to the filigreed underbelly of metal stair, Ben decided it was in his better interest to help out. Bending at the waist as much as his bindings would allow, Ben kicked and set himself to swinging, first away from the stairs, then back inward. The controlling spider was not cooperating, as it chose to yank a third time just as Ben swung inward. A third collision slowed his swing considerably, but his ferryman pulled again in quick succession and managed to get Ben past the first obstacle. Now, Ben was high enough that he could actually get a free foot, or knee, or even buttock onto or against the staircase to keep himself tangle-free as the spider continued to haul, thus avoiding more impact.

At the top, Ben did not flop over the edge, as expected, but dangled, suspended from the ceiling.

I feel like a Christmas ornament, thought Ben, *just not hanging from a tree.*

But as he spun around, surveying his surroundings, an unwanted, familiar figure came into view.

"Oh look," he said, "a tree."

His voice, he realized, had come out at a slightly higher pitch than normal. Tinged with a bit of surprise. A bit of panic.

"Tree *Lord*, fleshling," said the giant creature, which loomed over

Ben, even as he swayed several feet from the ground. "As I informed you on our last meeting. I am The Keeper. It is my charge to watch over the doorways. My charge to seek and quarantine. My charge to secure and inoculate. My charge to assess and annihilate."

"Wow," said Ben, "that's, uh…that's a lot of hats to wear. Keeper. The Keeper."

He pretended to mull the name over, screwed his face into a thoughtful, distasteful grimace. He was thinking fast, trying to buy some time to think of an escape. His last encounter with this creature had not gone well. Ben had barely escaped with his life. He already had misgivings about this meeting, for obvious reasons.

"Nope. No. I don't think it suits you. Keeper, I mean. Oakenpuss is better. I'm gonna stick with that."

The creature did not seem to realize the epithet was a slight, or perhaps it just refused to rise to Ben's gibe. It stood in unemotional study, slightly stooped and scraping the high ceilings with its erratically coiffed branches and leaves. Its breadth Ben estimated at five feet. Using that guess, Ben reached into the depths of his memory for the grade school formula of a circle's circumference. $C = 2\pi r$ or $C = \pi d$ so with a diameter of five, and pi being roughly 3.14, then Oakenpuss would be a little over fifteen and a half feet in circumference. Ben found that very interesting. The creature was bigger than the last time they had met. He was positive Oakenpuss could not make it down the spiral staircases any more, only the wide, grand stairways. And he was willing to bet the creature could only make it through the largest of doorways. No way it could enter the doorway to Earth. Too many small portals. Even the portal to Quilium should be safe now. If Ben could make it to either door, he could find refuge.

Movement behind the tree drew Ben's attention. The spiders, strangely enough, were staying clear of Oakenpuss. They did not scurry away, or avoid the tree's notice, they hovered on the fringes, maintaining a buffer, to be sure, but not fleeing in fear, and not attacking the giant talking acorn. That implied some sort of control on the Tree Lord's part.

"I see you've made some friends?" said Ben.

Information was always key. Ben wanted to stall for as long as he could, but also understand every dynamic, and every reason for his circumstance.

"Did you bring them here, or are they holding you hostage as well?"

Oakenpuss laughed, a low, rumbling, legato drumbeat, halfway between a low growl and the rolling pur of an enormous wooden tiger. It was sonorous and quite enchanting, if it were not emanating from an enemy.

"The crawlers, like all creatures, are inferior, and as such, are merely tools for my use. Useful tools, it turns out. They very neatly do my bidding, even if they do proliferate. No matter. That, too, is proving useful in an unforeseen way. As we do not approve of other species using The Crossings, these creatures will do an excellent job of deterring the occasional exploring race, such as yours. They pose no threat to my order, preferring to eat fleshly creatures. Therefore, I can allow them to thrive as they might. Besides, it does seem like they prefer their own world to these halls. So should we decide to cleanse this place of crawlers, we should be able to open the doorway and allow them egress."

"The Crossings? That's what you call this place? Man, we really need to get everyone together and decide on one name: Chathair Doras, City of Doors, The Crossings. It gets confusing." Again, Ben's flippancy elicited no response. "So, did you build 'The Crossings?'" Ben was pretty sure he knew the answer, but wanted to extract as much information as he could. Not to mention stall for time.

"We did not. We discovered them, eons ago and made them

ours."

"Ah, I see. So you know how they work? What science *The Crossings* employ to enable instantaneous travel between worlds which are physically separated by many light years?"

The tree seemed to crook it's head slightly. Perhaps puzzled. Perhaps interested.

"Do you understand what a light year is?" No answer again. "Hmm. Well, it's the distance that light can travel in one year—hence 'light year'—which is somewhere around six *trillion* miles. That's six followed by twelve zeros. A human in good shape can walk about fourteen hundred miles in a year, if she only stopped to sleep. I'll give you the benefit of the doubt and say you could walk two thousand miles in a year. So, if you started walking now, it would take you three billion years to cover the same distance light travels in one. And solar systems are at least four light years apart, so times that by four and you could walk to another planet in about twelve billion years. Give or take a billion. Of course, you can't walk through space, so you would have to build spaceships first. That's a whole other ball of wax. How's your chemistry? Physics? Calculus? Astronomy?"

The creature's brow ridges furrowed a bit in seeming agitation. Ben did not want him angry. Confused, certainly; interested, maybe; talking would be best.

"I suppose, with *The Crossings*, none of that really matters. But eons of walking these halls and you have never been interested in how they work?" asked Ben. "You must have explored the depths, categorized and mapped all of the doors and passageways?"

"We find the passages we need to find, when we need to find them," it replied.

"Of course, of course." Ben feigned respectful understanding. He did not want to give up the secrets he had learned about The City, but he wondered if Oakenpuss knew about the pixies, or the pins.

"So, you have never run across the creators of *The Crossings*? No sign of them? No writings, or libraries, or anything to give you some sort of clue about who they are, or were?"

"Clues abound, human. You have but to look. But Tree Lords care not for these trifling, dead hardscapes. Plants are life. Plants sustain, renew. We keep worlds in harmony, in balance, in growth and purity. It is the fleshlings that destroy, pollute, ruin worlds, again and again."

Ben secretly thought the plant had a point, but the conversation was taking a turn he did not want. The creature's bias could be an opening for detente, and his release, if Ben could just persuade along the right lines.

"I will grant you that humans have done their fair share of polluting and wounding of the land, but we have also done a lot to help plants and our planet." He was scrambling, now, to think of good examples. "We have found cures for many plant diseases. We have developed fertilizers to nourish plants in nutrient depleted soils. We raise plants inside our homes. We are also caretakers of the land. We have Arbor Day, a national holiday where we plant trees. We understand the biodiversity it takes to keep a planet healthy. You say we humans destroy, but I say we live in harmony. We breathe in oxygen and give off carbon dioxide gas. Plants—especially trees—need to absorb carbon dioxide to live, and in turn give off oxygen. Fleshlings may eat certain plants as food, but our waste from consuming food becomes fertilizer to feed more plants. If that does not describe a beneficial symbiotic relationship, I don't know what does."

"Nothing about your race is beneficial, human. Simpler fleshlings may bring benefits; they eat pesty insects and do drop fertilizer pellets. Those all come without destruction. I think we will limit our contact to those."

Ben felt a glimmer of hope. It had said, 'limit our contact.' Ben could work with that. At least it was not talking about annihilation.

"Well, I, for one, am happy to never visit your home world again. You will notice that I have never visited your homeworld since that first mistake years ago."

"True, but you have been visiting the sprites with regularity. And they you. You interfere in the natural order of things. We cannot have that. You must be removed."

"I beg to differ on your argument. If I may point out, it was your species that went to the sprite world and brought disease. Your people caused heavy losses to the sprites. It was my family and I—humans, fleshlings—who brought a cure to them and eliminated the Hollowing fungus. Talk about upsetting the natural order of things; once the fungus you brought took hold, it attracted the attention of underground dwelling creatures who attacked the sprites, further decimating their number. A chain of fatal reactions kicked off by one event: your arrival. If you are to be judge and jury to another race for the ignorant actions of a few, it would only be fair to hold your own race to the same standard."

"Ah, the Armillaria fungus. Yes, we had to carefully cultivate that into their population. It was no accident, fleshling. Sprites had shown their own interfering tendencies, and needed to be curtailed. And the Slizeg under the mountains were coaxed out just as carefully. They could smell the infected sprites; were drawn to the fungus and driven to grow more. The sprites became their medium, their gardening resource. It was deemed that reducing sprite numbers, and giving them something else to focus on would teach them to remain close to home, concentrating on their primary task of plant stewardship."

"You...planned all that?" asked Ben, incredulous. "Why? The sprites only came to this place after you and I came to their world."

"Yes, and they were only too eager to start exploring after that unfortunate day. Again, I blame you, fleshling. It was *your* action that started—how did you put it?—a chain of fatal reactions. You have only yourself to blame."

This was like arguing with a ten year old, Ben thought. "So, my accidental, innocuous, naive exploration that led me to the sprite homeworld for a brief period, where I touched little, interacted with no one, and left within minutes, caused you to attempt to wipe out their entire race?"

"Exactly. You were the catalyst." Ben sensed notes of rancor, subdued anger.

"Well, then, by that logic, I could take another step back and say your hostile actions of wanting to feed me to a plant forced me to flee to Quilium. To which, you will say your actions were warranted by my actions of coming to your world uninvited. To which I would argue that I only came to your world because your pet had come to mine, where I saw him, and followed him back.

How is Spot, by the way?" Ben looked around, knowing he would not see the creature, but putting on a show for having befriended the Tree Lord's pet.

"Unfortunately, *Groznyi* did not make it back from the crawler world. It was unfortunate. I did like that particular fleshling. He was beneficial to the trees, and useful to me. But, I have outlived many pets in my lifetime. There will be another."

Ben was saddened by the thought of these giant spiders feasting on that magnificent, intelligent, inquisitive animal. He had really liked Spot. And Groznyi? Such a harsh sounding name for such a graceful creature. Ben would never remember him with that name. He was Spot.

"That's pretty cold-hearted, even for you, Oakenpuss."

"I do not know what that means, fleshling, but I assume you do not approve of Groznyi's fate. So, I am sure you will be equally unhappy with yours, since you will be joining him. As I said, the crawlers prefer their own world. I'm allowing these to take you back with them to dispose of you as they will. That should close this loop once and for all. Good-bye, human." He waved a stickly appendage at the spiders, shooing them back.

Before Ben could respond, his cocoon swang away from the Tree Lord. His handler was on the move again, apparently traversing along the ceiling this time, for Ben continued to sway and spin. He was actually getting a bit dizzy. And nauseous. He wanted to keep his eyes open so he could map his travels, but he had to close them to keep down his breakfast.

Breakfast. It was only a few hours since he had been safely at home with his daughter and his dad, excited to be on another adventure through The City, to another world with unbelievable creatures that he called friends. It had felt like some fairy tale come to life. And he had almost brought Calliope; caved to her logical arguments that if it was just a quick overnight visit, there would be no danger. Thank God he had elected for caution and patience. He could not imagine his daughter in this situation, looking at such a gruesome fate.

No! He was not giving up that easily. He was getting out of this and going back home to his family. He just had to concentrate and get a hand to a pocket.

He closed his eyes again to curb the rising motion sickness, and focused on his left arm. It was trapped awkwardly along his side, his hand above the thigh pocket, but below his waist. He could feel his belt knife, snapped in its sheath at his waist, pressing into his forearm, so he concentrated on that. He could move his arm slightly inside the jacket sleeve, but the back of his hand was stuck in webbing, as was the outside of his jacket. He could only manage some up and down shrugging from wrist to shoulder.

He decided his hand was the weak link. If he could peel it away from the webbing, maybe he could suck it far enough into his jacket sleeve that he could manipulate the knife through his coat. It was not trapped by webbing, only by Ben's body.

He curled his fingers, digging them into his thigh. The webbing protested, came along for a fraction of an inch, then pulled his fingers back. Tough stuff. Ben tried again. And again. And again. His digits were cramping. His palms were sweaty. His skin hurt. And he knew he was running out of time. He pulled even harder and felt something give on his index finger, just above the nail bed. It was only a little movement, but he knew what it was. He had pulled the skin back from his cuticle, the skin's weak spot. Ben always got tears there during the dry winter months. And he knew what was next: blood. That could be useful, as long as he could rub it on the webbing, and not on his pants. He squeezed his fingers together and was able to get the tip of his index finger over the tip of his middle. He rubbed. Just a fraction of an inch, but enough to spread the blood. He could feel the moisture infecting the webbing, and then he felt the webbing release the nail of his middle finger. He bent his end knuckle, and the leverage was enough to tear the cuticle at that second digit. More blood. He repeated the process for each finger along his left hand. Once all fingernails were free, and bleeding, he worked hard to just make a fist, tearing more at the flesh of his hand.

Success! The last strands released his hand, so Ben sucked it up inside his sleeve, just far enough to rest over the belted knife. He used his jacket like an ungainly glove, worked at the button clasp of the sheath, popped it, then slipped free the folded knife. Careful not to expose it to the web and get it stuck, he worried at the handle until the blade swung open. A final flick, a telltale click, and his knife was free! He slid it down, letting the tip poke past fabric. He pushed and sawed, a little at a time, feeling the strands drag at the knife, but not capture; feeling them snap and recoil a fraction; feeling a slight movement of air making it through his cocoon. Progress!

Ben's ride came to a halt. He swayed and spun for a second, then dropped the few feet to the floor of the hallway. Unable to keep his balance, he toppled left and fell face first to the hard steel floor. It jarred him, sparked stars in his vision for a few seconds, and probably put a large goose egg bump above his right eye. Luckly, he did not drop the knife. Luckier still, he had not driven the blade into his own leg.

He bucked and scooted as best he could, polling his surroundings. He was correct. The spiders had come from the door he had seen on his first adventure through The City. The doorway with the uninviting insignia of large, angry spiders. Just like the large, angry spiders towing him around. This was the end of the road. They were going through. The doorway stood open; the light from The City spilled across the threshold, revealing a cave swathed in whispy silk. Behind him, the retinue halted again, impatiently awaiting...something. The crossing? A feast? An opportunity to steal this tasty meal (for Ben assumed he would be tasty)? They got none of that. Ben's chauffeur crossed over, then reeled him through like a fish on the line. He felt the tell-tale twinge in his mind and wondered if he tried to talk to the spiders, would they understand him? Could he understand them? Would it matter?

His cable ride stopped again, once he was fully on the other side. It seemed the others were loath to join him. He counted his blessings for that. If he could just have the one spider to deal with, that upped his chances considerably. Of course, the doorway was still open, so his advantage was in no way guaranteed.

"Hey... big guy," he faltered.

He was not sure of the correct honorific for an eight-legged monster. And, as he looked up into the black, fuzz covered face, he was unnerved by the four disc-shaped eyes reflecting the fading light from The City. Ben saw himself, four times over, wrapped in white thread, wriggling on the floor like a wounded caterpillar.

"I don't suppose you understand me? Can you understand that I mean you no harm? And I certainly do not want you to harm me? Is there some way we can work through our differences, perhaps? You let me go, and we both go our separate ways. No harm, no foul?"

The creature responded only with a jitter to the side; a herkie-jerky movement that, combined with the unblinking, obsidian eyes, struck Ben as being very mechanical, very robotic. This was extremely helpful, mentally. Thinking about his captors as robots, rather than the creepy-crawly, motley-haired killing machines they actually were, somehow fought back the near-paralyzing micro-phobia Ben harbored for arachnids.

Ben was not sure if the jittering was caused by his talking, but with no immediate attack, he was encouraged to continue. He put on his best, soft-spoken, unaggressive, but deep voice and resumed negotiations. The trick, he surmised, was to sound calm, confident, powerful, yet non-threatening. He thought James Earl Jones, Vader presence, but with Kenobi's subtlety. A bit of Jedi mind trickery. A "these are not the droids you're looking for" moment.

"I'm really quite trustworthy, and a most useful ally." He intoned. "I'm sure that if you release me, I could help you, some time in the future. Is there anything we could, perhaps, trade? Do your... people?... suffer from any disease, or fungus, perhaps? My people have many medicines."

The arachnid had one of the best poker faces Ben had ever come across. It showed no emotion, no blinking, no head turning or slumping shoulders. The only response this time was the raising of its frontmost legs. It moved them in a motion as if petting the air. Ben remembered that spiders could feel vibrations in the air with the hairs on their body. He also recalled that some spiders could "smell" with their pedipalps; chemical-sensitive hair sensors. He hoped it was hearing his vocal vibrations, and not smelling him, as one would sniff a particularly pleasant pork chop.

It stiffened, sank a few inches into a recognizable crouch that Ben's every instinct told him was preparation to pounce. This was it. It was going to spring on him like a puma on a rabbit, only not a tenth as cute. Of course, to the rabbit a puma was not cute, but Ben was pretty sure that while the rabbit would be terrified by the puma, it would be horrified into heart failure by a giant spider.

Ben, his heart racing just as fast as the proverbial rabbit, refocused his attention to the knife in his left hand. He bent his will—which was screaming to follow the escape option in his primal fight-or-flight response—towards pushing and pulling at the blade; to cut through as many of the sticky ligaments as quickly as possible; to free his left arm in time to drive home his tiny blade into the underside of this abomination. He was Bilbo Baggins, and his knife would be Sting, sinking deeply into this spider of Mirkwood! He would prevail to ride with dwarves and dance with the elves! He was going crazy, hysterical, and not just a bit lost in panic as he grabbed onto iconic heroes from his childhood.

His knife sliced upwards. His arm broke free. The spider sprang. Time slowed. Ben watched the eight stick-like legs open wide, like a giant hand coming to envelop and grasp. Unable to free his right arm, or his legs, Ben could only scrunch into a ball, left arm raised, knife pointed at the descending enemy, and hope the creature would impale itself and die before piercing him with its toxic fangs.

It seemed impossibly high above him, yet vividly close. He could make out individual hairs on its abdomen, even in the dimming light. They had a greasy sheen, like they needed a good shampooing.

Ben's eyes were transfixed as the creature descended. His adrenaline rampaged for the hundredth time in the last few hours. He took a giant breath and held it, ready to let out his primal scream in one last all-out effort of defense. He cocked back his knife arm, ready for the thrust to meet his foe. Its legs were just upon him, the abdomen almost within reach. Ben thrust, and growled like a king of the jungle, or a valiant knight crashing into the galloping hordes, knowing full well his odds of survival were slim, but honor, and courage, and faith could prevail.

A ball of green and brown slammed into the giant spider,

knocking it sideways, sprawling. Ben watched the shapes roll and clutch each other on the floor, one all black, the other earth tones, but then he realized that this was his chance to get free. He sliced the fibers trapping his right arm, and released that appendage. With both arms free, he made deft work of unwrapping his front. Back to mobility, Ben slipped free his machete, which still clung to his web-covered backpack. He also grabbed his small flashlight, and clicked it on. The light from The City was all but gone, as Ben's pin was out of range. Darkness was swallowing them whole, but his flashlight revealed hundreds of shining eyes still reflecting from the other side. Spiders were watching, and realizing that the prey was escaping, and whatever restraint they had shown in deference to the lead spider was now in question, as that creature was clearly in a struggle for its own life.

Ben evaluated his options. Escape back through the portal, back home, would be a battle surely lost. There was no way he could keep hundreds of creatures at bay, or defeat them completely. Combine that with whatever awaited on this side and he would never see his daughter again.

His decision made, Ben leapt for the door, leaned all his weight into it, and slammed it shut. The locking mechanism on this side was a spinning arm, a crank, rather than the usual wheel. Ben worked it like a meat grinder, heard the gears clank and swirl, heard the bolts moving into place and felt their solid clunk home. He held the door and waited, while glancing back to the figures rolling in the shadows behind him. Their battle was surprisingly quiet. Only the thumping of their bodies recorded their endeavors. And then, a crack, and a squeal, followed by more cracking. The earth-toned creature disentangled itself from the black mass, which remained on its back, squeaking and quivering on the cold stone floor.

"Spot!" Ben exclaimed when the green feather-furred face entered the light. "Come here, boy. Am I ever glad to see you!"

But Ben's Blinx friend was in no mood to get reacquainted. He was agitated and jumpy, scanning all around, from ceiling to floor, gazing into the darkness. He urged Ben to follow him down a side passage by running in that direction, then pausing to look back and wait for Ben, returning to grab Ben's pant leg in its jaws, when Ben did not move.

"Ok, ok. I get it, Spot. I'm coming."

He relinquished his hold on the door and followed the cat-bird-monkey creature, but not before he saw dozens of softball sized spiders scuttle from the darkness to descend on the wounded giant behind them. Ben heard muffled thumping, increased squeaks, then silence as the cannibals incapacitated their prey. That was motivation enough for Ben to stay close on Spot's tail.

—6—

Ins and Outs

Nigel threw the latch on the door. Instantly, the creature slammed into it with an intensity that Nigel had not expected. Luckily, the rubber wedge, and his foot behind it, stuck firm and prevented the steel slab from opening more than a few inches. Through those inches emerged four furry, stick-like legs, tipped with three claws each. Nigel could see two of the creature's eyes shining through the crack; unblinking black marbles that sparked with reflected ambient light. He brought the flamethrower up, pointed it into the opening, and increased the gas. With a greater roar, the flame grew another six inches, and the creature shot back from the tunnel at such a speed that the door slammed shut and Nigel fell into the wall. He righted himself and opened the doorway again, just as Emily's voice came over the speakers.

"It took off back down the tunnel. The doorway is clear." She said.

Nigel threw it open and charged through. He fanned the flamethrower around the tunnel, careful not to get too close to the root system that enveloped them. He scanned the walls and ceiling, then checked to see Garran right behind him.

"Let's push that thing back through to the other side," he said to Garran.

"I will follow your lead, Nigel Sullivan. You are doing excellent." His encouraging tone was not unappreciated by Nigel.

He adjusted the nozzle, reducing the blue flame to an eight inch torch, then engaged a slow, methodical pace along the tunnel, checking around curves, eyeing ceiling to floor.

"Did this spider shoot a web at you?" he asked Garran.

"No, it merely chased me through. Although, I did not stop long enough, nor let it get close enough to take action. It may very well be capable of casting its sticky material."

"Wonderful," mumbled Nigel. "I wish there were speakers down this hallway." He had spotted camera number six and wondered if the ladies could see the creature.

Unexpectedly, his wish was granted. HIs cell phone began its heartening chime: the upbeat theme from Bonanza, the original tv Western. He halted his progress and pulled his phone from his pocket. Glancing at the caller id, he saw his granddaughter's picture.

"Hi Calli. What do you see?"

"It's at the end of the tunnel, but hasn't gone back through the door. I think you're clear through to the end."

"Ok. I'm going to put you on speaker and continue down the hall. Call out if it moves." He switched the phone over, then dropped it into the chest pocket of his plaid shirt. "You still there, Calli?" He spoke into the air.

"Still here, grandpa," came the response from his pocket.

"That is a truly magical device," said Garran. Ben had shown him a cell phone before, and explained how they worked, but this was the first time Garran had actually heard voices emanate from it.

"It really is. Well, it's science, not magic, but sometimes the two are the same."

"Ok, Garran. Let's do this." He resumed his careful walk down the tunnel, trusting his granddaughter to warn him of an ambush. The sprite followed close behind, his obsidian sword held at the ready. They worked their way down the final few meters, and could see the portal chamber with its iron door, still open to The City of

Doors. However, they could not see the spider.

"Where is it Calli?" he whispered to his pocket.

"It's on the ceiling. Just beyond the entrance. It's waiting for you. It knows you're coming. Be careful!"

"Count on it," he replied, and raised the flamethrower, angled to the ceiling.

They were only a few paces from the chamber, now. Nigel knew the spider was waiting just above the entrance. He paused, trying to figure out the best way to attack, without setting the whole tunnel ablaze. But the spider solved that problem for him. Unexpectedly, it bent its abdomen around the tunnel's arched entrance and fired a volley of webbing through the air, a stream of silver gossamer that reached well behind Garran. Uncontrollably, Nigel let out a frightened howl, echoed by his granddaughter through the phone, and he waved the flaming canister in arcs above his head. The webbing did not burst into flame, as Nigel had thought it would, but rather shriveled upon itself, like nylon thread does when heated. That, unfortunately, did not stop the spider. It scrambled in, taking advantage of Nigel's panic, and continued to spray, and advance, spinnerette first. It was all Nigel could do to keep himself free of webs. He could not focus his flame on the creature itself as it bounced around. He retreated, hoping Garran was staying behind and out of his way.

Flaming high and low, Nigel was littering the tunnel with contracted pieces of webbing, still sticky, but relegated to blobs and balls that adhered to the floor and walls. He was stepping in them, forcing him to slow while wrenching his feet free. It was not easy. The stuff was tenacious. It pulled free from the dirt and root floor, but remained stuck to the bottom of his boots, making further steps awkward and wobbly.

That was distraction enough for the spider. It arched a spray over Nigel's head; a feint meant to draw his torch up. It worked. Afraid of being draped in a net, Nigel fanned over his head and shriveled the sheet of silk. But in so doing, left his lower body open, and the spider took advantage by blasting a zig-zag line from left ankle to right knee, to left knee, to right ankle, effectively binding Nigel's legs. He felt himself toppling backwards, and waved the flamethrower wildly in the direction of his attacker, but the creature was no longer in front of him. It had jumped to the ceiling, already in position to drop on its fallen victim. Nigel watched it let loose and flip, like a cat landing on its paws, fangs at the ready. He saw a flash of brown step beside him, and a black glint strike upwards to pierce the descending beast between its centermost pair of jeweled eyes. The body dropped with a dull, heavy thump, like a massive goose down pillow hitting the floor. The only sound remaining was Nigel's heavy breathing, and the roar of the still burning flamethrower.

"Damn. That did not go at all the way I had planned," Nigel huffed and puffed. "Thank you, Garran. That was a nice jab."

"You are welcome. I was merely waiting for the creature to become overzealous of you, and forget about me. Or at least, believe me to be unimportant."

"Well, he won't be making that mistake again," Nigel gave out a relieved laugh. He struggled, but could not unwrap his legs. "Uh, could I impose upon you to slice through these webs?"

Garran deftly flicked his blade between Nigel's knees, down to his ankles, allowing the older Sullivan to scramble to his feet.

"I guess we should close that door first and then figure out our next move."

"Too late, grandpa!" came Calliope's voice through the phone. "There are more spiders coming through. Three... No four of them! You'd better get back here and close the cellar door."

Neither Nigel nor Garran had any fantasies about being able to take on four of these creatures at once. They barely defeated one. In lockstep, the defenders retreated quickly back up the tunnel, keeping a wary eye for pursuit.

"Wait!" Calliope's excited voice came through again. "Ima just came through. And Sonam. And Kunga. And Tormad! They've shut the portal and locked it. You just have the four spiders in there, trapped between you."

Nigel and Garran halted, looked at each other and smiled.

"Let's take 'em," said Nigel.

****

It did not take long for the six to dispatch the invaders. They were half the size of the last spider, and not as cunning. Nigel assumed they were younger, and, thankfully, not as experienced at hunting. Pinned between the incoming sprites behind them, and Nigel and Garran in front, the creatures had nowhere to maneuver. They ended up getting in each other's way, and even managed to tangle themselves in their own webbing. Nigel had used his torch to corral the spiders and melt any threatening silk, but it was the sprites who did the killing.

Ima was graceful and quick. She avoided spraying silk, grasping legs, and biting fangs to stab one monster in its face. The two Dangjong sprites were just as efficient, using bows to pepper a spider a piece with arrows. Tormad, however, was messy. He was carrying his own shiny glass-like blade, but it was not the slim, graceful sword that Ima and Garran carried. It was more akin to a Viking battle axe; one crescent shaped, heavy blade balanced on the backside by a heavy hammer head, all attached to a solid shaft of deep umber wood reminiscent of wenge, and as long as the sprite's arm.

Preferring not to worry about grasping, clawing limbs, Tormad first used his weapon to chop at the front legs. This set up a fearful chittering in his foe, and an urgent retreat. But its effort to flee presented Tormad with the perfect angle to bisect the arachnid at its major body joint, dividing it into cephalothorax and abdomen, while spilling its bluish blood across the living tunnel floor.

It struck Calliope, as she watched on the monitors, that they would have to dispose of the spider corpses and clean the tunnel, otherwise, it was going to quickly smell of rotting corpses down there. Not a pleasant thought at all.

With their job done, and the doors secured, Garran made quick introductions between Nigel and the group, then they all made their way back up the passage. Kunga and Sunam collected their spent arrows from the carcasses as they went.

Calliope had already opened the vault door, and the ladies were waiting for their friends in the wine cellar.

"Hello twig," Emily greeted Garran. "It's good to see you, surprisingly."

She still had not completely forgiven the sprite for kidnapping Stephanie and Calliope, only months before.

"And Ima, Tormad, Sonam, Kunga, it is very good to see you, too. Thank you for coming."

Stephanie and Calliope had already made their rounds, giving hugs and greetings to their adventure companions.

"So, the gang's all here, it seems," said Nigel. "How do we go about saving my son?"

"The tunnels are overrun." Ima spoke with a matter-of-fact tone; analysis, not surrender. "We cannot fight these creatures all throughout Chathair Doras. They attack from all sides, above and below. We need a way to make them run from us. Nigel, your flaming stick will help, but it seems to only push them back in one direction at a time, then they return when you point it elsewhere. And, I must confess, I find the fire a bit unsettling."

"Aye, ye got tha' right," barked Tormad. "I nigh on leaked me sap when ye swung that 'round."

"I think I may have an idea," said Emily. "I need to do some research. Why don't we lock this place down and go up to the kitchen. I'll get online and look up a few things while everyone rests up."

They filed out of the cellar. Nigel closed the heavy steel door behind them, spun the wheel to lock it, then ushered everyone upstairs.

Calliope grabbed her laptop for Emily, who quickly got down to business, fingers flitting around the keyboard. Nigel slapped a coffee pod in the machine, which spit out a calming aroma and a mug of steaming dark liquid.

"Now that be a magical device!" Tormad eyed Nigel's cup of coffee longingly.

"That's right, Ben mentioned you had developed a taste for coffee," said Nigel. "Said you drink it through your fingers?" Tormad shrugged and nodded. "Here. You can have mine. I'll brew another. Anyone else care for a cup? Or water? Or...something else?"

Ima took water from the tap, as did Garran. Sonam and Kunga followed Tormad's lead and sampled the Sullivan coffee collection. Nigel popped a pod of his own in the machine and let the squelching fade out while his mind traveled the tunnel and opened the door to a multitude of arachnid attack scenarios. He wished he had his M-16 from his days in the Marines, and several thousand rounds of ammunition. Or better yet, he wished he had several thousand Marines, each with their own M-16. That would send those eight legged monsters back to whatever hole they crawled out of.

"I found some info," Emily interrupted Nigel's musings. "Listen to this. 'Many spiders have hair-like bristles, called setae, on the last segment of their legs. On some spiders these are chemosensory—used to smell—on others they are sensitive to both airborne and substrate vibrations, meaning they can 'hear' with their feet. These hairs are so sensitive they can feel the wing beats of a moth as it approaches.'"

"Ok, so how do we use that?" Stephanie asked her mother.

"Well, *Nigel*," she emphasized the older Sullivan's name, alluding that the girls would not be part of any operation, "can try using something really loud, like an airhorn, to overwhelm their hearing and make them run. That would work in all directions at once. Of course, it would also alert everything in The City that you're there, possibly calling more spiders to you. So, maybe only for last resort use."

"To overwhelm their sense of smell, he could use vinegar. I'll bet they would avoid walking over any place with vinegar on it, or around it. And we can buy gallons of it immediately."

"What about bug bombs?" Nigel asked. "I know those things fill a room for hours and kill bugs of all shapes and sizes."

"I thought about that, and maybe you can set those off as you leave an area, but those are also toxic to humans. I have no idea what they'll do to sprites. So, if you need to travel back through an area, best not to use one. I don't know how long the toxins last in an area that can't be aired out."

"Good point." Nigel said. "Still, maybe we can take a bunch and set them off down side tunnels we don't have to use. We can worry about cleanup after we get Ben back."

Emily nodded and started making a list.

"I think I'll run out and pick up a good bow and boat load of arrows." Nigel mused. "I appreciate the safety of killing these things from a distance, and the efficiency of collecting and reusing arrows. I'm more accurate, and faster, with a gun, but you can't reuse bullets. Eventually, I'd run out. Although, I could take about a thousand rounds with me, if I felt like carrying an extra thirty to forty pounds, plus the weight of extra magazines. Then there's the reload time once my magazines run out."

"Not to mention the noise," Emily broke in. "A bow is quiet. If you start firing a gun, every spider in that place is going to know you're there, just like the air horn."

"Good point."

"What about bug spray?" asked Stephanie. "Doesn't bug spray work to confuse a mosquito's sense of smell? Would it work on spiders, too?"

"That's a good idea, honey." Emily returned to the laptop, typed in a few search keywords, and waited.

"Yes! At least, there seems to be some research done that says Deep Woods OFF, or at least the DEET levels in it, are effective against spiders. So, Nigel can spray that all over himself and hopefully deter them." She scanned a bit more. "In fact, there is a spray made with pyrethrins, which are extracts from the chrysanthemum plant, that not only deters insects, but will kill them by..." She read a little more, then summarized, "by 'penetrating the cuticle and entering the nervous system, thereupon binding to the sodium channels that occur along the nerve cells,' blah, blah, blah, then 'leading to the overexcitement of nerve cells, and ultimately, death.' That sounds like just the ticket. It says it's safe to use indoors and out, safe around pets. Hmm. It does say the amount needed to become toxic to humans is way beyond normal use as a pesticide. I'm certain you're going to be using way beyond normal use amounts for these pests. You'd better wear a respirator, and gloves."

"Sheesh," said Nigel, "It sounds as bad as a bug bomb. But ten times as hard to use and carry."

"You know," said Emily, "let me check to see what the active ingredient is in bug bombs." More typing. More reading. "Yep. Pyrethrins. Same stuff. It's just delivered as a dense fog that penetrates everywhere. The difference being, with the spray, you can direct as needed, or spray it on the floors and walls to use as a deterrent, but it doesn't make the air toxic. It says UV rays break it down. I don't think you'll have a problem with sunlight in The City. It should last a good, long time. Long enough for you to rescue Ben and return, anyway."

"Right, then. I say we load up on this spray and a few dozen bug bombs. I'll get a respirator and gloves. I'll wear my outdoor gear, it's waterproof, so hopefully it will keep those pyrethrins away from my skin."

"We will be there to help, as well," chimed in Garran. "If these insect poisons are made from plant extracts, we should be able to handle them safely. Perhaps we should go in first and apply them liberally?"

"Indeed," agreed Ima. "We are adept at stealth, and are of no food interest to the spiders. Although, that does not seem to deter them from attacking."

"Let the blighters attack," said Tormad in his gruff manner. "We'll send 'em all back ta their Spirit forsaken world in pieces."

"Well said, Tormad," said Nigel. "But, I think stealth is our best bet against their numbers."

"Girls, let's go shopping." Emily gathered the girls and headed for the door. "Nigel, get what you need and figure out your plan of attack with the group. We'll buy every fogger they have in the store, every gallon of insecticide. We'll be back as soon as we can." They hustled out the front door without a backward glance.

"Well, my friends," said Nigel, "I hate to do this, but I need to run out and get some supplies of my own as fast as I can. Will you be all right here by yourselves?"

"Aye, we'll be fine," said Tormad, his root-like finger soaking contentedly in his half drained coffee mug.

"Indeed we will, Nigel." Sonam was enjoying his beverage as well. "But please do make haste. We are eager to go after Ben."

"You and I, both," said Nigel. He was out the door as fast as the girls, leaving the sprites to explore the Sullivans' home.

****

When Nigel returned, the girls were already back from the store.

Everyone was in the basement, readying their spoils.

"Grandpa," Calliope greeted him, "we couldn't find any air horns or other noise-makers, but we got four cases of bug bombs. At nine packs of six per case, that's two hundred and sixteen total. We also got four gallons of super-concentrated liquid insecticide. That was all they had."

"Yes, but, the mixing directions say for tough bugs, you mix one ounce per gallon of water, " cut in Emily. "We have extremely tough bugs, so let's do a little math. Say a normal spider has a half inch body. These spiders are like four feet long, so forty-eight inches? Let's say fifty for easy math. That's one hundred times bigger. So, we'd need about one hundred ounces per gallon of water. There are one hundred and twenty-eight ounces in a gallon, so let's just say we cut this stuff fifty-fifty with water. We have four gallons of insecticide, so we can make eight gallons."

"It's a good thing we have a bunch of two-gallon pump sprayers." Calliope pointed to four plastic pump sprayers sitting at her feet. "Dad's been taking them to the sprites for the past few trips. He stocked up."

"I hope eight gallons is enough," said Nigel.

"Me too," said Emily, a bit of worry showing. "And that's not the only sketchy news. The directions on the bug bombs say stay out of a room for two hours. After that, you can go in and open windows or ventilate in some manner. However, that's for a two-thousand square foot room. Those hallways are way bigger than that. So, the fog is going to disburse faster. Meaning spiders can run away, and safely come back well-within two hours."

"Ok. Not ideal. But, it also means Ben and I can come back through any fogged areas sooner. It also means I can set the foggers off closer to where I'm traveling." Nigel pondered the cases on the floor. "But we can't carry all of these boxes and pump sprayers. We need a cart."

"We have our beach wagon," chipped in Calliope. "It's one of those fold up wagons, but it holds a lot of stuff. It might be a little awkward getting it up the spiral staircases, but we've hauled it up normal staircases with no problem. We'll have to strap the stuff in so it doesn't fall out, but we have this cool, stretchy net thing, with hooks on the sides that will work. Let's go!" She took off like a shot up the stairs, Stephanie a step behind. Nigel followed only a fraction slower. The plan was coming together now, and he was itching to get after Ben.

****

Calliope thought her grandfather resembled a cross between intrepid explorer and determined Marine. From his floppy bush hat, cargo pants, and hiking boots, to the fully loaded pack bulging at the seams on his back, he was attached to his survival gear like a turtle to its shell. He had strapped a thirty-arrow quiver to the pack, the thirty fletchings flying just behind his right ear for an easy over-shoulder draw. To complete the image, and lend an angle of intimidating door-to-door salesman, his new Bear Kuma compound bow rested ready in his left hand, and the handle of a beach wagon, loaded with various insecticide delivery devices, was clutched in his right. He had also tied extra arrows to the outside of the cart; two bundles of thirty on each side, attached with bright pink string from Calliope's hoard of art supplies. With a tug on the tail of a quick-release overhand knot, Nigel could free a bundle and throw it in his quiver to resupply.

"This is going to be awkward," said Nigel, rolling the wagon forward and back. "But I'm afraid the wagon will be getting lighter, all too fast."

"Just try to sneak in as far as you can, grandpa," said Calliope. "If they don't know you're there, you can save the bug bombs for later."

"Calliope is correct," said Ima. "If Ben has indeed been taken to the spiders' home world, and we can follow, I expect we will need as much of this potion as we can bring."

"Well, one-hundred and twenty bug bombs, plus four gallons of insecticide is all we can fit in this cart. That's about half." Nigel shook his head, then shrugged in resignation. "If I have to, I'll come back for the rest. We can empty what's left in the cart outside the spider door, and I'll hustle back. Assuming we can keep the hallways clear."

"The doorway to the spider world is quite far," said Garran. "It is doubtful we will be able to make the trip more than once."

"Well, twice, if you count coming back with Mr. Sullivan," said Stephanie.

"Of course, Stephanie. Thank you for the correction."

"We'll make it," said Nigell. "I have no doubt."

"Should I get another wagon, load it up with the rest of the supplies, same as this one, and leave it on the other side of the Earth door?" asked Emily. "That way, you won't have to drag your empty cart back with you. Just hustle back. If you clear the other side, it should be safe enough for me to pop in for just a minute to stage the second."

"That's a great idea, Emily," Nigel nodded his appreciation. "But be careful. Crack the door, just a bit. If you see any movement, shut it fast and lock it tight. Leave the next wagon on this side. I'll make it through."

"We should get movin'," said Tormad. "We be losin' precious time."

"Right. Let's move out," said Nigel.

He hugged his granddaughter, then pulled his wagon through the vault door, past the wine, and into the tunnel. The wagon's wide, knobby rubber wheels rolled along with a muted thrum. Emily closed and locked the tunnel door. Calliope did the same with the vault as soon as Emily exited, then they joined Stephanie at the monitors, and watched the team's progress via the tunnel cameras.

"They're at the doorway," Stephanie observed. "Here we go."

They watched as Sonam and Kunga readied bug bombs. The others readied their weapons: Ima and Garran their obsidian blades, Tormad his black axe, and Nigel his modern, compound bow, arrow nocked and pulled back. Nigel also had a hardware store respirator over his nose and mouth, its bright pink canisters hopefully providing sufficient filtration against the aerosolized insecticide.

Sonam slowly turned the wheel on the door. Its internal gears rotated in rhythm, sounding a muffled, metallic clicking deep within the steel. He pulled the door open just a crack so Kunga could peek through the darkness on the other side. With a nod, Kunga indicated the all clear, and Sonam pulled the door open fully, the team still at the ready. Nothing greeted them but the usual darkened room with its iron spiral staircase. No creatures, no stray wisps of web.

Ima was first through, Garran by her side. Sonam and Kunga went next, then Nigel pulled the cart through with a little help from Tormad who lifted the back wheels over the threshold.

Through the monitors, the ladies watched as Nigel's pin activated the lighting. They saw the rescue party relax and gather at the staircase to the upper level. Nigel walked back to the door, and with a final wave to the camera, pulled it shut. The images on the screens turned still and lifeless.

Calliope could not help but feel a sense of foreboding, and failure. She wanted to be with her grandfather, saving her dad. Not stuck here on Earth with nothing to do but wait.

And something else nagged at her: The City. She did not know why, but she felt like they were missing something. Something that had to do with Chathair Doras. Why were the spiders there? There had been no sign of them at any other time. The sprites had been traveling the halls for years before breaking into her basement. They had told her dad that they had never seen other creatures in The City, besides the humans, the Tree Lords, and Spot that one time. So where had the spiders come from? And why now?

She was also worried about Poppie. Why hadn't their friend come to meet them? Was she in trouble, too? How could she not have known about the spiders? If she was taken by surprise, that suggested the spiders had arrived quickly. Through a doorway. But who opened that doorway?

So many questions, and Calliope was drawn to finding the answers. Determinedly, she promised herself she would.

—7—

Spiders in the Dark

Ben sat in silent darkness and stroked the soft fur under Spot's chin. Thankfully, for their safety, Spot did not purr like a giant cat. He just leaned into Ben's scrubbing fingers and enjoyed the attention.

Spot had proven himself an excellent watchdog. He could hear even the tiniest spider creeping up on them. Ben was not so adept. To him, the spiders were ghosts, appearing out of nowhere, prefaced only by a few seconds of light clicking before they descended with legs, webs, and fangs. He would certainly be a frothing bag of gelatine hanging from a wall by now, if it were not for his unexpected companion.

He thought about his new friend, and his recent conversation with Lord Oakenpuss while he had dangled from the ceiling. The Tree Lord had left Spot to die a horrible death on this world, all so he could unleash ruin on Ben and the Sprites, thinking that would be the end of anyone using The City of Doors. Ben boiled with anger and resentment over the revelation that the Tree Lords had released the Hollowing fungus on purpose, and had released the Slizeg against the sprites, just to 'keep them in their place.' Lord Oakenpuss was evil. Any creature Hell-bent on eradicating all other sentient species it came across, even to the extent of sacrificing their pets, was warped and wicked.

Spot stiffened, his head turned back down the way they had

come. Ben rolled from sitting to kneeling, his knives at the ready. When Spot stood up, Ben followed his lead. Not able to stand completely in this tunnel—it being about a foot shorter than his full height—Ben assumed a wide-footed stance, his knees slightly bent. It was not the most comfortable position, but he felt stable.

The Blinx padded backward, slowly, pushing Ben along. Unfortunately, this tunnel seemed to be a one way tube leading away from The City portal. The spiders were driving them deeper into their den. There was no choice, though. Every few minutes, more spiders found them, slowing only momentarily to cannibalize their fallen comrades that Ben and Spot had dispatched.

Ben had stowed his flashlight and replaced it with his Petzl Actik Core headlamp. Not only did it free his hands, but it had several light levels, from 450 lumens, down to 6, plus a red light for preserving night vision, and being stealthy. He was in red light only mode now. If there was ever a time to be in stealth mode, this was it.

Spot seemed better equipped to handle the darkness, but he did not seem to mind the light, either. They crept backwards as silently as they could. Ben let Spot guard their back, while he worried about possible dangers they could be walking towards.

It was not long before Ben, too, could hear the telltale clicking of spider feet on rock. More of the little ones were hunting. Little being a relative term in this place; a volleyball with legs. On Earth, a spider this size would have sent anyone running in fear. Truth be told, he was having the same reaction on this planet. But, there was also a sense of relief that they were not about to face spiders as big as dogs. Or bigger.

They continued on like this for some time. Ben's back ached, as did his legs from being in a constant quarter-squat, made even more difficult by his backpack.

The incessant clicking seemed always within spitting distance. That was assuming Ben could muster any spit. He had his water bladder in his pack, but it was unknown how long he would be trapped in this nightmare. Rationing his resources was prudent. He was thinking of Spot, as well. There was no question Ben would share what he had with his savior, and that meant depleting supplies that much faster.

As Ben's legs began to quiver under the strain, and his mind battled tired muscles, the dim light revealed their first intersection. It was a four-way, and Ben did not relish standing there long. It made them vulnerable from all sides.

"Psst, Spot," he whispered. "Which way, boy?"

Spot moved around Ben in the tight quarters and sniffed at each new branch. He stiffened at the tunnel which continued straight. Even Ben could hear a distant scratching down that route. More spiders ahead. Large ones, if Ben could hear them. The left seemed unremarkable to Spot, but not ruled out. The right, however, caused Spot to jump forward, his nose sniffing in circles, up and down. He rushed back and nudged Ben forward. They resumed their positions, Ben in the lead, Spot guarding their rear, but urging him forward with gusto. Before leaving the intersection, however, Ben used his knife to scratch an arrow in the dark rock wall, indicating the direction they were headed, and on another to indicate where they had come from. At some point, they would need to retrace their steps to get back home.

Ben strained his hearing to catch any early warning. He was reaching his physical limit; his breathing labored, his footfalls heavy, and his backpack scraped against the walls frequently. He was making too much noise. He needed to rest, but Spot was insistent that they hurry, and Ben was not inclined to argue. He would push on until collapse.

And that's just what he did. He pushed on, down a straight tunnel that, if anything, got a bit shorter. Thankfully, it never became narrower, nor necessitated Ben crawling along, nor shedding his backpack to be dragged behind. But the reduced height increased leg strain.

The wobbles began in his knees, so that each shuffling step hazarded a buckling, a final failure of sinew and muscle. Ben had long since braced his hands on his knees, to both bolster his bent back, and transfer weight off his thighs, redirecting it through shoulders, arms, and straight down his shins to his feet. Even this tactic was failing, now. The wobbles had spread, reaching his shoulders and elbows. His hands had a death grip on his knees, trying to keep everything steady. Finally, his fatigue so intense he almost welcomed the spiders, Ben faltered and dropped to the stone floor.

"I'm done for, Spot. I have to rest. Let the spiders come, and we'll take on this batch of little ones before we run into something larger and I'm too tired to fight."

Spot seemed to understand, and did not push further. He merely sank to his belly, like a cat watching birds through a window; seemingly relaxed, but coiled to pounce, keeping a stark alertness into the darkness behind.

It was then that Ben noticed the clicking was gone. Could they have lost the spiders? Shaken their tail? That seemed unlikely. They were in a straight tunnel. How could the spiders lose the scent? Maybe the spiders were territorial and would only range so far from their nest, or den, or web, whatever they called home turf. Could it be that easy? Just run until you reach some invisible border. Then again, the end of one spider's territory probably meant the beginning of another's. That was the safe bet. If those pursuing really had given up, Ben and Spot could be walking into something worse. Was it better to deal with the Devil they knew—smaller, manageable arachnids—rather than the Devil they didn't?

At the moment, Ben didn't care. He just needed to rest. He took a sip from his water bladder, unlimbered his pack so he could dig out a bowl from his mess kit. He filled it with some water and offered it to

Spot. Surprisingly, Spot sat back on his haunches and picked up the bowl to drink like a primate. Ben was immediately struck by Spot's resemblance to a lemur. His paws were furry on top, padded black on the palms and fingers. His thumbs spread at a greater angle than a human's, able to stretch almost one hundred and eighty degrees from his index finger, or close the gap completely. Ben knew Spot was an excellent climber. Between his foliage-like fur for camouflage, and his grasping paws, there was a good chance Spot was more comfortable living in trees than he was on the land.

Whatever Spot's preference, Ben was certain that they were both more comfortable living above ground than in these dark, barren tunnels. Like it or not, underground was where they were trapped for the time being.

With energy returning, Ben contemplated his options. They had traveled for hours in these tunnels. That meant that they were probably miles away from the doorway back. Unless they were walking in circles, which was also a possibility. If they kept going, they decreased their chances of getting home. There was no telling how far these tunnels stretched, whether they ever opened up to the surface. And if they did, would he and Spot ever find that opening. Ben had taken Calliope to Mammoth Caves in Kentucky two summers ago, and those caves had gone on for over four hundred miles. Some passages had been cool and dry, like these caves, so far, and some had been down-right wet, with water drizzling down the walls, or dripping from the ceiling, filling pools two or three levels below. In the Spring and Fall, the rains could raise the local water table, bringing flooding to the tunnels, trapping or drowning any life unfortunate enough to be meandering in the bowels.

Ben could see no signs that this cave system was a wet one. He had seen no stalactites, nor stalagmites. No pools of water, no dripping crevasses. But, the flip side to staying dry, was that he was also limited to the water he had brought, as well as the food. Which was not much. For that reason alone, Ben was beginning to think he and Spot should retrace their steps and make another run for the door. To do it now was their best option, before they got further away, before their supplies ran out, before they were weakened by hunger, thirst, and fatigue.

Spot had finished drinking and was lying down again. Ben felt as rested as he could be without an hour in a hot tub to relax tired muscles, followed by a two hour deep-tissue massage to work out knots upon knots all over his body. And sleep. He was going to need sleep. But a spa day was not meant to be. Neither was a nap. It was time to pack up and make their move. He squirmed into his pack, fastened the chest strap and cinched everything tight. Rolling to one knee, he scooted up next to Spot and whispered to the creature, hoping he would understand.

"Spot, we need to head back and try to make it through the door. If we keep going this direction, we may never get back." He pointed with his knives back down the tunnel they had just traveled. He made a motion like fighting. "We can fight through now, while we still have energy. We need to try." He nodded at his companion, attempting to discern understanding. Spot just blinked.

"Well, let's see if you'll follow." Ben rose to his usual quarter-crouch, the strain immediately tearing at his tired muscles. He motioned for Spot to follow as he slowly retraced his steps. "Come on, boy," he encouraged.

Spot immediately rose, and clamped his jaws on Ben's pant cuff, pulling him back.

"Whoa, boy. Take it easy," he whispered. "I know you don't want to head back into the mess we just ran from, but it's the only way home."

Spot seemed to disagree. He released Ben's cuff and headed in the opposite direction. A few feet down, just at the edge of Ben's dim light, Spot paused, looking back to see if Ben would follow. When

Ben did not, Spot came back and nudged Ben along again.

"No, buddy. We have to go back."

Ben resisted, but Spot was persistent. When it was clear that Ben would not be nudged, Spot tried another tactic; he walked past again, sniffed at the air in the tunnel, then did a little dance. He walked back to Ben, sniffed in that direction, and blew out a half-sneeze, half-raspberry. He repeated the sniffing and the dancing in the other direction.

"Are you saying you smell something better down that way?" Ben pointed.

Spot responded with an excited hop in Ben's direction, then back. Ben took a step or two after him, then sniffed the air himself. He smelled dirt, and stale air, and his own sweat. He reversed back down the tunnel a few paces, leaned his face into the dark and sniffed in that direction: dirt, sweat, and maybe it was his imagination, but the stale was staler, if that was a word. Maybe mustier? A morbid thought came to Ben: *tinged with death*. He returned to Spot, who was patiently waiting for Ben to figure things out. Ben sniffed again, concentrating hard. Yes. The air *was* fresher in the other direction.

"Ok, boy. I get it. Is there a way out this way?"

Spot perked up at the word "out." He hopped a few paces down the tunnel, encouraging Ben.

"Out it is, then. Lead on, Spot."

Their positions reversed; Spot in the lead, Ben in the rear. He was not sure how comfortable he was with this scenario; being the rear guard was dangerous without Spot's night vision, hearing, and sense of smell. Then again, rushing headlong into the dark unknown was no picnic, either.

Ben mentally repeated the phrase he was beginning to hate: better the Devil you know, etcetera, etcetera. He knew about the little devils behind them, so he knew what to listen for and what to expect. The devils in front were a mystery. Damn, he was tired of devils.

They encountered no intersections, no deviations. From what Ben could tell, this tunnel went in a straight line. Of course, with only a few feet of visibility for reference, the tunnel could be a large circle, for all he knew. One thing was certain, however: the air was definitely getting fresher. Ben did not have to concentrate, or second guess his imagination. It was clean, with maybe a touch of vegetation. He could not be sure what that vegetation was, but there were light, clean aromas, like Spring air.

Their tunnel ended in a surprisingly rough grotto, tall enough for Ben to stand upright, at last, and roomy enough for three more of him to stand side by side. It looked to have been chewed out of the rock by some giant, gap-toothed worm; craggly furrows ran top to bottom, while the intermediate columns retained the same natural smoothness as the tunnels. Ben examined the walls closer with his flashlight, and found nothing to explain the irregularities. Just more rock.

Except for one furrow, which turned out not to be a furrow, but a narrow passage. A crack that ran from the floor, far into the darkness above. A crack that Ben would normally avoid entering, as it looked dangerous, and tight, and scarier than a Florida storm drain hiding alligators, or snakes, or killer clowns.

"Stop it, Ben!" he cursed himself for letting his mind conjure up imaginary nightmares when he had real ones to deal with.

Without a delay for fear and doubt to blossom and bloom in his mind, he removed his pack and dragged it in after himself. It was a tight fit, but he could do it, shimmying sideways, scraping his belly and back along the rock.

Spot had no troubles, and he went through without hesitation. Ben prayed the blinx knew what he was doing. There was no room to fight wedged in this fissure, no room to run. They would be easy pickings for a squad of spiders.

That thought—along with imaginary clowns—sent shivers down

Ben's spine, and started a cold sweat. Paranoia was setting in, combined with claustrophobia. He could not help it, confined as he was, knowing what hunted them. His red light cast ominous, blood-rimmed shadows. Rounded outcroppings, bumps in the walls, they all became spiders clinging, waiting patiently for prey to wander in. He looked up and found only darkness. The crack could extend for a hundred feet above them, or mere inches beyond the sphere of illumination. For an instant, Ben considered flipping the headlamp to max illumination, and pointing upwards, but thoughts of awakening sleeping monsters motivated him to push forward as quickly as possible and leave the unknown alone. Spot seemed to agree. He needed no urging.

Their path gently curved. Ben could tell that much. After several hundred feet—Ben had been counting his sideways shuffling, estimating two feet traveled for every step— a literal ray of hope reached the rock wall ahead. A soft white, natural light brushed the rocks. There *was* a way out ahead.

A few feet later, they emerged into a grotto much like the one they had just left behind. Similar channels ran top to bottom, and the way out was a tunnel straight ahead. Ben could see trees through the mouth of a cave. Normal-looking trees, which Ben hoped meant fresh water as well. Fresh water would mean food, of one type or another. He and Spot could survive and take some time to plan their escape. Assuming he could muster the courage to reenter the spiders' warren.

They moved forward, Spot in the lead again, but as they reached the end of their tunnel, before it opened into a wider, taller cave, Ben spotted something that made him pull Spot back.

"Wait a minute, buddy." He grabbed Spot around the neck and chest, and spoke quietly in his ear. "Spiders," he whispered and pointed to large web sacks hidden in the shadows higher up the wall. The bones and remains of some long-dead animal protruded from the gray veil. Ben was crouched down next to Spot, trying to get a good look at the ceiling of the cave. He could see nothing but darkness.

"Back, Spot. Let's move back." He gently tugged Spot back down the tunnel, trying to be as quiet as possible. Back at the grotto, they stopped, and Ben dropped his pack to the dusty stone floor. He rummaged inside to find his bear canister, packed with dried rations, and his cooking kit: a small cook pot with lid, gas canister and MSR Pocket Rocket stove tucked inside. Setting aside the cooking kit, he emptied the food from his bear canister, filled it with some rocks for weight, then put the lid back on.

"Stay here, Spot."

Ben crept back down the tunnel, hugging the wall. At the end, careful to stay hidden, he rolled the canister into the middle of the chamber. It was immediately squelched in a blanket of webbing connected to a line that disappeared back into the darkness above. The webbing retracted, taking the bear canister with it.

"Damn it!" Ben cursed under his breath.

He had been hoping the web sacks were ancient, that the spider responsible had moved on. But deep down, he knew this cave entrance was the perfect hunting ground for a spider. Unsuspecting animals came in out of the weather, hoping for a safe harbor, to be greeted by a swift death. At least, Ben hoped it was swift for them.

He returned to Spot and contemplated his next move. Judging by the size of the dead animal bones stuck to the walls, this spider—or spiders—was big. Big enough to snatch up Ben and Spot, for sure. And it stayed out of reach, high above them, so no ambush. Well, actually, there *would* be an ambush, but the spider would be the ambusher. Ben and Spot would be the ambushees.

He contemplated his pack, its contents, and any other supplies or tools he had. Only one idea seemed plausible, but he had been hoping to save it for their final push back to the doorway.

Again, he wondered if that was the smarter move. Leave this threat behind and make a run back through the hordes of smaller spiders, back to the doorway home. Perhaps those spiders had moved on, left the tunnels clear. Perhaps he and Spot could just retrace their steps unassailed, all the way home. Perhaps there would be an ice cream sundae for him and a leaf salad for Spot waiting there, too. Pipe dreams.

He rationalized moving forward. It would be good to get outside and reconnoiter this planet. To find clean water and a source of food was the key. Eventually Garran and the other sprites would come after him. He knew they would. Then again, as far as they knew, he was spider food, wrapped up in The City of Doors. Would they even consider he had been brought to the spider homeworld? Unlikely. So he was back to saving himself, and Spot. And that meant going back into the tunnels. Eventually.

Strategically, it would be good to have a path of safe retreat. There had been no branching tunnels from this cave to their last intersection. And this had been the only spider encountered. If he could clear this end, then block off the intersection after going through, it would give him a sense of security at his back. For that matter, maybe he could find building supplies to block off other passages, too; further increasing his defenses, and decreasing the fronts he would be fighting. That idea appealed to Ben the most. Of course, it would take more than sticks and stones to shore up these tunnels.

One problem at a time. How to get out? Ben kept coming back to the same idea: his camp stove, and its pressurized canister. He needed to build a bomb. He emptied his cooking kit and assembled the single burner camp stove, screwing it to the top of the canister. As a test fit, he dropped the stove back inside the cook pot, and confirmed that the burner protruded above the pot rim by an inch and a half. Perfect. He put the pot lid on top of the burner, completing the heat trap. He pulled off his three dollar, gas station purchased, braided paracord bracelet and undid the braid, freeing nine feet of cord. He quickly wove a tight sling around the pot and lid, securing the stove inside. That was basically it; a homemade bomb from camping gear. At least, that was the theory. Ben had read about some camp stoves overheating due to wind screens being too close to the canister and burner, creating a heat buildup, which caused the canister to expand, breach, then explode. He was hoping that lighting his stove inside a closed pot would create the same reaction, much quicker. He guessed it would explode in about four to six minutes. Maybe less.

"Spot, you stay here. I'm going to give that spider his last meal." Ben grabbed a Bic lighter from his kit, struck the flame to show Spot, pointed to the flame, then the stove, then made a manic explosion gesture with his arms and a muffled *BOOM!* sound. Spot cocked his head to the side, in the universal animal sign for, "This human is crazy. I do not understand what he is doing."

"Right," Ben sighed. "You don't get it. Just stay."

Ben picked up his cook-kit-bomb, grabbed his pack by a strap and hauled everything down the tunnel, as quietly as he could. Thankfully, Spot stayed behind. The Blinx had understood that much, at least.

Ben placed his pack just inside the tunnel entrance, to be his shield, in case his timing was off and the canister exploded too soon. Next, he undid the wrapping around his pot, slightly, so he could reach inside and turn on the gas. He quickly re-tied his bundle, lit the Bic, and ignited the gas now boiling from beneath the pot lid. The *whoosh* of a medium fireball caused him to jump back, but the excess gas was consumed expeditiously, leaving the stove burning normally inside its aluminum cocoon. Ben hit the button on his watch, starting his timer, then pushed the pot to the other side of his pack, and prayed that he was timing this right. He guessed the heat would build to danger levels at four minutes. He would wait just over two minutes before pushing the pot to the center of the cave.

Ben pulled one of his trekking poles from the outside of his pack, and extended it to it's full four and a half feet. He wanted his hands nowhere near that pot when pushing it into the room.

One minute, thirty seconds. He readied for his deployment by inserting the tip of the pole into the looped metal handle of the cook pot.

Two minutes, thirty seconds. Long enough. Using the trekking pole, Ben pushed the pot towards the center of the room, it's bottom scraping along like fingernails on a chalkboard in the silent cave. At the extent of his pole, he gave the pot a quick nudge, shoving it another three feet. He yanked his trekking pole back as a glob of webbing *thunked* on top of the cook pot. It was then that Ben worried the webbing would cut off all oxygen, snuffing the fire, diffusing his improvised explosive. But, almost as alarmingly, the webbing shrank back from the pot, veritably melting away from the heat. He checked his watch: three minutes, twenty-two seconds. This was not good. He had no idea what would happen if the pot exploded on the floor instead of hanging in front of the hidden monster. Most likely, it would just throw shrapnel in all directions; not high enough to hurt the spider, but possibly far enough down the tunnel to impale himself, or Spot. Ben grabbed his pack, keeping it as a shield between himself and the explosive, and ran back along the tunnel to hunker down in the corner with Spot.

A massive *thump*, which he felt through the soles of his boots, caused Ben to drop to the tunnel floor and cover his back and head with the backpack. Lying there, his brain quickly analyzed the sound and rumble. It had not really sounded like an explosion. Nor did he hear the sound of shrapnel flying, or metal pieces striking stone. He rolled his pack onto the floor, then slithered around behind it, and snuggled to the wall. He felt Spot belly-crawl up next to him, and they both peered over the pack, towards the cave.

To Ben's horror, the spider had come down from its roost, and it was massive. The size of a teenage bull elephant. The thump that had reverberated through the very soul of the tunnel had been the force of the spider's massive bulk landing. And now, multi-faceted eyes, like the headlights on an antique Bentley, sparkled in the direction of the two hiding refugees. Ben's heart raced. He could feel Spot shivering in fear next to him, and was sure his own shivering provided no comfort to his friend.

He was rooted to the floor. To move would put them in the crosshairs of that beast. The only way left to them was a retreat back through the narrow passage, to the tunnels of smaller spiders. There was no way this enormous spider could follow them, but Ben was not sure they could make the entrance before being ensnared.

The creature, however, seemed not to care whether they ran or not. It slowly raised higher on its many legs, and curved its back end underneath itself, aiming two large spinnerets down the tunnel.

This is it, Ben thought. *It has us.*

The silver silk came at them faster than Ben could imagine. It splattered his backpack, arched over and around. Ben felt it land on his back, saw it glom onto Spot. He reached for his machete, but the creature was already hauling them back. His hands fumbled at the straps which held his blade in place. Fear, and the rapid dragging, blocked his attempts to draw the weapon. They covered the distance to the cave in seconds, coming to a rest under the monster's massive head. Ben's eyes were transfixed on the spider's fangs: furry, fuzzy, barbed black horns, glistening and wet. They were angled towards each other, like ebony calipers, ready to clamp down on prey; on Ben and Spot.

An ear-splitting roar erupted from the spider's backside. The creature flew a dozen feet in the air, partially from releasing its coiled legs in surprise, partially from the explosive force of the gas canister that had finally reached critical temperature, and ruptured. Ben grabbed Spot and rolled with him back into the tunnel entrance as the spider careened in for a landing.

The silk thread had severed, and so had the spider's abdomen. Or, rather, it had disintegrated. Only the head, thorax, and four legs landed in front of Ben and Spot, upside-down and continuing to twitch. The rest of the spider seemed to paint the walls and floor of the cave in a mixture of mangy black pelts and tinted turquoise gooey gel. Miraculously, he and Spot were unscathed, if covered in bits of spider blood.

They sat on the floor for a minute, taking stock of themselves, and watching the gargantuan head move, the remaining legs flailing at the air, the fangs pulsating. Ben finally freed his machete, and held it ready, just in case, but the creature was no longer a threat. Its twitching grew less, the parts stopped moving, and the head finally accepted its fate. The legs curled in, and what remained of the creature listed to the side, and died.

Not waiting for an invitation, Ben scrambled to his feet, grabbed his pack, beckoned to Spot, and ran for the mouth of the cave, for fresh air and sunshine, for an end to spiders in the dark.

—8—

A Second Rescue

Emily, Calliope, and Stephanie watched the monitors for fifteen minutes, not able to walk away, fearing that any minute the portal would re-open with Nigel and the other rescuers hot-footing it back in full retreat. Thankfully, that never happened. The monitors revealed nothing but quiet tunnels and closed doors.

"Ok, girls," Emily broke the silence. "We need to quick hit the superstore and get another beach cart and load it up. I want it prepped and ready in less than an hour."

The girls did not argue. They were eager to move, take action, do anything but sit and wait. They made it to the store and back with their purchase in less than half an hour. They packed it identical to the first—minus the arrows—within ten minutes. Now, it was up to Emily to roll it to the other side.

"I have to admit," said Emily, "I'm a bit nervous about opening that door."

"I'll do it," Calliope said eagerly.

"Over my dead body," Emily asserted. "On what planet do you think a mother would let her child, or any other, face danger before she did herself?"

"Well, with The City of Doors, we have plenty of planets to choose from," goaded Stephanie.

"Not funny, missy," said her mother. "No one's going down those tunnels, but me. Just give me a minute to work up the nerve."

She walked into the storage room and retrieved the Sullivan's older machete, slung it crosswise on her back; grabbed a City light-control pin from a drawer, clipped it to her shirt; snatched an extra folding knife, tucked it in her front pocket; hefted a sturdy flashlight in her left hand, just in case.

"I guess I'm ready," she announced to the girls. She grabbed the wagon handle, took a deep breath, then nodded to Calliope to open the vault door. Calliope obliged.

The wagon pulled easily through the wine room, out the back, and down the tunnel. The closer she got to The City portal, the more nervous Emily became. She could not help asking herself what she was doing. Why was she risking her life, and exposing her daughter to these risks? Sure, Ben and Calliope were good people. Sure, she wanted Ben to be safe, but he was in this trouble due to his own curiosity. She should not feel obligated to put her own life in danger.

She considered that. Did she feel obligated? No, not really. Then what was it? Frustration was a word that came to mind. She was frustrated with Ben for getting himself into trouble. Again. She was frustrated that he was pulling her into another crazy adventure. Again. Pulling *all of them* into another crazy adventure, she corrected herself.

But was he really? Was he pulling them in? He could not have known this would happen, obviously, and he would not want them putting themselves in danger. Then again, he should know that his daughter, of all of them, would never give up on him, would obstinately insist on planning and taking part in any rescue attempt. And his own father, as well. What father—what parent—in the true sense of the word, would not die to protect their child? Truly, Emily was now frustrated with Ben.

And how dare he not know that she would take risks to come to his aide? Did he not know her? Was she not a brave person? Had she not proven herself on the last adventure? And to top it all off, she had warned him not to go back into The City. She had warned him it was dangerous. Did he listen? No. Typical man, not thinking through the consequences of his actions. Rushing in all bravado and silly smile. Thinking he could just charm his way out of any trouble, or muscle through with those muscly muscles of his.

The image of Ben washing up, shirtless in the river back on Quilium, flashed in her mind. She immediately chided herself for letting her mind go there, but other images intruded: Ben at his open door, his genuine smile always greeting her warmly; Ben standing in a darkened field, facing a monster, gallantly placing himself between her and danger; Ben sleeping lazily, in a steaming mountain hot spring, so peaceful and, she admitted it to herself, handsome.

Her phone rang, yanking her from her musings with such shock, that she dropped the wagon handle, raised the flashlight like a club, and looked around for an attack. Realization dawned, and she pulled her phone from her back pocket. It was her daughter.

"Yes, Steph?" she answered.

There was some chuckling on the other end. "That was quite the karate move, mom," her daughter laughed. "Sorry, I didn't mean to scare you. We were just wondering if everything was ok? You've been staring at the door for, like, five minutes."

"Yes, everything is fine," she said, somewhat embarrassed. "I was just...going through my plan if anything was on the other side." She could feel her face turning red. She hoped the monitors could not portray her coloring, or if it did, the girls mistook it for embarrassment for being startled.

"Ok. Here I go," she told her daughter. "I'm hanging up so I can use both of my hands. Love you." Stephanie responded in kind, then Emily disconnected, and returned her phone to her back pocket.

With her heart beating like a rabbit's, and a cold sweat dampening her spine, Emily was surprised at the steadiness of her hands as she turned the wheel on the door. She took a deep, calming breath, then pulled. She kept her body behind the door as she stole careful glances around the edge. The other side was darkness. Light from the Earth-side spilled across the threshold, but did not penetrate far into the other room. It was quiet; seemed all-clear.

She bent down to pick up the handle of the wagon, removing her gaze from the other room for just an instant. That was the mistake made by most prey. With lightning speed, a web shot from the darkness, high to low, splattered across Emily's back, adhered, pulled taut, then retracted, dragging Emily through the doorway with a scream.

****

Stephanie watched the monitor in horror as her mother disappeared through the portal.

"Noooooo!" she screamed.

Calliope wasted no time, but ran to the storage room and grabbed two backpacks she had stashed in the back corner. The same ones the girls had taken on their last adventure.

"Here, take this," she threw one pack at Stephanie, who caught it, but remained stunned by her mother's capture.

"Put it on, Steph!" Calliope urged her friend. "And then put this on."

She tossed a spare respirator to her friend, then donned her pack and a respirator of her own.

"We're going after her now, before we lose her in that maze."

Stephanie snapped out of her shock, donned her gear and followed Calliope into the wine room. Calliope pulled the vault door shut and locked it behind them, then proceeded through the steel door at the room's rear.

"I packed everything we need in both packs, just in case," came her explanation, muffled through her mask. "You have a headlamp, knife, light camping supplies, dried food, hammock. We'll grab the bug bombs and close everything up behind us. We can't let those things through to this side. No matter what happens."

Stephanie nodded, but concern for her mother kept her quiet. She knew she had to snap out of it, focus, remain calm, and be ready for action, but the image of her mom being dragged through the door they themselves were about to enter had her in a slight panic. If she was honest with herself, she was half afraid for her mom, half horrified for herself. She had not let on to the others, not even Calliope, but she was *terrified* of spiders. Tiny spiders. These monsters had her petrified inside. It was all she could do to keep putting one foot in front of the other.

At the end of the tunnel, the dark maw of The City stood open and still, proving that the spider had already taken Emily from the room, otherwise her pendant would have activated the lights. The wagonload of bug bombs sat ready for its crossing, just this side of the threshold.

Stephanie steeled herself to cross over, while Calliope unhesitatingly shut the door with a forceful *clang*.

"I don't want anything sneaking up on us. We need to take these bug bombs, but we can't pull that cart, it'll slow us down." She looked at her friend and could sense uncertainty and fear.

"We've got this, Steph. Let's stuff this bag with all we can, and head out after your mom. We should be able to catch up to her fast." She said the last with a confidence she was not quite sure she believed, but fervently hoped to be true.

She had pulled a medium-sized duffle bag from her backpack and was frantically stuffing it with cans of bug bombs. When it reached its limit—the zipper pulling at its teeth with a strain not allowing it to completely close—Calliope deemed it full. She hefted it in her left hand with a satisfactory grunt.

"Here," she handed Stephanie a can from the few remaining in the wagon. "Just pop off the cap," she demonstrated by pulling off the black plastic cap and dropping it back in the cart, "shake it up," she shook it, "then when you're ready, press the button on top and it will start spraying, or fogging, or whatever. Ready?"

Stephanie nodded, still not able to find her voice. She popped the top off her canister and shook.

Calliope, while shaking her fogger with one hand, grabbed the handle of the heavy steel door, and pulled. She immediately pressed the button to start her fogger, tossed it in, and shut the door again.

"Let's let that marinate the room for a few minutes."

Stephane took deep breaths. Her mask felt stifling. The rubber straps pulled on her hair, the nose piece was digging into the skin under her eyes, and moisture was building on her upper lip—precipitation from her breath, to be sure, not nervous sweat. The valves opened and closed with her breathing, and she sounded, to her ears, like that Darth Vader guy her friends mimicked when they were trying to be intimidating.

"I can do this," she told herself. "I can do this. Just keep moving. Keep moving. Don't think."

"That should be good," she said to Calliope. "Let's get in there and save my mom." It had only been a few minutes, but she was afraid if she waited any longer, she would panic.

"Ok. Be ready to point and spray your can at any spiders." Calliope pulled the door open. Both girls stood behind it, but peered around the metal barrier.

"Looks clear," said Calliope.

"Yeah," said Stephanie.

"We should get moving," said Calliope, but she did not move.

"Ok," said Stephanie, who also remained still.

The darkness on the other side was not obscured by a dense fog, as Stephanie thought it would be. She could see the canister on the floor. It had rolled and wedged itself under the bottom iron stair and spewed its contents in the horizontal. A shimmering wet wedge blossomed across the floor, like a black on black, glossy on flat, abstraction. Stephanie hoped enough had made it into the air.

On the far side, against the wall, was the flashlight Emily had been carrying; dark and dormant, never having the opportunity to turn on. She had obviously dropped it when the spider grabbed her.

"Here we go," said Calliope.

She stepped across, another can held ready in her hand. The lights in the room glowed to life and revealed a relieving lack of spiders. Stephanie followed, close at her elbow. Calliope knew the relief on her friend's face mirrored her own. She quickly reached back and shut the door to Earth.

"Let's go get your mom."

The two pre-teens charged up the stairs, scanning above them as each revolution brought them closer to the next level. Nothing but darkness greeted them until Calliope's head was within three feet of the top, and then her pin activated the lighting in the room above. Not slowing down, Calliope pushed the button on her can of Raid, held it aloft like a torch, let out a primal war cry, only slightly muffled by her respirator, and sprang up the last few steps to face her enemies head on.

Fortunately, what met her was an empty space. Unfortunately, she stopped only a few steps beyond the stairs, and Stephanie sprang up behind her just as animated, spraying her own can of bug fogger in the opposite direction, not noticing her friend's stationary pose. Nor did either of them notice how wet the floor was. Stephanie crashed into Calliope, both lost their footing, scrambled like kittens on ice, then crashed down in a jumbled heap.

"Looks like Grandpa and the sprites soaked the floor to keep the spiders from coming down to our door," said Calliope.

"It didn't work," said Stephanie, bitterly.

"Maybe. Maybe there would have been more spiders if they

hadn't sprayed," said Calliope. "Either way, this area is clear, thankfully. And now we have insecticide all over our clothes, so maybe that'll keep them away from us."

Her eyes followed the wet trail across the floor, to the wide staircase. The ages of dust covering the stone treads was now dark sludge, wet with insecticide and dimpled with footprints from human and sprite. To the right of the staircase, the floor became dry, and faded into a dark archway with no evidence of a disturbance. To the left, smears of wet, swirly dirt patterns tracked into an equally dark archway the Sullivans had not yet explored.

"That way!" Calliope exclaimed. She popped up, pointing to the tracks on the floor. "Your mom was dragged this way. Look!"

"Let's go," said Stephanie. She dropped her can and pulled a new one from Calliope's duffle bag, then set off at a run.

The hallway lit up before the girls, revealing a doorless tunnel, dusted with uncommon cobwebs. With no intersections, no hiding places, no sign of giant spiders, or Emily, visible in the lit area of hallway, the girls sped recklessly along, hoping to gain ground on their quarry.

They ran for some time, the hall never presenting them with options, just continuing straight ahead, quiet and abandoned. Finally, just as their youthful vigor began to fade, their passage ended. Straight was no longer an option, but left and right opened as equal opportunities. Neither of which provided clues for guidance.

Stephanie turned to Calliope, "Which?"

But her question was interrupted by a woman's cry, echoing horribly from the depths of the tunnel on their left. Adrenaline pushed the girls to action. Mustering reserves of energy, they tore down the new branch, determination fueling the courage of youth.

****

Emily was pulled through the doorway with such force it knocked the wind out of her. She knew immediately what had happened, and what had grabbed her. A spider had been lurking and snatched her from the other side. And now, it was dragging her up the iron staircase, intent on tenderizing its next meal by pounding her into every step and baluster along the winding iron. It was with dazed relief that she popped through to the next level, and landed in an oil slick of insecticide.

She slid to a halt. The lights of the room, activated by her pin, were slowly burning to life. She squirmed sideways, on her belly, and spotted the mound of greasy fur that was her captor, also sprawled on its belly, and likewise in a puddle of bug spray.

Good, thought Emily. *Soak it all up and die, you disgusting monster.*

But, it did not die. The sparkling eyes rose up, to the level of an Irish Wolfhound. Its legs ranged from four feet long to six or eight feet, measuring from its furry toes to its backwards knees up in the air, back down to where they connected to its bulbous body. She found it hard to estimate their length as they twitched and moved and slipped a bit in the wet. Its head was like two basketballs glued together, side by side, and its abdomen was the size of that damn beach wagon full of bug bombs, now uselessly parked on the Earth side.

The Earth side, where the girls must have seen everything. Emily immediately imagined the shock her daughter must be experiencing, having seen her mother snatched, disappearing into a black otherworld. And Calliope! Calliope would be mounting a rescue, with no parent to hold her back. She had been itching to come in after her dad ever since the Twig sent that first email. Stephanie had slightly more sense, more caution, but Emily knew her daughter would be right at Calliope's side to save her mother. She had already done it, against a more unknown, and, in Emily's opinion, more disgusting foe.

But not this time. This time, Emily rallied, she would free herself and stop those girls from coming in. She quickly stood up to face the creature, and... *Clickity, clickity, clickity*, the spider's claws scratched out a rhythm on the slippery metal floor. It took off like a shot, headed for the darkened hallway to Emily's left. She turned to grab the iron railing, too late. She was yanked backwards again, dragged along the smooth, tepid metal floor of The City.

She scrabbled as she went, but found nothing to grab onto. They were traveling so fast that the lights would just start to glow before losing the activation signal and dimming out again. They sped down a long, straight corridor for quite some time, then a pause before a left turn—or Emily's right, since she was still facing backward—then more dragging. So, if the spider paused at intersections, then the next pause would be her chance to break free.

She reached back to grab the machete strung across her back. The scabbard was slathered in webbing, but not the handle. She worked the blade free, and made several attempts to swing it back and sever her tether, but to no avail. Two times she missed, the third struck the cable but just bounced off. The silk was strong, and worse, flexible. Unless they came to a stop, so she could grab a hold of the line and saw at it, she did not think her swings would cut it.

That did not mean she would give up, though. She kept making swipes as she slid along. She tried flipping herself over in a feat of acrobatics, wrapping a leg around the line and sitting up, but the spider could feel her flopping about. It took an unexpected route: vertical. It ran up the wall, then across the ceiling, while still moving forward. Emily slammed into the wall, flipped back to her belly, and pulled her arms in to protect her body. Then she was in midair while the spider ran above, then a hard reunion with the floor as the spider jumped down. This last move evoked an instinctive reaction; as Emily dropped, her arms extended to catch herself. The impact firstly smashed her fingers between floor and machete handle, secondly, slammed her elbow hard in the funny bone. Her weapon ejected from her stunned hand before she could react to grasp it. It clattered out of reach and faded into darkness as they moved on and the hallway lights dimmed.

Emily swore—a loud string of repetitive expletives—and pounded the floor moving beneath her. Her situation had become bleaker. She was counting on that machete to keep the spider at bay, once she freed herself.

But all hope was not lost. Her front pocket still held the folding knife, which had been digging into her hip this entire trip. She worked it free, and flipped open the blade. Using the same technique as before, she somersaulted-over, looped her leg around the line of webbing, and sat up. Knowing the spider would sense her movements and probably try its same counter-maneuver, she worked quickly, cutting under the web, sawing upwards between her legs. The shorter blade was easier to work with, this close to her body, but it was no better than the machete at cutting the tough cordage.

Finally, the knife bit. One small gap opened on the silk cable. She sawed harder, encouraged by her small success. The cut widened, the edges sprang away from each other as the elasticity reacted to its freedom. She was half way through.

The cord was less than a quarter of an inch in diameter, but she was tiring with the effort of sawing while not stabbing herself in the leg as she skated along, rolling side to side. All those years of yoga were paying off in a way she never thought to train for. She would have to thank Marta, her instructor, for pushing her so hard in class. If she survived.

They reached another intersection. The spider paused again and Emily slid to a halt. With the slack in the web, she doubled it around her blade and pulled hard. One slice, two slices, she repeated as the lights came up and the rear of the spider engulfed her vision. Its backside was a bulbous, dark brown, fuzzy fur mass ending in what looked like creepy monster fingertips arranged in a pentagram, and pointing in her direction. These were, undoubtedly, its spinnerets; evidenced by the silk rope extending from their center to Emily's tether.

This was an entirely too close and personal view of the spider's business end for Emily's liking, but she did not want to call attention to herself by scrambling away in any direction. The spider was currently occupied with deciding the best path forward. The hallway continued straight, but there were branches to the left and right. The creature was looking one way, then the next, as if sniffing out the correct path. Maybe feeling was a better term as it seemed to be testing the air with its front legs. Its indecision was working in Emily's favor, as she was almost through. Only a small strand remained.

The spider pranced right, tested the air one more time, then set its multiple legs in motion in a sprint down the chosen hall. Emily jerked forward, lost her balance and was flipped back onto her belly. She expected this, though, so held fast to her knife and stretched out into an easy glide. Once stabilized, she repeated her acrobatics, sat up, and gave one more vigorous cut to her leash. It snapped. She was free. She came to a halt and the lights responded to her presence. So did the spider. Recognizing that its prey had broken free, it returned, not on the floor, but on the wall. Emily bounded to her feet, knife at the ready, legs prepared to jump sideways, to avoid the launched snare she knew was coming.

The monster stopped twenty feet from Emily, its back end touching the ceiling, all of its evil eyes glaring in her direction. It had that stance she had seen on nature shows, and in her own home, so many times from smaller spiders. It stood there, studying her, first motionless, then a fast twitch coil as if ready to spring. Emily responded in kind, raising her knife, puffing up, crouching a bit, shuffling right. The spider twitched to follow, uncoiled, recoiled, uncoiled in a mechanical fashion, like its movements were gear driven, set sequences, as the hands of a clock.

They each stood their ground, for seconds, maybe minutes, Emily could not be sure. That old cliché of time expanding and losing meaning in tense situations was proven true. But for the sweat beading on her forehead, causing an itch she dared not scratch, she lost all awareness of anything but her enemy. And it seemed equally focused on her. She racked her brain, trying to think of her best course of action. She wondered if the spider was doing the same, or if it was acting purely on instinct. Was it sweating, or breathing heavy, or stressed in any way, or was it just hungry?

Emily decided to push her advantage. She puffed up to look as big as possible, then let out a bellowing scream, trying to overwhelm the creature's setae and send it scurrying. It did react. It backed down the wall, just a bit, and crouched, whether in preparation to flee, attack, or defend itself, Emily did not know. But when Emily did not advance, the spider stopped retreating. It surveyed its prey, and then shot. A silvery fountain of silk came in Emily's direction, filling the surrounding air. She dropped to the floor and rolled left, then sprang to her feet, knowing the spider would pounce if she stayed prone. Sure enough, the creature was on the move, skittering toward her, along the wall. She let out another bellow and waved the knife in the air.

The floor in front of her, as well as the wall to her right, was covered in sticky webbing. Her only safe path was to give ground backwards, which she was more than happy to do. And the spider was more than happy to follow. She kept backing up. It kept walking forward. As long as it did not attack, Emily was fine with this dance. But she knew the spider would lose its patience and test her ferocity, eventually.

She made it almost to the previous intersection, and then it attacked. Most likey, it wanted to keep her confined in this hallway, rather than allowing her access to three more escape routes. It fluttered across the wall faster than she expected. It leaped to the floor, but not like a cat's graceful leap that transitioned to a walk, or run, or stalking crouch. One minute it was on the wall, unmoving and glaring at her, the next it was on the floor, unmoving and glaring at her, standing between her and possible freedom.

There was no recourse. With the hallway behind covered in webbing, the hallway ahead was her only chance, attack her only option. She had to force the creature back, into the crossroads and beyond. She had little hope of killing it, but if she could just push it back and stay alive, there was hope.

"Raahhhhhh!" She screamed, raised both arms and ran at the creature.

It hopped backwards, retreated with her advance. Five paces, six paces, it was approaching the intersection. She just had to keep up her barbaric maneuver; be big, be bold, be loud and aggressive. But her foe was not completely fooled, nor unaware of its location. It did not want to be pushed into the intersecting hallways. It parried with an attack of its own. Silk rained through the air. It came from above, left to right, covering the entire hallway. There was no escape this time, no amount of acrobatics could avoid the downpour. Emily rushed forward, trying to avoid the majority, but that put her dangerously close to the spider's legs, fangs, and more webbing. She felt strands landing on her back, in her hair, across her arms. She danced to the side to avoid a straight on encounter. The spider rotated to match, but backed up even further to stay in front. Emily danced left, the spider repeated its move, and shot more silk, this time creating an artificial barrier from ceiling to floor, closing the hallway from that side.

Emily had glimpsed the opening to the hallway home, however. They were on the edge. She had to get around this spider. To her right, a fast break, non-stop, no matter what, would be her last chance. Undoubtedly, at the pace it was spewing silk, her enemy would soon close off this entire hall with a wall of silk, trapping her in a cocoon.

She ran, all out, swinging her knife as she went, hoping to deter, or cut, or knock away her enemy's tactics. It did not work. Webbing caught her legs. The spider had laid a tripwire across her path, and she blundered right into it. She was down, could feel more silk covering her, sticking her to the floor. This was it. The creature would sink its fangs in now, injecting a venom to end its efforts with this troublesome meal. Emily worked her knife arm free, alternated between cutting at the strands that bound her, and waving her blade in the creature's face, but neither was working. The creature was upon her, and would surely spray her one last time to trap that annoying flash of steel.

Cries of attack echoed around the hall, and then the spider reared up, its front legs scrambled in the air, and it emitted a high-pitched screech that Emily assumed was from pain. She saw something drop from its back end, then bluish liquid poured from its backside. Emily saw her daughter and Calliope attacking the creature from behind; Calliope with the machete, Stephanie with dueling cans of bug spray pointed directly at the open wounds. Calliope had cut off the spider's spinnerets, quashing the creature's most dangerous weapon. Fangs, to be sure, were dangerous, and horrifying, but the tactical advantage of throwing sticky thread was by far the greater threat.

The spider turned on the girls, warding them off with its long legs. As it spun, Emily was splattered with the translucent, foggy blue liquid draining from its abdomen. At the rate blood was draining, it could not live much longer. At least, Emily hoped that was the case. Wasting no time, not wanting the girls to be on their own, Emily dug her knife into the webs holding her to the floor.

Stephanie continued to spray her foggers in the creature's face, which was having as much impact as the blow to its backside. Its eyes had been coated, and it was no longer able to look directly at them. In fact, it was now stumbling around in an attempt to flee down another passage. However, it clearly was losing control of its motor functions. Its legs were slipping, unable to support its weight. It walked into a wall, used that as support to slide along for a few yards more, then even that was not enough. The creature slumped to the floor, legs twitching, but unable to move its bulk. Finally, it stopped moving, and died, in a pool of its remaining blood.

Calliope stayed to watch the creature, while Stephanie ran to her mother and started pulling at the net.

"Oh my God, mom, I thought it had eaten you! Are you ok?" Stephanie's voice was muffled by her respirator.

"Well, I'm covered in this sticky stuff, and spider blood, and bumps and bruises, but it never bit me, so for that, I'm thankful. I'm fine, really. But I don't ever want to go through that again. And this bug spray is killing my lungs." She coughed to emphasize the unpleasantness of the room's fumigation.

"Oh! Sorry," said her daughter. "We have a respirator for you, too." She dug around in her pack and pulled out a mask for her mother.

"Thank you," said Emily, as she donned the device. "We need to get out of here as fast as possible. There are bound to be more of those things around, and we have made a lot of noise. Something, or some *things*, are going to be coming our way soon."

"You don't have to tell me twice," said Stephanie. "I'm glad to get out of here. We just need to get you free."

They continued working to free her from her bonds for the next few minutes. The webs were tenacious; sticking to anything that touched them. The girls had it on their shirts, their bare arms, their pant legs. It coated their knives and fingers.

"We need some Goo-B-Gone," said Calliope. "That stuff would probably eliminate the stickiness."

"We'd need about a gallon of the stuff," said Emily. She was finally able to raise her torso from the floor, twist a bit on her side and use her body as a lever to pry the web from the floor. It worked, freeing her lower legs without needing to cut more strands.

"Thank you, girls. Thank you for rescuing me. Again." She smiled and hugged both girls. "Now, let's get out of here."

Calliope paused, as Emily knew she would. "We're already inside. And we've already fought off one spider—really easily, if you think about it. I mean, the bug spray did most of the work."

"No, Calliope," cut in Emily. "I'm sorry, but your grandfather did not want you risking your life, and your father would not want you risking your life, and I do not want you risking your life, or Stephanie's, or mine. And make no mistake, one spider we may be able to handle, *maybe*, but they will come in groups. You saw how they attacked in your basement tunnel. Any more than one spider, and we're done for."

Calliope struggled, mentally trying to come up with a persuasive argument, but every rationalization evolved into the same defense: she felt she was more than capable of battling these creatures, and she just plain wanted to go after her dad.

Emily, as a mother of a pre-teen daughter, and as someone who had been a pre-teen girl herself, knew the turbulent emotions battling in Calliope's head. She could see it written on Calliope's face, and in her body language.

"I know you think we can do this, Calliope, but we can't. That thing almost had me. If you girls had been one minute later, just a little slower, or had not been able to sneak up on it as it was focused on me, it would have sunk its fangs in, and I'd be dead right now. All bravado aside, I was terrified. I was dead. I was going to be eaten. Let that sink in for a minute. Picture all three of us, trapped in webbing as I just was, helpless, as those monsters come in close, then sink those giant pincers into your chest, or stomach, or maybe your face. It's horrifying."

"Ok, ok," said Calliope. The images Emily was conjuring up were exactly that: horrifying. So horrifying that Stephanie was white as a sheet and on the verge of tears. That, more than anything, was enough to collapse Calliope's ambition. "Let's get out of here, quick."

"Thank you, Calliope. I know it's hard, but these are the decisions you have to make as an adult. And that was a very mature choice."

Calliope was not sure she liked making mature choices. She knew it was the right thing to do; Emily was correct, they were outmatched by more than one spider, and more than one would come, but she felt compelled to go after her father. She looked over to the slumped mass of legs in the other hallway, and shivered. These creatures really were gruesome.

They headed back down the hallway Emily had so recently been dragged. The mood was tense. Emily could feel anxiety emanating from both girls, and herself. She was regretting her vivid description of their circumstances. Afraid she had put an overwhelming, if realistic, pall of dread over the girls, she searched for comforting words. But she was having trouble shaking her own growing angst.

"Girls, I..." Emily began, but she was not sure where to go from there.

"Shhhh," Stephanie interrupted her mother. "I hear something."

All three stopped, stood stark still, and listened. It was a distant sound, but definitely coming closer; that faint, frightening *clickety-clickety-clickety* of many, many claws tapping along the iron walls of The City, directly ahead of them.

"They're coming!" said Stephanie, her voice barely a strangled whisper.

"They've cut us off from the way home," Calliope whispered, too.

"Run!" said Emily, and pushed the girls back in the direction of their last battle.

They made it to the intersection and stopped.

"Which way," asked Stephanie. Taking action kept the panic down, but every time they stopped, she felt trapped. She wanted to just keep running.

"I don't know if the spider that had me was trying to stay away from other spiders, or take me back to his own pack," said Emily, "but he definitely did not like the left tunnel, and he was taking me down the right tunnel. I'm thinking enemies were to the left. And enemies to him probably means bigger spiders, so we're not going that way. To the right could be free of spiders, or it could lead to his pack. But he, or it, whatever, sprayed the entire hallway with webbing. I'm not sure we could get through without getting stuck. I don't think we should risk it. I think we keep going straight down this hallway."

"I like it," said Calliope. "Here," she handed a can of bug spray to Emily, one to Stephanie, and took one herself. "I grabbed about forty cans, and we've already used four, so maybe thirty-six left. We should only use them as a last resort. Run and hide first, fight if we have to, set off the foggers when trapped. I don't think even two are enough to take down one really big spider without having to hurt it physically, too. We should count on these only as a deterrent."

"Excellent thinking, Calliope," said Emily.

"I'm all for the running and hiding. I think we should do that now," said Stephanie.

Putting words to action, they took off at a jog down the hallway.

Each time the lights sprang to life, the ladies sighed with relief to see no sign of spiders. Emily had the strap to the duffle of lightly clanking tin cans draped over one shoulder. Calliope had woven a multi-loop nylon climbing strap through the bag's side straps, cinched it tight and locked it with a carabiner to keep the duffle compressed and the cans from banging around as much as possible, but they still emitted a clink now and again.

They had long since pulled their respirators down under their chins so they could breathe better at a jog. All-in-all, they were winded, their shoulders ached from their assorted packs bouncing around, but they felt they had gained a good lead on the pursuing spiders. If, indeed, they were pursuing. There was a very good chance they had been more interested in the dead spider and all the confusion at the intersection. Perhaps they did not even know the humans were in The City.

"Let's walk for a bit," puffed Emilly. "I think we may have lost them. Let's catch our breath."

"Oh, thank goodness," said Stephanie.

Calliope seemed lost in thought, which gave Emily mild apprehension. Now that they were moving away from an escape back home, Emily knew Calliope would be trying to meet up with her grandfather. That was not a bad idea, actually. Emily was thinking about that herself. But it was so they could join a larger group, then make a push for the doorway home, to get the girls out of danger. Emily knew Nigel would never allow his granddaughter to stay here, or go along on a mission to save Ben, but she would let Nigel handle that conversation.

"You know," began Calliope.

Here it comes, Emily thought.

"We haven't tried to contact Poppie since the last time we were in." She directed the comment at Stephanie.

"Hey, yeah!" said her friend. "We should call her."

"Whoah, hold on girls," Emily broke in. "Let's not make too much noise. We just lost those spiders and gained a bit of rest. There could be other packs not far away."

"Shoot!" said Stephanie. "There has to be a better way to call her. You know, we never did explore the consoles that give us the pins. Maybe they do more? We should try those."

"Well, first things first, we have to find one of those consoles, and they're usually in rotundas. We're long overdue for running across one of those. In fact, we're long overdue for running into any sort of intersection. This tunnel has been going straight, forever," said Calliope.

"Keeps us from getting lost, though," said Emily. "I've been thinking about that. I don't have one of your dad's notebooks handy for jotting down twists and turns."

"That's another good reason to find Poppie. She can guide us anywhere we'd like to go. And maybe help us avoid spiders, too," said Stephanie.

Emily could not argue with that logic.

They continued down the hallway for some time, without incident. They did pass two more intersections, the first branched only left, the other branched to either side. At each encounter, they decided not to deviate. Going straight was as good a guess for getting out as any other choice. They reasoned that they would walk straight until they found a stairway going up or down, then change levels and hopefully walk straight back to their starting point, all while avoiding spiders. That was the plan, barring any unforeseen mishaps. But in this place, unforeseen mishaps were quite commonplace.

After half an hour's walk, they entered a rotunda. It was smaller than others they had found; only five passages leading away around the perimeter, and it was surprisingly unadorned. The walls, usually riveted, or embellished with scrollwork, and showing seams of some sort, were invariably smooth here, revealing no breaks or joinery. The archways, too, were devoid of the ornamental flowers concealing control pins. They searched briefly, but found nothing to push, twist, or pull. Nothing at all stuck out as worth investigation for calling Poppie.

The center of the room did hold a spiral staircase that led both up to the next level, and down to the lower. The design of this staircase was different from others they had encountered. It did not emulate growing plants, nor was it ornately built of scrollwork. It was sleek, and smooth, and rose from the floor without standing supports, or a center pole, or even handrails. It seemed delicate, and magical, like a swirling ribbon lifting you up, or floating you down. The materials were the usual black iron, but somehow, it seemed lighter than air, and smooth as silk. It was elegant in its lack of detail, its simplicity, its ability to be, without much being.

"Do we go up, or down," asked Stephanie in a whisper. The room seemed to call for reverent silence, with its dark passages concealing the unknown, and the mystic central spiral leading to possibilities of salvation or damnation.

Calliope shrugged. They both looked to Emily for a decision.

"I think up," Emily whispered a reply. "Spiders are always in the basement."

"They're in the attic, too," reminded Calliope.

"Good point," said Emily. "Well, when we come in from home, we always go up two levels. Seems like we're more likely to find the hallway home if we go up one or two levels."

"Yeah, I think you're right, mom," said Stephanie.

"Sounds right to me, too," agreed Calliope.

Decision made, they ascended. The steps were wide, and silky-smooth, and gracefully lacking in ornamentation, matching the rest of the structure, which was apropos for this unembellished room.

There was space on each step for three to walk side by side. Their footfalls made soft scuffing sounds that did not travel far. There were no sharp edges on the steps; each being merely a wave in the metal ribbon that carried them higher. They walked bunched to the center, keeping from the unfenced edges, and the danger of falling off the sides.

As the ladies reached the third to last step, the lights above warmed, while the lights below faded. Slowly, they peered over the upper floor and around the new room. Their first impression: it was clear of spiders. Their second: it was not the level they wanted. Only two hallways branched from this room. One headed in the same direction as the lower hallway they had just abandoned, away from the path home. The other branched only slightly left of the first. This was a configuration they had not seen before, but had no desire to explore. They continued to climb.

Unnerving evidence of spiders greeted them on the next level. Webbing clung from ceiling to floor, and walled off all hallways, except for one leading to the right of where they wished to go. Cocoons of dessicated prey—smaller spiders, by the look of them—adhered to the walls. And on the floor were several carapaces, cracked open and empty.

"It looks like they shed their skin when they grow. Like a snake," said Stephanie.

"I think they do," said Emily. "I saw a spider documentary on The Discovery Channel a few years ago. I remember seeing a tarantula outgrow its outer shell and squeeze itself out. I think it took a day or two to harden its new skin."

"That's creepy," said Calliope.

"Got that right," said Stephanie.

"I think we'd better get out of here before it comes back. I think we're in its nest," said Emily.

"Should we go back down?" asked Stephanie.

"Might be a good idea," said Emily. "Let's try down."

They reversed direction and retraced their path. One level down, however, they froze. The telltale *clickety-click* of their enemy echoed from below. It was faint, but definitely rising up to meet them.

"Back up we go," said Calliope. "And quick like!"

The trio double timed it back through the spider's den above, and upward to the next level, and the next surprise.

—9—

The Stubborn and the Hungry

Ima crept along the passage, carefully avoiding the diaphanous sheets that blanketed the floor. They were shredded, as if some large child had thrown a tantrum, ripping and littering in an immature expression of frustration.

There was a dairy cow sized spider lying on the floor twenty feet ahead. It had not moved in the ten minutes the crew had sat quietly watching. When Nigel's brooch had activated the corridor lights, the spider had appeared at the edge of the light's influence, a massive shadow of undeniable shape. Nigel and the team had stopped, waited for a reaction to the light, to their movement. Nothing had happened. Even Nigel's pin, which had been glowing a deep shade of orange since entering The City, had remained constant. The consensus was, the creature was dead.

There was a chance it was playing possum. As its face was pointed away from them, looking down the hallway, in the direction the team wished to travel, all they could see was its enormous backside and a mass of legs, all resting motionless. Ima, being the quickest, most agile, and completely capable, volunteered to reconnoiter, while Nigel, Sonam, and Kunga stood ready with bows. Nigel, especially, dared not move forward, lest the hallway fully illuminate and awaken the slumbering giant.

Tormad remained his stoic self, content to watch and deal with whatever fate brought his way, but Garran seemed disinclined to let Ima take all of the risk. He crept along the wall, maintaining a twenty pace buffer behind Ima, fearful that his less-graceful movements might trigger a reaction. His sword held ready, Garran watched the dormant mass, but Nigel noticed that the sprite spared more than one glance in Ima's direction. An interesting development? Or a human's romantic imagination? Nigel was not sure, but he did find it interesting.

The creature was fully resting on its belly, which seemed an odd posture, indicative of death. All eight legs curled close, but the tips still impacted the floor. It could be dead, or sleeping, or extremely patient, resting its bulk, ready to spring at any moment. It made no reaction to Ima's approach, but she was extremely stealthy.

Still, Nigel thought to himself, if spiders could feel a moth's wings beat from a mile away, surely they could sense Ima's footfalls on this metal floor. For the creature to not react, it surely had to be a corpse.

Ima moved closer, then leaned forward a few inches to peer around a leg which rose taller than herself and blocked the spider's face. The first glimpse told Ima all she needed to know. The beast was dead. Its eyes were completely gone. Sucked out of their sockets, probably by its hungry brethren.

"It is dead," she whispered back.

"Thank God," mumbled Nigel.

Garran closed the distance and was at her side immediately. The rest of the team relaxed a bit and made their way to Ima as well. Nigel took up the wagon handle and pulled along his arsenal of poisons. While he could step carefully over, or around the scattered webbing, the beach trolley was not as maneuverable. Its wheels thumped and bumped over the remnants, a muted rattle of liquid filled cans following along. Bits and pieces of the sticky thread tenaciously attached themselves to the rubber tires, making the cart even more ungainly.

He reached the group, bringing light with him, and they could clearly see that the creature had been in a battle. It was covered with multiple tiny scratches and bite marks.

"Death by a thousand cuts," said Nigel, referencing the seventh century Chinese torture tactic known as lingchi. However, whereas lingchi was usually administered by a single executioner, in a long, drawn-out manner designed to extend punishment, this spider's wounds, and the surrounding mess, seemed to suggest a chaotic battle with multiple enemies. Enemies much smaller than this monster.

"This is not good," whispered Ima, voicing the conclusion Nigel was also drawing. "If we extrapolate the size of these bite marks, compared to the size of this spider's fangs, it would mean that the spiders which attacked were no bigger than choocha."

"What's a choocha?" asked Nigel.

"It is a small animal on our world that lives along the riverbanks," supplied Garran. "A fully grown animal is a little smaller than my head."

"My point," continued Ima, "is that there must have been many of them, hunting in a pack, that swarmed and overwhelmed this much larger creature. Smaller creatures do not usually go after something so much larger, especially when the larger is just as aggressive and dangerous. They would need to be fast, and vicious."

"Great," grumbled Nigel. "As if the big ones weren't trouble enough. I'd rather deal with one big one than multiple little ones."

As if his words were a summons, the hulking mass in front of them shuddered, and the legs moved.

"It lives!" spat Tormad. He reacted instantly, swinging his onyx ax laterally to sever the limbs closest to him, neatly through the tibias.

Several arrows thunked into the creature at the face, along the cephalothorax and abdomen. Sonam and Kunga had been lightning fast with their bow work. Nigel was grabbing cans of bug spray, preparing to detonate, but the creature ceased moving.

"What, by the spirits, was that?" whispered Garran.

"It cannot still have life," said Ima, considering. "What if it did not move itself, but was moved?"

"Yeah, from the inside," said Nigel, his eyes wide. "They're inside him, eating. We gotta move!" he whispered.

Nigel stuffed the two cans of bug spray unceremoniously inside his jacket. The chest strap of his backpack had created a storage bubble he found useful for temporarily jamming things he needed quick access to. He retrieved his bow, and the wagon handle, then backed away from the carcass, continuing in the direction of the arachnid homeworld.

As Nigel was the slower, having to haul the rumbling wagon along, the rest of the gang peeled off in reverse order. Tormad followed close to the wagon, Sonam and Kunga came next, bows ready, then Garran, and finally Ima. They eyed the hulking mass, once again still. It was not until Nigel had passed into the next zone, and the lights around the spider's remains began to dim, that the excitement began.

Nigel's brooch changed from orange to fire engine red.

"Oh no," said Nigel. "That's not good." He pointed to the brooch with his chin when the others looked at him. Then everyone looked back to the corpse.

A dozen sparkles of light appeared on top of the dead body. More rose over the back and around the edges. A veritable river of glitter began issuing from between the dead creature's fangs. In seconds, the floor was infested with jittery, jumpy, reflected lights from the eyes of a hoard of softball-sized spiders.

"Nigel Sullivan," whispered Garran, "I think now would be a good time to set off several of those canisters."

"Aye, old-timer. Blast those buggers afore they swarm!" said Tormad, evidently not so intent on engaging these smaller beasts in battle.

Nigel had attached a short loop of string to his bow, then used a carabiner to quick-clip it to the speed loops on the straps of his backpack. That freed his hands, but kept the bow within reach. He grabbed the two cans from his jacket, pressed their buttons, and tossed them to the floor a few feet in front of Ima. The reaction from the small arachnids was instantaneous. Like flocks of birds, they split into two flowing masses. One congregation swam up the left wall, and broached the ceiling. The second undulated along the floor, a sea of hopping, springing creatures, cascading over each other like rolling waves. It seemed their previous meal, whether completely emptied or still retaining some gruesome morsels, was not as appetizing as the newcomers. Nigel guessed cannibalism was not the first choice of these creatures, merely a necessity. The chance for a new entre on the menu was too much to pass up, even if bellies were full.

The swarm on the floor encountered the foggers and recoiled. As the fog from one can sprayed dead center, and the second can sprayed at the right wall, the attackers moved left. Nigel grabbed two more cans and set them off more strategically. He set one upright by the left wall to bathe the creatures clinging there. The second, he put on its side in front of the first, pointing straight towards the ground gathering. They had no choice now, but to push through the poison. Those at the front emerged drenched, and dripping, and drunk with the chemicals. They weaved and stumbled. They were overrun by those behind. Nigel hoped they were crushed and no longer in the fight.

Those on the ceiling fared better, as the fog was having trouble reaching the high ceilings quickly, but spiders at the back of both lines were getting a decent amount of exposure. Nigel was starting to cough, himself. He quickly donned his respirator, then set off another two bombs as the team continued to back quickly down the hallway.

Sonam and Kunga moved past Nigel, to take the lead. They did not want to waste arrows on the smaller creatures, then blunder into a larger foe and have no ammunition. Their eyes had proven well-equipped for the darkness, so they ventured to the edge of illumination, making sure the escape route was clear.

Ima and Tormad formed the rear guard. Tormad, being a bit shorter, was wielding his ax like a scythe, cutting the floor spiders into pieces, or launching them back down the hallway, to disappear in the darkness. Ima's blade was deftly flicking the creatures from the wall, almost faster than Nigel's eyes could register. Her movements were a dance of retreating steps, each accentuated by smooth swipes that cleared a row of spiders, then pecked and chopped upward at the strays, like a chef dicing furry beets.

Tormad was overrun first. Several spiders flanked him, avoiding his swinging blade, to pounce and attach themselves to his legs. They tried inserting their fangs, but found his scruffy bark too hard to penetrate. They skittered up his back, searching for chinks in his natural armour.

Garran leapt forward, his sword flashed with skill almost as adept as Ima's, and Tormad's back was once again clear. Garran remained to bolster the defense from the right.

The ceiling, however, was out of everyone's reach, which the spiders quickly learned. They surged past the battle line to drop like black rain all around them. It was too late for retreat, too late to abandon the wagon and outright run, there were too many, in all directions. Nigel dropped the handle, kicked a spider with his left foot, then stepped on another. It made a surprising crunch under his boot, instead of the soft smoosh he had expected.

He reached into the cart and activated four bug bombs where they sat, then grabbed his granddaughter's pristine machete from its scabbard, nestled handle-up inside the wagon, and christened the blade with the bluish blood of the nearest spiders. He stabbed and hacked at the creatures on the floor, maintaining a distance from the walls, so the jumpers could not reach him. They still dropped from the ceiling, but any that dropped close to Nigel, he used for batting practice.

In minutes, his arms were coated in slime, as were his boots and pant legs. He worried that all this blood would dampen the effects of the DEET with which he had coated his clothes. The chemical did seem to be keeping the buggers at bay. They would approach, ready to pounce on him from the floor, then pause and skitter back a bit. By then, Nigel would zero in and either step on them, or slice through their exoskeletons.

The mess accumulating on the floor was growing. It was like a coating of guacamole-layered nacho chips; slippery and crunchy and dotted with the salsa of mashed bits and pieces of spider innards.

The older human was huffing and puffing from a level of exercise and excitement that he was not accustomed to at this juncture of retirement. His fatigue, and the increasing level of muck, was causing him to slip more often, and miss his target. If not for his thick clothing, and thick layer of bug repellant, the little monsters would have bitten him many times. As it was, their numbers around him were increasing, and their fangs were getting closer. He spared a glance for his companions, and saw Tormad once again covered in a moving, fuzzy carpet of arachnids.

Ima was still free, but only because of her untiring speed and grace. Her sword struck like a viper's tongue, her feet danced over spiders as graceful as any ballerina: a jeté, an assemblé, a sissonne, each accompanied by a strike of her black crystal blade. She continued to be where the spiders were not.

Garran, surprisingly, was also free of spiders. He was proving to be gracefully athletic in his own way. Rather than a dancer, he was more akin to an arborescent Jackie Chan. Just when a group of spiders were poised to overwhelm him, he would execute a crouching spin, sweeping out one branch of a leg, punting spiders sideways into the wall, or backwards over their comrades. He would skewer several spiders with one jab, then fling their corpses from his blade, directly into the surging mass, scattering the creatures, and disrupting their momentum. When three spiders did manage to latch onto his legs, Garran cartwheeled to the right, and with legs at the apex, flung the spiders from his ankles. He landed with the grace of an acrobat and continued the fight.

Then Sonam and Kunga were at Nigel's side, knocking spiders away with their bows like golfers driving down the green, then firing their arrows far down the hallway, in the direction the team wished to move; another bad sign.

"We have a disappointing development," Sonam delivered his news in his usual calm demeanor. "A very large spider is headed our way. Nigel, you may want to throw a few more of those fogging canisters in that direction." He pointed into the darkness, the way they wanted to escape.

"I would," grunted Nigel, "if I could get these spiders off me. Unlike you sprites, I'm pretty sure one bite from these bastards and I'm a dead man."

"We will keep them off of you for the moment," chimed in Kunga.

He used his bow as a staff, and began knocking spiders away, left and right. Sonam joined him, and Nigel found that the immediate area was quickly cleared, but the sprites were facing a growing black tide of voracious eaters.

Nigel took a deap, steadying breath inside his sweaty, stifling mask. He itched to take the thing off, and breathe normally, but he knew the air was thick with toxins. His eyes were starting to burn, and he was worried about damage to his sight. He could not believe the spiders were still attacking through the haze.

Trying not to overthink the situation, he grabbed two more cans, pushed the buttons, and tossed them down the hallway into the darkness. He heard the first can hit the floor and rattle on. The second thunked into something, and bounced back into the light. It was immediately followed by a monster of epic proportions. Nigel found epic to be an apt term, as he was suddenly reminded of the 1981 classic movie, *Clash of the Titans*, where Perseus had to fight off scorpions the size of a grizzly bear. However, this demon, more the size of a Volkswagen Beetle, did not move with the stop-action jitters of that claymation classic. This evil walked with the heart-stopping, slow-stalking, deliberateness of a real life predator.

"Forget the fogger!" cried Nigel. "Time for the big guns."

He unshackled his bow, pulled an arrow from his quiver, and swiftly unleashed a four-hundred grain projectile at three-hundred and forty feet per second, to slam into the creature with about one hundred foot-pounds of kinetic energy; more than enough to drop a water buffalo. It struck the creature dead center of one of those shiny, unblinking orbs. Its reaction was shocking. It spun around, thrashing and lashing out with it's legs, while swiping at its damaged eye with its pedipalps. Webbing began spraying everywhere, covering everything, from walls to ceiling. With no rhyme or reason, the sticky substance blurted through the air, grabbed onto walls, coated the smaller spiders on the floor, and created anarchy and chaos for all living things in the hallway.

A fortunate side effect, was that a full quarter of the remaining small spiders broke off and immediately swarmed the wounded creature. They did not use webbing. They leapt onto the careening body and began biting; injecting their venom to either kill, or put it to sleep. At this point, that was probably the most humane thing, since Nigel's shot was most likely a mortal wound. He almost felt sorry for the creature, and then he remembered it had been all too ready to eat them only a moment ago.

Satisfied that the larger arachnid was no longer a threat, Nigel returned his attention to the smaller foe. Maybe it was his imagination, since Kunga and Sonam were keeping him safe, but the spiders seemed to be slowing. Maybe the fogger was finally taking effect. In fact, Nigel noticed a spider drop from the ceiling, no longer in a controlled descent, to land upside-down in a leg-twitching mass on the floor. Finally, the bug spray seemed to be working.

Then Nigel remembered the sprayers. He traded his bow for one of the two-gallon canisters, and let loose with a shower of insecticide, dousing anything that moved on floors or walls. Within minutes, those on the floor were crawling lethargically, or twitching, or still. Those on the walls were dropping, and those further back were retreating from the imminent threat they could sense heading in their direction. The hallway was won.

"Let's move out!" Nigel barked through his mask. "Sonam, Kunga, back on point. Ima and Garran, rear guard. Tormad, with me."

He jammed the sprayer back in the cart, retrieved his bow and started pulling the wagon. Then he remembered he was not in command, and these were not his Marines.

"Please!" he added, unnecessarily, for everyone was already taking their positions.

Sonam and Kunga had disappeared into the darkness ahead, Tormad was at his side, scanning the walls, ceiling and floor for anything moving, Ima and Garran were bringing up the rear, watching behind to ward off any followers. Thankfully, the smaller spiders seemed to be in full flight, never looking back. The crew had reduced their number by more than half, and those remaining may have been poisoned beyond survival. Nigel could only hope.

The next section of hallway lit up, revealing the final resting place of Nigel's trophy kill. Kunga and Sonam were retrieving their arrows from a dozen, now dead, smaller spiders. Nigel cautiously walked up to the face of the dead giant to retrieve his own arrow, which had buried itself up to the fletchings.

It was unnerving to be standing in front of those monster fangs and many unblinking, jeweled eyes. But it really made Nigel's skin crawl when he rested his left hand on the fuzzy face, just under the ruined orb. A mushy padding, like jello under a layer of moss, surrounded the eye socket. A hard ridge encircled that; a bony ring the thickness of Nigel's wrist . He shifted the heel of his hand to the ridge for a firmer base, then pulled on the arrow with his other hand. There was some resistance, as the triple blades of his arrowhead backed their way out of the skull. A lot of squelching, some crunching, but he was relieved when it pulled free, and seemed undamaged. He wiped the arrow clean on the carcass, then hurriedly backed away and continued down the hall.

"I fear the closer we get to the portal of the spider world, the more dense the population of these creatures," said Garran. "I am not sure we can handle another attack, such as the last one."

"I be absolutely sure we can *no* handle it," harrumphed Tormad. "Those blighters nigh on chewed me bark ta shreds. I'll have sap scabs fer weeks."

"Perhaps, if you were to move a little more, and not wade into the fray, relying on brute force alone to tackle our foe, you might avoid becoming their climbing trellis," said Ima convivially.

"Ah, sure, lass. If I be a hundred turns younger, maybe. But, I do no think me parts ever moved like yorn. Me branches be never that nimble."

"That is easy to believe," said Kunga.

"Watch it, monk," growled Tormad.

Kunga chuckled.

"Well, should the opportunity arise," added Garran, "a good molting can shave a few centuries off your tired limbs. And bark, and roots. I feel like a sproutling again." He demonstrated a flip, mid-stride.

"Great idea," Tormad replied, sarcastically. "All I do is get me-self broken so bad I can no heal, drag me bits te water, then remain motionless n' vulnerable for half a day while I regrow. Sounds wonderful."

"The day is young," said Kunga. "There's still a chance all that could come to pass."

"Ye monks be always so cheerful."

They passed down hallways as empty and clean as before the spider infestation. It gave Nigel a sense that they could reach Spiderland without another major battle. He was hoping this would be the case, and that they could save the rest of their insecticide payload for "the other side," as he thought of it. Having never really crossed over to another planet—an idea he still found incredulous— he was unsure of what to expect.

Even though, once he thought about it, he must be on another planet now. It just did not seem like it. He had merely walked through a door into a massive building. There was no purple sky, or three moons, or strange plants, or aliens. Well, ok, he was traveling with five strange alien plant-creatures, but they were extremely human-like. And, yes, they were fighting monsters straight out of some B-rated horror movie from the 60's, but that was sort of the point, as well. All of this seemed like a movie; unreal, impossible, but incredibly familiar.

The hallway opened to a foyer similar to others in The City of Doors; a large open space twice as wide as the hallway, and twice as tall. Their hallway picked up again on the far side, through another iron archway lightly embossed with leafy vines and florets. To their right, a grand staircase led down to a lower level. Constructed of mahogany treads rather than stone, they were layered in the usual dust. But this time, the dust was peppered with disturbances; silver-dollar-sized dots had been cleared of their gray blanket by a hundred not-so-little, hairy spider paws.

Interestingly, Nigel thought, it looked like these spiders had three toes, or pads, or whatever. And around the toes, there were slight scratch marks that he assumed were the tips of claws cutting through the dust. Suddenly, Nigel remembered one of Sun Tzu's more famous teachings:

> *"If you know the enemy and know yourself, you need not fear the result of a hundred battles. If you know yourself, but not the enemy, for every victory gained you will also suffer a defeat. If you know neither the enemy nor yourself, you will succumb in every battle."*

Now, Nigel had the urge to study these creatures more closely. At least, a dead one. He also realized that he and his companions could stand a little more team building. They seemed to fight well together, but Nigel was a new addition. He needed to work his rhythm into theirs, help out if he could, but maybe follow their lead a bit more.

It was hard to judge their ages. Except for the scruffy Tormad, they all had relatively smooth bark, which gave them a youthful appearance, for little trees. But their earlier conversation led Nigel to believe they were all at least a hundred years old, if not several hundred. That was a lot of knowledge earned.

Then again, Nigel had been trained in the greatest military ever known on Earth. He had fought in wars between nations. He had been directed by great leaders, and led men into battle himself. He might not be a hundred years old, but he had his own valuable experience.

Turning that valuable experience to the situation at hand, Nigel focused on the last feature of this foyer: the second grand staircase that led to the upper level. The sprites were already studying this, as the stairs themselves were no longer visible. The entire structure—stairs, railing, upper balcony, even the ceiling—were ensconced in webbing. They could still walk up, but they would have to walk through a narrow tunnel of silk, created to slow down any approaching enemy, or prey, and force them into single file formation. It was a very effective defense, and hunting technique.

"That is the way we must go," said Garran. He had traveled these hallways longer than any of them, since he was part of the first contingent to Earth, originally hunting for Ben, several years ago.

"That is most definitely a trap," said Sonam. Kunga nodded in agreement.

"Well, o' course it be a trap," gruffed Tormad.

"Yes," cut in Ima, "but it is a trap we must spring." She looked serious, but determined. Nigel liked her. She was calm and fearless. She kept a clear head in battle. She was an excellent leader.

"I agree," said Nigel, "But, if we spring it correctly, it could be a trap for the spiders, not for us. You see, that tunnel can work in both directions."

"Clever, Nigel," said Ima, "I see what you are suggesting."

"Yes. As do I," Garran stated with some skepticism. "And in order to flip this trap, I assume there must be some bait?"

"Well, that would be a down-side to the plan, yes," said Nigel with a grimace.

"To be clear," chimed in Sonam, "you are suggesting that one of us go up that tunnel, somehow attract the spiders—or maybe one giant spider—draw them back down this tunnel, so that we may dispose of it, or them, while trapped in their own trap?"

"Exactly," said Nigel.

"Yes," said Ima.

Garran made a sigh and shook his head in dissatisfaction, though not disapproval.

"Aargh, why do we no just chop the cursed thing apart an' walk in," Tormad proposed, hefting his ax.

"Sure," answered Nigel, "Give it a shot. Swing at that section there." He pointed to the leading edge of the tunnel.

Tormad smiled a confident, menacing smile, stomped over to the offered wall of webbing, and gave a mighty swing of his crystal ax. The blade rebounded back with an equal amount of force, sending Tormad into a spin, and landing him on his backside.

The rest of the team stifled their laughter as the gruff warrior picked himself up off the floor, and swore heartily.

"Did ya know it were gonna do tha?" he accused Nigel.

"I had a suspicion," Nigel admitted. "Sorry about that. But our scientists have studied spiders for centuries, and marveled at how strong and resilient their webs are. It is said the silk they spin is stronger than most metals. We might be able to cut through this, in time, but we would wear ourselves out, and undoubtedly be attacked long before making any real progress."

"Fine," stated Tormad, ignoring his friends' grinning. "I'll go up the tunnel, an' bring those buggers."

"I do not think that would be wise," said Ima. "This will require stealth, speed, and agility. And while I know you can move quickly when you so desire, and can be quite agile, you are not built for stealth as much as I."

"You do not always have to be the one taking risks, Ima," countered Garran, guessing she was the next to volunteer. "I will go in and lure the monsters out."

He quickly turned to Sonam and Kunga who were about to interject and, presumably, offer themselves up as being just as competent.

"This is the most sensible. You two must stay out here with your bows, to strike these creatures from a distance. As will Nigel, since his bow is much more powerful, and a single arrow can kill one of the larger creatures. Tormad can wield his ax, and Ima her sword, guarding your flanks against any that escape into the room, at which time I should be back to join you in battle."

"That is a sound plan, except for your ability to get any and all creatures lurking beyond this tunnel to follow you," said Ima. "We two should go, and take with us as many of these," and here she struggled with the phrase she had heard the humans use, "bug bombs? as we can. We will creep in as deep as possible, activate the toxin, sound the alarm, and drive the creatures to the tunnel."

Nigel felt like he should make his own offer to be the bait, but if he was honest with himself, he was not very fast, not very nimble, and his bow would certainly be best used firing at the spiders as they emerged from the tunnel. Ima must have sensed his thinking, for she looked at him kindly, and shook her head.

Nigel smiled and shrugged.

"Ok. I'm not thrilled with putting you two in danger, but that does seem like our best bet. Now I'm wishing I had dragged that flamethrower in here. I'm wondering if fire would melt all this webbing back in on the spiders. Then again, we could end up facing ten times as many of those vicious little ones. If that's the case, even this plan is going to backfire. My bow will be overkill, and I'll quickly run out of arrows. All these bug bombs may not work fast enough, either. Remember how many we set off and how long it took for the spiders to feel the poison? We'd never survive."

"Nigel is correct," said Kunga. "Perhaps we should rethink our plan?"

"The backup plan," said Nigel with resignation, "is to run like Hell if those small devils come pouring out."

He considered for a few minutes, then added, "In fact, I think that's exactly the right thing to do. If we get overrun, we need to run as fast as we can back home and retrieve the flamethrower. I'm starting to think that would have been more effective than all of these bug bombs. When the smaller spiders come at us in hoards, I could light up quite a few all at once. And it does a number on this webbing, too, I'll bet."

"And what of the wagon?" asked Garran. "Do we retreat with this in tow?"

"No, we leave it right here," answered Nigel. "And to that point," he unlimbered his pack and leaned it against the wagon, "there's no reason to haul this pack back, either. If we high-tail it out of here, I'm not going to need anything in this pack." He grabbed the machete from the wagon and clipped it to his belt. The quiver he detached as well, and slung that across his back.

"I'm about as ready as I can be," he told the team. "If anyone has a better idea, now's the time to speak up. Otherwise, we might as well get on with this."

Silence ensued as everyone looked at each other and saw the same determined resignation and lack of an alternate plan. With no further comments, Garran grabbed two cans from the wagon and held one to each hip. To Nigel's amazement, thin vines emerged from Garran's bark, to wrap around each can, holding it in place. He repeated the action two more times, creating a belt of bug bombs around his middle. Ima did the same.

"Well, that's a neat trick," commented Nigel.

"It takes some effort, but we do find it handy," responded Garran.

"If it takes effort, maybe you should consider clothes?" suggested Nigel. "Pockets are down-right useful."

"Indeed," chimed in Sonam. "You humans are quite adept at making useful clothing. The trend has started to catch on in some communities, since Ben's arrival."

"Actually," said Ima, "Calliope and Stephanie have been the true fashion inspirations."

"Aye," chimed in Tormad. "Those two fireflies be a force o' nature, ta be sure."

Nigel thought he actually saw a smile crack the gruff sprite's facade. He could relate. His granddaughter had the same effect on him.

With their small arsenal attached at hips, Ima and Garran headed for the tunnel. Nigel unpacked one of the sprayers, and set it next to the wagon, ready to douse the tunnel opening if a horde of smaller spiders emerged. Then he knocked an arrow to ready his bow for a larger enemy. Tormad stood by his side, his ax waiting. Sonam and Kunga split to the outer edges, covering the room from all angles.

With a final look back, Ima gave a nod to her team, then she and Garran entered the trap.

—10—

A Prayer Answered

B en and Spot emerged into the fresh, clean air of a mountain forest. Maybe forest was not quite the correct term, but they were certainly in the mountains. Ben could see that the wall of rock behind him rose many hundreds of feet, and continued left and right, far into the distance.

In front of him, the land sloped downward, covered by strange trees; short, twisted and bent. Packed tightly together in a flowing river of color, each plant was adorned with bulbous, succulent-like petals, their hues ranging from yellows to oranges to reds. The river stretched on for quite some distance along the mountain chain, always remaining at this same elevation, replicating a veritable sunset swimming to the horizon.

As beautiful as it all was, Ben remembered the defensive reactions of plants in the Tree Lord sanctuary; he was, understandably, reluctant to approach these new specimens. Spot, however, wandered into them with a devil-may-care attitude, and received no reaction. Well, Spot did seem to know best when it came to vicious plants.

Looking up, Ben gauged that they were nearer the base of the mountain than the peak. He could not even see the top, for all the juts and misshapen angles on this face of the mountain. He could see the snow line, though, still a thousand feet or more above him.

Below, the succulent forest covered the sloping land for quite a distance before merging into taller versions of itself, and interspersing with some sort of conifer. From this distance, it looked most like a white pine, flush with pinecones. Of course, they could be miniature pineapples, for all Ben knew. Or—the frightening idea struck him— the egg sacs of another alien monster.

Spot did not seem worried. He loped between the short trees, heading straight for the taller. Ben kept pace, but drew his machete, just in case. They were on an alien planet, after all.

Ben checked his watch; a new toy he had purchased only a few weeks ago, a hockey-puck-tough, solar-powered behemoth with built-in thermometer, altimeter, barometer, and compass functions. He switched to altimeter. The display showed 1,786 meters above sea level, which was just under 6,000 feet. He wondered how accurate that was on an alien planet. He knew the watch judged altitude by air pressure—the less pressure, the higher above sea level you were—but it gave that measurement based on the average pressure stored for Earth's sea level. On this world, the chemical composition of the air could be different, and the atmosphere could be thicker or thinner, therefore its weight would be different, making his watch completely inaccurate. Still, gazing out on the vista before him, Ben could imagine there was a mile of mountain beneath him, so that aligned.

More clues to this planet's Earth-like atmosphere and geological composition came from Ben's breathing, and weight. Years ago, on a trip to Seattle, he had hiked to Panorama Point in Mount Rainier National Park. The trailhead parking lot was at around five-thousand feet. Two hours of hiking later, he had gained just under two-thousand feet of elevation, and his body had felt it. Being from Michigan which averaged eight-hundred feet, he was not used to even sitting in a car at five thousand, but walking up another two thousand had him huffing and puffing and taking breaks whenever he found a nice boulder or suitable log. He remembered that feeling of not having enough oxygen to fill his lungs. He had a similar feeling here, so he imagined that his watch was close to accurate. That meant increased dehydration and fatigue while at this elevation. He would have to watch out for that.

As for his weight, well, he did feel a bit bouncy, sort of light. But that could be jubilance over escaping from those tunnels of terror. The air was fresher, the sky was bluer, he had a smile on his face, and a bounce in his step. It could be hope, and a positive disposition. Whatever the cause, he was not floating away, and his footfalls planted firmly on the rocky terrain, so some sort of gravity was working just fine.

He surveyed the area before him, choosing his path forward. The ground was interspersed with hard rock and gravelly patches. It was in the gravelly patches that the small trees found root, but their bent trunks tended to meander over the rock slabs, perhaps for support when the mountain winds blew, perhaps to escape sitting in water during a rainy season. Ben hoped it was the former, or at least, if it was the latter, this was not the rainy season where he had to worry about flash flooding. For now, the skies were sapphire blue and free from clouds.

Ben wondered about this, too. This was the third planet he had been to—well, fourth if you included The City of Doors, but there he never left the halls—and on all three, the skies had been blue. He understood how the Earth's atmosphere split the sun's rays, scattering the blue wavelengths more than other colors, most of the time, but he thought other planets would have variations. Then again, it made sense that whoever built The City, would connect its doorways to worlds with similar environments. Environments conducive to life. Environments with a similar sun, or suns, that did not irradiate the planet. Environments with water, and weather, and plants. And plants made oxygen. And oxygen, along with nitrogen, made up most of Earth's atmosphere, which absorbed and scattered mostly blue light. So, Ben reasoned to himself, it made sense that these planets had blue skies. And if they did not, he would probably be dead, or dying as soon as he looked up and wondered at the strange new color painting the skies of a strange new world.

Popping out of his revery, Ben noticed that Spot was now a hundred yards ahead of him, statue-still in that frozen state animals use when they detect movement; enemy or prey.

Ben stopped as well. Tensed and ready, he scanned the treeline, then the area around them. These stubby, voluminous trees were perfect cover for anything wanting to sneak up. He suddenly felt extremely vulnerable. Exposed and hunted. Visions popped into his head of spiders scuttling beneath the trees, closing in from all sides, ready to wrap him in a cocoon. That jubilant feeling vanished. Gravity pulled on his growing dread.

He dropped to a squat, machete ready, and scanned under the trees, looking for movement. He spun in a circle, but all was quiet. A constant breeze whistled through the colorful forest, but the stiff structures held steady, and the fleshy leaves never waved or rustled. It should have been easy to notice anything moving between the motionless boles. But nothing crawled, nothing climbed, nothing slithered along the ground.

He stood back up. His thigh muscles were quick to quiver, and still burned from the extended workout he had given them in the caves. If he could make a safe camp, he would sleep like a baby from exhaustion, then probably wake up too stiff to stand.

Spot had not moved, so Ben walked slowly, quietly up behind him.

"What is it, boy?" he whispered to Spot. "What do you see?"

Spot did not acknowledge. He kept still, scanning the area ahead. There was a good view under the succulents, from Spot's lower angle. Ben crouched down again, and followed Spot's gaze. Forward, towards the larger trees, Ben saw nothing of concern; more brown, stocky stems and colorful, bubbly petals. He scanned left. More of the same.

Except... Something caught his eye. It was a "something" that the human mind was good at: picking out patterns, or, in this case, irregularities in a pattern. Not five feet away, one brown succulent trunk was growing from a stone slab, not from the gravelly area in-between. His eyes traced the trunk upwards, but could not discern where that dwarfed tree's leaves emerged. In fact, that tree's trunk seemed to just reach up into the canopy of the tree next to it, but not add additional volume to its crown. Ben focused deeper on the many colored leaves, their matte finishes blended and overlapped each other, as if the creator of this world had painted by pointillism; adorning her canvass with tiny dots of color, insignificant by themselves, but taken all in from a distance, they formed a picture of amazing detail, like Georges-Pierre Seurat's '*A Sunday Afternoon on the Island of La Grande Jatte,*' or Vincent van Gogh's '*Self Portrait.*'

But Ben had just discovered that this portrait—which he was naming, somewhat unimaginatively, '*Succulents*'—had two tiny flaws. Above that curious brown trunk, growing where it should not be, and in the fringe of the neighboring tree's canopy, were two glossy leaves among the matte. And those glossy leaves, though bulbous, like their neighbors, were twice as big, and shaped like yellow eggs, standing askew on their pointed ends. A single black dot adorned each, as well. No other leaves seemed to have this mark, and this, more than anything, screamed a verdict in Ben's mind: eyes! They were eyes! And the trunk was not that of a tree, but of some creature, with natural camouflage, suited to this forest of color.

Ben gazed around with this newly formed knowledge, and it was like he had donned magical lenses. For now, everywhere he looked, in all directions, he saw more anomalies. They were layers-deep throughout the dwarf forest. He and Spot were surrounded. That was why Spot had stopped. Maybe he had seen them. Maybe he could hear the movement. Maybe he could smell them. Whatever the reason, he seemed unsure of what to do. But Ben knew. He knew the creatures were closing in. He knew they were outnumbered, and out of their element. He knew that if they could not see this new enemy, they could not effectively fight. They needed to reach the forest of conifers, and hope that the open spaces between the taller tree boles would at least bring this new threat into the open, and make their enemy visible. They needed to run.

"I see them, Spot," he whispered to his friend. "We need to make it to that larger forest ahead. To the tall trees. I think we need to run for it."

Ben was not sure if Spot understood, but his feather-furred head dipped, his lemur-paws grabbed the ground tighter, and his crouch deepened. Ben figured he was ready to run, or ready to attack. Taking the initiative, Ben barked, "Run, Spot! Run!" and took off like a shot for the tall pines. Spot bounded past him by his second stride. The blinx was fully stretched out, galloping for all he was worth. Ben wondered when his friend would notice that his human companion was dreadfully slow, and had been left behind. He wondered if the creatures in the trees would make their move before he reached his destination.

The answer to the last question came immediately: yes, they would. All around, the air erupted with sound and color. An explosion of greens and browns, of yellows and oranges and reds, was accompanied by the humming of a thousand cellos playing a low C note. The sky filled with hundreds of creatures, each with four wings a-blur with motion as they carried bodies most definitely akin to giant praying mantises. With definitive triangular heads, and those segmented arms sporting giant barbs, the resemblance was unmistakable, and terrifying.

Ben pumped his legs like a man possessed. He could hear the mantises in pursuit. The thrumming grew louder as the insects dove lower to track their prey. Ben expected them to swoop in, to land on his back and Spot's, as an eagle on a rabbit, snatching them from the ground, hooked with those horrific spikes.

Not today, thought Ben. *I'll not escape a den of spiders just to become a meal for a different pack of insects.*

He ran with his machete ready to swing at the first creature that came within reach. Miraculously, however, no mantis came closer than a dozen feet above. They seemed content to let Ben and Spot run. In fact, Spot had already reached the pine woods, and was dancing side to side between the tall boles, watching and waiting for Ben, clearly distressed that the human had not reached safety yet.

Ben was two hundred yards out, and closing fast. It helped that this was a downhill run, but dodging between the trees, trying to keep his footing on the rock plateaus, and out of the stone-filled crags was difficult to do while ducking between low branches, and watching for an attack from above. His backpack caught on the bulbous leaves, breaking them off. Their insides were, indeed, like a succulent. A gooey, mucusy sap leaked from them, coating the outside of his pack, splattering the ground behind him. The air filled with a sweet smell, like mango. Ben hoped this goo had no adverse effects. He hoped it was syrup, like from an agave plant. Or medicinal, like aloe. Whatever the verdict, for the time being it was not hindering his running.

His heel landed on the edge of a rock slab. His toe dug into the unstable gravel of a crag, and he went sprawling, head first down the slope. The weight of his pack slammed his chest into the stone and knocked the wind from his lungs. Careening into the bole of a tree with his shoulder, the crunching impact spun him around. His legs now faced downhill, and his boots caught the rock, stopping his descent.

Yes, gravity here was close to that of Earth. The pain in his body verified that.

He pushed himself up quickly and looked for the enemy. Surely they would attack a fallen prey?

No attack came. He looked around for his machete, which had

flown from his hand when he landed. It was twenty yards down the hill, the tip skewering the ground at a thirty-degree angle. With a grunt for his tired bones, he scrambled to his feet and continued his run. He grabbed the machete as he passed, feeling that much safer to be reunited with his longest weapon, and still amazed to not be embroiled in battle.

He was in the taller succulents now. Ben no longer needed to stoop to avoid branches, or see beneath the canopy. He had a clear view of Spot waiting for him, only a few dozen yards away. He could make it. He would make it.

What were the bugs waiting for? Did they want him in the open? Did they prefer to attack once he had cleared the shorter trees? It made no sense to Ben. They could have attacked his legs at any time back there. They could have taken him out before he even knew they were close. It was a mystery to which he was not sure he wanted to find the answer.

He skidded to a stop next to Spot, just inside the edge of the pine forest. Close up, these tall trees did indeed look like Scots Pine; straight trunks, free of boughs for the first seventy feet, then populated with branches and dense needles for the next thirty. The scaley, craggly bark was covered in dried pitch, so Ben kept from rubbing up against the trunks, but he did hide behind one. He took a knee next to Spot. The forest floor was covered in layers of long brown needles that provided a surprising cushion.

The companions remained huddled and watched the flying color show. Spot, evidently happy that his human had made it to safety, proceeded to lick Ben's backpack, while still watching the insects. Ben realized it was the succulent sap that Spot was sampling.

"Ugh, Spot," Ben scolded, "you really should not eat that stuff until we figure out if it's safe."

Spot paid no heed. So far, he seemed none the worse for wear, and Ben fervently hoped that the juice proved edible. He was much too weary to be carrying a sick blinx around an alien planet. And he refused to consider losing his friend to poison. If Spot's enthusiastic licking revealed anything, however, it was that the sap was just as tasty as it smelled.

No matter the verdict on the succulent sap, he and Spot had bigger problems at the moment. The creatures remained, hovering over the polychromatic field. It was unnerving to see the sky filled with so many flying insects the size of his daughter. Hundreds of opalescent eyes shimmered in the daylight, all trained on Spot and himself. The air reverberated with a thrumming so loud, Ben could feel it in his chest. He did not move. Spot kept licking, but remained otherwise still as well. The creatures just watched.

After a minute or two of this, one creature advanced. It fluttered to the ground, just outside the edge of pines, fifteen feet away. Ben stood ready.

"Who be you?" its multi-parted mouth screeched. More of an order than a question.

Ben was surprised to hear the creature speak, especially after the unintelligible spiders, but he was even more shocked at its voice. It was high-pitched and grating. Almost painfully so. It gave Ben the feeling of fingernails on a blackboard; raising uncomfortable goosebumps, and setting his teeth on edge.

"We escaped the spiders in the cave. We mean no harm to you. We just want to rest a bit before returning to the caves and trying to get back to our own home."

Ben spoke slowly, just loud enough to be heard above the droning wings, but he tried to be as non-threatening as possible while still projecting strength. It was a hard combination of traits, and he was not sure he was pulling it off.

"Spi-ders?" the creature asked. "What be they?"

Ben got the feeling this talking mantis suspected what a spider was, but wanted to confirm. He thought he detected hope, maybe, in its body language, if not the pitch of its voice. It had straightened a bit, twisted its head on the diagonal, much like a human would when considering.

"The creatures that inhabit those caves," he pointed back up the slope to the dark opening. "Eight legs, round bodies, fangs. Many spin or spray sticky, silvery threads to ensnare creatures to eat."

The mantis seemed to evaluate Ben's words. "How you escape?"

"We fought them. We killed them."

Ben hoped these insects were not allies of the arachnids. On Earth, they were enemies. He hoped the same held true here. Then again, on Earth, praying mantises ate just about any insect they could catch. Ben had even read that some of the larger mantises would eat mice, snakes, or even birds, if they could catch them. It did not take much imagination for Ben to scale a battle of this mantis versus himself to an Earth mantis versus a mouse. He was beginning to wish they had never left the caves and the spiders.

"How do you kill?" screeched the mantis.

Ben deliberated his answer. Did they want to assess his strength? Or did they not believe he had killed such a large predator?

"With fire," Ben said.

"Show," ordered the creature.

Ben realized that this was a Cold-War moment. He faced an enemy with greater numbers, but held them at bay by fear of his prowess in battle and ability to wield a powerful weapon. They were demonstrating their show of force. Now, it was his turn to match their might, or become a meal.

Looking around, he found a stick the length of his forearm, used that to scrape a blob of sap from his tree, plopped it on a bed of pine needles, and covered that with more dried tinder. He then cleared the area around the pile, so as not to create a forest fire. Using a magician's sleight of hand technique, Ben's motion of clearing the area masked his hand grabbing the butane lighter from his pack's waist pocket. He knelt down and covertly pressed the igniter on the lighter concealed by his palm. Blue flame seemed to fire from his hand, as if by magic. The dried pine needles caught immediately, and the pile soon bloomed into a nice fire. The pitch underneath was quick to catch as well, and Ben was amazed at the tall blue flame that erupted from that. He knew pine pitch was flammable, but this stuff seemed incredibly so.

A cacophony of squawking and chittering came from the hovering insects; either fright, or excitement. Their spokesperson took several steps back, rose up tall, extended its fearsome forearms wide and fanned its wings in an impressive display of size and color. Ben knew this tactic, as most animals did this, even humans to some extent. It was a defensive posture meant to scare enemies, fool them into thinking the mantis was larger than it was. Not that being large would help against fire, but Ben was sure it was an instinctive reaction to any threat.

Ben stood as close to the fire as he could. It was giving off quite a bit of heat, but he wanted to show these creatures that he was not afraid of fire, that he was the creator and controller. And now that he could see their fear, he planned on keeping this fire going as long as he could.

"You see," Ben called to the strutting mantis, "I can create fire. I vanquished the spiders this way and escaped their lair, but I wish to go back, for the doorway to my home is on the other side of their tunnels."

Ben was reluctant to tell them more. It was important that they knew he had no desire to remain in their world, but he sure did not want them in his, either. He and Spot needed to return to the cave as soon as possible, but not without a plan against those spiders. This pine pitch, though, seemed like an excellent weapon to add to his arsenal. Perhaps a few torches made from this stuff. He could gather bunches on sticks, then cover the sticky substance in easily ignitable needles and grasses, for fast lighting, and to keep the torches from sticking to everything they touched.

"Make it go, now," screeched the mantis, clearly agitated by the fire.

"I cannot," said Ben. "It must burn through its fuel before it goes away." He could easily cover the fire in dirt to put it out, but he claimed helplessness as an excuse to keep the fire going.

"Dangerous," the creature called back. "Forest sparks and burns easy. Burn for many dawns. Cover sky in dark cloud. Makes breathing hard. Kills crops." It motioned with its long arms to the colorful succulents behind it.

"These trees, these succulents, are your crops? Your food?" Ben asked the creature.

"Yes. Only grow here. Our only food. Crop burns, we starve," it replied.

Ben was skeptical that such fearsome creatures were herbivores that ate soft, juicy succulents. With pronged limbs clearly evolved for catching prey, and scissor-like mandibles adept at cleaving through all sorts of materials, they appeared the perfect carnivore. The Earth version sure was.

"Weavers hunt us here. Crops only grow here. We protect crops. We fight weavers. Fire scares weavers. You help us control fire."

Well, that added some credibility to their claim of being plant eaters. If they had to constantly fight giant spiders to survive, they would definitely need to evolve effective defenses. Still, Ben was uneasy with the demeanor of their spokes-mantis. Its attitude was blunt, overbearing. He got the impression that no creature but a mantis was welcome in the vicinity of their crops, and that they enforced proximity rules with deadly ferocity. To say he was reluctant to hand these creatures the power of fire, was an understatement.

He needed to assess his options. He needed time to rest, and form a plan. But there was no way he could rest while surrounded by an army of praying mantises.

"Fire may not be something I can teach," he called back. "I must consider if it is possible. But first, my companion and I must rest. We will retreat into this forest, away from your crops. Please allow us our privacy while we do so. We will return here when we have rested, and call for a meeting."

The mantis' only response was a jittery head bob that Ben took as "yes."

The pine needles of his fire had all burned to ash. All that remained was the branch with the burning blob of pitch. Ben picked it up, as a torch, and with an attempted friendly, yet cocky nod to his insect hosts, retreated deeper into the conifer forest, Spot trotting close at his heels. Ben tried his best not to look backwards, tried to stand tall and proud, as if he had no concerns at all of a hundred deadly insects attacking him. He could feel their eyes following his movement. His skin prickled and crawled. His shoulders were so tense, he thought his bones might snap, yet still, he did not turn.

Spot, thankfully, was not so reckless. He spared many a glance backwards, and Ben was relying on him to give fair warning of any danger. What fair warning might allow, he had no idea, except maybe dropping his torch to the needle-strewn floor, planting him dead center of the largest forest fire he had ever seen. Mutually Assured Destruction - MAD - was an appropriate Cold War acronym.

Ben and Spot traveled deep into the pine forest. So deep, they not only lost sight of the colorful succulents, but tree-tops obscured all views of the mountains as well. He took several readings from the compass on his watch, which, thankfully, did register changes as south, west, and east, so this planet also had somewhat of a magnetic pole. Or perhaps the mountain contained huge deposits of iron ore. Either way, he took sightings from several points along their path, and the compass stayed true. He tried his best to follow a straight line to the west, continuing down the mountain, so retracing his path east would return him to the cave he knew.

The mantises seemed to honor Ben's request for privacy, but he assumed they were tracking him with spies. The creatures he had seen were patterned for camouflage while tending their crops, but he suspected there were others, equally camouflaged for these woods. He could be looking at one right now, and assuming it was just another branch on a tree, covered in green needles. No, tonight would be spent around a fire. A very large bonfire.

Ben's watch ticked off an hour since departing their insect comrades. The pitch torch was, surprisingly, still burning; low, but constant. He was anxious to find a place to stop for the night, but he wanted a more strategic campsite.

This planet's rotational, and revolutional orbit appeared Earth-like. The sun was sinking to the horizon in what registered as the west, and its rate of descent was comparable to Earth, if a bit slower. It dropped three fingers for every hour, as opposed to four fingers an hour back home, giving this planet a longer day by about eight hours, if Ben's logic was correct. At this rate, Ben had about three hours until sunset. He wanted his camp fully set up by then.

Half an hour later, Ben found what he was looking for. The conifers ended abruptly, and a field of shin-high grasses opened before him. Fifty yards of sage green dissipated into the pebbled shoreline of a large lake, fed by the cold runoff of mountain snow. He could set up camp on the shore, away from the camouflage of the trees. It opened him up to possible aerial attack, but at least he could see and hear them coming. He was counting on a fire to instill enough fear to keep an attack from happening.

To that end, he quickly found a spot to pitch his trusted four-season tent, where the field ended and the pebbled shoreline began, still twenty yards from the water. After all, there was no telling what lived in this cold mountain lake. Images of the Loch Ness Monster came to mind, as well as extremely large bears trolling the shores for fish.

He gathered a dozen large rocks in a circle to form a fire ring in the pebbles, just outside the tent's doorway and vestibule to keep the heat and protection close to his shelter. Normally, after a long day of activity, he looked forward to crawling into his portable home and getting a good night's sleep. Here, he was unsure how much sleep he would get. He needed to stay vigilant in this strange place.

On the other hand, he was exhausted. It seemed like weeks since he had left his home and daughter, not just a single day. He wondered if Garran was searching for him, or if the sprite had journeyed safely through The City to inform Calliope. Ben hoped not. He knew his daughter. She would be planning a rescue. And he knew his dad. Nigel would be executing that rescue. Ben hoped the sprite was blocked by the spiders—safely blocked—and that he had more sense than to tell Calliope.

Spot was at the lake, walking the damp stones, eyeing the gently lapping waves with untrusting eyes. Ben was glad to see his friend exercising caution, for once. After much scrutiny, Spot leaned close, sniffed the liquid, then took a long drink. Ben found that a pretty good endorsement of potability. It did not necessarily mean it was pathogen-free, but at least it wasn't salt water, or sulfuric acid, or some other alien chemical.

With water concerns settled, Ben returned to the forest, keeping an ever-cautious eye on the trees for movement, and gathered enough wood to keep his fire burning all night. Once he had that, he doubled it, following the camping rule of thumb. Campfires always seemed to consume more wood than one expected.

He gathered a ball of dried grasses and weeds from the field, layered on a bunch of sticks and twigs for kindling, then topped it off with a pine cone he had found. It was the size of a Jeffrey Pine's cone, like a small pineapple, as large as Ben's hand. It was dry, its scales curling open, and the seeds inside were a rich, mustard yellow.

Ben had planted his torch in the stones before gathering wood. Its flame had died in the meantime. He added the stick to the pile, then surrounded the bundle with a teepee of larger sticks. Careful to keep his lighter hidden from spying eyes, he repeated his magic trick and lit the dried grasses, bringing fire to life. Flames spread from grass to twigs quickly. The twigs themselves had enough sap in them to create an even, hot flame that brought welcome warmth in this cool mountain air.

Something about fire brought a sense of security and comfort to the great outdoors. Ben already felt safer, like his first line of defense was in place; a big sign that could be seen from a distance, saying 'stay away.'

With his camp set up, he slowly inhaled the crisp mountain air, and relaxed with the terpene perfume that drifted from the pine-like trees behind him and the telltale aroma of a vast body of clean water that rolled in with each breeze off the lake.

He let his shoulders relax, and took a moment to scan his surroundings. Sheer mountain ranges stretched from the northern horizon to the southern, and punctured the sky with their imposing peaks. There would be some great rock climbing up those verticals, if it weren't for the scary neighbors.

Miles to the south, dark thunderheads and flashes of lightning engulfed the snow-capped spires. Thankfully, the skies above his lake remained blue and speckled with innocuous cotton ball clouds. Ben hoped that all the bad weather stayed to the south. He had enough worries without spending the night in a thunderstorm. That would surely put an end to his crackling fire.

He stepped closer to the campfire and hovered his hands over the heat. The scales of the pine cone were now surrendering to the flames. He watched them turn to glowing embers, then gray ash as the burning ate its way to the cone's center. He heard a slight sizzling— the moisture steaming free—and then the whole thing exploded with a rapid *bang, bang, bang* of a dozen miniature hand grenades. Flaming branches flew in all directions. Ash spewed into the air. Hot coals became glowing projectiles. One barely missed Ben's head as he dove for cover.

Crawling on the ground, he scrambled back from the fire and scanned for Spot. The blinx crouched at the water's edge, legs coiled and ready to react, eyes wide as he watched the debacle Ben had unleashed. Sparks and flaming debris pelted the tent, most bouncing off with no damage, but a few were hot enough to glom on and melt their way in.

Ben whipped off his jacket and swatted the tent, swiping away the hot coals. Small explosions continued, but they were growing infrequent, like reluctant corn kernels in a microwave popcorn bag.

Spot approached cautiously. Ben could sense the animal's confusion, and maybe disappointment in Ben for creating such pandemonium. He sat a good ten yards from the fire while Ben assessed the damage. All in all, it could have been worse. Ten coals had burned holes the size of a dime or smaller into the outer tent. Luckly, the material was woven such that Ben was not overly concerned with tears developing. But he would have to patch these spots once he got home.

And he would get home. Because this unexpected incident was a fortunate development. Ben now had a plan.

With the fireworks ended, Ben regathered his security fire. Several rocks from the ring had blown back a few feet—an interesting display of force. His kindling and teepee logs were scattered along the beach. Luckily, the field of grass behind him was too wet to ignite, as twigs were still burning in the weeds. He used these to build up a new fire, using branches only this time. No pine cones.

An hour of daylight still remained, so Ben grabbed a small mesh bag he packed for airing out wet clothing, and returned to the forest. He gathered as many pine cones as he could find, discarding any old, dried-out ones with missing seeds. His plan: to harvest as many seeds as he could, and make grenades. The effectiveness of his camp stove exploding and taking out that massive cave spider gave Ben confidence. This would get him home to his daughter.

Half an hour later, Ben was sitting by a stable campfire, using his knife to pluck seeds from cones, plinking them into his coffee mug. Each cone yielded half a cup of seeds. Each seed had the explosive power of three firecrackers, roughly. Ben evaluated the power of a single seed by carefully dangling one from a long branch, over the fire. Within a second or two of the flames licking the kernel, it exploded with a percussive force Ben felt from eight feet away.

The next step was to figure out a container. It had to hold enough seeds to be powerful, and flammable enough to ignite. The answer was easy: dried grasses. The field had an abundant amount of shin-high grass, blades as wide as Ben's pinky. He could collect it, and weave it into mats about six inches square. From there, he would tie it into a roll with more grass, creating a tube; sew up one end, fill it with seeds, pack it with a little more grass, then sew up the other end, leaving a few blades of grass poking out for an easy to light wick. Piece of cake.

He was in for a night of work. Or at least a few hours. He wanted a proof of concept completed, and a few production models sewn up before turning in. He could assemble more tomorrow, in the daylight.

A nice bundle of grasses was piled by his log bench by the time the sun's final glow vanished below the horizon. The star had descended between two mountain peaks in the distance, bathing the edges of their snow-covered cones in gold as their backsides faded to black. Ben did not stop to enjoy the show, so intent was he on his task.

The first mat came together sloppily. He laid out twelve blades in one direction, then wove twelve more crossways, over, under, over, under. Each time he added another to the weave, it pushed out others. He grumbled and swore, while Spot sat close by and watched.

"You know, Spot," Ben said, "I used to weave mats like this out of paper with my daughter, Calliope, when she was younger. You remember Calliope? You allowed her and her friend Stephanie to escape from the sprites when you attacked them a few weeks back." Spot just blinked back at Ben.

"Well, you will love Calliope. She is amazing; full of fun and fire, and such a warm heart. I miss her already, and I haven't been gone a day. But, that's why we have to hurry. If Garran hasn't already told her and my dad what happened, they'll start to worry. I was only supposed to be gone for one night. That means, if I don't get home tomorrow, Calliope will push to come looking for me. My dad will probably hold her at bay for another day, but after that, he'll come looking himself, and then there'll be no one to hold Calliope back. She's just too clever and too headstrong for her own good sometimes."

"There. Finished!" Ben finally had his woven square. He bent the ends of each grass frond backwards and wove it back into the mat, locking everything tightly in place. He held the mat up for Spot to see. "What do you think?" Spot gave his usual response: a puzzled head tilt.

"Well, you'll see what it's good for in a minute."

Ben rolled the mat into a tube an inch and a half in diameter and tied it in place with another blade of grass. More weaving across the bottom pinched the tube closed. Now, he had a small pouch. Wispy cotton balls of shredded grass came next, stuffed inside to plug any holes and add quick burning tinder. Next came two long blades of dried grass running up the side and poking out the end as a fuse. Then the seeds piled on top of the fuse. He added only an eighth of a cup. This first one was a prototype, for testing. No need to blow up the beach. More cotton grass on top, then he sealed the open end as he had the other, leaving six inches of grassy fuse poking out.

It was done. A camp-made firecracker with deadly potential. One that would surely be illegal in any town back home, but would hopefully save his life by allowing him to pass unmolested through the spider-infested tunnel system.

He hefted it. It was very light. He might want to add some gravel to it for better throwing weight, and, he thought gruesomely, shrapnel for deadly projectiles.

"Stay here, Spot. I'm going to light this on fire and there will be a big boom." He made a whooshing noise and exploding motion with his arms. Spot sat up and looked alarmed, so Ben surmised that his meaning was understood. At least, Spot stayed where he was.

Ben grabbed a burning stick from the fire, walked thirty yards down the beach, set the grenade on the stones, and lit the grassy fuse with the flickering twig. He ran like Death itself was chasing him, and reached a safe distance by his campfire. He pulled Spot close beside him, and they both hunkered down behind his backpack.

The fuse burning down was a flickering firefly on the dark beach. Five seconds later—Ben was counting—the pouch was consumed by flames. Not a second later, an explosion lit up the darkness, its echoes ricocheting across, and around the mountain lake. The sound was such that Ben worried it might trigger an avalanche in the distant peaks. He heard stones splashing into the water, and landing all around, but none close to himself or spot. All in all, it was an impressive test.

He flipped on his flashlight and walked back to the detonation site. The firecracker had created a small crater, about two feet wide and a foot deep. That was an eighth of a cup of seeds. If he packed future pouches with a quarter cup, plus stones, it would be plenty of firepower to take out a huge spider. Probably equivalent to his camp fuel canister exploding. But the fuse took too long. Five seconds allowed too long for a spider to scurry away. The next fuse should be half as long. Two or three seconds was plenty of time for Ben to light and throw, or run away. He had his design. Now, he just had to make about ten more.

His stomach growled, reminding him that eating was a priority. A quick forage into his backpack yielded the anodized alloy mug from his now-defunct cook kit, and a packet of freeze-dried beef stew.

He siphoned water from his hydration pack into the cup. To set it to boil, he placed it on two large branches, which spanned the campfire, their ends resting on the tallest opposing rocks of the fire ring. The fire was just able to lick the mugs base, providing sufficient heat to start a boil in minutes. Ben dumped the water into the dried meal bag, mixed thoroughly, then set it aside for a few minutes to rehydrate. Once ready, he sporked a sample into a bowl for Spot. But like the jerky Ben had offered back when they had first met, the blinx merely sniffed at it, then turned away, uninterested.

"More for me," Ben said.

With his belly now full, Ben sat on the ground by the fire, his back against a driftwood log, and the backpack as a worktable. He quickly got busy weaving mats. Spot snuggled in close to his side for warmth, and fell asleep.

Ben revised his weaving tactics and finished the next mat in half the time of the first. He set that aside and started another. All in all, he was finding this chore somewhat relaxing. The night was cool and, thankfully, calm. Even a little wind would have made handling the grasses a challenge. As it was, if Ben was not on an alien planet, surrounded by imposing, and suspectedly deadly giant insects, cut off from his home by a mountain of enormous arachnids intent on cocooning him and sucking his insides dry, he would be enjoying himself immensely, and planning his next camping trip to bring Calliope here.

"Oh well," he said to himself. "Earth has places just as beautiful. And there, I can bring company." This time, his mind drifted not to

Calliope, but to Emily. He was remembering the morning with Emily, drinking coffee, watching the sunrise in the Beinbiodag Mountains on Quilium. It was nice, sharing those moments with someone who appreciated them. He let that scenario play out in his mind while he worked.

Ben was able to finish a dozen mats before exhaustion finally set in. All stayed quiet while he wove, and kept his fire stoked. Checking his watch, he saw it was well-past midnight, Earth-time. Funny that here, on this planet, night seemed to align with Earth's Northern hemisphere.

He was dead tired, and ready to crawl into his sleeping bag. After adding a few more logs to the fire, he set an alarm on his watch. His plan: to get up every hour, check the fire, and assess the area. He was also trusting Spot's senses to alert them of imminent danger approaching. But he was in no way trusting that those giant mantises were not keeping an eye on him. Popping out of his tent every hour would show them that he was ever vigilant.

He crawled into his tent, leaving his boots in the half-open vestibule. Spot took a walk around the tent—apparently doing a perimeter security check—then came inside as well. Ben bundled inside his sleeping bag, and Spot relaxed at his feet with his head at the doorway, looking out. Perhaps the blinx had gotten a good enough nap. He seemed to be on watch, now. That made Ben feel a little more secure. A minute later, the tent's human occupant was fast asleep.

The electronic cricket chirping of Ben's alarm was an unwanted intrusion, jerking him from a sleep so deep it was painful to break free. He fumbled at the buttons to silence the noise, then sat up to prevent falling back into the welcoming arms of slumber. Spot swiveled his head backwards and gave him a look of "all's well," which Ben appreciated, but the fire had burned down a little low, so he crawled out of his sleeping bag, out of the tent, and placed a few more logs on the fire.

He sat for a bit, just to listen to the night, but he knew Spot's ears were better equipped to hear danger. He heard nothing unusual. Just a bit of wind blowing through the grasses, small waves lapping at the rocky beach.

A quick walk around the tent, away from the light of the fire, revealed nothing moving in the darkness. Ben gazed up at the stars above this new planet and was amazed at their density. Wherever he was in the universe, this galaxy was flush with alien suns. The thing missing, however, was a moon. Or moons. So far, Ben had not seen a moon rise in the night sky. Perhaps it only rose every other day, or once a month, or maybe it flew through the night sky so fast, he missed it while he slept. He knew Saturn's moon, Titan, took something like fifteen days to orbit the giant planet. Something similar could occur here.

With welcome peace in the night, Ben returned to his sleeping bag. He reset his alarm for another hour, then fell asleep, dreaming of strange moons and maps of new solar systems.

—11—

Dirigible Discovery

Daylight greeted the trio, as they gazed up the dilapidated staircase. Emily, Stephanie, and Calliope had climbed twelve flights, had even zig-zagged deeper down clear hallways to new vestibules, new spiraling stairs, but always, the clicking found them.

For the last three levels, all had been quiet. They had outpaced the hunters, once again. Unfortunately, the previous three floors had also been devoid of any branching hallways. Only large rotundas greeted them, with doors that, judging by their hieroglyphs, lead to unwelcoming planets: a world of snakes; a world of either boiling water, or tar; a world of acid rain. Emily wondered why anyone would create doorways to such dangerous, inhospitable places.

Another unnerving development was becoming more frequent: rust and dust. The higher they climbed, the more neglected the rooms and stairs became. Dirt and mold gathered in seams between walls and floor. Rust formed in telltale patterns of draining moisture; two-dimensional, reddish-brown stalactites painted themselves down the walls, from ceiling to floor. Water was definitely reaching these higher levels. And the lights had stopped responding to their presence four stories below, forcing the ladies to pull out headlamps again. Whatever maintained the lower levels, it did not extend up here.

But on the previous floor, they had seen a dull halo of pale light drifting through the ceiling egress; just enough to dust the top stair in a curious glow. It was not the amber of The City's lights. Not the warm glow of fire (thankfully). Not a moving, shifting, active glow of Nigel carrying a flashlight, or a sprite with a saluna leaf. It put Emily in mind of daylight, and she wondered if the next level had an opening to the outside. Would they finally get a glimpse of the world that spawned The City of Doors?

She was unsure if excitement or apprehension was more appropriate. She had vaguely imagined this collection of hallways living inside a dead rock, floating in space. But sunlight, dust, and mold suggested otherwise. What sort of world would it be? What other creatures would they encounter? Frankly, Emily had had her fill of other-worldly creatures and monsters. She would rather everything was quiet and uninhabited.

They had climbed, and entered another chamber even more in disrepair than the last. Another round room with no branching hallways, and only four doors leading to uninspiring worlds. Another spiral staircase leading upwards, made of iron, but this time so caked with ancient rust that it seemed fragile and dangerous. But a room most definitely illuminated by an indirect light coming from a strong source on the next level.

They could see the ceiling of the room above through the top of the stairwell. It looked immense, tall, and slightly dome-shaped. A larger room with changed dimensions gave Emily hope for a new route home.

"Do we go up?" asked Stephanie.

Calliope looked to Emily for direction, as well.

"We do," affirmed Emily.

She led the way up the decomposing steps which crunched under her boots as the corroded iron flaked and fell away. Emily consciously monitored the supports on this spiral flight. It was delicate in its strength, with scrolling vines and designs forming a metal grate, and nothing but air in the gaps between. If any of those ornamentations were rusted through, their weight could send them plummeting.

The structure held. They reached the top, and were greeted with a view that none of them could have anticipated. An expansive observation deck spread out before them; a room most definitely larger than the one below, but just as circular and indeed capped with a high dome. Instead of steel, however, this room was dedicated to copper and glass. Half of the room was composed of massive windows secured in frames of patina-green. One of those windows was shattered, its crystal pieces scattered at its base like a field of diamonds. It seemed they had found an explanation for the poor state of the lower levels. As the wind howled by the breech, Emily could imagine all sorts of water and debris being sucked in during a storm.

No glass stood in soldier rows on the back half of the room. Solid copper panels connected in uninterrupted succession, mirroring the design of the great transparent panes of the front, and completing a three hundred and sixty degree rotation without a hallway, or portal, or any helpful factor. Not even another stairwell. Just a dead end.

The ladies' feet tapped along a copper floor, smooth as glass; not panels or tiles fitted tightly together, but one seamless, smooth sheet, as if molten metal had been poured to fill the room, then cooled to ice-rink perfection. The only interruption being the stairwell rising in the middle.

The dome above them was a jig-saw framework of rhomboidal sections; front half glass, the back in copper. Concentric rings of diminishing size formed an intricate flower effect while bringing strength to the structure. The crystal panes revealed a dismal sky of layered ash, pewter, and graphite clouds, ready to burst with a torrential storm.

The daylight that filtered through that grouchy atmosphere came from two suns, the largest being equal to Earth's. The smaller was easily a third the size. It was an amazing concept to Emily, looking at two suns, and she wondered about their beauty, and intensity, were they in a clear blue sky.

"Oh, my goodness!" exclaimed Stephanie. "Mom, look at that." She had moved closer to the windows, and was pointing to the expanse below.

"Holy cow!" Calliope echoed her friend's astonishment.

Far below them, but extending to the horizon, were buildings of pure metal. Not concrete, not wood, not stone. Just metal. Rusted steel boxes stood ten stories tall next to dark iron mounds that looked like mottled snakes hugging a hundred yards of dirt. Oxidized copper spires sprinkled the vista, reaching up like fingers pointing accusingly at the heavens. Here and there were mirrored chrome buildings in various geometric designs, reflecting the dull gray of the clouds above.

Adorning the buildings were all manner of gears, pistons, and camshafts, all working furiously at some unknown task, for some unknown patron. There was no smoke, no smog, no waste that they could readily see, but something kept those pieces in perpetual motion. It was a flurry of curious chaos.

The composition and configuration of buildings went on and on with no recognizable pattern. What was recognizable, interestingly, were accents of precious metals painting the scene below. Details of gold, silver—or maybe aluminum, or platinum—and the smoky gray of titanium, formed rooftops, and wires, and whirligigs, and doodads throughout the movement below. Was it a careless display of wealth, or a utilitarian use of precious metals that mostly resisted decay? Perhaps it was neither, for nowhere in that chaos did they see a single living creature to covet or control those treasures.

"What in the world is this place?" said Emily.

"Do you think all of these buildings are connected?" asked Stephanie. "Do you think all the hallways have been leading us from building to building?"

"Could be," said Emily. "I don't see even one window out there. We could have been walking all through those buildings and never known."

"It doesn't seem like it, though," interjected Calliope. "Remember the stone walls and fresh water springs, and the Garden of Life? I always pictured The City of Doors being inside a mountain or something."

"Yeah, me too," echoed Stephanie.

"You know," added Emily, "I kind of did as well. Maybe these buildings are part of the system keeping all The Doors working."

"You mean like big motors, or batteries?" asked Stephanie.

"Exactly," said Emily. "They sure look like a bunch of motors working at something."

A clanking echoed up the staircase, pulling the ladies back from speculation, to the more immediate problem.

"The spiders are coming!" Stephanie's phobia always simmered just below the surface. She was battling to keep it from coming to a boil.

"Alright," said Emily, sounding all business. "Let's spread out, and look for anything that can help us, or get us out of here."

They scattered, as the room was quite large. Stephanie, being the self-defined math nerd, counted her steps from the staircase at the center, to the outer edge. Her typical stride spanned about two and a half feet. Quick math gave the room a radius of fifty feet. With that, she solved for the circumference: $c = 2\pi r$.

"Three hundred and fourteen feet around," she said to herself. "Approximately. Cut that in half, and there is about one hundred and fifty-seven feet of glass. Each pane is about four feet wide, so divide one-fifty-seven by four and get thirty-nine and a quarter windows. Taking away a window and a quarter as space the frames take, gives me thirty-eight windows. Seems about right."

"Not that that fact helps in any way," she mumbled.

She began at the first window left of the stairs, and walked around to the right, giving a wide berth to the broken pane and its pieces on the floor. She alternated her gaze from the vast expanse of motorized buildings outside to the empty copper floor beneath her feet. She could not say she saw nothing of interest, but she could not say she saw anything helpful, either.

Emily started at the back of the room, where she hoped the shadows secreted something useful. It was dusty and dark, but otherwise plain. The lack of any type of bric-a-brac, or garbage, or writings, or castoffs of anything from the creators of The City of Doors, was an enigma to Emily. The spiders had been here less than a month, and already their detritus filled every hall they traveled. Why couldn't the creators have left more clues, or a manual, even? Frustrating, that's what it was. Just plain frustrating.

As those thoughts rebounded around her head, her eyes spotted a lump of shadow on the floor. It was the size of a Scottish Terrier, and her immediate conclusion was, *spider*!

She froze, watching and waiting for the shadow to react. Nothing happened. She glanced carefully around the room, looking for the girls, making sure they were safe. Stephanie was still walking along the windows, nothing hunting her from above or behind. Calliope was on the other side, walking towards Stephanie, equally safe. Emily turned her attention back to the lump. Thinking it might track her movements, she sidestepped to the right. No response.

Maybe it was dead? She fished her flashlight from her pocket and pointed it at the mass. It glimmered, not with the reflective eyes of a nocturnal creature, but the leaded dullness of oxidized aluminum.

"Well, blow me down," Emily muttered to herself.

She hurried to examine the mass, but being closer only brought more questions.

"Girls, come look at this," she called in an amplified whisper.

"Whoa! That's cool," said Calliope, reaching Emily first.

"What is it?" said Stephanie.

"No idea," said Emily. "I was hoping you girls might have an idea. It looks a bit like a clarinet attached to a football; built along the same lines as Poppie. Look at the detail on those tiny gears, and the wires."

Composed of two opposing sections, the object was another steampunk creation. One piece being a flattened, oblong canvas bag of mottled tan but little to no other detail. The second piece was a narrow pipe some two and a half feet long with flared ends, like funnels, or the bell of a clarinet. The entire thing was made of dull gray metal, but much more interesting than the canvas bag. Mini, pencil-thin arms were attached along opposing sides of the clarinet tube. Each arm had three sections separated by rotating joints, each section tethered to the previous with thin wires—no doubt allowing the sections to move and perform functions similar to a human arm. Some of those mechanical arms were tipped with four small fingers at opposing angles, perfect for clamping onto things. Tiny things, to be sure, as the fingers were quite dainty. Other arms ended not in fingers, but in stiff, fuzzy balls the size of Emily's thumb. All in all, there were twenty arms; ten on each side of the clarinet.

Emily grasped the object at the center of the tube and picked it up. "Oh, my goodness!" she gasped. "It's so light. It barely weighs a pound."

The cloth bag remained connected to the contraption, even though deflated. Two rings—one at each end—extended from the cylinder and looped around the football. The bell at one end of the tube was larger than the other, and was filled with a series of dainty fan blades. Peeking inside the other end's smaller opening, Emily saw a metal cone nestled inside a larger, hollow cone.

"Incredible!" Emily exclaimed in further amazement. "I think this is a tiny jet engine, or, more likely, a turbofan."

"What?!" Calliope and Stephanie said together.

"It is. Look. The fans in the big end suck high pressure air from the front, the engine compresses and heats some of the air, then shoves low pressure, hot air, forcefully out the back to create thrust. I think this bag must be a balloon. It inflates, either with hot air, or helium, or hydrogen, or something, to create extra lift. Kind of like a mini zeppelin. I think this machine flew its way up here, then stopped working. It's a drone."

"Maybe it's smart like Poppie!" said Stephanie.

"But it's not working," said Calliope. "I hope that doesn't mean Poppie stopped working, too."

"Oh, I think this guy stopped working a long time ago. Look at the dust on the balloon. It might even have a little mold in these dark patches." Emily pointed to some black speckles on one side of the cloth.

"I think we should take it with us," said Calliope. "I can strap it to the outside of my pack. Maybe if we find Poppie, she can get it working again."

"If you think you can, I don't see why not. I'm kind of curious about it myself," said Emily.

"Cool," agreed Stephanie.

Calliope turned around and let Emily tuck the contraption behind the cinch straps on her backpack. The weight hardly registered.

"Perfect," she told Emily. "I don't even know it's there."

"Ok. Let's keep looking," said Stephanie. "Maybe there's more up here."

"We need to hurry. The spiders..." Emily trailed off, not sure what else to say.

They continued on as a group; headlamps back on for the girls, Emily with her flashlight. Three beams cut into the deep shadows at the rear of the room.

"Look!" Stephanie ran to the back wall, where another lump was leaning. "It's another one!" She picked up the second device, showing it to her mom and Calliope as they caught up.

Of a different design, this one was shaped like an egg cup large enough for an ostrich egg. But instead of a stem and foot at its base, it had a shorter version of a turbofan tube attached, and below that, a fin that could swivel. Instead of holding an egg in the cup portion, it had a deflated cloth balloon, like its partner, but this one was more mushroom-shaped. The same pencil-thin, jointed arms sprouted around the ring of the egg cup; some with fingers, some with those fuzzy, spinning balls.

"It looks like an egg soufflé in a giant ramekin," said Emily.

"What's a ramekin?" asked Calliope.

"It's a small bowl you bake stuff in. I usually bake desserts like custards and chocolate soufflés, but traditionally, a soufflé is a puffed up egg dish that looks, well, something like this contraption. Just smaller."

Emily was pretty sure she knew the purpose of these machines, now. "They're maintenance drones," she said to the girls. "I think these machines are what keep The City clean and operational. But for some reason, they stopped working up here. These two came up, and died. And no more have come up since. That's why these last few floors have been in such a state of disrepair. No workers to fix and clean."

"OMG. I think you're right, mom"

"Makes sense to me, too," agreed Calliope. "Do we take this one with us as well?"

"I can carry it," offered Stephanie. "It's just as light as the other one."

This new device seemed better suited to go inside Stephanie's pack, rather than strapped to the outside, so she carefully packed it in with her other gear.

They finished searching the remaining area, but found nothing else of interest. More dust, more mildew. No more flying machines, and certainly no hallways or stairs.

Calliope made her way over to the broken window. The massive ten-foot pane was shattered to the edges, leaving a jagged doorway to the elements. The wind rushing by the breach went at a speed and direction to create a vacuum effect, sucking Calliope's hair forward. Stephanie and Emily came over, and they all carefully poked their heads outside.

The air smelled of damp earth, and rain, but no other distinguishable odor presented itself; no smells of smoke or burning diesel, or any type of pollution from all those working machines. Emily wondered what could possibly power all that motion. It didn't seem to come from plant life, for there was no vegetation as far as they could see. It could be that this entire planet was covered in machines. Maybe they were one big machine, like a clonal colony of aspen trees back on Earth, all sprouting from one parent tree's root system and spreading for miles. Maybe all the smaller buildings below were children of this larger building from which the humans now gazed. If that were so, would those smaller buildings eventually grow to equal their taller parent? And how would their growth intersect their peers'?

This world presented nothing but questions. But right now, the only answer Emily was interested in was how to escape the pursuing spiders, and get the girls back home safely.

Outside did not present any solutions to that dilemma. Their rotunda did, indeed, seem to be attached to a mountain, or some massive cliff face. Directly below was a straight drop of hundreds of feet to the tops of more mechanical buildings. Behind them was a sheer face of granite, shiny with condensation acquired from the passing storm clouds or a recent shower.

Holding on tight to the window frame, Calliope craned her head and shoulders outside and around to look behind the copper half of the dome. She saw the cliff face continue up above them so high that it disappeared into the angry clouds.

"Well, looks like we were right," Calliope pulled herself back inside, "The City *is* inside a mountain. And we're only at the base. It looks like it goes up another thousand feet, at least."

"Is there any way down? Or even up?" asked Emily.

"Maybe, if we had our climbing gear, and a ton of rope," answered Calliope. "Without that, we'd have to free climb. And I'm not wearing the right shoes for that."

"Oh, yeah. The shoes are totally the only problem with that idea," Stephanie's sarcastic banter made Calliope chuckle.

"Ok, girls. Let's think. We need a way out, or a way through the spiders."

"We still have the bag of bug bombs. We could set one off and throw it down each flight of stairs then sprint down after, never stopping, but keep going through each level as fast as we can, until we don't run into any more spiders," suggested Calliope.

"Could work," Emily considered the plan, "but those big spiders usually resist the bug bombs at first. We might have to set off a can or two, then wait and hope. Otherwise, they could snag us with a web, or just drop down the stairs after us. Then we'd have spiders in front and behind. Let's leave that for last resort."

"I can't think of anything." A hint of worry laced Stephanie's voice.

"That's ok. Why don't we take another look around. Spread out and just think of any crazy idea. There has to be a way out. Or maybe we can block the stairs."

"In fact, Calliope, you are right about setting off bug bombs. That's the first thing I should do." She grabbed four bug bombs from the duffle bag.

"I'm going to head down two levels, set off two bug bombs there, then I'll set off two bug bombs on the level below us, and head back up. That should deter the spiders, mask our scent, and buy us a few hours. Maybe. If we're lucky, the spiders will lose interest and just go away."

Emily descended. Calliope and Stephanie leaned over the railing and watched her light move around in the darkness below. They heard the soft hissing of foggers being activated, then the *tap-tap-tap* as Emily ran up the stairs two levels below. Two more hissing canisters were activated in the room underneath them, and Emily quickly popped up the stairwell.

"All set. That's some stinky stuff. I wouldn't want to go through there, if I were a spider. No matter how hungry I was."

By the looks on their faces, Emily could tell both girls were not convinced by her cavalier attitude.

"Don't worry, girls. We'll figure this out. Come on, let's take another look around this place."

They spread out again, not so much searching this time, but meandering. Emily wanted to give their bodies something to do while their minds worked the problem. There was a solution to their dilema, she could feel it. She just had to work all the angles.

Stephanie made her way over to the windows, again. The city below was fascinating to her. All that movement. What were those buildings doing? Where was all that effort going? And even more interesting, who was running it all?

She scanned the vista, looking for movement that was not a machine. Surely there were people down there. Or aliens. Maybe they were like the sprites, and that's where all the plants were: they were alive. Or, maybe they were rock people, and had no use for plants. Maybe they were more like the Slizeg, and prefered the dark. That would explain the lack of windows. She hoped they were not like the slug people. Maybe they were bat people. That was scarier. Or mole people. Not so bad. Or worm people. Gross, but not dangerous.

She ushered her mind away from that topic, since it was not helping her anxiety, and thought about the other glaring point of interest out there: the gold, and silver, and other precious metals that seemed to adorn everything. All that wealth. If they found a way out of here, maybe they could get down there and just pick up some scrap. They could be rich!

Stephanie let her mind wander through a world where money was not a barrier to dreams. She could travel to places she had only seen in movies. She could go to math camp. She could meet new and interesting people. She could get a pony!

Then realization dawned on her; she already *was* traveling to places she thought only existed in movies. She *was* meeting new and interesting people, and plants. She *was* doing math (sort of), and sometimes camping. Who needed gold and silver when one had magical doorways? Now, all she needed was the pony.

She smiled, feeling much more confident about their situation, and turned to share her newfound outlook with her friend. But Calliope had not joined her by the windows. She was on the other side of the room, in the shadows. Well, Stephanie could share her epiphany later. Right now, she would turn her positive attitude towards finding an escape.

Calliope's mood, while not as uplifted as her friend's, was nonetheless determined and hopeful. She was studying each and every panel at the back of the rotunda. In particular, she was examining the mock window frames dividing the panels. That was usually where controls were hidden, in the decorations on the frames. Alas, these surrounds were all smooth, unadorned. She ran her fingers over each and found no scrollwork, no flower designs, no runes or writing of any kind. She went from one copper-clad side of the room to the other, with disappointing results.

"All right," she said to herself, "I'll just have to go back over the wall again. Maybe the panels have something useful."

She reversed course, slowly examining panels this time. Calliope ran her hand over the copper, trailing it behind the illuminated spot from her headlamp as it traveled up and down, left and right. The metal had been created perfectly; not a crack, a dent, or imperfection. Her fingers did feel tiny wrinkles atop the glossy skin, but not from the design. That remarkable green patina—where it had sprouted and spread, like moss across stone—raised tiny waves here and there upon the copper. Calliope found it aesthetically interesting, but useless to their endeavors. Where were the extras? The decorations? The hidden Easter eggs of helpful technology? There had to be more. She just knew it.

Again, she reached the last panel with no revelations. There was nothing special about this wall. Nothing to help them. They were trapped up here. They were going to have to make a mad dash back down the stairs, through the hordes of spiders waiting below.

"There's nothing here," she pouted to the others. "We're stuck."

"I'm afraid I haven't found anything either." Emily had been zig-zagging back and forth across the room, from front to back, looking at the floors, then looking at the dome above. "Just a room that's half windows, half panels."

"Well, not quite half-and-half," said Stephanie.

"What do you mean?" asked her mom.

"Just that there are forty window panels in the front, and forty-one copper panels in the back. I counted." She had tested her original hypothesis of thirty-eight windows, found she was off by two, and chalked up the error to inaccurate measurement by pacing.

"Hmmm," said Calliope. "That's interesting."

"I'm always counting things," said Stephanie, shrugging off her friend's comment as sarcasm. "It gives my mind something to work on."

"No, I'm serious," urged Calliope. "That *is* interesting. Why would there be an odd number on the back side? Why not make both sides the same? That seems more logical."

Calliope quickly counted off twenty panels from the edge, into the shadows of the back, then stood in front of the twenty-first.

"What is special about this panel?" she asked the wall.

Emily and Stephanie joined their lights to hers, illuminating the wall from dome to floor. It looked like the others. No markings anywhere. The baseboard was plain, the frames were plain. Nothing moved when they pushed, pulled, tapped or even kicked.

Emily took a few steps back and widened the beam on her light, trying to take in the entire panel. The girls carved shadows from the beam; silhouettes of fragile youth on a copper canvas. They moved aside, allowing Emily an unobstructed view. She saw nothing helpful. Another step back, and her light spilled over to the other panels for comparison. They looked identical.

"I don't see any difference in the panels," she told the girls. "If this one is special, I'm not seeing it."

Calliope had been watching Emily, hoping to see the dawn of her "aha!" moment as something jumped out. But as her eyes dropped in disappointment, they landed on a blemish on the floor between Emily's feet.

"What's that?" she pointed to the spot.

Emily aimed her light down. "A hole! There's a hole in the floor! A diamond-shaped hole!"

The girls rushed over, and all three dropped to hands and knees to examine the spot.

"It's like a keyhole in the floor. And a keyhole suggests a key, which suggests a lock, which suggests a door!" Calliope exclaimed. "But where?" She instinctively looked at the twenty-first panel. It had to be there. Calliope was certain. They just had to find the key.

"So, if this is a keyhole, where would the key be?" Stephanie voiced what Calliope was thinking.

"Not here," said Emily. "We've looked over the entire place. All we found were the drones."

"The drones!" exclaimed Calliope, as she swung the pack from her shoulders.

She hurried over to the windows for good lighting, then unstrapped the clarinet drone from her pack and examined it from top to bottom.

There! Along the bottom of what Emily said was the turbofan, were two parallel lines. Seams. She dug her fingernail into a crack and pried. It moved. She needed something stronger than her nail. Her knife would do. She pulled her red pocket knife from her pack and used the tip to gently work the seam. The bottom opened. A pencil-sized section of the casing pivoted down, its tip shaped like a diamond. It was a match.

"This is it," she said. "The drones must hover over the keyhole and lower the key in."

What happened after that, Calliope was eager to see for herself. The look on the others' faces told her that they were just as anxious to test the theory.

"Go for it, Calliope," said Emily. "Try it in the floor."

They scurried to the keyhole with the drone. Stephanie grabbed Calliope's pack and lugged it along. Without pause, or a second guess, Calliope carefully dropped the key into the hole. There was a little pressure, a little bounce, as if a spring-loaded plate pushed back, but a satisfying click told her the maneuver had done... something.

A high-pitched scraping echoed around the room and raised the hackles on Calliope's neck. Metal dragged across metal. This was not the well-oiled movement that other doors in The City exhibited. This was the creak of neglect, of old bones, of dust and age and disuse.

But the middle panel did recede, herky-jerky into the wall a few inches, and then squeaked and screeched its way behind the panel to the left, revealing a breakfast-nook-sized alcove. Three walls and a ceiling, but no hallway, no stairwell, no doorway.

Calliope lifted the drone and stood. "I was hoping for a way out," she said, a little disappointed.

"Maybe there is," Emily was shining her light at the floor, where a large hole was the only thing of interest.

"That doesn't look like a staircase," said Stephanie.

"Let's see." Emily walked to the alcove, but before she could enter, the panel began its return.

"It's closing!" cried Stephanie.

"Uh oh," said Calliope. "I was wondering how to close it. Looks like it's on a timer."

"So, we have to leave the drone here?" asked Stephanie.

"No, we can't leave the panel open," answered her mom. "The spiders will just follow us in. We have to close it behind us. That's assuming we can escape this way."

She moved over to the wall. "Calliope, open the door again, please, but leave the drone plugged in. Let's see what's in here."

Calliope complied. The door opened easier this time, but squealed loudly, nonetheless. They all winced at the noise, fearful it would announce their presence to the enemy below.

Emily swung her light around the alcove, along the walls, up to the ceiling, but the only thing of interest was the hole in the floor; like a well, or a mine shaft, descending into darkness. Her flashlight's beam penetrated a few dozen feet and glinted dully of the well walls which were, not surprisingly for The City, more dark metal. Interestingly, though, narrow, shadowed rectangular recesses created perforation lines traveling down into darkness.

"It's a ladder!" cried Calliope, hopefully.

"Maybe." There was something about the design that made Emily think its purpose was something other than a ladder.

The hopeful part was that the vertical tunnel descended way beyond three floors. It did have potential as an escape route. What gave Emily pause was that there were four perfectly straight, evenly spaced lines of those small alcoves on opposing sides: north, south, east, west. Her immediate thought was that they were tracks for gears to climb up and down. Not that the humans couldn't use them as hand and foot holds—rungs on a ladder—but it made her wonder what they would encounter that was also traveling the tunnel.

"Should we climb down, mom?"

"Maybe," said Emily. "First, I want to make sure nothing comes up the tunnel, or down, when the wall closes. What can we hang in the tunnel that we can lose if something squishes it?"

"Squishes it!" said Stephanie, alarmed.

"I don't think it will, but best to make certain," assured her mom.

Calliope searched through her pack. Food packets, clothes, and first aid kit were all ruled out as too important. Digging further in was her two-person survival tent—basically a tarp with twenty feet of paracord—and her sleeping bag. Nothing that could be wedged inside the hole. The best she could do was to set a smaller item inside one of the tracks. But Emily wanted something that spanned the tunnel.

"I don't know," Calliope said. "Maybe I could somehow hang my sleeping bag in there, although I'd hate to lose it."

"What about the drone," suggested Stephanie. "I mean, if we have to risk something, let's put that in there."

"That's an idea," agreed her mother. "The long one might wedge in there. Does the other drone have a key, too?"

Stephanie pulled the second drone from her pack and flipped it upside down. The seams were there. She copied Calliope's action with her own knife and popped the key out. They swapped one drone for the other, keeping the wall agape, and carried the clarinet drone to the hole. The bell end barely wedged into a niche four tracks down, while the "mouthpiece" rested one rung higher on the opposite side.

With their test configured, the ladies backed out of the alcove, and Stephanie removed the egg cup drone from the keyhole. A minute later, the panel closed.

They heard no crushing sound, although the squealing and creaking of the panel could very well have obscured it. They listened for a few minutes. Calliope put her ear to the panel, trying to hear anything moving behind the wall.

"It's quiet. I don't hear anything."

"Ok. Steph, open it again," directed Emily.

The panel once again slid back into the mountain. The humans converged on the alcove. Three lights lit up the shaft. The drone was still there, wedged as it was before. No harm done, no disturbance whatsoever that they could see.

"Hmm," said Emily. "Assuming the drones use this shaft to travel, then how do they open the door from inside?"

Everyone jumped to the same conclusion and turned their flashlights to the floor in front of the door. There, just to the right of center, was another keyhole."

"Bingo!" said Calliope. "Good thinking Ms. LaPointe."

"Ok. Next test," said Emily. "I will put the blade drone in this keyhole. You girls go out there, and take the egg cup drone out. Let's see if the door stays open."

The girls hustled over to the other drone while Emily prepped the drone on her side. When everyone was ready, the girls removed their drone from the keyhole.

They waited. Sixty seconds. Two minutes. Three. The door did not close.

"I'm going to test opening and closing from this side," Emily told the girls. "If the door doesn't open, you can open it for me. Here we go." She lifted her drone. After a minute, the panel squawked its way into place and sealed shut.

"I'm still ok back here," came her shuttered assurance from behind the metal wall. "I'm inserting my key now."

The door repeated its maneuvers and opened to Emily's triumphant face.

"There we go," said Emily. "That's how we get back out once we find an exit. Come on in and let's get on our way."

"Eggy and Clare to the rescue," said Calliope.

Stephanie raised an eyebrow. "Eggy and Clare?"

"Because they look like an egg soufflé and a clarinet. Best I could do on short notice," Calliope shrugged. "I thought about Thing One and Thing Two, but those names are taken."

"Oh, I like Thing One and Thing Two," said Emily.

"Too hard to remember which is which," said Calliope. "Eggy and Clare are pretty self-explanatory."

"If you say so," joked Emily.

"Ok, for now" said Stephanie, "but I'm going to keep thinking about it."

Calliope shrugged, then returned her drone to its place on her pack. Once she and Stephanie were inside the alcove, Emily pulled up the egg drone and placed it in her daughter's pack. The door closed, sealing them in and the spiders out. With their lights illuminating the small room, the three stared down into the pit, apprehension delaying their descent.

Emily broke the silence. "I guess I should go first."

"First, let's do this," interrupted Calliope. She dug around in her backpack and pulled out a ring of carabiners, and removed one. "Let me clip your flashlight onto you, so you don't drop it into the pit."

Emily's flashlight had a hole for just such an attachment at the end. Calliope fished the carabiner through the hole, then Emily clipped that onto the dufflebag's strap, still crossing her torso.

"Excellent, Calliope. Thanks."

Emily sat down on the rim, poked a foot into a rung, stepped into it, then lowered herself further.

"Not too bad. I wish my toes could go a little deeper, but at least I'll get a nice calf workout like this." She smiled up at the girls to give them a moral boost.

"Are you two ready to do this?"

The girls quietly nodded, their expressions a mixture of excitement to be moving forward, and fear of the unknown. Emily could relate. She was less than comfortable climbing into a dark tube where they would be clinging on for God-knew-how-long until they found a way out. But the spiders would be coming, or at least blocking their way down via the staircases. They could not just stay here to starve, dehydrate, or be eaten. This was their way out.

"We're going to make it girls. We'll be fine. This shaft is going to get us safely past those spiders.

"We know we came up thirteen flights. Let's say each flight was about fifteen feet tall, so we need to climb down one hundred and ninety-five feet to get back to the level where we killed the first spider. Let's say an even two hundred for easier math. Shouldn't take us long to climb down that far."

"And how do we know what two hundred feet are?" asked Calliope.

"Well, we'll guess. Right now, I'll estimate that these notches are two inches tall, with a one-inch gap between. So, say for every four rungs, that's one foot traveled."

"So eight hundred rungs to climb," Stephanie chimed in the math.

"Right. Let's see how many I go down with each step," Emily continued the story problem, and moved several steps down, then back up.

"Each step is about five or six rungs, depending on stretch. Let's say five because I'm a bit taller than you two."

"Before you ask, mom, five rungs per step, means we have to take about one-hundred and sixty steps before we are close to the level we want," Stephanie smugly explained.

"Thank you, Steph. Nice math. That's not bad, girls. One-hundred and sixty steps is easy. Especially for you rock climbers. It'll be your yoga mom that has trouble holding on that long."

"Don't worry, mom. We'll talk you through it," Stephanie joked. She knew her mom was in great shape.

"Ok. Should we do this?"

"Ready," Stephanie and Calliope answered together.

"Then follow me."

Emily started her slow descent, giving the girls room to enter above her. Stephanie slid over the edge next. Calliope brought up the rear. She panned her headlamp around the small room one last time and saw nothing new. All was quiet. She took a deep, calming breath, then followed her friends into the shaft.

—12—

A Trap Sprung

Inside the spiders' lair, the amber lighting of The City was diffused and muted. It scattered through the layers of webbing, warmer in some spots, darker in others. It gave the impression of walking through a cave on fire, glowing with the molten core of the planet. An event which Ima had witnessed once on Quilium with mixed terror and fascination, knowing that to even approach the glowing substance would ignite her bark.

Thankfully, the similarities here were limited to the lighting. The tunnel remained at The City's ambient temperature. The air, however, tasted stale to the sprites. It suggested a restriction in flow, and too many creatures breathing in a small space. That did not bode well for their mission.

They reached the top of the buried staircase, for the tunnel leveled out. Straight was their only choice to continue forward. Garran had explained that there was a foyer at this level, with five archways to choose from. Fortunately, the corridor that led to the spider doorway was the one directly across from the staircase. The cocoon they traveled was funneling them to their desired destination. Ima was in the lead, as usual, but Garran was close behind. The tunnel was large enough for them to walk side-by-side, but that left them no room to maneuver.

With Nigel, and his pin well behind them, the light soon began to fade. They had decided not to use their saluna leaves, or find another pin to activate The City's lights. The sprites could see well-enough in the dark, and they did not want to send any more alerts to the spiders. This was to be a stealth operation, after all. At least, the first part.

Garran knew they had reached the archway to the hall, there was a definite squareness to the webbing in front of them, and the darkness was deeper. They were entering the final passage to the spider door.

"Are you ready," Ima whispered back.

"No," said Garran, "But I go where you go. Let us do this thing, and retrieve Ben Sullivan."

Ima smiled to herself, then stepped deeper into the tunnel. If the previous section had seemed stagnant, this section was fetid and stale. There was the sense of things rotting, and the waste of fleshy creatures. It was not pleasant to Ima, or Garran, but they continued on. Sprites did not breathe, as animals did, but they did respire through their bark. Some of the gasses they could sense were akin to fertilizer, but others were toxic. Of that, Ima was certain.

The tunnel continued on for some distance, not broadening, but not narrowing, either. Ima thought it strange that they had encountered no spiders, as of yet. This was a very deep trap. She was just wondering about its effectiveness when they came upon a clear doorway. The portal was free of all webbing, closed and locked. Its embossed design depicted an all-too recognizable picture: menacing creatures, eight-legged, fanged, hairy, and standing in tunnels constructed of webbing. Tunnels identical to where the two sprites were currently standing. It seemed the spiders were transforming The City into a semblance of home.

"We have reached it!" Garran whispered excitedly. "Do we go back and get the others?"

"Not yet," said Ima. She was looking further down the tunnel. "We have not sprung the trap, and there is something ahead."

She continued walking, and Garran followed. He could see it now, as well; darker lumps in the dark tunnel. They were not spider shaped, just mounds of differing sizes, from shin-height, to chest height on a sprite. And they reeked of rot. Ima need not get any closer to realize that these were decaying corpses, wrapped up and stored for later feasting.

"We have entered their pantry, it seems," she said. "This would be an excellent place for Nigel to spray the liquid poison. If we drench their food, perhaps they will ingest it."

"Or, we spring the trap, and kill the beasts. We can just walk in after that," replied Garran.

"Yes. That is probably the most expedient," Ima sighed. "I am just not comfortable with all of this killing."

"I understand." Garran rested his hand on her shoulder. "It is not our way. But these creatures seem to exist merely to kill, and eat, and breed. I think it best we exterminate them from Chathair Doras. The risk of infecting other worlds seems great."

Ima merely nodded solemnly.

Garran walked forward, allowing Ima time to gather her thoughts. He empathized with her. Death was a sacred passing for sprites. Barring disease, such as The Hollowing, or attack from others, such as the Slizeg, sprites lived many hundreds of sun cycles. They had no need to kill for food, since they obtained all of their nutrients from soil, sun, air, and water. They only fought to protect, to defend their homes and loved ones. Otherwise, they preferred to live in peace. But all too often, they found that fate forced their hand.

The hallway was quiet. Cocoons were everywhere; on the floors, stuck to the walls, even hanging from the ceiling. Up ahead, Garran could see that the tunnel branched right. If memory served, that was the hallway to another level, and ultimately, the door to the Tree Lords' world. He wondered at that. How would the Tree Lords respond to these creatures being so close to their homeworld? Would the spiders even attack the Tree Lords? They were quite large, and, like the sprites, plants. Not flesh creatures, as the spiders seemed to desire.

Garran turned to pose this question to Ima. To his horror, she was bound and muffled, and being dragged backwards down the hallway by no less than five choocha-sized spiders. More were emerging from the ceiling. It appeared they had smaller tunnels behind the webbing that coated everything. More than likely, the creatures had been tracking the sprites the entire time they were in the tunnel, just waiting for them to get deep enough, and surrounded.

Garran sprang forward, blade slicing, and severed the tow lines hauling Ima. He skewered the first creature to pounce, flicking its body at the others. Ima struggled against her bonds, but was making little progress. Garran tried to spare a second to free her arm, but every time he dropped his defenses, a spider jumped, or sprayed its silken snare. It was all he could do to not join his friend in bondage.

Spiders were emerging from behind, as well. In desperation, Garran straddled Ima, danced over her wrapped body, and struck the enemy in all directions. His blade was draped in silk, waving like a banner, or some ghostly scepter. He struck two spiders climbing high along the wall, and on the downward stroke, deftly followed through, flicking the tip along Ima's side. It did not free her, but it did sever a few threads. He continued to fight, keeping the creatures at bay. Another downward swipe, and more threads separated, but she was still not free.

More spiders were emerging from around the bend, and something large was coming, as well. Garran could tell by the increased darkness, and a pushing of air, as if a great plunger were making its way through the tunnel.

A spider landed on his back, and sunk its fangs into his bark. It was uncomfortable, but its toxin had no effect. He reached back, grabbed the creature, tore it from his neck and threw it down the hallway. He was being overwhelmed. It was time to get Ima out of here.

Abandoning defense, Garran swung twice at Ima's bonds. Finally, they severed enough that she could work her arm free. She tore at the silken threads, unwrapping enough to sit up and grab the cans at Garran's waist. She activated the buttons, pointed the streams first in the direction of the exit, then at Garran's back, to free it of the half dozen parasites latched on. Tearing the webs from her mouth, she screamed, "Gooooo!"

Garran unceremoniously grabbed the trailing tow lines still attached to Ima's back and dragged her down the tunnel. Ima dug into her bonds and fished out her own cans of insecticide, then tossed them as far into the spider pantry as she could, hoping, and fearing, to drive the monsters after them. Once her eight cans were launched, she used her weapon to saw at the strands binding her legs. Nigel was correct, these seemingly delicate threads were unbelievably tough, but her sword was sharp, and it claimed victory.

Her legs and sword free, Ima joined the fight.

"Garran, toss your remaining canisters! We must drive them all out."

Garran obliged. Each container hurled, end-over-end, spitting its contents into the depths of the spider pantry.

The noise of battle, the toxic fumes, the temptation of prey within reach, all bewitched the countless denizens hidden behind their silken drapes. And the walls boiled with spiders of all sizes, skittering and jumping and climbing over each other, each in an effort to get their fair share of the prize. Each eagerly chasing the bait.

The trap was sprung. The horde was coming.

****

"Gooooo!"

Nigel heard Ima's scream escape the muffling effects of the silken tunnel, and knew the spiders were coming. He and the sprites stood ready. He did not draw his bowstring, yet, as it took strength and energy to hold it back that long, but he did practice drawing a few arrows from his quiver, transferring the motion from mental awareness to unthinking muscle memory.

"The small ones are coming!" they heard Garran's warning, closer than Ima's.

Nigel changed tactics, set his bow on the wagon, grabbed a pump sprayer, and hustled to the right of the tunnel opening.

He could hear Ima and Garran coming. Their footfalls were muffled, but accompanied by the crystalline ring and eggshell cracking of their swords cutting through spider exoskeletons. They were being overrun, but Nigel knew they would make the exit.

Ima burst from the tunnel, three spiders on her back, and more at her heels. Nigel drenched them in chrysanthemum juice. Garran burst free a second later, even more encumbered by arachnids. Nigel bathed him as well.

Thankfully, these spiders seemed to be a different breed than the small army of their last battle, and more susceptible to the toxins, for they quickly fell to the floor, wobbling and wandering in various directions. Tormad took advantage of their confusion, and dispatched them with his axe.

Nigel turned his sprayer to the tunnel entrance just in time. The floodgates had opened. Dozens upon dozens of spiders, the size and color of large sewer rats, were exploding from the silken mouth. He tried to drench them all, but the sprayer only covered so much area, and he had to continually pump to keep up the pressure. The spiders seemed to fear the liquid instinctively, for they avoided coming for Nigel, but they streamed after Garran and Ima.

Sonam and Kunga fired their bows, raining arrows into the fray. Their aim was impeccable, each arrow felling a spider.

Tormad's axe was as a scythe, reaping swaths of spiders from his vicinity.

Two gallons did not last long. Nigel's sprayer ran out before the enemy finished pouring from the tunnel. And something else was coming. Nigel could see the edges of the silken walls bulging and moving, as if a snake were regurgitating a bowling ball. He knew what that bowling ball must be. A very, very large spider. Something three or four times bigger than anything they had yet seen. Something elephant sized.

The small spiders were noticing his sprayer was empty. Throwing the plastic canister at the closest, he retreated to the wagon and grabbed his bow.

"Retreat!" he yelled. "Something huge is coming. We can't fight these little ones and that big one at the same time in this large room. We need to get to the hallway for cover. We need to go back home."

"I have another idea," yelled Garran over the din of battle. "We were at the spiders' door. We are close. If we can draw the spiders into the tunnels, further away from this room, we can circle back via a different path, then use the remaining bug bombs to poison this room. That will buy us time to reach their door and get to Ben."

Nigel's desire to reach his son outweighed his instinct to run. If Garran's plan worked, they could get back here, and through that door much sooner than if they retreated all the way home. But, how would they make it back through this army? And most likely, there was another army on the other side of the portal. What then?

"Nigel?" Tormad's question cut through his thinking. "What say ye?"

"Let's try. Garran, lead the way!"

Garran took off down the same hallway from which they had come. Nigel thought that was a plus. If this plan went south, at least they were headed in the right direction for a complete retreat.

"Not too fast," said Ima. "We do not wish to outrun them. We need to tease them after us."

"Leave that to us," said Sonam with a smile. "We will ask them politely."

He slapped Kunga on the shoulder. His friend returned his smile, and shrugged at the team, as if to say, "Well, what can I do? I must follow."

The two took up positions on either side of the tunnel, and fired back into the mass of spiders, stoking their ire. The rest of the group continued on at a slow jog.

In no time, the team was swerving around the Volkswagen spider carcass and through the slippery, crunchy remains of their first major battle. They passed the hollowed out shell of the cow-sized victim, and Nigel gained an inkling of Garran's master plan.

"Garran," Nigel asked, "are you thinking to introduce the spiders we are running from, to the spiders we barely escaped in this hallway?"

"Indeed I am, Nigel Sullivan," Garran replied. "Do you remember how this first batch immediately attacked that other large spider when it came into view? I am hoping that they do not suffer any other spiders intruding upon their territory. I am hoping that the two flocks will battle each other, and forget about us."

"And if they end up being friends, and more interested in eating us than each other? We would have just doubled our enemies, and trapped ourselves between the two."

"Yes," Garran admitted, "that is a gamble. But, I am reasonably certain they will not choose to be friends."

"I hope you're right," said Nigel.

He did not comment further, not only because there was nothing more to say, but also because this section of hallway was still steeped in toxic fog. He donned his ventilator, and waded through.

Further reasons for silence came, as curled up corpses of small spiders, who had not escaped the foggers and the spray, began to dot the hallway. They should soon be catching up to the first pack, assuming the spiders had only escaped to the edges of the fog.

Everyone in the group was tense, and ready for confrontation. Ima, once again in the lead, held up a hand to slow them down, then brought them to a halt.

"There is a moving mass, up ahead, on the floor," she whispered.

"We need to pass through them," said Garran. "Another one hundred paces or so, a hallway branches to our left. If we take that, we will come to a room with a staircase leading down. From there, we travel two more hallways to another staircase leading up, which will have circled us around to the room we just left behind. If all goes well, it should be emptied of spiders."

"Here come the monks," Tormad's gruff whisper broke in, "an' the second part of yer plan. Assumin' the first part was ta be runnin'."

Sonam and Kunga quickly overtook the group, and continued past Ima.

"I would not linger here, friends," said Kunga, over his shoulder. "There are hostiles on our heels!"

"There're 'bout ta be hostiles on yer chin!" cried Tormad, as he took off after them.

Nigel spared a look backwards, to see a tidal wave of spiders rolling over the floor and walls. He, too, threw aside any doubt about what to do. It was obvious. Run. Run away. Run fast.

The party of rescuers charged into the beaten band of spiders, which lay licking their wounds in the hallway. They did not slow, did not fight, did not attempt to engage. They ran through, over, on top of any creature in their path. A battle cry escaped from Tormad, that infected the others. Soon, they were all yelling, and running, and batting at spiders, like a squad possessed. There were spiders everywhere; to the front, the rear, the sides, and above. At first, the creatures seemed too shocked to react, then eager for revenge, as they began to follow, and jump, and reach. But then they sensed the bigger threat; the torrent of newcomers, their unwelcome cousins.

Garran's gamble paid off. The black nibblers from the first battle reacted savagely towards the incoming brown rats. They seemed to find new life, new energy, as they scrambled over the incoming spiders. And the brown rats reacted in kind, with fangs, as well as webs. It was not long before the hallway behind Nigel's crew became completely plugged by a silken stopper.

"It's working," said Nigel with surprise. "Much faster than I would have thought. They must really hate each other. Like the Hatfields and McCoys."

"I am not familiar with those animals," said Kunga. "Are they only on your world?"

"They're not animals, as you might think, but two human families," explained Nigel, as they watched the battling arachnids. "Clans of relations, actually. They had a bitter feud that lasted almost thirty years. Their hatred for each other was so intense, it drew in others around them, and became almost a mini-war. It happened over a hundred years ago, but we still reference it to this day."

"It sounds barbaric," said Ima.

"Aye," added Tormad. "There be mountain clans that do no get along, but killing? Never."

"Well, humans can be many things, including barbaric," admitted Nigel.

"Let us keep moving, while our enemy battles itself," interjected Garran.

The juniper sprite took the lead, guiding the group along the hallway. They encountered a few sickening spiders along the way. Tormad, Sonam, and Kunga ended their suffering without slowing their pace.

In no time, the crew reached the turn, and followed it to the chamber with the staircase; this one a wide, stone spiral, carved—or grown?—from solid white and black speckled granite. Chips of quartz sparkled as the room's lighting bloomed, and Nigel wondered at the weight of this giant formation. He fervently hoped the underlying substructure could support such mass.

They raced down the steps, Nigel almost tripping in his haste, and his waning energy. So much adrenaline, so much activity, and so much work left ahead of them. He would need a break, soon. He was getting too old for this. With grim determination his only fuel, he huffed and puffed on. Thankfully, they were past the fogged areas and into cleaner air. His respirator was once again pulled down around his neck, and swung backwards, out of his way.

The lower level was clear of threats, so they passed uneventfully into the next hallway, then the next after that. They reached the staircase leading back up, and Nigel recognized the silver dollar spots of spider footprints decorating the dust. At the top would be the spider tunnel, and hopefully, a room devoid of arachnids.

They climbed as a tight group. Nigel's brooch was already activating the lights to the room above. So far, all was quiet and still, but everyone had weapons ready.

The ceiling was the most visible from the stairs, its black iron clear of webs and creatures. The team hugged the left wall, and a few steps later were able to train their eyes on the silver tunnel at the far side of the room. No longer a perfect tube, but sagging and somewhat tattered from the stampede of a hungry horde, it was free of movement, having hopefully disgorged all of its contents. It seemed their plan had worked, for the moment. Surely one of the two combatants would prevail—most likely the brown rats, since their numbers were greater—and the winners would make their way here. The saving grace to that was, it would be a much smaller, wounded army that returned.

At the last step, Garran motioned for them to stop, and indicated that he would enter the room first and the others should wait for his all-clear. He stepped onto the landing and moved furtively around to the left, towards the hallway leading back to the battlezone. Without warning, Garran flew backward across the staircase and was plastered in webbing, cocooned to the far railing and the wall behind it. It seemed the room was not so empty after all.

Ima sprang to Garran's rescue. Tormad, true to his nature, dove and rolled into the room, a Bristlecone tumbleweed, too fast for the gossamer projectiles that dogged his path. Kunga, then Sonam sprang in after, peppering the far end with their spritely arrows. Nigel, being the larger, and juicier, of the team, kept to the cover of the stairwell, but popped his head around the wall, then back, to gauge his target. It was a monster of a spider, the elephant he had seen pushing its way down the tunnel. It was too large, by far, to enter any of the hallways and still maneuver. Too large, even to make it down this wide staircase. Well, maybe it could squish itself, but it would be severely cramped while doing so, and find itself in an even smaller passage at the bottom. No, this beast was limited to the upper lobby, and the spider tunnel beyond that.

Nigel drew back on his bowstring, spun around the corner on one knee, then let fly. He was (not completely metaphorically) shooting at the broad side of a barn. The spider was faced away, its enormous hind end, with its spinnerets like a strange bristle-studded bear paw, pointed at an enemy it must sense through vibrations.

Nigel's arrow struck that bulbous abdomen high and to the right side. But rather than sink in, disappearing into the soft digestion engine, as Nigel assumed it would, the arrow glanced off, as if it had struck stone. It seemed that this beast was armored.

Nigel dropped back to the cover of the stairwell and its walls, as a blob of silver thread was fired in his direction. Armored or not, the spider did not appreciate the attack.

"We must attack the joints!" yelled Sonam as he danced around the room, avoiding webbing.

"Or the thread firing orifice," said Ima. She had Garran free, and the two were now beside Nigel.

"That's it!" cried Nigel. "I need to hit it in its spinnerets. Even if it does not kill the spider, it might keep it from shooting webs. That alone will give us an advantage."

Nigel nocked another arrow, drew back, and spun around the corner. The spider was pointing its firing butt towards the far corner of the room, where the two monks were shooting arrows, and drawing its attention. Tormad was trying to sneak closer, to get his ax within striking distance. Nigel did not have a clear shot at the spinnerets, but he could see the side of one. He took aim, and let loose his arrow. It hit just left of its mark, but the impact was solid, and they heard a crack. The creature felt it, too, for it immediately jumped four feet high, slammed into the black iron ceiling, then came down in a spin to face Nigel. It charged faster than Nigel thought possible for a creature of such bulk. Apparently eight legs could move even a fanged and furry brown elephant with speed.

Nigel remained on one knee, steadfast, reached behind his ear to grab another arrow from his quiver, nocked it, and fired directly at one of the large eyes sitting high in the creature's forehead. The arrow missed its target, glancing off the hard armor to disappear behind the creature, which now loomed over Nigel.

Garran and Ima leapt to his side, swords flashing and slashing at fangs and legs. They beat the creature back, being too fast for its lunges and swipes. Tormad, too, had taken advantage of the spider's ire. He rushed the creature from the backside corner to hack the spider's legs. He swung at the creature's many knees, hoping the joints would be weak spots, and easier to cleave.

Sonam and Kunga moved to its front. They, too, shot for the creature's eyes, and their aim was better. Two of the shiny black orbs were as pincushions, filled with the sprites' needles. This angered the spider more, but did not slow it down. In fact, possibly sensing its danger, it turned again, hiding its face, and resumed its rain of webbing. The team scattered and dove for cover, lest they be glued to the spot.

Nigel was back on the stairs, but Garran and Ima continued to push their advantage. With their speed and agility, they were able to remain close to the spider's sides, following Tormad's lead and working to damage the log-like appendages. It was working. A bluish, opaque liquid oozed down several legs. The beast tried to crush the sprites with its bulk, tried to keep them off balance and moving, but the stocky Tormad was not so easily herded, and the two juniper sprites were too nimble.

Nigel was up again. The others were providing ample distraction. He had plenty of time to take a deep breath, draw back on the bow's string, aim for the spot where silver thread emerged from furry black, then calmly let the string slip through his fingers on the exhale. He watched with unblinking hunter's eye as the arrow slid through the air, a blur of black shaft and white fletchings, to sink deep into the spider's backside, skewering one of the spinneret fingers, folding it inward, pinning it to the spider, and lodging itself up to its feathers.

The spider was not pleased. It ran forward this time, away from the team, towards the tunnel its children had taken. It was trying to escape, or reach them for help, or hide. But try as it might, it could not fit its armored bulk into the hallway.

Nigel had a straight shot at the hind end now; a clear target. He fired another arrow, directly at the white flag of his first, waiving like a tail, pinned to the harried beast. The second arrow struck next to the first. This one, too, drilled deep, and the spider reacted as Nigel expected. It turned, in desperation, like a cornered animal—which it was—and charged for its lair. Nigel was already aiming with his third arrow. This time, his vision narrowed with laser focus to a single gigantic eye. He fired. The bolt struck true. The eye exploded. The arrow disappeared. The creature fell. Silence came.

Nigel sat down on the floor, breathing heavily, and realized he was dead tired.

Sonam and Kunga busied themselves collecting their arrows.

They had fired their entire supply, but recovered them all. They were not able to retrieve any of Nigels, stuck as they were, deep in the beast. But Nigel had extras strapped to the wagon, now knocked over, its contents scattered around the room.

Ima and Garran came over to Nigel, and joined him on the floor.

"That was well done, Nigel Sullivan," said Garran in a hushed tone. "We are close now. We should continue on. Reach the doorway to the spider homeworld and find our friend."

"Yes," said Nigel. "Let's get my son."

He forced his tired muscles to lever his bones off the floor. His knees gave a pop and a crack in protest, but did their duty. He righted the wagon first, then the team gathered the spilled supplies and repacked. Nigel donned his backpack which had spun to a far corner, and he pulled the wagon after the sprites, into the silken tunnel.

They reached the next level, and traveled to the far hallway outlined in webbing.

"Eee-gads," exclaimed Nigel. "That is a foul smell." He pulled his respirator around and secured it over his face, attempting to block out the smell. It helped.

"There are many decaying creatures further into this tunnel. It is the spiders' larder," said Ima.

They continued on, encountering no spiders. Minutes later, the team stood in front of the doorway decorated with the beasts they had just battled.

Garran grabbed the wheel and turned it, releasing the locking bolts.

"Ready?" he asked the team.

Everyone nodded. Garran pulled on the door. Nigel pushed the buttons on two canisters of poison and tossed the foggers into the darkness.

"Here we go again," said Nigel.

—13—

The Enemy of My Enemy

The night passed without event. Ben's alarm chirped for his seventh security check at just after eight in the morning, Earth time. The sky was still dark, but he expected the sun's glow would soon brighten the sky. With flames still licking away at last hour's half-bundle of wood, Ben decided to start breakfast. Hot water was heated to rehydrate a breakfast skillet packet, then another cup serviced his coffee.

Spot was napping, now. He had been on watch throughout the night, and must now trust that Ben was up for the day, as he had rolled onto Ben's sleeping bag and pulled the end over himself. Ben hoped the blinx did not have fleas. So far, his friend seemed itch-free, and was probably less aromatic than Ben himself. If not for the unknown dangers of what lived in this mountain lake, Ben would have a wash up before setting out. As it was, he didn't fancy becoming breakfast for some giant otherworldly salmon, so he would make do with a few personal hygiene camp wipes and a toothbrush.

Once breakfast was done, and all garbage cleaned and stored in a compressed plastic zipper bag, Ben set about finishing his spider grenades while contemplating the praying mantis situation. He was confident he could find some flint in these mountains, but quartz or another hard stone would also spark when struck, so it was just a matter of trial and error, then teaching the mantises.

The real question was, should he? Ben could not help but

compare this situation with Star Trek's Prime Directive rule when encountering alien civilizations. The Prime Directive strictly forbade members of Starfleet from revealing or sharing advanced technology with developing civilizations. To do so disrupted their natural evolution, could unfairly change the balance of power between nations, or even bring about the civilization's untimely end by giving them destructive power they were not ready for.

Ben imagined handing fire to these mantises, and in their haste to use it as a weapon, unleashing massive, explosive forest fires in these combustible pines. They said themselves that such uncontrollable fires had darkened the skies with ash, and wiped out their crops in the past. Did he want the responsibility of wiping these creatures out? And who was to say the mantises would not take the knowledge Ben gave them, and use it to eradicate all the spiders? Not that Ben had any love for the spiders, but it seemed the spiders kept the mantises in check. Take either creature out of the equation on this planet, and the other species would dominate. Just the type of unnatural imbalance the Prime Directive was made to prevent.

With too many variables and unknowns, Ben made up his mind; he would feign inability to pass along the knowledge of fire. He would assure the mantises that he would clear many of the spiders from the cave before returning to his world, but that was all the help he could give. Hopefully, that would be enough for them to allow him safe passage.

It was another two hours before the sun crested the mountains to the east, and full daylight sparkled across the cold mountain lake. Spot's soft snores drifted from the tent, as Ben sat by the fire, enjoying a second cup of java. He had a baker's dozen spider grenades finished, and ready to go. He had also made four small torches by sticking goose egg globs of pine sap onto the ends of sticks, then wrapping the tar in more dried grasses until nothing tacky was left exposed. These, he bundled together with a few strips of green grass, used as twine, and set them by his pack. The grenades were packed in the same mesh bag he had used to gather pine cones yesterday. Once he finished his coffee, his plan was to wake Spot, pack up camp, extinguish the fire and head back to the caves. It was time to head home.

****

Ben and Spot stood at the edge of the praying mantis farm, the conifer forest behind them. All seemed as quiet and empty as the day before, when they had first emerged from the very cave Ben could now see further up the mountain. However, Ben knew better. He knew there were hundreds of creatures hiding in the colorful forest before him.

"Hello," Ben called out. "Are you there?"

His voice echoed off the distant mountain wall. No immediate reply came. He was just about to call out again, when a distant droning caught his ear. A familiar bumble bee thrum rose in volume from the south, up the mountain chain, over the succulent forest; a single mantis flying in their direction. Ben could not tell if it was the same creature he had spoken with the day before, but its coloring was similar. He waited and watched. The mantis had spotted them, no doubt. It landed in front of them, maintaining the same five yard gap.

"You rested. You teach us fire." Yes, it was the same imperious mantis. Ben nicknamed him Napoleon.

"We have rested. Thank you. I have considered how to teach you to make fire, and I cannot. It is something my race is adept at, but it is difficult to master. Perhaps, when I return home, I could gather teaching aids and come back. I may have devices that would allow you to create fire. I would have to do much research."

The mantis did not move, did not speak. Ben took this as a bad sign. Being a contractor, he had long recognized silence, and patience as tools of a negotiation. He let the silence build, hoping it added stress to the mantis, making the creature speak first and offer a clue as to their next move. Alas, the creature seemed frozen in place. The silence extended from seconds to minutes. Ben was beginning to feel nervous, now; his negotiating tactic was backfiring.

A thought hit him: what if there was a reason this mantis was unmoving? Didn't they sit motionless when hunting, just prior to attack? They waited for their prey to get close, then used lightning speed to clamp in their barbs.

Ben felt very exposed. What if more mantises were creeping up from behind? Spot had not moved. He had not sensed anything. Or had he? Ben moved only his eyes to look at Spot by his side. The blinx was standing, not sitting; legs slightly bent, ready to move; ears perked and swiveling slowly, not relaxed; head low, but slightly tilted, as if he was concentrating on something. Ben wanted to look behind himself, but he also did not want to turn his back on the mantis. He imagined another mantis poised behind him, about to strike; possibly hanging from a tree, ready to sink its tibial spines into his neck. Ben scrunched his head down, and cinched his backpack higher, trying to create cover for his tender neck.

He felt a bead of sweat trickle down his temple. This situation was untenable. Ben was going to snap. He had to move, assess the situation, maybe retreat and regroup. He could come back again tomorrow, try to sneak through the colorful glade and avoid the mantises. Maybe he should press forward now. He could light one of his torches quickly and force the mantises back.

His hand moved slowly towards his machete. Why had he not drawn that before reaching the glade? The move was obvious now, and no matter the situation, it would be construed as aggression.

Spot moved. Like the big cat he sometimes resembled, the blinx pounced, not at the mantis in front of them, but slightly to the side, at something smaller; a gray-brown baseball that moved under the nearest succulent. A spider.

The mantis moved, too. It scrambled into its crop on all six legs, staying low, disappearing into the color. Ben was no longer hesitant. He drew his machete and spun around, checking in all directions. Nothing to the sides. Nothing creeping up from behind. He looked up.

"Jimminy Christmas!" Ben shouted and stumbled backward several steps. Far above him, but sinking down fast on shimmering belay lines, were no less than a dozen spiders, varying in size from plum to watermelon. Permission be damned, Ben was running through the succulents, and heading to the cave. This planet made his skin crawl and frayed his nerves. He wanted out. He was headed home.

Turning into the field of colors, Ben quickly plotted his path. Keeping low both to avoid getting hung up on the succulents, and to peer below their boughs for spider and mantis alike, he charged forward, and called for Spot to follow.

"Spot! Let's move!"

His encouragement was hardly necessary, as the blinx bounded past him, once again taking the lead. It appeared Spot merely needed the ok, and he was happy to return to the cave.

Ben spotted movement in the short trees. Mantises appeared from camouflage hiding to pounce on what Ben had mistaken for rocks. Pale blue jelly squirted from those rocks, and furry legs twittered in death. A war was raging around him, and Ben wanted no part of it.

Concentrating forward, Ben saw Spot jump high and flip around in the air to land facing him. A melon sized spider lay between them, but Ben's momentum had him upon it before Spot could return to help.

"Aaaahhh!" Ben screamed in panic, and slashed with his machete. The spider split in two, three, four pieces, and was kicked into the succulent field. He shook off the heebie-jeebies and kept on running,

Spot already leaps ahead.

They reached the cave entrance with no further battle. Ben paused to look carefully inside. Most likely, these spiders had come from this cave. With the death of Gigantor, there was nothing to fear for the smaller. They had raced to occupy valuable real estate, and begin the hunt. That could mean even more were waiting to pounce once they entered.

Perhaps Ben had miscalculated. Perhaps he should have brought more firepower.

A humming reached his ears. The mantises were airborne. That did not bode well for the battle in the fields.

A mantis flew in fast and landed hard next to Ben, slamming itself into the wall. It was Napoleon.

"You help. Bring fire. Too many little ones." Its screech of a voice, uncomfortable to hear when calm, was intensified to painful in panic.

"Bringing fire to the battle could ruin your crops," Ben fired back, but thought hard. "I think they are coming through this cave, now that the enormous one is dead. If you bring me wood from the forest. Lots of wood, I can build a fire in the cave, kill them all in here. Can you do that? Then, you will only have to deal with those that remain."

"Yes. We bring wood. You start fire." And with that, Napoleon launched itself into the air, screeching to its companions what Ben hoped were directions to bring truckloads of sap-laden combustibles.

Minutes later, an aerial convoy began dropping sticks and branches and logs of all shapes and sizes in front of the cave entrance. Ben began organizing and chopping kindling, trying to ready a fire that he could push into the cave entrance. He was fairly certain that a large enough blaze would create enough smoke to fill the cavern, and drive the spiders out or back into the catacombs. Once the cave was clear, he and Spot would charge through and make their way home.

Ben had a fire going in no time. It started small, then he added larger branches, with the most sap. Once those were burning steadily, he tossed them, carefully, about ten feet inside the entrance, creating a secondary bonfire just behind the carcass of Gigantor.

Light from the growing fire flickered in the cave, illuminating the gaping cavity of the dead spider's abdomen. Ben's camp stove explosion had really done some damage, and apparently created a meal opportunity for Gigantor's relatives, for there was massive movement inside the corpse. Small spiders, in relation to those in the fields, scuttled back from the heat of the fire, but did not cease their feeding. There was a lot to eat here, but there were also a lot of mouths to feed. Hundreds of small spiders seemed to already inhabit this cave. They could not all have come through in just a day, could they? Ben was beginning to think maybe these were Gigantor's children.

Firewood kept coming. Ben fed both fires. The one by himself was both a controlled ignition source, and a defensive weapon. The one inside the cave was gaining volume, and producing quite a bit of smoke. Already, there was a haze in the air, and some of the very small spiders were escaping from the cave, crawling up the mountain face. The mantises saw these refugees readily, and dispatched them with fearful ferocity.

There was a nice bed of red-hot coals under the cave fire, now. Ben chucked wood onto it like a tender, or fireman, on steam engines of old, feeding fuel to the boiler, powering the great mechanical beasts to life. But this fire was bringing death, and a cleansing, of sorts.

The stench of burning hair wafted from the cave. Gigantor's corpse was being consumed by the fire, now. Anything still inside that cavity trying to eat, would be roasted alive. Ben could not imagine any arachnids hiding in the cave, either. The smoke was dense, and the heat was intense. The very stones would be getting warm, burning the feet, melting their webbing. There was a cleanse occurring, and when it was done, Ben and Spot would go home.

No spider that emerged from the cave survived. The mantises were thorough in their exterminating. The fields still hid eight legged intruders, and there was no telling how many spiders had escaped into the conifers before their invasion was detected. Ben had a feeling that as long as they stayed away from the succulents, the mantises would not pursue them overtly. And perhaps the cold mountain air would be the end of those exiled arachnids.

Ben kept the bonfire burning full for another hour, and then let the fuel burn down. He planned to continue through as soon as it was cool enough, and the smoke had cleared enough for Spot and him to pass. In the meantime, he kept his outside fire, by his feet, fully stoked. He wanted the protection, and the warmth. The mantises had brought enough wood to keep it lit for a day or more. Ben planned to be long gone by the time it ran out. If the mantises chose to keep it stoked, or tried to move the fire, keep it going as an eternal flame, that was up to them. Ben would not feel responsible. After all, they could do the same thing with a natural forest fire, or lightning strike. Ben had merely shown them it could be controlled, with care.

Napoleon flew back. He—it—landed as far from Ben's fire as it could without being hidden in the succulents.

"Weavers escape into tall trees. Leaving our crops. What do you now?"

"Now? Now, it is time for my companion and me to return to our home. We will venture back into the caves, taking fire with us to keep spiders away. I will leave this fire burning, but if no more wood is added, it will burn itself out—the fire will disappear—before the sun goes down."

Napoleon's only reply was that jittery head bob that Ben took for agreement.

One more survey of the cave revealed significantly less smoke in the air, and heat at tolerable levels.

"Spot, it's time to go," he told his companion.

Ben checked to make sure his bag of grenades and bundle of sap torches were strapped securely to his pack, then heaved the gear onto his back. He had set aside a branch covered in a goodly amount of sap, and he used this now as his first torch. A few seconds with the sappy end in the fire, and it blossomed into a giant candle.

Ben gave the mantis one last farewell. "Good-bye, and good luck. I wish you well. May you defeat the remaining spiders, and find peace with your crops."

Napoleon stood tall, and maybe relaxed a bit. "Luck to you. Kill many weavers on travels. Return and teach fire."

Imperious to the last, Ben thought to himself. In response, he took a page out of Napoleon's book, and merely gave a curt nod, then he entered the cave, with Spot by his side.

—14—

Top Floor. Going Down.

Calliope was definitely in her element. Emily was right; for a rock climber, this was easy. She immediately tested out a resting position by leaving one foot on the rung of the track the others were on, then stepping across the tube to the opposite track and tucking her other foot in tight. As suspected, she could stand easily without having to hold on with her hands, her legs just slightly wider than shoulder width apart.

"If you get tired, just step across the tunnel and put a foot on the other side. Then you can stand, sort of normal, and let go with your hands," she called down to the others.

Emily and Stephanie looked up.

"Well, that's good to know," said Emily. "I'm going to need a break at some point. But let's be careful with our movements. One slip, one wrong placement of hands or feet, and we fall down this tunnel a very long way. There are no second chances, and no safety ropes in here."

Calliope carefully returned to climbing position. Emily's words were very sobering. The thought of falling was now forefront in her mind. Concentration, she told herself, that was key.

They climbed in relative silence, focusing on firm footholds and hand grips. Stephanie kept count, giving them a report every ten steps.

"Fifty," Stephanie announced. "We're almost a third of the way there."

"Easy-peasy," said Emily.

"Yes, except for the fact that we have not seen any other alcoves or doorways," Calliope pointed out. "We should have passed at least three floors by now."

"I did notice that," said Emily. "But that's ok. On the other side of this wall are the spiders. We don't want to get out here anyway."

"Yeah, but what if we don't find another door?" chimed in Stephanie.

"I'm confident there will be another one soon. Perhaps they are only every ten floors or so. If that's the case, we'll try for a door below the level we want."

There was not much of a choice, really. They either climbed back up to the top and returned to be trapped in the Overlook Room, or continued down, hoping for another door. It made sense that there would be another door, or an exit of some sort, somewhere. Why create a shaft for something to travel, if there was nowhere for it to travel to, or from? They continued their climb in silence.

"One-hundred," Stephanie quietly reported.

The darkness above was now as eternal as the darkness below. Emily was sure there was another doorway. Whether they would reach it before their strength gave out, was another matter. Already, her calves were burning, her toes tiring, and her fingers were getting shaky.

"Girls, let's take a break for a minute. My hands need a rest."

They each copied Calliope's move of earlier, straddling the emptiness, relieving their hands of responsibility. Emily sighed in relief, shook her hands, and wiggled her fingers. It would not be so bad if she could grab the track like grabbing the rungs of a ladder, but there was no hole on the backside of these, so she could only squeeze the rung between her thumbs and fingers. That was not a grip she exercised often. It was natural enough; in fact, it was how humans grasped most things throughout a normal day, but not necessarily heavy things. She likened this to her project of last summer, relocating a flower bed from one side of her yard to another. She had to transplant seventy-two cement pavers as the edging for her garden. They were easy to carry, at first; one in each hand, pinched between fingers and thumb. But by the twentieth, her forearms burned, and her fingers weakened. She had switched to carrying them like a serving tray.

There was no such relief here, but taking a break, and taking the pressure off her fingers helped. Even if she did have to put them back to work momentarily.

"How are you girls doing?" she asked.

"I'm good, mom, but I was ready for a break, too."

"Same here," agreed Calliope. "I'm ready to keep going whenever you both are, though."

They started again, the monotonous climb. Near step one-hundred and twenty-six, Emily's toes pushed through the rungs all the way to the top of her foot. The tension was released from her calf. It was heaven. She took another step and found additional relief.

"Girls," she could not keep the excitement from her voice. "One second. Let me adjust my light. Something's changing."

Her flashlight was hanging in front of her, focused on the rungs. She flipped it over her hip and pointed it down.

"We did it!" she whispered up, excitedly. "There's another alcove!"

She quickly climbed down. The tracks they were climbing continued through the alcove, floor to ceiling, like the actual ladder they were using it for, on all four sides. Emily squeezed herself between two ladders, and stepped off onto solid floor. She helped Stephanie through the tracks, backpack removed and passed through first in order to provide enough room. Calliope followed in the same manner. All three ladies took a deep breath, and shook out tired hands.

"This is early, though, isn't it?" asked Calliope.

"Definitely," insisted Stephanie. "My math was correct. I've been double checking it while climbing. We need to go at least one-hundred and sixty steps to the level we want."

"So, what level are we on?"

"Maybe level eleven or twelve?" suggested Stephanie.

"Any level above the one we were shooting for is spider-land," said Emily. "Of course, they could all be on the upper levels, looking for us up there. Maybe we should take a look."

Emily turned her light to the floor. There, just to the right of the wall they assumed would slide open, was the now-familiar diamond-shaped hole. She motioned for her daughter to turn around, and then pulled the egg cup drone from her pack.

"This thing seems warm," she commented.

"Well, I'm sure sweating," said Stephanie. "I'll bet everything in my pack is getting a little warm."

Emily thought nothing more of it. She pried the key down from the bottom, and inserted it into the hole. This panel, apparently, was better maintained. It slid back a few inches with just a whisper, then transitioned right, into the wall, with no more than a low hum. Immediately, on the other side of the doorway, The City's lights began their warming glow, activated by the girls' pendants. And immediately, Emily realized it was not empty. The hallway beyond was consumed in webbing which shrouded the light, allowing no more than a candle's worth to lend a sinister, haunted house ambience to the way beyond the door.

A dozen creatures, varying from baseball-sized to loaf of bread, scurried for cover. Lucky for the ladies, these creatures were spooked by light, and had not noticed a new food source popping so conveniently from the wall. Emily snatched the drone from the keyhole and held her breath, waiting for the door to close. She counted the seconds. Ten, twenty, thirty; the humans did not move, did not breathe. Fifty, sixty. Why wouldn't the damn door close?! Seventy, eighty, one-hundred. Finally! The panel slowly emerged from the wall, closing the cupboard door. It slid into place, and everyone let out a relieved sigh.

"Ok. They are *not* all on the upper levels," said Emily.

"No. Definitely not," Calliope shivered.

Stephanie was silent, and staring at the closed doorway. A look of panic creased her forehead.

"Honey, you ok?" asked Emily.

Her daughter nodded, but the expression lingered.

"We'll keep going down. We'll find a clear exit," she assured the girls.

A clicking noise came from the drone, and Emily almost dropped it.

"What was that?" She held the drone up and away from her body. They all watched it closely.

Another click came from inside the cup section of the drone; a soft click, like a clock tick. Then another a second later. And again.

"It's trying to wake up," whispered Calliope.

Emily quickly set it on the floor. It listed sideways, the finned bottom preventing a stable stance. The clicking became faster. And then it stopped.

"Maybe it really is broken," said Calliope, "and it can't start itself back up."

Stephanie squatted next to the drone and listened. "It's humming."

Emily and Calliope knelt down to listen. There was a soft thrumming, like a tiny engine was purring along inside.

"Look!" Stephanie pointed at the cloth bag attached to the cup. "The bag is filling up."

Ripples disturbed the strange cloth, and the bladder was

definitely gaining volume. They watched in interest as the bag inflated. At two thirds full, the bag stood tall, and the drone started to rock slightly on the floor, like an invisible string was tugging it upwards. At three-quarters full, the drone rose to balance on the tip of its fin. Seconds later, it left the floor altogether, and continued to rise to four feet above the floor. It hovered, the quiet hum of its internal engine barely registering in the room.

And then, an arm moved. One thin appendage straightened, then bent at all three joints, clicked its little fingers, and went still. The adjacent arm repeated the maneuver. The third had a fuzzball instead of fingers, and when its joints fully extended, the ball whirred with a blurring spin. It retracted, then came to rest. The process continued until all arms had performed their warm-up.

"I think it's going through a systems check," said Emily. "It's making sure everything is in working order."

A whisper of a whir started in the drone's miniature jet engine. The dirigible moved forward, slowly, then the fin and engine rotated beneath it, and it flew in a tight circle, as if surveying its surroundings.

"Hello there," Calliope spoke to it. "Is there anything we can do to help you?"

The craft did not respond. If it considered them at all, it was only as obstacles. It wound its way around the perimeter of the small room, and hovered over the shaft for a few seconds. The ladies thought it would descend or climb the tube—hopefully not climb, as it seemed to go inert at the upper levels—but it changed its mind and instead drifted over to Calliope. It swiveled around to her back, and hovered by Clare.

"Oh, you want the other drone," Emily said.

Calliope quickly dropped her backpack and detached the clarinet drone. She set it on the floor, and they all backed away to give the egg cup drone room to work.

"Clare is still cold," whispered Calliope. "I don't think she's trying to wake up."

"Maybe Clare was the main drone in charge of caring for the upper levels, and when it broke, Eggy went to fix her, but he lost power, too," suggested Emily.

They watched while the working drone hovered over the other, emitting soft clicks and pops. There was no response from the prone drone, if indeed the egg drone was communicating. After five minutes of trying, it seemed the nurse drone gave up. It sank even lower, grabbed the inert drone with a few of its twiggy armes, and dragged it over to the pit. Once it reached the edge, it stopped, thankfully. Calliope was afraid the tube was their version of a trash shoot, and the egg cup drone was sending its companion to the dung heap. Not a very dignified way to go.

As it turned out, however, Eggy hovered to the back track, extended an arm, and fiddled with something. Then it waited.

The humans looked at each other with questioning glances. Calliope shrugged her shoulders. Stephanie shook her head, indicating she had no idea what was going on either.

They walked around the pit to get a look at what the drone had poked at. Along one track, were familiar designs; small scrolling vines and flowerettes that often hid buttons or levers. The drone must have activated one such device. So they waited, too, to see what responded. Calliope hoped it was Poppie.

After a few minutes, everyone could hear something rolling up the tube. It was definitely not Poppie making that much noise. To Emily, it sounded like the elevator in her first apartment building back at college; a contraption built at the turn of the twentieth century, and not maintained since its installation. Not exactly a trustworthy transport mechanism.

When the source of the clacking arrived, however, it was not an elevator car, or an ornate cage, or a basket. It was just a metal plate that, when it came to rest, fit so snugly into the shaft, there was a barely discernible crack between it and the floor of the room.

Eggy pulled Clare onto the platform.

"Wait!" cried Calliope. "Can you help us get out of here? We just want to go home."

The dirigible did pause this time. Perhaps Calliope's desperate appeal reached something in the drone's programming.

"Can we go with you? Or can you show us a way out first?" she continued.

Eggy just hovered for a bit. Calliope hoped it was considering and not just confused. But then it flew back to the track, and extended one twiggy arm to a flower design at about chest height. It dropped to the bottom of the track, it's fin only an inch from the platform, and pointed to the very bottom flowerette. It repeated the action: back to the upper flower, down to the lower. Then it faced Calliope, and waited.

"Directions," said Emily. "It's showing us how to use the elevator."

Calliope directed her question at the drone. "Is that right? Are you telling us to push the top button first, then the bottom button? The top one brings the lift up, the bottom one directs it down?"

The drone twirled once. They took that to mean yes. Then it tapped the center of the bottom flower with its appendage, and returned to hover above Clare. A second later, the platform descended into the pit and they watched it drop until the lights from their flashlights could no longer reach it.

"Ok. There's no way we can all fit on that," said Emily.

"And where did it go?" Stephanie sounded skeptical. "It seems like it just went to the basement. I don't want to go to the basement."

"Cool," said Calliope. "I'd love to see what's in the basement."

"Oh, no," said Emily. "I agree with Steph. We do *not* want the basement. We just want to go down to the next alcove with a door."

Emily thought for a minute. "We just climbed down twelve

floors, I wonder if the next door is another twelve. We could climb to the next one. If we don't hit an alcove after—What was this one, Steph? One-hundred and forty steps?—then we climb back up."

"I'm all for another climb," said Calliope, "but remember, we were already tiring when we reached this one. Add the strain of another downward climb to the fatigue we've already built up, and then maybe have to climb back up the same distance? It is way harder climbing up, than climbing down. We are going to get a serious workout."

"We can take breaks," reminded Emily. "Stephanie, what do you think? Could you make it?"

Stephanie had only been partially listening. She was considering the vinework on the iron track, careful to not fall into the once-again gaping pit. "I think we don't need to go to the basement. I think that's where Eggy and Clare went, but that's because he pushed the bottom flower. But there are ten flowers in between. Thirteen flowers in all. He pushed the twelfth flower to call the elevator up, then the first flower to go down. I'm guessing the thirteenth flower goes to the observation deck. I say, we call the elevator, and press the eleventh flower, and see where we end up."

Her mom and Calliope joined her to study the pattern.

"You're right!" said Calliope. "Nice job. Whoa. That means there are over a hundred floors in this place?"

"Only one-hundred and forty-four," supplied Stephanie. "The bottom one is the basement, so twelve floors for each of the other twelve buttons. Twelve times twelve is one-forty-four."

"Whoa. This place is huge," Calliope was thinking through all the halls they had traveled, and those had only covered a handful of floors.

"It sure is," said Emily. "Way bigger than I thought it was."

She looked at her daughter. "Ok, kiddo. Should we call the elevator?"

"Definitely," said Stephanie, and she pushed the twelfth flower.

They waited, peering into the hole with their flashlights. Nothing seemed to be coming.

"Maybe the button is broken now?" Calliope voiced the concern they were all feeling.

"Or maybe you have to be a drone to make it work," said Stephanie.

"Or, maybe the elevator is still dropping off the drones, and we just need to wait for it, just like we wait for any elevator already in use by someone else," supplied Emily. "Patience, girls. Patience."

"Speaking of needing the drones to make something work," said Calliope, "I just realized we lost both drones, and they were the ones with the keys to open the walls on these alcoves."

"Oh, crap!" gasped Emily. "You're right."

They stood quietly, thinking of what to do. Calliope pulled off her backpack and rummaged through each pocket. She found nothing to solve the problem. Stephanie followed suit.

"Here's a pen." She held up a worn ballpoint; the run-of-the-mill sort swiped from the junk drawer of any kitchen, anywhere.

"See if it fits," shrugged Calliope.

They moved to the keyhole in the floor, and Stephanie tried to insert the pen. It was too big.

"Round peg, square hole," said Emily. "Nice try, girls."

"What if we take it apart?" suggested Calliope. "The ink cartridge will fit."

She accepted the pen from Stephanie and worked the black plastic tip free. The flexible ink tube, only a third of the ink remaining, came with it. She held the tip and jammed the other end in the hole. The cartridge bent, and wobbled, but fit.

"I can feel it wanting to move, but the plastic isn't strong enough to force down the button in there."

"What now?" asked Stephanie.

"Hmm," Emily thought for a minute. "Let me see the outer tube from the pen."

She accepted the white plastic from her daughter and squeezed it in her hands. Too tough. She set it on the ground, and carefully stepped on it. It squished a bit, going more oval than round. She stepped on it again, and bounced a bit on one foot, then examined her work. The pen's outer casing was now very misshapen; past oval, but not quite flat.

"Give this a try," she handed the implement to Calliope, who tried it in the hole.

"It fits," she said excitedly.

She pushed the pen down. It stayed firm, and she felt the internal lever begin to give way.

"I think it's working!"

"Stop! Don't open this door!" Stephanie's forceful whisper made Calliope freeze. "Spiders."

"Right," Calliope extracted the pen. "We can do a full test on the next floor. Here, you keep the key." She handed the dismantled pen back to Stephanie, who put it in her backpack hip belt.

A distant clacking alerted them that the lift was returning.

"Hallelujah!" said Emily. "Let's do this."

When the lift arrived, they agreed that Emily should go first. If she did, indeed, reach the next level at twelve floors down, and there was another control panel, she would disembark, and send the elevator back up for Stephanie, with Calliope coming third. Emily hugged both girls, then stepped onto the platform.

"See you both in a minute," she smiled in reassurance, then pushed the center of flower number eleven.

The platform descended at a comfortable rate. Emily hugged her duffle bag of bug spray close, as to not snag on the walls. It was an uneventful trip. Her flashlight unveiled nothing new in the tube; smooth, charcoal steel walls, inlaid with uninterrupted tracks on north, east, south, west sides. She looked up, and could still see the lights from the girls' headlamps shining from above. She waved her flashlight above her head.

A minute later, she arrived. Her daughter had been correct, there was another alcove, and logic said she was now twelve floors below the girls. She pointed her flashlight up again, clicked it off, on, off, on, to signal the girls, then stepped off the platform. After a quick look around the room, making sure there were no surprises, she pushed flower twelve again, to send the elevator back up. It worked. It ascended, and Emily got a good view of its undercarriage. Reassuringly, the thing was beefy. Four feet tall, at least, it had three iron gears running up each track: twelve in all, and each as wide as the track itself. The lift must be able to haul quite a bit of weight. Much more than a few drones, or a single human. What else could possibly fit up such a narrow tube?

Just one more mystery for this place.

She waited, and worried only a bit, as Stephanie descended. But descend she did, joining her mother within minutes. Calliope followed, and the threesome were once again ready to see what was behind another door. Everyone prepped two cans of Black Flag. Stephanie set hers in front of her on the floor, and readied her plastic, makeshift key.

"Ready?" she asked them.

"Ready," they answered.

Stephanie pushed the pen in. The door opened. On the other side was another rotunda, with the usual spiral staircase running through the middle, archways to hallways leading in several directions, and everything blissfully free of spiders, and webs, and carcasses, and detritus.

Emily laughed in relief.

"Yes," said Calliope, quietly.

"Thank God," said Stephanie.

The three moved out into the room. Stephanie tucked the penkey back in her pack. The door eventually sealed itself behind them. They looked around the room. Five new hallways presented themselves.

"Ok," said Emily, "Which way do we go?"

"I think straight ahead." Calliope pointed to the hallway directly across from the alcove. "When we first started going up, we came from that direction. I say, since this level looks clear so far, we take that hallway about the same distance back and see if we find a staircase leading up to our door."

"I think so, too," said Stephanie. "Straight back, no turns."

"Ok. Lead the way, girls."

They walked for over an hour, and passed several branching hallways on this level. They chose to continue straight each time. The halls remained free from any trace of spiders.

With much relief, their hallway finally encountered another foyer. This one had only one other hall, exactly opposite the one they were exiting, and the rest of the walls were covered in doorways. No one was even remotely interested in exploring the new doors. Their attention was on the expected, wide, iron staircase rising in the middle of the room.

"I say we take this up," Calliope said before anyone could ask. "We must be close to our door. I think we go up and scout it out."

"I'm good with that," said Emily. "Steph?"

"Sure. Why not."

They climbed. Cautiously, they poked their heads above the next floor, as the lights above warmed. Another room free of spiders. And the stairs continued their rise to the next level.

"Keep going up?" asked Calliope. "Ten more levels to our level."

"Absolutely," answered Stephanie, more emboldened by the lack of spider presence.

The next few levels were more of the same. Some rotundas were all hallways, some mostly doorways. All were free from spiders.

It was not until the seventh floor up that they began to see the unwanted. Small webs in the corners of the ceiling. Just a dusting from the tiniest of arachnids. If they did not know the potential, and the warning signs, they would have thought them normal, unthreatening spiders one would find in one's basement. But the ladies knew better. These were the young, escaping the cannibalistic tendencies of their older cousins by pushing the nest out further, expanding the colony in generational waves. Much as humans did, actually; chopping down forests and paving over farmlands in never ending urban sprawl, destroying every natural ecosystem in hubristic construction. At least humans did not eat each other. Yet.

The eighth level up—or three levels away from the floor where the spider had dragged Emily—the spider presence grew. Webs were bigger, and a few spiders the size of matchbox cars skittered down darker hallways as the room's lights spun up.

"Do we keep going?" asked Stephanie.

"We do," said Calliope. "We're so close. Only three levels to go. We can make it."

"I think so, too," said Emily. "Just keep your foggers ready, and your machete loose."

Stephanie looked none-too-confident, but she nodded that she was ready, a can of fogger in each hand, a finger on each button.

They climbed the next staircase warily. Emily flipped her watchfulness from above to below, keeping a cautious eye behind to avoid a rear attack. Those spiders stayed hidden in the dark.

The room above was free of moving spiders, but the webbing on walls was thicker, and in a few places, contained cocooned meals from obviously larger hunters. They were now near arachnids of a size to avoid.

"Two levels to go," whispered Calliope. "If the rooms stay empty, we can sneak past."

Emily and Stephanie nodded their agreement. Everyone was sweating a little more, breathing a little heavier. To say nerves were on edge, would be an understatement. They climbed.

Halfway up, Stephanie stopped. "Wait," she whispered urgently. "Look over there." She was pointing above the entrance to a branching hallway. A cocoon near the ceiling held another meal.

"More dead spiders," said Calliope. "Good riddance."

"No," said Stephanie. "It's shiny. I think it's Poppie."

Everyone stared, and studied. It was difficult to make out the exact shape and color of whatever was trapped behind all that webbing, but there did seem to be something different.

"I don't know," said Calliope. "I can't tell."

"We need to get her out," said Stephanie. "I know it's her."

"Honey, we really need to get ourselves out of here, fast," said Emily.

"Mom, Poppie can help. I know it. We have to free her."

Emily looked at Calliope. "Do you think it's her?"

"It could be. And if it is, Steph is right. We have to free her."

Emily sighed and shook her head to herself. Every motherly instinct told her to take the girls and run. They could come back with a larger rescue party and free Poppie. It was not like the spiders could eat her. She could wait.

"Ok. Let's be quick about it," she gave in. "And quiet!"

The three wound back down the stairs and moved quietly over to the wall beneath the cocoon. Emily cupped her hands and motioned for Calliope to step up, then reach her machete up to cut the webbing, and free their friend. It was hard work. The tip of the machete was all that could reach the cocoon. Calliope tried sawing at it, then slashing, but she needed greater hand and arm strength to work that far above her head for any length of time. She finally settled on jabbing the blade between the wall and the webbing, and twisting to pry the sticky stuff free. If she could just get the cocoon down, it would be much easier to extricate Poppie.

Stephanie kept an eye on the room, sparing a glance now and then to check Calliope's progress. This was taking too long. She knew it was her idea to rescue Poppie, but being back in spiderville and not moving forward gave panic a chance to germinate and fester.

"Almost there," whispered Calliope.

She had to hop to reach the last strands. Emily tried pushing her higher, straining her biceps to lift the younger Sullivan. The unchoreographed maneuver was successful in freeing the cocoon, but unsuccessful in maintaining balance. Calliope toppled to the ground, and Emily fell backwards. The cocoon was left to freefall. Luckily, Stephanie was there to catch it.

"Are you all right?" she asked her friend.

"Fine," Calliope said, picking herself off the floor. "Let's get Poppie out of there and get a move on."

They could see, now, that Poppie was, indeed, in the cocoon. Stephanie held the bundle tight while Calliope cut the strands with her pocket knife. It was slow going, but much easier than working over her head. Soon, their friend was free, if still unresponsive.

"Poppie," Stephanie whispered, "can you wake up? Can you move?"

There was no response. Stephanie turned the pixie over and examined her. Webbing clogged her tiny gears. It would take some time to clean her out. Time Stephanie would rather not spend in the middle of a spider den.

"She needs to be cleaned. I need some Q-tips and toothpicks, I think. Maybe a little soap and water?"

"I say we take her with us," suggested Calliope. "We can take her home and clean her up, then bring her back."

Stephanie nodded, held Poppie close and headed for the stairs. Near the top, before the upper lights could activate, Emily stopped the group.

"Masks on, girls," she whispered. "Stephanie, why don't we put Poppie in your pack, so your hands are free for bug spray. Let's be ready."

Masks came back out. Poppie was safely ensconced in Stephanie's pack. They each prepped two foggers. With a final nod of agreement, they ascended the last few stairs, slowly and quietly.

Moisture from Calliope's breath was condensing on her upper lip. All of them sounded like petite Darth Vaders, climbing stairs with backpacks and a duffle bag, sporting their masks, and under heavy stress for hours. Calliope imagined this as the next reality tv show: *Shed, Shred or Dead*; or maybe *Are You Smarter than a Spider*; or *The Great Spider Chase*; or *Aeroba-rachnophobia*. All great ideas, she was sure. However, she was not sure that anyone would be willing to participate in a second season.

The City's amber lights did not greet them for the next level. Their eyes rose above the floor to find a room cocooned in webbing. Feeble wisps of light burped through cracks in the silk fabric that adorned walls, ceiling and floor, affording a shadowy view of a dead end.

The staircase continued to rise to the next level, but it was encased in spider trappings, and walled off at the ceiling. No entry, no exit. Of branching hallways, they could only see one, and that one had been transformed into a webbed tunnel that no doubt led into the maws of a waiting beast. No creature in its right mind would walk into that feeding funnel.

If there were spiders present, they were camouflaged in the shadows. Regardless, continuing on was not an option. Emily touched both girls on the shoulder and shook her head, no, then pointed back down the stairs. Neither girl argued. Their eyes above their masks were wide in apprehension and fright. They retreated hastily down to safer levels.

—15—

Making an Entrance

Darkness greeted Nigel's crew on the other side. Fuzzy light from the open door crawled across the threshold, but was unable to penetrate to any useful depth. Nigel dug his headlamp out of his pack and slipped it on. The high beam pushed back the black, giving them a first look at this new, hostile world. They were in a small cavern, roughly formed of non-porous, non-sparkling, indeterminate rock of indiscriminate dark tones. The curved and craggily ceiling arched twelve feet above and the undulating walls wrapped around them at twice that diameter. The room was empty, except for pieces of a large spider lying on the floor. Very few pieces: a leg, a segment of shell, pools of gelatinous spider blood, crusty on top. Whatever had killed it had departed some hours ago and dragged off the rest.

They were alone. Nigel had expected hordes of spiders, like demons waiting at the gates of Hell. But this cave appeared old, and unused. There was webbing hanging from the stone, sagging weakly, covered in ages of dust. Nothing lived here, or had visited in a long time. Except for the dead spider on the floor. And whatever had eaten it.

"Over here," whispered Sonam. "Footprints. Human. And something else."

Human-shaped footprints with a boot tread disturbed some dust on the uneven stone floor. Additional tracks stamped in spider blood, and definitely *not* human, were interspersed with the boot prints.

"Yes, those are Ben's," agreed Garran. "And I recognize these others as well. They are from the pet of the Tree Lords. It is a creature not unlike a large feline, but more nimble in the trees. It is strange that it would be here. However, I do not think it means Ben harm. In fact, Ben told a tale of this creature saving his life, years ago."

"Oh, the Blinx! Spot, he named it," said Nigel. "He told me about that. He also said it helped Calliope and Stephanie escape when you sprites kidnapped them."

"Yes, that is correct," said Garran. "We are still very sorry for that error in judgement."

"Water under the bridge, at this point, my friend," said Nigel.

"They went down this smaller tunnel." Sonam indicated the low passage Ben and Spot had used to escape.

The oblong opening in the stone was more evidence that they were in a cave system. Their search was evidently going to be through crude tunnels. Nigel debated about leaving the wagon. If there was ever a chance they would need a wagon-load of bug bombs, it would be in these caves, on the spider homeworld. He suspected that a closed-in cave system would work to trap the toxic fog for quite some time, giving them more bang-for-the-buck, so to speak. Still, the wagon was loud, and slow, and cumbersome. It might get caught, hung up on rocks, or wedged in a smaller tunnel. It would definitely block their retreat should they encounter an enemy of sizable proportions.

That last was the deciding factor for Nigel. The wagon was a liability. It had to stay.

"I need to repack," he told the others. "We can't drag this wagon through tunnels."

After unlimbering his backpack, he divested it of a few of the bulkier items: tent, cook kit, sleeping bag . He adjusted the cinch straps to allow more space in the pack, then stacked it full of cans.

Once the pack was full, he stuffed two more into his jacket, clipped the machete to his waist, and grabbed his bow. No more than a dozen bug bombs remained in the cart, which Nigel hoped would be enough to get them back through The City, and safely to their doorway home. That was assuming they made it back to The City.

One obstacle at a time.

Following footsteps in the dust, the group entered the tunnel in the usual order: Ima and Garran in the lead, Tormad next, then Nigel, followed by Sonam and Kunga guarding the rear. No one spoke. The caves were quiet. No water dripping, no wind whistling. In fact, the space seemed dead. Dark and dry, cool and quiet. The loudest sound came from Nigel's footfalls; his hiking boots thumping a muffled rhythm; *ker-thunk, ker-thunk, ker-thunk.*

The sprites made little noise, which surprised Nigel. They were, after all, wood. Why would they not make clip-clopping noises when walking on a hard surface? Did they have some sort of soft bark on the soles of their feet, like slippers? If it were just Ima and Garran, he could attribute it to being graceful, but Tormad was just as quiet, and he stalked along much like Nigel himself.

A question for a safer time, he supposed. For now, he needed to concentrate on finding his son.

Nigel's Black Diamond headlamp was set at a medium burn, bathing the low tunnel in one hundred and fifty lumens of artificial light. When the path continued straight, the light tickled at forty or fifty yards, but turns and bends in the tunnel cut that short.

The floor rolled and pitched like a gentle ocean swell. Every once in a while, Nigel's foot found an angle beyond the norm. Thankfully, his boots wrapped his ankles in supportive cocoons, keeping good alignment, preventing twists and sprains. Good gear could get a person through any hardship. Nigel wished he had good gear for encountering giant spiders. A tank, maybe.

While the sprites ghosted along the tunnel in relative ease, Nigel walked wide-legged and slightly stooped to keep his head from knocking on the now-and-again nodule or outcropping. Nigel's best guess, since he was not a geologist, was that they were walking through a mountain of basalt. Close-up to the stone, he could see that the dark gray, almost black rock was shot through here and there with streaks of rusty-red, probably oxidized iron deposits carried here by eons of water seeping its way through cracks and voids. How these tunnels formed, he could only guess. Maybe they were ancient lava tubes. Maybe they were formed by running water; underground rivers that wore away the rock for millions of years before earthquakes or shifting tectonic plates altered the flow and left the caverns to dry out for the next billion centuries. Or maybe, some creature on this alien planet just ate its way through rock, like a worm through garden soil.

Whatever had created them, the spiders lived here, now. And that was enough to worry about for the time being. That, and cracking his skull on the roof. Fortunately, his thick crop of gray hair, tucked inside his Marine bucket hat gave him a modicum of protection. He knew his son did not benefit from that same gene. But Ben had a hard head, and knew how to keep it down.

They walked for an hour, sometimes finding a footprint, but mostly continuing forward because there were no branching tunnels to agonize over. Just an endless tube of black, filled with stale air. Still air. Silent air, just sleeping endlessly underground, waiting to be stirred once an eon by wandering creatures, lost in the dark. The exciting current of movement would last a few minutes from their passing. The dust would rise, float, spin, slow, settle, and remain in its new resting place for another eon, incurious and unconcerned.

The sprites had begun relaxing their guard, due to the lack of any spider signs since that first cavern. Nigel was thinking about calling for a break. His lower back was starting to ache, and the pack was chafing. One of the cans was pointed at a bad angle; the bottom rim scrubbed his hunched spine, even through the backpack's padding.

"Gang," he spoke softly, "I need to stop for a minute and rest. And I need to rearrange my pack."

The sprites halted, not seeming to mind a break themselves. This was the first quiet stretch since they had left Ben's house hours ago. It was a good bet they were all running low.

"It is very encouraging to know that Ben escaped, and we have seen no signs of pursuit," said Sonam. "I am very hopeful that we will find him alive. And soon."

Nigel nodded while dropping his backpack. He sat on the cold stone and rummaged around in the pack, digging for the errant can, and trying to keep the rest in order. He shifted a few cans, but finally settled on using a fleece sweatshirt as another layer between himself and the cans. It had the added bonus of dampening their sporadic clanking.

After a long pull on his water tube, Nigel realized his companions might need hydration.

"Do any of you need a drink of water? I'm happy to share."

"Thank you, Nigel," said Ima, "but we can go many days without water. We took nutrients before leaving our world, not knowing when we would find sufficient soil on this journey."

"Well, that's a neat trick," said Nigel. "Sure makes for lighter packing. I'm lugging around five pounds of water and food packets. Guess that makes us humans a little more fragile."

"I would not say fragile," added Garran. "You humans are quite adept at handling fire. That is a powerful force to control. We sprites are somewhat fragile in that area."

"I guess we all have our strengths and weaknesses," said Nigel.

Nigel leaned against his pack and straightened his sore legs, one knee popping and cracking in protest.

"I just need another minute to rest up, then we can get back to it."

"I am not sure we have a minute," whispered Ima from her position a little further down the tunnel. "I hear something ahead of us, but moving in our direction."

"Could it be Ben?" asked Kunga.

"I do not think so," answered Ima. "I hear clicking. As of many small claws tapping the stone. Many, many small claws. I believe the spiders have found us."

Nigel gave his two cans of Black Flag to Tormad, who hugged them against his body with one arm, while readying his axe with the other. The old marine snatched four additional cans, then squirmed into his backpack and locked the chest strap. He stuffed three cans inside his jacket, readied the fourth to detonate and throw, and grabbed his bow.

"Should we back away, or charge through?" asked Nigel.

"If we retreat, we may lose Ben's trail. We have not seen any other branches, so this tunnel is our only guide," said Garran.

"Charge through it is."

Nigel secured his mask and made his way to the front. He pressed the button to release the insecticide, then threw it as far as he could down the passageway. The can banged and clanged and rolled into the dark. They could hear it hissing away. Ben grabbed the next can, and let that fly. Two should create a sufficiently dense wall of fog in this low tunnel. If the spiders walked into that, they would be sorely discombobulated.

Nothing approached except traces of fog rolling along the roof. Even as Nigel watched, the misty gray dissipated, attaching itself to the stone walls, or floating to the floor. Maybe two was not enough. He readied another.

Everyone was still. The foggers had stopped their hissing after about forty seconds. Ima strained to hear the clicking approach, or hopefully fade away. Nothing but silence came. She turned back to Nigel and mimed moving forward to investigate. Nigel shrugged, and looked to Tormad for his opinion. The bristlecone nodded, then looked to the monks behind. Both of the willows, bows at the ready, nodded resolutely.

Ima motioned for the others to stay while she moved ahead. Garran, of course, ignored her request, for which he received a very human eye roll from his juniper protectorate.

That young sprite is trapped in his own web, thought Nigel. *But what a great web love is.* And then he remembered, Garran was supposedly over a hundred years old. Not so young at all. *The old fool should know better.*

The two evergreen sprites moved down the tunnel, around the bend, and out of Nigel's dim light. Everyone else remained as statues. Holding their breath. Straining to hear.

Ima and Garran were back within seconds, their eyes wide with fear, which, Nigel realized, was in itself extremely alarming.

"There are hundreds of them," Ima whispered. "The small, voracious version. They blanket every surface of this tunnel, like moss consumes the Lower Craglands back home. We cannot win this one. We must retreat."

"Damn!" Nigel swore. Quietly.

Clicking echoed, an exclamation point and starting whistle to the race now begun. Sonam and Kunga took off, their dreadlock branches flailing and bouncing about as they ran. Nigel was next, hustling as best he could, still wide legged and unsuccessfully not bumping his head. Tormad jogged backwards, keeping an eye on Ima and Garran who now guarded their rear. Since Nigel was retreating down the tunnel, his light traveled with him; the pursuing spiders were left in perpetual darkness. At least, for as long as the rescuers could maintain the lead.

"Tormad," Nigel barked a whisper to the gnarly sprite, "set off a can and drop it. We need to keep them drenched in poison."

Obligingly, Tormad activated a can and let it fall, never missing a step or slowing the team. Nigel had no troubles skirting the can, as his legs straddled it with his gate. The mist blasted his right pant leg, but he didn't mind. Anything that made him less tasty to the spiders was welcome.

They made it to a section that ran straight for several hundred yards, so Nigel reached up and flicked his headlamp to high beam, adding another two hundred lumens to his light. He called a halt, and turned to spotlight the enemy. Ima and Garran had not engaged. Could the foggers be working to hold the spiders back? He pulled another can from his jacket and made ready to throw. The clicking had not resumed. Yet.

Kneeling down, he whispered, "Tormad, can you open the top of my pack and grab four more cans for me?"

Tormad complied. Nigel re-stuffed his jacket. The ticking returned.

"That's our cue."

Two more cans sailed down the tunnel. Another bath for their tenacious followers.

Nigel left his headlamp on full as they resumed their retreat. He did not want to stumble blindly into a second group of marauding arachnids. Every one hundred steps or so, he dropped another can. Before long, he was empty again. At this pace, however, they would arrive at the cavern soon. He planned on tossing a dozen cans back into the tunnel, once they did.

Another hundred yards passed, and he felt Garran tug at his pack. "Keep runnin', Nigel Sullivan. I be grabbin' another can to detonate. I believe it be workin'."

Nigel kept scuttling along, but each time Garran rummaged in his backpack, he would stand a bit taller, and inevitably smack his head on the rocky ceiling. There would be bruises. But bruises were better than bites.

The group burst into the original cavern, and spread out. The doorway to The City remained closed, and the spider bits remained untouched to the side. Two other passageways left this chamber. Nigel prayed they would not be attacked from those angles. Especially while dealing with their immediate threat.

He dropped his pack and grabbed can after can, detonated each, and chucked them as far back into the tunnel as he could manage. The metal clanged and rang against the rocks as the canisters ricocheted off the walls and tumbled along the floor.

"Wait, Nigel!" Ima implored. "Save them. I believe the toxins we have already released have done much damage. Let us see what makes it through. We still have to return down this tunnel to find Ben."

Nigel dragged his pack back to the cart and dropped it in, along with his bow. He unsheathed his machete and waited with the others. His headlamp blasted the entire wall around the tunnel, and as the fog billowed forth in silvers and grays, vapor particles caught the light, sparkling like glitter. Nothing followed the fog. It dropped and faded from their vision, lacing the rocks with chemicals that Nigel hoped would deter any spider from following once they returned to the tunnel. But no spiders emerged from the poisoned hole. No clicking echoed. They waited.

"We must check again," whispered Ima, meaning she and Garran.

The two scouts entered the tunnel, quickly disappearing into the dark. The rest of the team closed ranks near the wagon. Nigel resupplied his pack, keeping four cans reserved in his jacket. The supply was running low, now. He should not have released so many in his last panicked salvo. But there was no use crying over spilt milk. Best to move forward and hope for the best.

Ima and Garran returned.

"They are dying." Garran motioned for the team to follow them.

Everyone fell into position and entered the cave. Forty yards in found them stepping around a smattering of spent cans. After Fifty yards, they met the leading edge of dead spiders. The sprites, with their smaller, unclad feet, were able to step between the carcasses, but Nigel waded through, like pushing through a field of thistle, not sure if a thorn would bite his ankle, or catch a pant leg. Many of the creatures were still twitching, battling the poison that attacked their nervous systems. And careful as Nigel was being, every so often, his boots would crunch a fuzzy leg. They felt like pretzels under his feet. Gross, fuzzy pretzels.

Nigel tried to count as they walked, but the creatures were piled along the edges, where spiders that had been climbing the walls had fallen on those crawling along the floor. It was hard to visually separate one black softball from another. Following the legs helped, especially if they were still twitching.

He passed one hundred in his first ten steps. From there, he guestimated ten more for every step he took, knowing it was probably closer to fifteen. His steps reached five score and the bodies still carpeted the cave, although the carnage was thinning. Over one thousand spiders in this roving cluster. Ima and Garran had been correct; there were way too many for them to have fought head on.

A few crawled along, stutter-stepping, wobbling, not yet having succumbed. The sprites dispatched these quickly. It was mercy at this point.

They reached Nigel's original two cans—the start of their retreat—and continued on with renewed caution. What were the odds they would encounter another pack? Nigel felt it odd to find clusters this large. Back on Earth, he never saw spiders in groups, just solitary rovers. He knew some arachnids lived in colonies, but over a thousand hunting together? That seemed out of character. Then again, this was not Earth. And these were not necessarily even spiders. They looked like spiders, and acted like spiders, but they were on an alien planet. They were aliens.

Still, Nigel thought, *if it walks like a duck, and talks like a duck. It's a duck.* That was a saying his granddaughter liked. *Thank goodness she's safe back home, and not subject to this nightmare,* he thought.

The tunnel continued for hours. No branches intersected their path. There were curves and sections where the tunnel got taller, or wider, but it never gave them any choices. Ever forward.

Every once in a while Garran found a boot print, which proved they were still on Ben's tail. But those prints were inevitably surrounded by those of spiders as well. He was hunted.

Nigel called for another rest. His third since re-entering the tunnel. He was slowing down the rescue, he knew, but he was also taller than his wooden companions, and carrying a heavy pack. Where they could walk normally, he was forced into a constant partial squat. He had not had a workout this strenuous since his basic training days.

Even though the cave was quite cool—he judged it to be low fifties, high forties—Nigel had stripped off his jacket long ago. He was generating plenty of heat. He did not want a jacket wet with sweat should things get colder. That was a recipe for hypothermia. At rest, he would drop his pack, cool off for a minute, then slip the jacket on to stay warm. He did that now, and took a few sips of water. He also munched on a protein bar that Calliope had stuffed into the belt pouch.

Thinking of his granddaughter gave him an extra boost of energy. Calliope, capable and smart as she was, had experienced enough loss and pain already with her mother's passing. She could not lose her father. Nigel was motivated to save his son because he was his son, for sure, but fathers and daughters had a different bond; emotionally closer, and eminently fragile. Nigel felt a renewed surge of urgency and drive. He needed to step up his game, get moving, and find Ben. For Calliope.

A rumble echoed down the tunnel, a distant thump that reverberated through the rock and made the cave growl low.

"Hell's bells," Nigel jumped up; threw his pack on. "That was an explosion."

"Yes," agreed Sonam. "I wonder if that is good, or bad. I do not relish being buried under a mountain of rock."

"It has to be Ben," said Nigel. "Spiders don't make explosions."

"It could also be a third player," said Garran. "We know nothing of this world."

Nigel gave it a thought, then, "We have a saying on Earth: 'The enemy of my enemy, is a friend.'"

"Ach, I havnae found tha' one ta be entirely true," scoffed Tormad. "There be one time, whin I were but forty turns from a seedling..."

"Tormad, perhaps another time," said Ima. "I would surmise that any animal's instinct would be to run from such an explosion. Ergo, if the noise came from in front of us..."

"Aye, lassie. Tha' be bettin' on the rain. We be gettin' company. C'mon then! Bring yur best, ya wee furries!" he growled.

Nigel held two cans at the ready. The willow monks knocked arrows and watched both front and rear. Ima and Garran stood with swords level, pointed forward. But all of them knew that if a stampede was headed their way, retreating was again their best option.

Nothing came down the tunnel. The rumbles faded, and no chittering or clacking echoed. They seemed no worse for wear.

"Shall we continue forward?" It was more of a suggestion than a question, as Ima just glanced at the group to make sure they were ready, then resumed her cautious push down the path.

Half an hour they walked before they came to their first crossroads. And with the crossroads, came much confusion. They had definitely found ground zero for the explosion. The floor was covered in fallen debris: chunks, slivers and dust shaken loose by some detonation that had blackened the ground and smoked the walls. Nigel could smell pine pitch, and creosote. And there were many, many spider pieces. Dozens upon dozens of legs. Burnt heads with hollow eyes. Scorched and crispy carapaces. There had been a battle here, but other than the spiders, there was no sign of another party.

"Here! Another boot print in the ashes," said Garran.

It *was* Ben! But by the prints, he was headed down a side tunnel, to the left of the tunnel leading back to the portal.

"Damn! He's headed the wrong way," Nigel cursed. "He's probably lost down here."

"I do not think so," said Kunga. He was pointing to Ben's hastily scratched arrow on the cave wall, pointing back in the direction of the portal cavern.

"Then why did he go down that tunnel?" asked Nigel.

"Perhaps the spiders that escaped took something he wants," suggested Garran.

"You think they have Spot?"

"I do not think Ben Sullivan would leave a friend behind," said Garran.

"Hell no, he wouldn't," Nigel said with pride and conviction. "Let's go help him."

The older Sullivan stalked down the tunnel, tracking his son's sooty boot prints. The sprites fell into formation, ready for the battle to come.

—16—

Poppie to the Rescue

They descended to the lower level, but Emily pushed them further, down to the next, then the next. Finally, she stopped, and they all removed their masks.

"We're stuck, girls. We need to travel further down to a lower level and find another hallway headed in the direction we want to go. Maybe we can pop back back up on the other side, where the spiders hopefully haven't reached."

"Yah, ok," said Stephanie, somewhat dejected.

"Sure," said Calliope.

Stephanie pulled Poppie out of her pack. "I'm going to keep trying to clean her up. We could really use her help. She was able to tell us when you and Mr. Sullivan, or the sprites, were in The City. Or not in The City, anyway. Maybe she can help us find a clear path home."

"Sure, honey," said Emily. "We need all the help we can get." She thought her daughter might be focusing on Poppie to take her mind off of the spiders. Emily was fine with that. Whatever kept her going.

They continued traveling down, well-past the level where they had found Poppie. Emily wanted a bug-free buffer zone between them and the spiders while they looked for another staircase going up. She also had to find a hallway traveling east-west, which is how she thought of the hallway back to the elevator. She was trying to keep her bearings in this maze. As it turned out, returning to the level of the elevator was their only choice.

"Can we take a bit of a break, and eat something?" asked Calliope when they reached the elevator level.

"Yes, please," agreed Stephanie. "My stomach has been growling for the last hour."

"Sure," said Emily. "I didn't know you girls brought food. And I'm not eating spider meat."

"I dumped a bunch of protein bars in each pack, and filled the water bladders. We need to ration, but we have supplies to last a few days, if we're careful."

"Well, let's hope it's not a few days. I don't even want it to be a few more hours," said Emily.

"I hear that," said Stephanie.

Calliope distributed a chocolate chip whey protein bar to each. They sat on the floor and munched in silence. Stephanie continued picking sticky thread from Poppie's gears. She had found a safety pin in her first aid kit, and was using that to carefully clear out the pixie's innards.

"This is like playing Operation," she told the others. "Trying to insert the pin without touching anything but the webbing. I don't want to scratch Poppie's insides."

Calliope and Emily watched her delicate work. The gummy threads stretched and adhered with tenacity, but Stephanie had a steady hand. After a few minutes, she flipped the pixie and began cleaning her other side. It was a wadded web the size of a grain of rice that was the final saboteur. As Stephanie cleared that glob, Poppie's gears and levers and springs sprang into motion. Her soft ticking and clicking spun up to a smooth rhythm, and her copper eyelids fluttered open.

"Poppie!" Stephanie exclaimed. "You're awake!"

The pixie sat up in Stephanie's hands, her tiny legs dangling.

"Pop."

Poppie test-fluttered her wings, their amber glow already looking healthy and warm. She rose from Stephanie's hands and did slow revolutions while climbing above their heads. Everyone rose to watch.

Calliope gave her friend a hug. "Nice job, Steph."

"Thanks," Stephanie said.

Poppie flew back to hover at eye level.

"Pop, pop, pop, pop."

She rattled off a beat, threw her hands in the air as she spun around, then gave them a mid-air bow.

"I think she's saying thank you," Emily said.

"You're welcome," said Stephanie. "But now we need your help. The spiders are still here, and they have overrun The City. Can you help us get back to our door without running into any spiders?"

"Oh, and my grandpa is in here with the sprites: Ima, Garran, Tormad, Kunga and Sonam. They might need help too," added Calliope.

"Yes, but right now, *we* really need help. The others are better equipped to fight these monsters," interjected Emily.

Poppie pondered for a minute, then flew up to the ceiling and extended her antennae to drag along a central, art deco line of silver inlay. The fine design sparked blue where she flew. She traveled twenty feet down the hallway, then returned.

"Pop, pop."

"No?" asked Calliope, confused. "Do you mean you won't help us get home?"

"Pop, pop."

The pixie did a zig-zag in the air.

"So you mean you can't get us to our door without running into spiders?" asked Stephanie.

"Pop."

"Yes. Oh, crud," said Calliope, crestfallen.

"Ok, well, we have plenty of foggers," said Emily. "Poppie, if you can lead us down the hallways with the *least* amount of spiders, or the smallest, we can fight through them with bug spray."

"Pop, pop."

"No," translated Stephanie. "I think maybe she's scared to get trapped again."

"Can't say I blame her on that point," said Calliope. "After we go through our door, she has to stay here and fly her way back. Without us to help fight off the spiders."

"Pop, pop." The tiny sprite seemed to have a disapproving tilt to her tiny eyebrows.

"Looks like she disagrees," said Emily. "She's not afraid of the spiders for herself, it seems."

She directed her comments to their mechanical friend. "Poppie, are you worried that there are too many spiders for us to fight through?"

"Pop."

"Are they big ones—give us one pop—or are there a whole lot of little ones—give us two pops?"

Poppie pointed her hands down and gave one pop, then she hopped a foot down the hallway and gave one pop, then she hopped another foot and gave two pops, then another foot and another pop, then another foot and seven pops, before floating back to them.

"Well... crud, indeed," said Emily. "Poppie, you may be right. Those are a lot of spider clusters to fight through. Girls, I really don't like those odds. We barely beat one of the large ones."

"So what do we do now, mom?"

"I don't know, honey," Emily shook her head and started pacing.

"Pop, pop, pop."

Their pixie friend flew down the hallway in the direction of the elevator. She stopped to make sure the humans were following, which they quickly did once they recognized her excitement.

For another hour, they walked. Straight back the way they had so recently come. Emily began to suspect she knew where Poppie was leading them.

"Poppie, are you taking us to the elevator?"

The pixie stopped and peered at the older human, but did not answer. She did not appear to understand.

"We came down a tube hidden in the wall," supplied Calliope. "There is a platform that travels up and down the tube. One of the floating cleaner drones that work in The City showed us how to use it. We sort of fixed him, but we couldn't fix his friend. We call them Eggy and Clare."

Poppie executed her usual excitement pirouette to indicate they had hit on an excellent idea. Whether that was what she had originally planned or not, they were headed that way now. Their clockwork guide continued forward. Not long after, they reached the final foyer; the elevator room.

"Should we just take the stairs?" asked Stephanie. "Poppie, which way do you want us to go?"

The pixie pointed down.

"How far down?" asked Emily.

The pixie pointed down, over and over.

"All the way to the basement?" asked Calliope, with a little more excitement in her voice than Emily wished the girl would have.

"Pop."

"Cool," said Calliope.

"Ay yai yai," muttered Emily. "Why do you want us to go down, Poppie? We are eventually going to need food, water, a bathroom."

"Pop."

"Yes?" asked Emily, confused. "Can we find food in the basement? And water?"

"Pop."

"Maybe it's another Tree of Life room," said Stephanie.

"I hope it has more than plums, or we're going to really, really need a bathroom," Calliope quipped.

"Ok. *If* we go down," started Emily, "can you also guide the sprites and Nigel Sullivan down to rescue us? We are eventually going to have to leave this place and get home."

"Pop."

"Is there something else in the basement to help us?" asked Calliope. "I mean, that's where Eggy and Clare went. Are there other drones down there? Can we get an army of drones to fight the spiders?"

"Pop."

"Pop."

"Pop, pop, pop."

"That was a yes to something in the basement, yes to more drones, and maybe to fighting spiders," Stephanie translated.

Emily weighed her options, a frown played across her face as she considered Poppie's cryptic plan.

Finally, she sighed, "Fine. Let's do it. Poppie, how do we get to the basement? Should we take the elevator?"

Poppie flew over to the keyhole in the floor, and landed. She looked at the hole, and emitted two pops.

"No key," clarified Stephanie. "She can't open the door. But that's ok, Poppie. We can open the door." She fished out the crushed pen and held it up for their friend to see.

Poppie took flight again, and hovered near the back wall. She gave one pop, indicating they should use their key. Stephanie obliged, and the wall slid open to reveal the lift room just as they had left it. The lift still present.

"Now what?" asked Calliope. "I mean, do we go down one at a time?"

Emily did not like the idea of anyone being left alone with more than a hundred floors of separation from the rest of the group, but the lift could not hold all three of them. The girls, however, could maybe fit in there together, tightly. They would have to leave at least one of their packs with Emily, the other could squish between their feet. If they went down first, with Poppie, Emily could wait by herself for the elevator's return. She relayed her plan to the girls.

"It took almost fifteen minutes for the elevator to take the drones down and make it back to us," said Stephanie. "Should we be apart that long?"

"We won't all fit at once. The only way to keep everyone together is if we take the stairs. And that's how many levels?"

"I think about one hundred and thirty-one," supplied Stephanie.

"My legs hurt just thinking about it," said Emily. "And it will take way longer than fifteen minutes. This will be fine. You girls stick together, and don't go anywhere, or touch anything until I get there. If you end up in another alcove, don't open the door. Just wait for me."

Stephanie passed her pack to her mom, then she and Calliope stepped onto the platform, Calliope's pack tucked between their feet. Stephanie pressed the lowest button, and the platform began to sink into the floor.

"By mom," Stephanie waved nervously. "See you in fifteen minutes."

"Fifteen minutes," Emily waved back.

They sank out of view, but Emily could still see their lights descending down the tube. In fact, although it dwindled to a pin-sized star, Emily was sure she could see their light step out of the tube, leaving the elevator. She waited patiently, staring into the dark pit, hoping the elevator was indeed returning to her.

Her alcove was quiet. Her flashlight, shining down into the shaft, lent the room a subdued ambience with its peripheral glow. As the seconds ticked by, a sense of vulnerability percolated. She scanned the room with her light. The wall was closed, the room empty but for her. She thought of the observation deck twelve floors above, and the spiders they had left behind. Could they have gotten through the wall up there? Could they be coming down the shaft now? Reluctantly, her heart beating faster, she aimed her light at the ceiling and up the shaft. She leaned over the pit, holding onto a track spanning floor to ceiling. Nothing but the empty tube could be seen as far as her light reached. No glinting eyes. No furry, eight-legged creatures. She was still alone, it seemed. She breathed a little easier.

A soft grinding noise drifted up the tube. The elevator was coming. She stepped back and watched the platform slide into place. Eager to join the girls, she flopped Stephanie's pack onto the platform, then stood over it, while tightly clutching her bag of bug bombs. With a push of the lowest floral button, the elevator descended.

Except for the spooky lighting, and the close quarters, Emily found the familiar experience of an elevator ride comforting. The only thing missing was a little Muzak playing from a monophonic speaker in the ceiling. She briefly considered tapping the music app on her phone, but then remembered where she was, and what she was running from, and the unknown she was being delivered to. Best to remain quiet, and alert.

She counted the elevator alcoves as she passed through, knowing that there should be ten of them before hitting the basement. At the tenth, she prepared herself for a fight, just in case. Her left arm was busy holding the duffle bag tight, but her right made ready to detonate a can of bug spray.

Warm yellow lighting spread across her feet, then her legs, and on up her body. She had reached the basement, and apparently the girls' pendants had activated The City lighting. Both girls and Poppie were there to greet her.

"Welcome to the basement, Ms. LaPointe," said Calliope.

She was wearing a big grin, and swept her arm wide, directing Emily's attention to the enormous room to which the elevator had deposited them; a cavern, more than a room. The walls to their immediate left and right were two dozen feet high. More steel wrapped the room, but where the upper levels were smooth metal sheets joining a metal ceiling, these walls were rougher, as though steel or iron had been sprayed over rough rock, but the spray had run out after fifteen feet, leaving the rock exposed and curving into a ceiling of equally rustic rock.

Wide rows of tall boxy appliances adorned with knobs and wheels, gears and pulleys, littered the floor. Glass and copper vacuum tubes glowing amber or electric blue, stuck out of the boxes like patches of blooming flowers. A soft humming and light clicking noises filled the room, but not so loud as to be overwhelming. The ladies could converse at normal levels.

"Look, mom," Stephanie pointed down one of the aisles, "I think that's Eggy."

Indeed, there was a dirigible drone floating effortlessly ten feet above the floor, polishing and fidgeting with the gears near the top of a steampunk mainframe.

"It does look like him, doesn't it," Emily agreed.

"And over there," Calliope pointed down the right side of the room, "is one we're calling Ollie the Octopus. For obvious reasons."

"Oh, my," exclaimed Emily. "I'm not sure I like the looks of that one."

A dirigible with a more bulbous balloon attached to a metal bowl like Eggy's, dangled six arms, instead of the eight of an octopus, as it floated a few feet above the floor. One of its arms was emitting a blinding light, and a spattering, crackling noise as it apparently welded a small fissure making its way diagonally from the top edge to the middle of a wall.

"Looks like a repair drone." Calliope stated the obvious. "So, there are cleaners, and repairers. I wonder if there are builders."

Poppie gave a pop, answering Calliope's rhetorical question.

Then, the pixie flew along the outer wall, and over to a barrel-shaped contraption just shorter than a fifty-gallon drum. It looked like nothing more than a tightly packed bundle of black pipes. She hovered over the unit, waiting for the humans to catch up.

"Is this a builder?" asked Calliope.

"Pop, pop."

"Hmm. Is it something to help us?" asked Stephanie.

"Pop."

"Ok. What do we do?"

Poppie landed on top of the appliance, where two coils the size of bendy straws protruded. She leaned over, extended her antennae, and touched one to each coil. A winding, zipping noise started from inside the barrel, and then it moved, apparently on castors. It glided and spun itself off the wall, into the middle of the aisle. Poppie again took flight, and the thingamajig began to unfold itself. It expanded exponentially until it had grown into a rectangular frame, ten by fifteen feet. Each side had a joint in the middle, and at each corner. Piping extended from each middle joint to the middle joint of the adjacent side, creating a diamond inside the rectangle. And those four pipes had joints in their middles, each with a single pipe extending to join a final knuckle, dead center of the entire contraption, creating an "x" inside the diamond.

A hissing came from the pipes, and Poppie warned the girls to back away, which they gladly did. Flames puffed and sputtered all around the frame structure, until they blossomed into a steady blowtorch-flow four inches around the outside, and consumed the inner lattice.

"What in the world is that supposed to do?" asked Emily. She could feel the heat ten feet away.

"I have no idea." Stephanie was dumbstruck by the machine.

"I think it is meant to disinfect the hallways," said Calliope in awe. "Look, it's about the same size as the hallways. This thing could roll along, and burn the spiders and their webs out of The City, hall by hall."

"Pop," came Poppie's confirmation.

"Is that what this machine does?" Emily asked the pixie. "It rids The City of unwanted... things?"

"Pop."

"Oh my," said Emily. "I hope it never considers us unwanted."

"Pop, pop."

"Thanks, Poppie. That's comforting."

Emily wanted to trust the pixie, but she had a robot vacuum once that roved around her house, indiscriminately sucking up anything in its path: socks, power cords, Stephanie's toys, her dog's tail. She had her doubts that this walking welder knew human from spider. Or even cared.

The flames died, the hissing and sputtering snuffed out, and the heat dissipated. The winding and zipping noises wound up, and the pipes began folding themselves back into barrel form.

"Well, that didn't last long," said Calliope.

Once the apparatus had completed its origami executions, it glided its way past the girls and over to the elevator. The girls expected the lift to rise, carrying the exterminator upwards. Instead, the barrel extended its own cogs and walked itself up the shaft's tracks.

"It seems the elevator shaft is used by more than just the elevator," said Emily. "We'll have to keep that in mind, if we get back in there. I don't want to be going up when something like that is coming down."

"Me either," agreed Stephanie.

"It's going to take a long time for one robot to clean the entire City," said Calliope. "And I think the spiders will just run around, avoiding that thing, won't they?"

"Pop, pop."

Poppie fluttered past the ladies and around a corner. They

followed, only to find the next wall lined with more of the iron drums. Dozens of barrels rested quietly, waiting for their call to arms.

"Whoa," exclaimed Calliope. "That's a lot of cookers."

"The Cookers," said Stephanie. "That's a good name for them. We have Eggy, Clare, Ollie, and The Cookers. Oh, and Poppie, of course."

"Sounds like a jazz band from the sixties," said Emily. "Ollie and the Cookers. Eggy's on bass, Clare on the sax. Poppie as lead singer. Ollie is on drums, obviously, with all those arms."

The girls chuckled appreciatively.

Poppie was flying from one Cooker to the next, waking them from their slumber with a tickle of her antennae. Each sleeper whirred and zipped a yawn, stretched to full height, belched a menacing good morning, then collapsed into its travel size as it made its way to the transport tube.

Thirty-five Cookers rolled past and crawled their way to upper levels. The one from the other wall made thirty-six. Stephanie had been counting. Just thirty-six machines to clean the entire City. It seemed a daunting task.

"So, if there really are only twelve exits from the elevator to the hallways, each placed twelve floors apart, for one-hundred and forty-four floors," she was doing the math out loud for the others, "and thirty-six of those Cookers just left to start cleaning, that means each Cooker has to clean four floors."

"*If* they split up," said Emily. "You girls know how big each floor is, how many branches and stairs. Maybe they will clean a floor in pairs. Or triplets. Or maybe they all went to the same floor and are going to clean one at a time."

"Yikes!" said Calliope. "That would take forever."

"Exactly," said Emily. "I think we're going to be down here for a while."

"Well, then I think it's time for a snack." Calliope tossed a protein bar to Emily. Stephanie had her own supply, pre-packed by Calliope when she had prepped the backpacks. Stephanie shared water from her water bladder with her mom.

"And while we munch," Emily said, "let's check out this basement."

She looked around the massive warehouse, not sure where to begin. This strange building inside a mountain had mysteries on top of mysteries. And Emily was afraid one time, they would find a mystery that would prove their undoing.

—17—

Saving Spot

Ben was there, in the thick of the fray, fighting off a dozen beagle-sized spiders at his feet, while five more descended from the darkness of the huge cavern's ceiling. Their all-black forms floated down like a movie S.W.A.T. team dropping through the skylights of some grotesque art gallery of horror.

"Ben! Above you!" Nigel yelled out.

"Dad?!"

Ben's head spun around in shock, which was all the opening the spiders needed. They pounced. The first attached itself to Ben's chest and knocked him off balance, to tumble to the floor. Two more floated in the air towards his legs, but were skewered by an arrow each from Sonam and Kunga before they could reach their prey.

Nigel rushed to his son's aid, but Ima was infinitely faster. She reached Ben and lunged, sinking low. Her sword deftly slipped between Ben's chest and the spider. With a twist of her body and an upward push of her blade, she separated the spider's cephalothorax from its abdomen. A return twist with a horizontal slice and the spider's limbs were all that remained stuck to Ben. The rest of the creature plopped in pieces to the floor, neatly quartered like a hunk of furry tuna.

Nigel pressed the button on a can of Black Flag and tossed it to the right of their exit. He launched another to the left. It was imperative that their exit remain clear.

"Ben, put this on." He shoved a respirator into his son's hand, then nocked an arrow in his bow and fired at a wolf spider above their heads.

Ben grasped the significance of the respirator and donned it without question. But instead of holding ground or even retreating to the obvious exit, he charged towards the other side of the cavern; the side teeming with arachnids of alarming size.

"Ben!" Nigel yelled, and fired his arrows. "Where are you going?"

"They have Spot," he growled back. "I'm not leaving him."

"Damn it," Nigel swore. The rescue just got harder.

The older Sullivan retreated to the area by the return tunnel, now clear of spiders that were focusing on live bait that had moved so conveniently into their den. He dropped his pack and started pulling out more bug bombs. This was a big room. It would need at least ten cans. He grabbed, pushed buttons, threw as far across the room as he could, trying to concentrate the fog near the back wall, where Ben was now chopping with his own machete.

Sonam and Kunga continued to fire their projectiles into the darkness, eying targets Nigel's eyes could not pick out. Tormad stalked brazenly into a swarm and swung his axe with efficiency and aptitude. Garran joined Ima at Ben's side, keeping the area around him as spider-free as possible while he worked to free his friend.

The spiders ignored the cans at first, but they soon realized that the mist was something bad. Those closest were quick to shudder, then crouch down in confused defense mode. By that time, it was too late. They wobbled and fell over. Others started to retreat, but the rescue party was waiting. Tormad's axe was once again a scythe slicing wheat, separating the creatures from life. Ima and Garran spun and danced around Ben in a whirl of death. Sonam and Kunga stood to the side, calmly and rhythmically releasing arrow after arrow into the morass of skittering bodies. Each bolt found its target. Each bolt took its prize.

The fog was doing its job. The spiders retreated either up into the darkness above—a disconcerting thing, losing sight of the enemy—or down other passages, leaving the back wall of the cavern clear of creepy-crawlies. Nigel could see, six feet up the wall, a silver cocoon with a strange paw sticking out of the side; an almost human hand, but fur-backed and with a leathery palm, and the angles of the fingers were not quite right. That had to be Spot.

Ben reached up with his machete and scraped between the cocoon and the stone, but he could reach only half of the sticky sack.

"Dad, I need your help. I need a boost."

Nigel hustled to assist his son.

"Man, am I glad to see all of you," he said to the group, now gathering around. "You came in just the nick of time. I wasn't sure where Spot was, so I couldn't set off another bomb, but now... Help me get him off the wall, will you."

"Here," Nigel set down his bow, then clasped his hands together and locked his elbows stiff, arms down by his thighs. "Step up and let's get this done."

Ben put a foot into his dad's hands and stepped up. Nigel grunted under his son's weight, but held firm while Ben got to work. It only took a minute for Ben to cut Spot's cage loose from the wall. Sonam and Kunga caught it as it fell, and eased it down to the floor. With his survival knife Ben quickly sliced through the silk wrapping and had his friend free. But Spot was not moving.

"He still breathes," said Ima. "I believe he is just drugged. He will have to be carried."

"I have him," said Ben. And with that, he hoisted the unconscious animal over his shoulder in a fireman's carry, easily clasping Spot's front and back ankles together in one hand.

"Let's get the Hell out of here."

"Amen to that, my boy," agreed Nigel.

As they filed back into the tunnel, the spiders chittered, enraged that so much fresh food was escaping. Ben was concerned that the creatures would charge, poison fog in the room or not.

"One second," he said, and shifted Spot around.

Reaching into his jacket pocket, he pulled out one of his homemade grenades.

"I'm going to discourage them from following, and maybe take a few more out while I'm at it."

"Whoa, Ben! What is that?" asked Nigel.

"Sort of a pipe bomb I made outside these caves yesterday. I already set one off in here. It'll be ok."

"We saw the damage. My worry is the bug fogger. It's explosive, too. You set that off in there, it could double the blast."

"Excellent!" said Ben. He lit the fuse, and threw it deep into the cavern. "We'd better run, then."

No one asked questions. They all ran. Two seconds later, a stuttered duo of explosions erupted from behind, one a split second behind the other. Nigel surmised the initial flame had ignited the fog just before the actual bomb had exploded. Of course, it could have been the other way around, but at this point it did not really matter. A concussive blast of hot air pushed through the tunnel, knocking them all flat. Luckily for the sprites, the humans were in the rear. Their bulkier frames blocked most of the force and the few licks of flame that reached them. Had Sonam and Kunga still been in the rear, Nigel was certain their willowy dreadlocks would be charred and quite a bit shorter.

"God almighty!" Nigel groaned and pulled himself off the stone. "What in the world did you make that out of?"

"Pinecones," Ben gave him the abridged answer.

"Everyone all right?" Ben asked the sprites.

"All good here," said Garran, helping Ima to her feet.

"Why, fer th' luv o' dirt, does ye humans always be burnin' things!" grumbled Tormad. "Damn near popped me bark."

"It was a bit unexpected," said Kunga. "But not unwarranted. Any spiders remaining alive behind us will think twice before coming down this alley. I expect the noise alone would have rattled their senses, based on the information Ms. Emily found on how sensitive these creatures can be to noise."

"Emily?" Ben perked up and looked down the tunnel. "Did she come, too?"

"Oh brother," Nigel shook his head. "No, Ben. She didn't. She's safe at home, watching the girls. Which is where I'd like to be, so can we get going?"

"Absolutely. Let's go. Did I mention how glad I am to see you guys?" He hoisted his still sleeping companion back onto his shoulders and headed out.

****

The group reached the portal chamber without encountering another roving pack of arachnids. Five sprites, two humans, and one sleeping blinx stood before the iron gateway back to The City, and took stock.

"Isn't that my garden wagon," asked Ben, eying the disheveled cart, which held the remaining dozen bug bombs, and was now camouflaged in crusty spider blood.

"That it is, my boy."

"Well, can we use it to haul Spot? He's getting kind of heavy."

"You bet."

Nigel quickly emptied the cart, and Ben nestled his companion in. The blinx filled the interior, but not uncomfortably. Nigel repacked his abandoned gear into his pack, then topped it with the remaining cans of bug spray. It was tight. Ben took five cans for his own pack, then pulled his first aid kit from the top compartment.

"How is your friend," Ima asked Ben.

"I think he'll be ok. I only see two puncture wounds on his hind quarters. Looks like a single spider bit him and injected him with a sedative. He's lucky. With that many spiders, I was afraid he'd have multiple bites. Then I'd be worried about his recovery. As it is, I expect he'll wake up in an hour or two. Of course, some spider venom has a necrotic effect that can make flesh sicken and die, but I'm hoping these were not that kind of spider."

"Shoot, seeing as how they're from a different planet, they may not even be spiders. Their venom could do all sorts of things we know nothing about," said Nigel.

"Let's hope not, dad," Ben shook his head in worry for his friend.

Ima gave Garran an alarmed look, but kept her comments to herself as they watched Ben pour antiseptic into the puncture wounds, then cover them with gauze pads.

"That's about all I can do for him, myself. He really needs a vet. But what vet could we possibly take him to?"

"Not a human one. That's for sure. Not unless you want your secret out," said Nigel.

"Well, let's see if he gets better," said Ben. "Then we can decide on next steps. First, though, we have to get back home. And that means getting through the spiders hunting the halls of The City. And Lord Oakenpuss is their leader, by the way. That Tree Lord I ran into all those years ago. The one who also brought The Hollowing to Quilium, and believe it or not, admitted that he sent the Slizeg to turn the sprites into zombie slaves. That tree is bad news."

"A Tree Lord has targeted us?" asked Garran. "That is troubling, indeed. They are formidable, as we have said before. Very troubling."

"Burn tha' blighted stump!" Tormad growled.

"Mostly, he said he does not want any creature except Tree Lords using The City," continued Ben. "He calls it 'The Crossings,' but that's neither here, nor there. He said they don't even use it much, just to search for new plants, and put an end to the occasional 'fleshling,' as fleshlings are *not* good for plants. He decided that included me, and by association, you sprites, since you followed me into The City. Sorry about that, again."

"I believe you humans have a saying: 'Water under the bridge.'" Garran nodded at Nigel, who smiled and nodded back.

"Peace does not mean an absence of conflict," chimed-in Sonam. "Peace means solving differences through dialogue, education, and knowledge. We should attempt to engage the Tree Lords in peace."

"Gah, you monks," scoffed Tormad.

"Ok, then," Ben made ready to pull the wagon. "Let's worry about the Tree Lord later. For now, let's get out of spider town."

Nigel stationed himself by the door and waited for the others to get ready before pulling it open.

"We cleared the other side of spiders, but there is a good chance they have returned by now," Nigel advised. "Oh, and the stench is horrible, so you may want your mask back on." He secured his own, and Ben followed suit.

With everyone ready—Ima and Garran, as always, were at the front; Tormad backed them up; Sonam and Kunga ready to fire arrows as necessary—Nigel spun the wheel, and unlocked the door. Taking a deep, steadying breath, he pulled it open.

A blast of furnace-hot air pummeled them. Ima and Garran were thrown back. Both evergreens sparked and caught fire. Nigel was momentarily knocked off balance, but he quickly righted himself and pushed the door closed. Sonam and Kunga jumped to the aid of Ima and Garran, but were understandably cautious of catching fire themselves. Ben quickly pulled his water bladder from his pack and wielded it like a mini-bagpipe, squeezing the bladder while pointing the drinking tube onto his singed friends. The flames were squelched.

"Are you both all right?" asked Ben.

Sonam was helping Ima, while Kunga tended to Garran.

"I am not quite sure," panted Garran. "That was unexpected and unpleasant. I, for sure, have lost some bark. And some foliage. But I do not think I will have lasting scarring. Not like last time." The sprite turned to his companion. "Ima, how are you?"

"My initial thoughts are that I am as you; singed bark and foliage, but nothing permanent."

"Thank the spirits," sighed Garran, and without thinking, he entwined his arms with Ima's.

Ima herself was quite shocked by Garran's show of affection, but Nigel noted that she did not pull away. The two sprites looked at each other while the silence became obvious.

Nigel cleared his throat. "I suppose we should figure out what to do next?"

"Yes," said Kunga. Nigel noticed a soft smile bend the monk's wooden mouth. "The flames are a definite problem. No sprite can make it through there. We may be trapped on this world."

"Ahk, curse this place," said Tormad. "I'll no be stayin' 'round these rocky tubes. I need sun."

"We have to assess what's happening on the other side," said Ben. "I mean, there is nothing to burn in The City. Everything is metal and stone."

"Except for the spiders and their webs," said Nigel. "And on the other side of that door is one Hell of a lot of webbing. The walls, the halls, the stairs, entire rooms were cocooned in the stuff."

"The spiders will be coming for us, eventually," added Kunga. "It seems we are trapped between a fire and a chasm. Somewhat literally, in this instance."

"I think we need to open the door again," suggested Ben. "We need to gauge just how bad the other side is, and if it is cooling down. How about all of you," he indicated the sprites, "retreat to the mouth of the tunnel with Spot. Dad, you stand far back from the door, and I'll open it. You get a good look. Yell at me if I should close it. If it's bearable, we'll keep it open to gauge intensity, and maybe the heat and light will scare away any spiders that come after us."

Everyone nodded—the sprites a bit apprehensive—and moved to their places. Nigel stood a good twenty paces from the door, while Ben grabbed the handle and pulled. Heat rolled into the room immediately, along with the warm illumination of a robust fire. The ceiling of the cavern was high, and rounded, so as the heat rose the cooler air moved out of the way, creating a bit of whirling wind in the cave.

"There is quite a bit of flame," said Nigel. "And heat. I can feel it from here. But the fire is back into the hallway beyond. I can't see what's burning, but I can see patches of the iron wall that was coated in webbing when we left. It's my guess, at this rate, the fire will burn out all the fuel in about thirty minutes to an hour. However, it's a metal room, so everything is going to be pretty hot for a bit longer after that. It'll be like an oven. Go ahead and close the door, Ben, or this room is going to cook. We can check it again in half an hour and reassess."

As the door closed, the wedge of light compressed. Darkness ate away at the glow, until the egress shut tight, and the cavern was once again consumed by pitch. They returned to working between the shadows. The palid spotlights from Ben and Nigel's lamps, which seemed so bright before, were timid workers now, leaving so much of the room, and its many hallways, shrouded in the unknown.

"And now, we wait," said Ben.

"An' hope the beasties no find us," Tormad said, quietly.

—18—

Fire and Ash

They waited in the spider cavern for five hours, opening the door every thirty minutes to check on the fire. It had lessened each time, but did not die out all at once, as Nigel had hoped. It sputtered and lingered, and the heat remained intense. Too intense for wooden sprites, if not humans with equal temperature limitations.

During their waiting, both Ben and Nigel extinguished their headlamps in order to conserve the batteries, only igniting one when taking turns to open the door for updates. The rest of the time they sat in the dark, waiting and listening for any sounds of approaching spiders.

Tormad had a soluna leaf tucked somewhere in his brambles. He pulled that out, giving them enough glow to illuminate their faces in a spooky, campfire-story, ominously-shadowed way. Nigel, as a grandfather who had told many a campfire story, found the situation comforting, and almost comical. But then he saw his son checking on Spot. Nostalgia and mirth evaporated.

The blinx was doing better. After the third hour of waiting, Spot began to stir. He did not wake, but he did seem to be dreaming; twitching his paws, making huffing noises, as if putting up a great battle in the dream world. An hour after that, he opened his eyes to lethargic slits. Ben greeted him with a whisper, letting him know he was safe, and to keep resting. He gave his friend water, slowly dribbling it into the blinx's mouth. Spot gratefully smacked and slurped, then closed his eyes, returning to a more restful slumber.

At hour five, Ben declared the fire dead, and the heat bearable. Spot was sitting up, but had no energy to walk. He was happy to stay in the cart. The group stepped through the doorway with cautious optimism. Everything was covered in soot, the floor covered in an inch of ash, but there was not a trace of spider presence anywhere. No webbing, no bones, no creature of any kind. The City lights were activated by either Nigel's pendant or Ben's, giving them a clear view of the hallway for fifty yards in both directions. Empty. And in further recognition of the spiders' eradication, Nigel's pendant light remained dormant. No yellow or red glow giving warning.

Ben closed the heavy door to the spider world and spun the wheel shut, locking the cursed portal, hopefully for all time.

"What do you suppose caused the fire?" asked Sonam.

"It could have been us," said Nigel. "We set off a lot of bug spray in here. Maybe The City sparked somewhere and poof! It started a chain reaction of fire."

"Possible, I suppose," said Garran. "But back on Earth, when you burned the webbing with your flaming wand, it did nothing but shrivel. It did not ignite."

"On Earth?" said Ben, alarmed. "Is Calliope ok? Did spiders get to the house?"

"She's fine," Ben's dad assured him. He nodded at the sprites. "These guys all came through and we took care of the spiders and closed the door. I left Calliope at home with Stephanie and her mother. Emily knows what's going on and is watching Calliope until we get back. Don't worry. She's as safe as can be."

"Thank God," said Ben. "Although, she's going to be really upset now. I won't be bringing her back into The City for some time. If ever."

"So, if we did not set the fire, who did?" continued Nigel.

"We may never know. Just be glad it is out now," said Kunga.

"Just be glad it seems to have eliminated all of the creatures," said Ima.

"Amen to that," said Nigel. "I was not looking forward to fighting through more of those roving hordes."

"Nor I," agreed Tormad. "Filthy blighters."

The crew wandered back the way they had come, the ash muffling even the humans' footsteps, as well as the wagon's wheels. Each step puffed dust into the air. It was not long before the hallway behind them was obscured in a gray haze. Spot sneezed, then put his head down in his paws. Ben and Nigel put their masks back on, to keep the fine particles from getting into their lungs.

"These things are sure coming in handy," Nigel's voice came out in a muffled mumble.

"Yeah, they are," agreed Ben. "Good thinking, bringing them along."

"It was Emily that figured out the bug bombs. After that, we needed a safe way for you and me to breathe. Hence the respirators. Anyway, this whole endeavor has been a group effort; from the sprites, to Emily, to Stephanie and Calliope."

"Well, thank you, to all of you. Spot and I really appreciate you coming to save us. We were in quite a pickle."

They crossed through the now-open grand rotunda. The thick tunnel of webbing was completely gone, turned to ash upon the floor. The stairway down had a new dusting of ash, completely concealing the old footprints from humans and spiders. And, assuming Nigel had not missed it before, the stone of the staircase sported a new crack running through three steps. He wondered what other structural changes the intense fire had wrought.

"Great Spirits," exclaimed Garran. He was pointing to a mound of ash three feet deep to the right of the staircase. "I believe that mound is what remains of the giant spider."

"I think you are correct," said Sonam. He walked around the back side of the mound, bent down, and stood back up, displaying the tip of one of Nigel's arrows. "Here is the felling blow." He handed the tip to Nigel, who inspected the blades briefly. It seemed to be in good condition, so he dropped it in a backpack pocket.

"Never know. Might be needed," Nigel shrugged.

"Sounds like you did some hunting," Ben said to his dad.

"More like surviving as the hunted," corrected Nigel. "That spider was as big as an elephant."

"I am not sure all the hallways will be this clear. We should continue on before any remaining spiders decide to reclaim this space," said Ima. She was eying the various exits and staircases.

"Good idea," said Ben. "I am more than ready to be home. Although, we're not that far from the first doorway I found all those years ago. We would come out in the Upper Peninsula of Michigan, but at least we'd be away from the spiders. For that matter, we're not that far from Quilium, either."

"That is true," said Garran. "But, it would be best to get you back to Calliope by the fastest route."

"I agree, but if we need a fallback plan, I'd rather escape to northern Michigan than take a chance on an unknown planet."

With Ima once again in the lead, they retraced their path from several hours earlier. The entire level seemed to have endured the same blistering fire, for which the group was grateful. That meant no more spiders. No more fighting. At least, until the next level, perhaps.

They reached a wide spiral staircase transcending floors. They needed the next level down. Those hallways lead, eventually, to the doorway for Ben's basement.

With Ben at the front, and Nigel at the back, they were able to navigate the cart and its cargo down the steps. Spot was not too sure about all the bumping and tipping, but as he was still not able to walk, he endured.

"This level has seen the same burning," said Ima. "And more recently. It is hotter than above."

"Too hot for us?" asked Ben.

"I think we will be fine," she replied. Garran nodded his agreement.

"There seems to be very little ash," said Sonam. "I wonder why it is so hot, for having less to burn?"

"Could it be residual heat from the fire above?" asked Garran.

"Well, heat rises," said Ben. "I would expect the fire above us to have heated the next level up, not this level. However, this whole place is made of metal, and metal does conduct heat, so maybe it traveled down."

"More likely, there was, or still is, a fire burning below us," said Nigel.

"That could get uncomfortable for us, then," said Ben. "We'd better keep moving before it turns into an oven."

The ash was indeed less in these hallways. Sparse enough for Ben and Nigel to gratefully remove their respirators. It was hard enough breathing in the oppressive heat without adding the confining masks. Spot was panting, and had lain back down, still weak and sleepy.

Ben's prophecy seemed to be coming true. The further they walked, the hotter it became. It was a gradual increase, but after thirty minutes, Ben had sweated through his shirt, his jacket long since removed and stuffed in his pack.

"I hear something ahead of us," said Garran. "It is a hissing, and crackling."

"Crackling? Like fire?" asked Ben, straining to hear.

"Possibly. But different."

They continued forward with caution. Before long, their pins turned on the lights revealing the end of the current hallway, and the intersection of another, traveling left and right. Even before the lights had activated, however, they could see a glow emanating from both directions.

"I think we're about to catch up to the fire," said Nigel. "And I'm more and more guessing we did not cause it."

"I do not think we should go any closer," said Garran. "It is too hot, and too dry for us to continue. I fear we are in danger of the fire."

"Aye. I no wish ta pet the manx today," added Tormad, with an unusual waver to his usual gruff manner.

"I'm not sure what a manx is," said Ben, "but I'm going to go take a look. You all stay here. I'll see what we're up against."

Leaving the cart behind, Ben hugged the left wall and hurried to the turn. At the corner, he stopped, then carefully poked his head around for a quick glance before pulling back. The group saw him scratch his beard, wipe his brow, then take a second, longer look. He then leaned forward to look down the hallway on his right. Seemingly satisfied, he jogged back over to his team.

"Well, you definitely did not cause the fire," he told them. "I think The City is cleaning house. And we're not getting home by these hallways."

"What's going on?" asked Nigel.

"There is some sort of metal contraption spanning floor to ceiling, wall to wall, spouting flames and charring the entire hallway. There's one in each." He waved from side to side, hall to hall. "We'll need to find another way."

The group reversed course. All of them happy to return to decreasing temperatures, but concerned that their path would be forever thwarted by obstacles.

"Why do you think The City is purging the spiders now?" asked Garran. "Why burn them out, but not us when we wandered around here for years trying to find you, Ben Sullivan?"

"Maybe it's their sheer numbers," supplied Ben. "A few sprites wandering around are allowed, but those spiders were transforming the entire City. Coating walls, covering all the lights and buttons and things. I think we can assume this place has sensors of some sort—maybe more creatures like Poppie—and the spiders would definitely be interfering with how they function. Maybe it reached a point where The City needed to clean out its ports."

"Speaking of Poppie," he continued. "I called for her when I first entered The City, but she never came. I assumed she was too far away to hear me, but now, I'm wondering if she was dealing with all of this."

"We didn't see her either," said Nigel. "Just spiders. Everywhere."

"I hope she's ok. The girls will be extremely upset if anything has happened to her."

They retraced their steps, returning to the wide staircase that had dropped them onto this floor. Instead of climbing back up to look for an alternate route, however, they chose to continue on this level. It was Ben's hope that the floors were laid out in concentric rings, of sorts, and that eventually they would find an intersection leading home. He had his journal out, and was studying the hand-drawn maps of hallways visited. They remained sketchy pieces of a very large puzzle, and only stretched from his doorway to the doorways on Quilium, the Tree Lord's world, and the second portal to Earth, in Michigan's Upper Peninsula. The spider homeworld was on that path as well, of course, but the only mapped return route home was now blocked by flaming contraptions. Time to expand his cartograph.

"I'm hoping that somewhere ahead of us, we will find another intersection. If at all possible, we should head to our immediate right, then right again. If we can do that, we should run into our staircase."

"Let's hope," said Nigel.

The crew set out. Spot sat tall, now, looking much livelier. Ben suspected he was almost ready to leave the cart.

The hallways were once again the quiet tunnels Ben had come to expect in The City. Dark iron floors, smooth to the touch, and walls adorned with architectural filigree: scrollwork and vines, flowerettes and ferns, the occasional unreadable lettering.

The ash lessened, along with the heat. He added a new section to his drawing every time the lights turned on. Before long, he had a string of twenty with no new intersection. There were more doors, though. He did not pause to mark them all on his map, but a few drew his eye like a child to a toy store window.

A wooded landscape with a massive stone monolith in the distance—like Yosemite and El Capitan. Could be a climbing challenge, but definitely a beautiful hike. Assuming no monsters interrupted the day.

A mountain slope with a single path clear of trees; an excellent ski adventure, should the relief's shading represent snow.

An island paradise with beaches, and palm trees, and rippling waves lapping the shore; his mind conjured grass huts, and swimming, and lying on the beach with a special someone, drinks with little umbrellas close at hand.

The City could be his own personal travel agency, were it not for the Tree Lords, and the Slizeg, and the giant praying mantises, and spiders the size of elephants.

Maybe Earth travel was better.

A rotunda presented itself with the next section's illumination. Another room with a huge spiral staircase leading down and up, and branching hallways in five different directions.

"Well, none of these is exactly at a right angle, but this one is close," Ben pointed to an archway on their right. "Or we could try going down."

"I think not," said Kunga, who was looking down the spiral. "The heat radiating from below suggests the fire still consumes that level"

"Right it is, then," said Nigel.

They did not pause, or debate the route. It was a logical choice, given that none of them had been down these halls. They simply, quietly, trundled the wagon down their new path, leaving tracks of human, sprite, and cart in the sporadic patches of ash that sometimes popped up in their path.

The hallway took them on the diagonal, away from their desired goal, but on track to intersect a tunnel leading back to the staircase home. And they knew a hallway existed that ran on an intercept course. They had never explored it, so maybe it curved, but so far, all hallways had been straight, only turning when connected to rotundas. Ben was reasonably confident they would find the necessary hall soon.

Their path continued to have little ash, and no spiders, nor fire breathing boxes. The heat was gone, the iron back to comfortable. The lights lit, revealing no surprises, which, lately, was quite the welcome surprise.

Their pace was considerably slower now. They were exhausted. At least, the humans were. Nigel could not tell about the sprites. Did they tire? Did they sleep? Did they dream? He had a lot of questions for this lot of interesting creatures. One thing was certain; he owed them a huge debt for helping to find his son. He was thinking he might have to come with Ben on his next trip to Quilium and see if he could help restore the balance. If there *was* another trip. It seemed The City had cleared the spiders, but what other surprises were lurking? And would The City tolerate any more visitors? Time would tell.

A light appeared far in the distance; a twinkle of white at the end of the tunnel. It was not like The City's amber illumination. While it was cooler in color, it sparked a warmer feeling, a sigh of relief, and a sense of hope. It was the comforting color of natural daylight.

No one spoke, but their pace quickened. Ben imagined he would finally see what was outside this underground city. He imagined windows overlooking... what? A huge, bustling city? That seemed unlikely with these hallways either deserted or teaming with spiders.

Desolation? Perhaps. But desert? Mountains? Forests? Natural disaster or man-made? What if it was nuclear? What if this entire planet was irradiated, and this entire time they had all been getting exposed? He quickly ruled that one out. Partially because he figured he would feel those effects by now, partially because he thought the sprites would be able to sense it as well, and partially because that fate was too gruesome to consider.

Ben did not get his answer when they reached the light. The window he hoped to see was not looking out over some great vista of a foreign planet. It was in the ceiling. And it was not a window, but a skylight molded into the iron, like a reverse funnel, spewing light instead of draining it.

And under that light, like a stage prop in "A Midsummer Night's Dream," stood a tree, twelve feet tall, with a canopy twenty wide. It was teeming with fruit, which Ben knew to be plums. Could this be the same tree Calliope and Stephanie had found? He did not think so. He got the feeling from their tale that their garden had been on a different level. But the resemblance was there. The tree stood on a mound of grass, and behind it was a rock wall, dripping with water.

There were differences, too. Calliope had mentioned that her garden's light came from a giant crack in the ceiling, like a natural break in the structure of the place had created the sanctuary. This room's light was clearly invited by design. And where the girl's garden had a staircase, this room had only branching hallways; five, including the one the group now stood in. One other important difference between the two garden rooms: with this room, mechanical boxes burned in the archways of each exit, except for the one the team currently occupied.

"They're blocking the other passages," said Ima. "How do we get past?"

"Why are they blocking the passages?" asked Ben. "They're not moving. Not coming in, not leaving. Just sitting there."

He was thinking, and looking closely around the room. And then he saw it; translucent threads stretching from the back of the tree to the ceiling, just at the edge of the skylight. Spiders. But where were they?

"There are spiders in here." He pointed to the webbing.

"Perhaps the flaming mechanisms do not enter because they do not want to harm the tree," suggested Sunam.

"Or perhaps they are afraid of the water," countered Kunga.

"Well, whatever their reason for not entering, maybe they would leave if the spiders were gone," said Ben. "We may have to clear this room for them."

"We could throw in our last cans of bug bombs," suggested Nigel.

"I would really like to not poison the water or the plums," said Ben. "I was hoping for a drink."

"Aye," chimed in Tormad. "We sprites are no poisoned by tha' gas, but it do leave a right foul taste in the air. I'd be glad ta be rid o' it."

"Ok, then. What next?" asked Nigel.

"A repeat of the spider's nest, I think," said Ima.

Garran sighed. "Ima is correct. She and I will flush them out. The rest of you, be ready."

Ima and Garran drifted into the room, their eyes scanning up and around, but finding no quarry. They waved the all clear to the rest of the group, who then spread out around the grassy mound, but well clear of the inflamed archways. The only remaining hiding place was the tree. The canopy would conceal the dark bodies. Plural, of course, because it would have to be the little ones, to hide in the dense branches and foliage of the tree. A large one would not fit. And the smaller ones seemed to always be in packs. How many could the tree hide? A few dozen? A hundred? More? It all depended on how small, really.

Ima made a move to climb the grassy mound. Garran blocked her.

"No, Ima. This time, I go first. You watch my back."

Nigel was positive he saw a smile twitch on the lady's bark this time. Ima gave Garran a slight nod, and let him proceed. He stalked cautiously up the mound, eying the canopy warily, but nothing moved. The dark purple leaves did much to conceal any dark bodies. Spiders could easily be hidden by shadows in the foliage. Garran watched for movement; a leg twitch, a scurry, a pounce. All was still.

But his eyes caught something out of place. A patch of white nestled deep in the tree, near the top, close to the bole. A cotton cloud, a wispy collection of webbing gathered into a ball as large as a human head. And it was pulsating.

"Friends," Garran whispered over his shoulder, "I think we have a dilemma. There is an egg sac."

"I don't think that's much of a dilemma," said Nigel. "Let's cut it down and feed it to the flames before they hatch and eat us."

"What Garran means," supplied Sonam, "is that we sprites only kill in self defense. And babies of any species are usually not a threat. However, this is clearly a unique circumstance."

"At present," continued Kunga, "they are eggs, in a sac. Clearly not a threat."

"Not so much just eggs," said Garran. "The sac is moving. I believe they are hatching and working at getting out."

"Hell's bells people!" growled Nigel, seeing even less of a choice to ponder and more of an imperative. "Spiders can have hundreds of eggs in each sac. We need to get rid of that fast, or we'll be in a worse scenario than when fighting that horde in the hallway. We all remember how that went. Someone needs to climb up, cut that sac loose and toss it into the fire."

"Aye, that's a right nasty piece o' werk, that," said Tormad.

"I'll do it," said Ben. "You've all done enough coming to rescue me."

He dropped his pack and left it by the wagon with Spot. The

blinx watched him curiously. Ben loosened his survival knife in its sheath and stepped up the hill. Garran stayed by his side.

"We still have not ascertained where the mother is," Garran said to him.

"Good point," muttered Ben.

The two reached the trunk and stared up. There was not just one sac, but three. Each one a little higher, and opposite the next. And on the middle one, sat mother. Watching. She was the basketball-sized variety, all black, but for a stripe of off-white on her underbelly. Ben was not sure if the stripe was significant, but on Earth, spiders with unique markings were best avoided. Here? All spiders were best avoided.

"Oh, crap," said Ben. "She is not going to be happy. But we need her to come down before I go up. Because I'm not fighting her in the tree. She definitely has the advantage."

"Perhaps an arrow would be best," suggested Garran. "Sonam? Would you be so kind as to dispatch the mother?"

"Are we sure we cannot coax her down, and maybe take her babies with her?" asked the monk.

"You are welcome to try," said Ben. "I'm sure if you get up close to chat, she will force your hand and make self-defense your only option."

A brown and green blur flew past Ben and Garran, and scrambled straight up the tree.

"Spot!" Ben cried, but the creature was already weaving through the boughs.

Spot navigated like a fish swimming through the coral. He dodged twigs and slipped around branches with grace and ease. The mother spider watched him, jittering around her sacs, tempted to attack, yet fearful of leaving her brood. As Spot came closer, not slowing his ascent, but revolving around the trunk, looking to keep her moving, she sank into a telltale crouch, announcing a pending attack.

"Sonam, please!" cried Ben. "Shoot now!"

The monk released his arrow, just as the spider launched. Spot dropped from his branch as if stepping off a bridge, appendages tucked in tight so as not to snag as he fell through the canopy. Sonam's arrow led the spider's trajectory perfectly, and skewered her as she passed through where Spot had been. She flipped and bounced through the branches, an inert bundle in a game of Kerplunk.

Spot popped into view, clearing the foliage briefly, before reaching out an arm to grasp the lowest branch, swing neatly around, and sit like a bird. Mother spider kerplunked past Spot, who once again dropped, swung like a monkey, kicked out and sent the dead spider flying into a flaming doorway to his left. The spider was engulfed immediately.

"Well, that was dramatic," said Nigel.

"Yes, well... Spot, glad to see you're feeling better," Ben said to his friend. "I guess it's my turn to take care of the eggs."

Spot climbed with him, with obvious patience for his larger, slow-climbing human friend. Ben made it to the first egg sac with little effort, even while scanning the branches, wary of hidden companions to the spider they had just dispatched. None emerged. He set to, carefully slicing the egg sac away from the trunk of the tree as Spot observed; a silent supervisor assuring that work progressed with the necessary efficiency and skill.

Ben was equally aware that a slip of his knife could open this slowly undulating sac and release hundreds of ravenous miniatures. The fates only knew what kept the spawn contained. Ben assumed they were too young, too newly born and fragile to eat their way through the silk. But how fragile? How newly born? Best not to linger.

The last strands of adhesive split from the bark. Ben held the first sac free, admitting to himself that he was a bit repulsed, a bit fearful of the moving mass. Spot, however, had no such afflictions. He snatched the sac and repeated his plunge, grab, swing, and throw maneuver to toss the offending silken pouch into the same oven. It melted and shriveled, and then there was popping, like peas exploding in a microwave. It was over in an instant, and the flames concealed any carnage, but the sounds were gruesome.

Spot was immediately back at Ben's side, giving no further thought to his deeds, ready to move on to the next.

"Right you are Spot. I suppose," Ben said to his companion. "Best to keep moving. Get the job done."

They moved up a few branches to the next. Ben sliced, and freed the prize. Spot snatched and performed acrobatics. Another task completed. One remained.

As Ben began separating the final puffball from the tree, he mused aloud.

"In the movies, this is where things always go wrong. The heroes successfully pass the first few tasks, and the audience thinks they are home free, everyone breathes a sigh of relief, and then something goes terribly wrong. The heroes are attacked, or hurt, or maimed. Sometimes, they even lose one of their party. Let's not be the cliché, Spot."

He cleared the sac. Spot again relieved him of the tacky bag, and consigned it to a fiery end, as he had its siblings. No surprise mishaps. No hidden traps. No cliché story twist. Just a clear room.

Ben and Spot exited the tree, to rejoin their friends, who had remained stationed around the room, wary of returning spiders, or advancing fire engines, or anything unexpected. No one was quite ready to let down their guard.

"Well, what do we do now?" asked Nigel.

"I'm not sure," said Ben. "I had hoped the removal of the spiders would be enough to clear those flaming contraptions, but they look unsatisfied. Or stuck. Or something. Maybe they're waiting for a sensor to tell them this room has been cleared. Maybe, as long as there's movement, the machines will guard the archways."

"Should we go back the way we came, for a bit? Wait in the hallway and see if they leave then?" asked Nigel.

"Garran? You've been in these halls longer than most. What do you think?"

"I may have spent more time here, Ben Sullivan, but you and Calliope have discovered things we never have. The pins. Poppy. But, I believe your guess is a sound one. Chathair Doras obviously sensed the spiders in here. If we leave, perhaps it will register this room as clear of any creatures, and call the machines away."

"Afore we exit this fine room," butted in Tormad, "I'll be needin' a refresher in tha' crisp lookin' water."

The bristlecone pine set his axe against the plum tree, then walked over to the stone wall glistening with liquid. He stepped into a puddle and put both hands against the rock, letting water stream over his knobby fingers.

"Ah! Now tha' be a right proper drink. Brothers, and sister, this here'll put the green back in yer boughs."

The other sprites joined their ancient friend, soaking up the mineral infused water through hands and feet. Spot drank for a minute from the puddles, while Ben and Nigel examined the plums, picking a few for their packs, and eating one or two after careful inspection. The girls had been correct, they looked like plums, and tasted like plums. Must be plums.

After the sprites had declared unanimous rejuvenation, the group retreated in usual alignment; Spot now by Ben's side, rather than in the cart. They shuffled from the room, and returned to the hallway that had led them there.

After watching for several minutes, with no movement from the flames, the group settled in for a break. Nigel pulled out a snack bar. Ben rummaged through his own stash and found a bag of peanuts.

The sprites, as comfortable standing as sitting, chose to remain on guard. Sonam and Kunga returned further up the hall, making sure no unwelcome visitors approached from behind, while Garran and Ima kept a watch on the garden room.

"I do no suppose ya have a spot o' coffee on ye?" Tormad whispered to Ben.

"Sorry, Tormad," Ben chuckled. "I have a few packets of instant left, but I don't think I should be brewing coffee right now. We may have to move quickly."

"Aye, tha' be a shame," said the bristlecone sprite.

"But the second we get home, I'll brew you a fresh pot," he assured the sprite.

"Well, let's be ta gettin' ye home, then."

"Amen to that, my friend." Ben said.

They waited for some time, with no changes. Nigel was glad for the rest period, but now he was ready to move on. He was about to suggest they travel back to the staircase, go back up, then try for another route, when Sonam came back to the group.

"Something approaches."

"Spiders?" asked Nigel.

"No. This sounds mechanical in nature."

"Maybe Poppie," suggested Ben.

"It very well may be," said Sonam. "But we have been caught unawares before. I suggest caution, and vigilance. It could also be another of those fiery beasts."

The team made ready. Ima and Garran abandoned their surveillance of the room and joined the defensive line. Tormad hefted his axe, while the willow sprites had bows ready to draw. Ben had his machete out, while Nigel hefted his own bow.

"That's a nice bow, dad," whispered Ben. "Did you just get that?"

"Just this morning, as a matter of fact. And it shoots like a dream. I'll be taking this out on a real hunt, of something I can eat."

"What? You don't find spider tasty?" Ben quipped.

They could all hear the approaching mystery machine now. And it most definitely was a machine. It was emitting a whirring and clicking that Ben found all too familiar.

"It's Poppie," he said.

A smile creased his face, and he let out the breath he had not realized he had been holding. A few seconds later, the fairy floated into view. She seemed just as healthy as ever. Her silvery form maintained its mirror-like shine, and her copper face still sported that saucy smile. Of course, Ben was sure her mouth was permanently cast in that shape, but it was nice to see she had not been damaged.

"Poppie! We are so glad to see you. And so glad you are all right. We were worried the spiders had eaten you," Ben greeted the sprite.

"Pop, pop." The sprite popped to the negative.

Ben assumed that meant the spiders had not eaten her. Obviously.

"Poppie, can you help us get past these fire breathing machines that are blocking the other halls? We are trying to go home."

"Pop."

"Thank you," Ben said.

The mechanical pixie fluttered into the garden room. The others followed her in. Ben assumed she would fly over to the flaming machines. Instead, her furiously pumping wings lifted her to the ceiling. She circled once, and aligned herself with a silver art deco inlaid line pattern in the ceiling. She flew so close that her antennae touched that line; and where they touched, an electric blue glow blossomed. She held that connection for only a few seconds, then drifted back down to hover in front of Ben and the group.

And they waited.

"Poppie, is something supposed to be happening?" asked Ben.

"Pop."

"Did you tell those machines to leave?"

"Pop."

"Do you think they will listen?"

"Pop."

"Ok. We'll wait," said Ben.

He looked at the group and shrugged. He was not sure how long they should wait, but Poppie seemed sure the machines would leave, so it was only right to give her some time.

Before Ben could suggest they all relax a bit, the flames in each archway dimmed, and then extinguished. The torch contraptions were revealed to be a matrix of pipes. Pipes which, now, were folding back in on themselves; compressing, and contorting, even as the contraptions as a whole were turning around and receding down their respective hallways.

"You did it, Poppie!" exclaimed Ben. "Not that I doubted you would, of course." He gave her a conspiratorial grin.

"Pop."

"Excellent. Can we go home now?" suggested Nigel.

"Pop, pop."

"No?" Ben was surprised, confused. "Why not?"

In response, the pixie flew to the hallway opposite the one Ben would have chosen. One that led them away from the path home, if her popping was an indication.

"You want us to go somewhere else in The City?" asked Ima.

"Pop."

"But why?" asked Ben.

"Pop."

Ben was a bit frustrated with the pixie's binary responses. "Is it too dangerous for us to go home?"

"Pop, pop."

"Do you want us to do something in another part of The City?" chimed in Nigel.

"Pop."

"Poppie, we really want to get home to Calliope and Stephanie," said Ben, knowing that the pixie would remember the girls and hopefully want to see them as well.

"Pop!"

She let out an exceptionally loud response, then twirled twice in the air, and pointed down the tunnel. The action clicked in Ben's mind. He suddenly had a clue as to what Poppie was trying to tell them, and his heart sank.

"Poppie, are Calliope and Stephanie down that hallway?" Ben asked her.

"Pop!"

"Damn!" he swore, and looked at his dad.

"I swear, Ben, we left the girls with Emily back home. With explicit instructions to under no circumstances follow us in," Nigel defended himself.

"Dad, I believe you. Something else must have gone wrong. But we need to move."

"Absolutely," Nigel agreed.

"Unquestionably," echoed Garran.

"Unreservedly," said Ima.

Tormad, Sonam, and Kunga agreed in unison.

The team set out at a jog down the hallway. Ben's mind was racing through scenarios that would have led the girls into The City. He quickly gave up. He knew that was wasted energy. Whatever happened, happened. The point now was getting to the girls to figure out if they were injured, or in trouble. He mentally checked his first aid kit, noting what he had used on Spot, and what he had left. Not that he could do much for spider bites except swab with disinfectant and throw on a band aid, but they could have other scrapes and cuts from running around in here. His frustration mounted as the hallway stretched on.

Twenty minutes of jogging, with a lot of huffing and puffing coming from Ben and Nigel, and they reached another room skewered by the expected central spiral staircase. This place was certainly predictable.

What was not predictable, however, was Poppie's next course of action. Ben had assumed they would continue down a side corridor, or even go up. But Poppie was going down. Down would take them to a level Calliope and Stephanie had never been. He was surprised they would go there. Obviously, spiders or circumstances had forced them.

"The girls are down a level?" asked Ben.

There was a bit of a pause before Poppie replied. "Pop, pop."

No? thought Ben.

"But you are leading us to them?" he asked.

"Pop."

"Are they down several levels?" asked Nigel.

"Pop."

The human fathers looked at each other, worry clear on both faces.

"How far down?" asked Ben.

Poppie spiraled from her hovering height of six feet, all the way to the floor, where she sat for a second before rising again.

"The bottom?" asked Nigel, incredulous.

"Pop."

"Why, in God's name, would they go all the way to the basement?" Ben asked no one in particular.

Poppie did not wait for them to discuss more. She started her swirling descent down the stairs, assuming the rest would follow. Which, of course, they did, without hesitation.

A Family United

D ad, Grandpa!" Calliope exclaimed, and ran to hug them both.

"Easy, Calli," Nigel said, clearly out of wind. "Hug your dad first. I need to sit down." He disengaged from his granddaughter, dropped his pack and slid down the nearest wall, taking a seat. "Whew. These old bones have not seen this much exercise in years. My thighs are going to be sore tomorrow. We must have done a thousand stairs."

"Two thousand six hundred and twenty," Stephanie said. "Assuming you were on the same level as the door home. I did the math."

"Oh, well, my legs concur with your math."

"What in the world are you doing in here?" Ben pushed back from his daughter, to look her in the eye. "It was foolish for you to come in."

"That was partially my fault," Emily stepped up, and Ben noticed her for the first time. "I just opened the door to put more supplies inside for Nigel and the gang, but a spider was waiting. He snatched me and pulled me through. The girls came in and rescued me, just before the spider was about to sink his fangs in." She looked at the girls proudly.

"We couldn't just leave her, Mr. Sullivan," Stephanie said, a pleading tone to her voice.

A gasp and an "Oh my goodness, Dad! Is this Spot?" came from

Calliope, and the conversation turned. Stephanie joined her friend to kneel on the floor and greet the Blinx.

"Hello, Spot," Stephanie said. "I don't know if you remember us, but earlier this summer, you saved us from the sprites, who were kidnapping us. Even though, as it turns out, they are really nice and we probably didn't need saving. Still, it was very nice of you."

The Blinx just blinked.

"Can we pet him, Dad?"

"Sure. He likes his chin scratched, just behind the jaw," said Ben. He had a feeling that Spot and the girls were going to become good friends.

"How did Spot get here, Dad?" asked Calliope.

"That is a long story, Calli. And I especially want to hear your story, but there will be time for everyone to tell their tale after we make it home. Can we go home now?" he asked Poppie.

"Pop, pop."

"No? Why no, still?"

"We set off a whole bunch of Cookers to clean The City of spiders," informed Calliope. "We saved Poppie, and she brought us here, then turned on the Cookers, and sent them up the elevator."

"Elevator? There's an elevator!?" perked up Nigel. "Then why the devil did I just climb down two-thousand and several hundred bloody steps!"

"Two-thousand six-hundred and twenty," said Stephanie.

"Yeah! That many!"

"Well, it's not a real elevator, as such," clarified Emily.

Calliope explained about the Cookers, and the shaft they crawled up, and that they were waiting for the Cookers to return, meaning The City was clean, and they were safe to go home.

"Cookers eh?" Ben chuckled at the name. "I guess that name fits. Ok, then. We wait," said Ben.

"Have you discovered the purpose of this room?" Garran had

been looking curiously at the boxy metal machines, with their gears and levers and vacuum tubes and diodes.

"I think we're in the control center, Twig," Emily greeted Garran in her usual manner. "These look like crazy mainframe computers, or something. Kind of steampunk, if you ask me."

That perked up Ben's interest. He strode over to the first row of boxes. The rest of the group followed. Calliope and Stephanie walked with Spot, reaching down to scratch or pet him frequently. Spot did not seem to mind the extra attention.

As they wandered around the large room, the group began to spread out a bit. Ben took the opportunity to walk next to Emily, although he suddenly found an alarming lack of words. He stuck with flashing her a smile, which then seemed awkward and out of place, given their current predicament. Was that sweat he felt on his brow? He quickly turned his attention back to the machines.

They passed row after row of the steel boxes. Things were whirring inside, and ticking, and clacking, and ratcheting. Ben could not imagine what these contraptions could be doing, but they sure were busy doing it.

They reached the wall opposite the staircase and the girls showed them the elevator. It was silent; nothing going up or down, so they continued on, rounding the corner and past the wall where Emily indicated the Cookers had been lined up. It was then that a mini dirigible came into view, dusting and preening around the vacuum tubes and gears.

"Holy cow, what is that thing!" Ben exclaimed, drawing his machete. Spot crouched, and the sprites all brandished their weapons, ready for another battle.

"Whoa, whoa, whoa!" cried Calliope, stepping in front of the group and holding up her hands. "That's Eggy. He's just a cleaner. He belongs to The City."

"Eggy? A cleaner?" asked Nigel. "I think we missed part of your story."

"Yes, yes," said Calliope. "We should probably back all the way up to following Emily through."

Calliope, Stephanie and Emily spent the next several minutes relaying their adventures. They recounted the finding of Eggy and Clare, the discovery of the elevator, the rescue of Poppie, and how they had been forced to retreat at all stages, leaving the basement as their only escape. In return, Ben recounted his adventures, from capture, then delivery to the spider world, Spot's rescue of him, their escape outside Spider Mountain, their encounter and interactions with the Mantises, as well as Ben's pinecone grenades. He showed them the few he had left in his pack.

Nigel and the sprites gave a brief review of their adventures, sparing the gory details. However, their tale gave a much more dire picture of the spider infestation. Everyone wished the Cookers well on their job of purging The City. With the size of the building, and the prolific nature of the eight-legged monsters, missing even one could mean another invasion. Time would tell if the extermination was a success. For now, all the humans and sprites could do was wait.

Attention turned back to watching Eggy do his domestic chores. Ben was fascinated by the discovery of the different dirigibles. He took a tour up and down the aisles of mainframes looking for Ollie. Clare was not too far behind Eggy, and the girls spent a minute letting the lankier airship know they were glad to see it back to good health. Clare gave no reaction that it heeded their good tidings, however. It remained focused on its job.

Ben eventually found Ollie. The hexapod was on his continuing mission of crack repair, this time bonding a corner of a mainframe, a dozen feet up. Ben had his notebook out, making notes and drawings. Eggy and Clare had already been immortalized in his memoirs. Now Ollie had his place.

As Ben sketched and scribbled, something skittered past his feet and he jumped. His first instinct told him it was a mouse. But he had never seen a mouse in The City, so his second thought was, *spider!* The Cookers had missed this level, not surprisingly, since it was full of ancient machinery. The spiders had infiltrated all the way down here, and not been noticed.

"Everyone! I think I just saw a spider down here," he called to the crew.

Footsteps clattered from all directions. Everyone had wandered off, gazing at gizmos and thingamabobs, trying to get some clue as to what this place was about. But they all crowded around Ben now. Even Poppie.

"Where?" asked Garran, the first to reach him.

"I think it crawled into that hole in the bottom of this mainframe." He pointed to an opening, about an inch and a half square at the base.

Poppie gave a "pop, pop."

"No? You don't think it went in there? But I saw it," Ben asserted.

"Pop." And after a pause, "Pop, pop."

"Yes, then no?" Calliope was confused, too. "Are you saying yes, he saw it, but no it didn't go in there?"

"Pop, pop."

"Perhaps she is suggesting it is not a spider?" commented Ima.

"Pop."

"Ah, whew. Well, how can she be sure?" asked Ben.

In response, Poppie held up her little copper hands, in a gesture to wait, mimicking Calliope's actions from earlier. She then twirled around and flew across the aisle to a different mainframe. She hovered next to a bank of what looked like giant spark plugs with a fan of copper coils attached. Unceremoniously, Poppie yanked one of the coils free. Immediately, an alarm clock beeping emanated from the unit, and a red diode began flashing from the end of the spark plug.

"Oh, my," said Nigel. "That doesn't seem good."

"Pop, pop," came the pixie's response.

She pointed back to the hole where Ben had seen the mysterious creature. A second later, something rolled out that was infinitely more interesting than a spider. Another robot. A small one. The size of a mouse, or a spider, but square-ish in body, this one did not hover or fly, it walked on four stumpy legs, somewhat projecting like a spider's might, from the side of its body. For feet, it had little metallic discs. It skittered, rather than walked, across the floor, quickly, but inefficiently. Ben wondered at the design, when compared with Poppie's complex watch-like mechanisms.

"Awe, it's kind of cute," said Calliope.

"You would think that," said Stephanie. "It reminds me of a big beetle. Yuck."

"We could call him Beetle!" said Calliope.

"Oh, no, no, no," said Emily. "If you're going to name him after a Beatle, we'll call him Ringo."

"Who?" said Calliope.

"Oh my goodness, Ben!" Emily turned to Calliope's father. "You have failed as a musical educator. Shameful."

Ben had the good grace not to roll his eyes. "Not everyone worships The Beatles, ya know."

Emily gasped in exaggerated affront. "Take that back," she whispered in mock hurt.

"I mean, I like most of their music," he backtracked. "But if stranded on a desert island, I would go for something else."

"Oh really? Like what?"

"Well..." He thought for a bit, discarding a few bands that quickly popped into his head, not settling on one in particular. "I don't know. I'll have to think about it when we are not... well... here."

"Hmmm. Fine," she said with an air of "this conversation is not over."

Throughout their band banter, Ringo had made it to the alerting metal box. Surprisingly, the critter began walking up the outside. Its little metal feet were sticking to the smooth metal, and Ringo was navigating cogs, levers, and tubes as easily as walking across the floor. Ben guessed its feet were magnets.

When it reached the disconnected coil, it did a surprising thing. It ate it. With a *snap*, and *sproing*, Ringo split itself down the middle, opened up to a hinge on its backside, then clamped shut around the still-connected end of the copper coil; at which point, Ringo proceeded to chew the free end of copper into itself like an over-exuberant pencil sharpener grinding away at a writing implement.

"That did not seem helpful." Nigel's right eyebrow quirked upwards.

"Indeed," agreed Sonam.

"Pop," countered Poppie.

With a quarter of the copper consumed, Ringo began emitting a now-familiar electric-blue glow through fine lines which decorated its body. Ben found the patterning somewhat resembled a circuit board, and somewhat resembled a Lemarchand's Box from the '80's movie Hellraiser. Ben preferred not to dwell on that latter resemblance.

As the last of the copper noodle disappeared into Ringo, the tiny robot sat, and hummed, and the blue glow grew brighter. A static white noise slowly percolated from it, and it began to rise. But not on its legs. It was being lifted away from the metal chassis of the mainframe by a new copper wire emerging from underneath. It seemed Ringo was rebuilding.

"Whoa," said Emily. "How in the world is he doing that?"

"Ah, it appears to be a similar device to that which builds doorways," commented Garran. "We found larger cubes—much in shape like this Ringo—at the base of an unmarked doorway. When we detached them and planted them in that tunnel on your world, they spent over two sun-risings emitting a similar blue light, which leached metals from the surrounding soil and built the portal we use today."

"Incredible," said Nigel. "So much cleaner than the digging, smelting and extruding we do to make metals. This technology alone would be worth a fortune, and save the environment along the way."

"Easy, dad," said Ben. "We can't just bring this tech back. First off, we don't understand it. Secondly, we can't explain where we got it."

"I know, I know. I'm just thinking of the possibilities."

They all watched Ringo recreate the copper coil. When it reached the end of the giant spark plug, its feet stuck tight, Ringo sat over the hole, and completed the connection. The alarm ceased, and the diode stopped flashing. Ringo stood up, walked his way down the box, across the floor, and back into the little hole Ben had seen him enter earlier.

"Busy little guy," said Emily. "He didn't even stop to admire his work."

"Pop."

"So, what do we do now?" asked Calliope.

"Kunga and I found another hallway towards the back of this room. We were tempted to explore down there when we heard Ben's call."

Ben finished sketching Ringo, and snapped his notebook shut. "I'm game. This place is incredible."

"Ach. Dead metal an' stone. No plants. No dirt. No water, " said Tormad. "Ye can keep it. I'm fer home. I'm needin' a cool mountain breeze an' icy glacial water, brimmin' with nourishment."

"Soon, my friend. Soon," said Ima. "I think we are all a bit homesick. But for now, we must wait for those Cookers to finish their job and vacate the hallways. We may as well learn a bit more about this place, in the meantime."

The other sprites nodded, or shrugged. They set out as a group, with Poppie leading the way.

The hallway lay at the back corner of the mainframe room. It was rougher than the hallways of the upper levels. Not cave rough, like a natural formation, but not the smoothly refined, artistic iron they were used to seeing. This tunnel was carved stone; smooth, to be sure, with no tool marks or jutting edges, but not polished or embellished with decorations. It was ten feet wide, and the walls rose another ten before arching over to the other side. Certainly overkill for a group of humans and sprites to traverse. Ben imagined machines as big as large SUVs driving through with no trouble. He thought of the Cookers, and wondered what this tunnel was actually built to accommodate. Whatever it was, he hoped it did not come through while they were using the tunnel.

They emerged from the other end into another cavern, the lights just warming up to their presence. They stood for a minute, taking in the view, for it was extraordinary. They were on a landing, thirty yards deep, and a hundred long. A railing guarded the edge, broken to the left and to the right by two staircases leading down. The lighting continued to activate down this much, much larger cavern, glowing far into the distance, and revealing massive objects on the floor beneath them. Calliope and Stephanie, ever rushing to the curious, sprinted to the railing.

"Whoa!" exclaimed Calliope, looking down. "Dad, check this out."

Ben and the others joined her. Forty feet below, they saw that the objects were built into the floor, in three neat rows. All identical. All circular, black metal cylinders about twenty-five feet tall, and thirty feet in diameter, with all manner of copper pipes, tubes and wires sprouting from their tops, like shiny, shaggy toupees. A humming, as of a giant nest of electric bees, came from each device.

"Good lord," said Ben. "Do you know what these are?"

"Generators," Nigel answered his son. "They are all generators."

"There must be a hundred of them." Ben was gazing down the long cavern, where the lines of giant machines dwindled, but their end could not be seen."

"I'm thinking more like two hundred, or more," said Nigel. "That's a lot of power."

"Well, there would have to be, to power a place as big as this, with all these doors, plus the city outside. Assuming the other buildings don't power themselves. They all seem to have moving parts, doing some sort of work," said Emily.

"City outside?" Ben turned to her, his mouth agape. "You saw outside?"

"Oh, yeah," said Calliope. "When we were on the top floor, it was all windows overlooking a huge city of machine buildings. Not a living creature in sight. Just all sorts of weird mechanical pistons and gears and contraptions attached to what looked like buildings, along sort of streets, but not streets. It was really weird."

"Kind of creepy," added Stephanie, nodding her head.

"That, I gotta see," said Ben. "Think we can take that elevator thingy up while the Cookers are busy?"

"No way," said Emily. "You don't want to be going up while those things are coming down. They'd crush you. Best to wait till they get back. And then, we should go home, not wander around more in this place."

"But the spiders should be gone now," said Ben, almost pleading.

"Yeah, I'm with dad," said Calliope. "I could show him real quick. Up, then down to our level in the elevator. Then we go home."

"Ben, I think Emily is right," chimed-in Nigel. "We're all tired. And covered in spider guts. We need to get home, lock all the doors, and sleep for about a week."

"An' have a coffee," Tormad added.

"I would love a shower," said Stephanie.

Emily could see Ben wavering, so she put a final nail in the argument. "And don't forget that Lord Oakenpuss is still out there. What do you think he'll do when he finds his pet spiders are gone?"

"Well, I'm hoping he thinks I'm dead and gone, too," said Ben. "And I'm hoping he never sees us again, and we never see him. I know I'll be staying far away from his doorway."

"Still. Maybe it's best to leave this place quiet for a while," she finished her argument.

"Pop, pop, pop, pop." Poppie let out an alert. She was pointing back down the hallway.

"I think something's coming," said Stephanie.

That put everyone on alert. Thoughts of home were set aside, replaced with images of Tree Lords having found them. Nigel's team fell into formation. Ben took Nigel's spot behind Ima and Garran, Emily and the girls went behind him, with Tormad at their side, then Nigel covered from behind. Sonam and Kunga brought up the rear, their bows already trained ahead of the group.

They reached the mainframe room and heard the normal buzzing and clicking and whirring of the machines. Eggy was floating and dusting around the end of the sixth row, not seemingly concerned about anything other than cleaning. Poppie flew straight down the outer wall to the far corner, where she hovered for a few seconds, then did a pirouette mid-air, and let out more excited pops.

"I think she's saying the Cookers are back," said Stephanie.

"Thank God," said Emily.

Everyone joined the pixie, then relaxed from their battle-readiness. The fiery exterminators had returned in barrel form and were rolling out of the elevator in intervals, aligning themselves along the wall; rows of blocky tin soldiers, awaiting their next call to duty.

"Twenty-eight," said Stephanie. "We're missing eight."

On cue, two more Cookers rolled out of the elevator, like giant Pez candies ejecting from their dispenser.

"Twenty-nine, thirty," counted Stephanie.

The group waited patiently for the stragglers. Two more came a minute later. The next two, five minutes after that. The final two took another fifteen.

"Well, the band is back together," said Emily.

"Ollie and the Cookers," chuckled Calliope.

"Seems like they were working in pairs on each floor," said Emily. "We were wondering how they were going to tackle the work."

"Think it's safe to use the elevator now?" asked Nigel. "I don't relish having to walk *up* two-thousand stairs."

Emily shrugged, but Poppie "popped" an affirmative, so the group moved past the sleeping flame throwers to stand around the small lift in the corner.

"What do we do now?" asked Ben.

"We push one of the flowers," said Emily, pointing to the designs molded into the metal track.

"Actually, down here, the buttons are inside a bunch of nested diamond shapes," said Stephanie.

"Sort of art deco," Ben noted as he looked closer at the patterns. "But which one do we want?"

"We think there are one hundred and forty-four floors, with an elevator opening every twelve," supplied Stephanie. "And when we were climbing down from the one hundred and forty-fourth floor, we were trying to hit the one hundred and thirty-first. That would be one floor above the floor our door is on. But that's the floor we always walk up to when we come here. So, we can either take the elevator up to floor one hundred and thirty-two, then walk down a flight, or take it to floor one hundred and twenty, and walk up eleven flights."

"That's a no-brainer," said Nigel. "We're going to one hundred and thirty-two."

They split off in pairs. Garran and Ima would go up first, then Emily and Stephanie, followed by Ben and Calliope, Nigel and Spot.

Ben was going to go with Spot, but Nigel insisted on a father-daughter pairing. Then Tormad, Sonam, and Kunga would squeeze in for the final run. At fifteen minutes per trip, it was going to take over an hour to get everyone up, but that was still shorter, and easier, than walking up one hundred and thirty-one flights of stairs. The sprites started off.

While they waited, Ben took the opportunity to pull Emily aside.

"Emily, I just wanted to say how sorry I am that you got pulled into *another* insanely dangerous situation with this place. I know you warned me not to come back here. I'm sorry."

"Yeah, you definitely owe me, Sullivan. You're racking up quite the list of I.O.U.s with me."

"Well, when we get home, and have a day or two to rest, how about I take you out for dinner? Someplace nice. You choose."

"Dinner?" she said in mock disapproval. "You think taking me to dinner is payback for almost being eaten by giant spiders? Mister, you'll need to throw in dessert. And you better believe you'll be wearing your dancing shoes." She poked him in the chest to emphasize her point. "That might—just might—be a start."

"Dancing?" Ben's uncomfortableness was evident in his face. "Can't we do something easier? Like skydiving? Or lion taming?"

"Dancing." Her tone indicated there was no negotiating.

As they returned to the group, Ben muttered, "I think I'd rather visit the spiders."

—20—

Custodian 452

Beneath Platform 18 of Generator Room 1, a warning light was blinking. It had started some time ago in response to the entire complement of thermal sanitation units being mobilized. In such circumstances, protocols dictated a complete maintenance inspection and threat assessment of the Planetary Bridge Terminal, and all power plants. For that purpose, Custodian 452 was activated.

An ungainly stunted snowman, composed of two stacked copper tubs, each studded with nickel arms, sat on iron castors. Custodian 452 whirred and hummed and let the friction of gears in his too-long-dormant servo motors heat up his cold copper carcass. Time did not rule him as it did biological units, but he knew it had been ages since he had performed his duties. His castors presented rust. The lubricants in his bearings had dried up or drained away. Twisting his crown section elicited an insufferable screeching, with a reverberation and jittering that set his sensors on edge. The ball joints in his many arms were all but frozen in place.

He was dust-free, at least. Thankfully, the cleaning drones appeared to be keeping up on their tasks of polishing and sweeping. It seemed, therefore, that his first order of business would be a visit to the greasing chamber. He had his own private room. Just around the corner. Little more than a cavity in the wall, but his alone. He was important, after all. Head Custodian for Generator Room 1. He could not be expected to leave his post for greasing. Unthinkable.

He rolled heavily out of his docking bay, castors squealing in distress. The vibrations sent shivers through his gear train.

Oh, he absolutely craved his greasing unit. It sported twenty-six omni-directional F39L General Lubricant injection nozzles which delivered a refreshing splot to several key rotational sprockets and pivot points. Not to mention his rusting castors. And he would not mind a fine sheen of S22L across all internal gears and drive chains. That unbearable itch of bare metal on metal grew worse as frictional heat increased unabated. Unacceptable for one of his stature. But for that treatment, he would have to travel to Maintenance Building 18, which did mean leaving his post. And that would have to wait until the warning light was addressed.

He really must remember to transmit a request for the creation of a mobile lubrication drone. Yes. That was a fine engineering addition. He set aside processor 7 to work asynchronously on developing an initial draft schematic for just such a drone. Requests had a much higher probability of production approval when accompanied by schematics. Not to mention, if his schematic was chosen, so was the *name* on his schematic. What an honor that would be. A drone of his design, sporting for all time a name of his choosing. He would certainly be more creative than the maintenance unit that had named him. Maintenance Unit 6 was the culprit. Mechanical units in those days lacked an imagination algorithm.

He pondered names for his new drone design while he rolled to the lubrication chamber. *S22L Hovering Lubrication and Maintenance Unit? Hmmm. A very practical name, but limiting in lubricant.* His design would allow for lubrication updates. Aeronautic Multi-lubricant Delivery Unit? Oh, much better. He sent the data to processor 7 for addition to the schematic, and turned his full attention to his surroundings. He had reached his greasing chamber.

He found it exactly as he had left it, nozzles already set to his own lubrication inlet levels. He rolled neatly into place. The pressure plate beneath the floor activated precisely 25 centichrons after entry. Alas, whereas the F39L General Lubricant *should* have begun flowing, nothing happened. Lubricants did not splot as expected. Perhaps he was dormant longer than he had presumed. He had not interfaced with the command console as of yet to check the temporal reading. Perhaps the lubricant nozzles were clogged with dried grease plugs. F39L did have a moisture life of only 67.29 megachrons.

He would have to summon a special cleaning drone to fix the greasing unit. Really! How was a Head Custodian—*THE* Head Custodian—supposed to perform his duties during such an inconvenience.

If Custodial Units could groan, then 452 surely would have let out at least a weighty sigh of frustration. As it was, he merely rolled himself out of his personal greasing chamber, and back over to his docking bay, dead center of the command and control ring for Generator Room 1, where he could summon a Cleaning Cricket to ream out the grease tubes, and possibly a Tube Worm to crawl deep inside, should the obstructions be deeper.

While he waited for the cricket, he verified that the thermal units had not yet returned. That was good. And bad. Good that Custodian 452 still had time for that lubricant injection, should the cricket be quick. Bad that there had been a need for so many thermal units, and that they were still scouring the Bridge Terminal. It put Custodian 452 in mind of that biological incursion of megachron 4031. *That* had caused quite a lot of damage. He hoped this would not be similar.

The Cleaning Cricket arrived. It was a small drone, with an aluminum chassis, etched with surprisingly detailed scrollwork and decoration. Custodian 452 wondered about that. *He* was not etched with such decorations. He wondered at their purpose. Why would drones need such etchings? Perhaps it was merely a gift of the creators, to make less significant units feel more important? No matter. It surely must weaken the chassis. He was glad to not have etchings.

About the size of a large insect—hence its name—the Cleaning Cricket had four legs, each double-jointed with gears at the segments, allowing the unit to lever its appendages in any direction independently. Its face consisted of a very bright white light emitting diode below a smaller optical lens. The devices worked in tandem to analyze ports and determine cleaning requirements. On its head, were two extendable, stiff wires which it inserted into ejection tubes to dig out frozen grease plugs. It was very efficient and speedy for such a small drone. Custodian 452 sent it on its way. Anticipation of relief almost made his gears tremble with delight.

Precisely 14.330 chrons later, the cricket reported successful completion. It identified twenty-six ejection ports sealed with dehydrated F39L General Lubricant, to depths ranging from 1.25 to 3.61 standard units. Custodian 452 recalled the chemical specification list for F39L, calculated the dehydration coefficients, and came up with an estimate. Between 230 and 252 megachrons had passed since he had last used the grease unit. Not terribly long. But a greasing was definitely overdue.

He squeaked and squealed, most embarrassingly, across the glossy iron floor, towards the open chamber and its welcoming twenty-six multi-jointed flexible hoses just waiting to provide slippery satisfaction. Custodian 452 was not disappointed. F39L flowed freely. The itch disappeared. The sticking gears unstuck. He rotated his crown section one hundred percent in a negative arc while rotating his base section one hundred percent in a positive. He reveled in the smooth, almost soundless operation. Ah, the fluidity of movement regained. An electrostatic shiver ran across his chassis. Pure lubricant bliss. Now, he was prepared to handle the rigors of his duties.

It was then that Custodian 452 heard sounds above him.

Something... Some *things* were moving around on Platform 18! And from the sound, they were *biological* somethings! Now that was simply not done. And unacceptable! The thermal sanitization units had unsuccessfully sanitized the entire Planetary Bridge Terminal. That was highly irregular of them. And inconvenient. Regulations were very clear. No biological units were allowed into the Bridge Control Chamber, nor Generator Room 1. These levels were strictly off limits.

Now Custodian 452 would have to enact Protocol 38. And he really did not like enacting Protocol 38. It was such a bother. A complete shutdown and recalibration, after summoning a Tactical Engineer to complete sanitization procedures. That could take some time. Not to mention he really did not get along well with Tactical Engineers. They had no social graces, and they always left the Bridge Terminal in such a mess. Quite destructive units, actually. Such a bother.

He almost managed a real sigh of frustration as he plopped back into his docking bay and gently connected his 64 pin integrated data cable to the master control console. Light pulses flashed back and forth inside the cables. Data was transferred. Algorithms executed logic sequences. Records were tabulated and assessed.

It seemed there had been a quite serious biological incursion throughout the Bridge Terminal hallways. The thermal units were reporting all invasive species exterminated. However, they also reported two sentient biological species working in coordinated fashion with a Monitoring and Reporting drone. That was unusual. MaR drones did not tend to interact. They just, well, monitored and reported.

No matter. That would be an item for the Tactical Engineer to investigate. The thermal sanitization units had all returned and placed themselves back in standby mode. It was time to enact Protocol 38.

After a last centichron to enjoy the routine rhythm of his

humming power plants—he did find the thrum of 66.3 oscillations per centichron comforting—Custodian 452 sent the command sequence necessary, initiating the shutdown of the entire Planetary Bridge Terminal, and all but three of the enormous geothermal power plants.

Behind him, a concealed steel panel unlatched and inched open with a drawn-out *crack* of ancient airtight seals breaking their adhesion. The Bridge Control Chamber would now be accessible to the Tactical Engineer. 452 hoped his terminal would not get *too* messy.

—21—

The Shutdown

The lift platform returned, having delivered Ima and Garran successfully to the one hundred and thirty-second floor. Emily and Stephanie stepped on next, and hit the twelfth button. Poppie fluttered above them, having apparently decided to join the lead teams. Stephanie, wearing a big grin, waved goodbye to those still waiting, as if she were clanking away on an amusement park roller coaster. The optimism of children never ceased to amaze Ben.

They chit-chatted while waiting for the elevator's return. Ben got more details from everyone about their adventures, and he shared more information about the world outside the spider caves. He was still unsure about the mantises intentions, friend or foe. He thought that they were enough of an ally to ask for help if he ever needed them again, but he would work hard to never need them again. Calliope was definitely disappointed she would not get a chance to camp at that mountain lake, but she agreed with her dad that it was not worth fighting through the spider caves.

The elevator returned, right on time. Ben and Calliope stepped on, dropping their packs between them, at their feet.

"See you in about thirty minutes," Ben nodded to his dad.

"Right behind you," Nigel said.

The lift rose and soon all light from the basement was cut off by the elevator shaft. Calliope and Ben pulled out their headlamps and clicked them on.

"This is pretty tight," said Ben.

"Yep. It is," said Calliope. "Keep your arms and legs in the vehicle at all times."

"Got that right," agreed her dad.

They rose at a steady pace, passing an exit chamber every twelve floors, about every thirty seconds or so. Calliope counted them as they passed, gauging how far they had come. Ben found the softly rumbling ride to be quite relaxing, compared to all the other travel he had done in The City.

He pondered that name for a minute. Maybe 'The City of Doors' was not appropriate anymore, if there was an actual city outside this building. And 'The Building of Doors' did not sound right. No rhythm. Too many syllables. Of course, they could always use the Sprites' name: Chathair Doras. That was a lofty name, a chunky name that one had to wrap one's mouth around to pronounce. But this *was* a lofty building, even a chunky building that one had to wrap one's mind around to understand and respect. Hmm. Maybe he would give this problem to the girls to solve.

"One more section to go," said Calliope, as they passed the tenth chamber.

Only a few seconds above that, the elevator let out a soft whine, then ground to a halt.

"Oh, no," said Calliope. "What's going on now?"

"I have no idea," said Ben. "Maybe it will start back up. Let's give it a minute. Maybe it has to charge its batteries."

"Maybe," said Calliope. "Poppie seems to need recharging. Maybe this is similar."

"Except," interjected Ben, "I would assume it would return to a defined recharging station, not stop in between floors like this. Like our robot vacuum cleaner at home."

"Yeah, it should be going back to the basement, probably," agreed Calliope. "This isn't right."

Ben thought for a minute. He was pretty sure he knew what their next steps would be, but he did want to give the elevator—or The City —time to work out whatever kink had stopped the mechanism.

"Dad, nothing's happening," said Calliope.

He sighed. "Nope. I think we're on our own here, Calli."

"So we climb?" Ben detected a little more excitement in her voice than he felt himself.

"We climb, kiddo. But carefully."

"Always, dad."

Calliope stepped onto the rungs and began the ascent.

"No rest for the weary," Ben said to himself, then followed behind his rapidly scrambling daughter.

****

Stephanie had already inserted her squashed-pen door key and opened the way into the halls. Garran and Ima were out and about, scouting with Poppie, verifying the spiders had been eradicated. So far, it all looked clear, except for the ash.

Emily sat against the wall. Even though Stephanie's pin had activated the hallway lighting, and the soft glow was bleeding well into the elevator room, she still held her flashlight. Every few minutes, she clicked it on and gazed down the shaft, trying to see Ben and Calliope on the rise. So far, nothing. It had been ten minutes since they sent the lift down, it would be a few more before it returned. Assuming they had gotten on and started up immediately.

The City lights began to dim; a slow fade of their bright, flame-colored tones to a low-burning amber, to a dying candlelight. The usual signs of a control pin leaving the area.

"Stephanie, honey, you should probably sit closer to the door, so your pin keeps the lights on for Ima and Garran."

"Sure," Stephanie said.

She moved through the doorway and into the hall. But the lights did not grow brighter; they fluttered out with a final, somewhat unusual sputter and a flicker, like they had tried to burn brighter, to obey the control pin, but had spent the last dredges of whatever fuel supplied their power.

"That's weird," said Stephanie. She stepped further into the hall. "The lights won't come back on."

"Ugh. What now."

Emily climbed to her feet and joined her daughter. Her light lit up the hallway for about twenty feet. Stephanie had stowed her headlamp in her pack, but she pulled it back out and added its light to her mother's.

"Garran? Ima?" Emily sent a loud whisper down the hall.

"They may not have noticed the lights going out," said Stephanie. "They went pretty far down the hall, and they don't use pins, so it was already dark for them."

"Right," said Emily. "Well, they should be back in a few anyway. And Ben and Calliope should be here soon."

"Uh, what if the elevator stopped, too?" asked Stephanie, suddenly worried for her friend.

"Shoot!" Emily spouted softly.

Both ladies rushed to the elevator. They pointed their lights down the shaft. Two staggered and waving lights pointed back, still several floors below.

"Ben!" Emily repeated her loud whisper into the pit. "Ben, can you hear me?"

The lights below stopped moving around, pointed straight up. From a distance, Ben answered.

"We hear you. The elevator stopped. We're not sure why, but Calliope figures we can climb the eleven or so floors to you. Be there in a minute. Or ten."

"The lights went out up here, too," said Emily. "Do you think the whole City shut down?"

"Maybe," his answer drifted up. "Let's figure it out when we're out of this hole."

"Right. Sorry. Good luck," she whisper-shouted.

The wait seemed interminable, even though it was only a few minutes. Stephanie kept poking her head down the shaft, whispering encouragement to the climbers. Emily kept a wary eye on the hallway, not trusting that the spiders were all truly gone, but also hoping Ima and Garran would return soon.

Finally, Calliope's hand slapped onto the chamber floor. Stephanie reached down to grab her pack and helped haul her friend over the rim. Calliope rolled and sat on the floor, shaking the strain from her hands, rolling her ankles to relax the muscles through to her cramped toes.

"Whew. Good thing we hadn't had to climb back up after climbing down last time. We were right, it is much harder coming up."

Ben's head popped over the edge. Emily repeated her daughter's maneuver, hauling on Ben's much larger pack.

"Damn it, Sullivan! Can't anything be easy in this place?" Emily huffed.

"Tell me about it," he said, a bit out of breath. "It's looking like I'm going to have to walk down two thousand stairs to get my dad and the others, then walk back up those same two thousand. My dad is *not* going to be happy."

"I'll come with you, dad," offered Calliope.

"Oh, no," Ben said. "You are going home with Emily and Stephanie. I want you three safe and sound before anything else happens. We're too close to home to get waylaid now."

"But dad!" she began.

"No buts. We are not sure the spiders are gone. I don't want to worry about the three of you. I want you out of here."

"I agree with your dad. We need to get home. We've had a long, long day," said Emily.

Stephanie remained quiet. She was torn between supporting her friend, and her desire to get home and never see another spider again. She also had no desire to make a round-trip on two thousand six hundred and twenty stairs. Uh-uh, no thank you.

"Unfortunately, it seems you will have to postpone going home," Garran's voice came from the doorway. The sprites' quiet return had gone unnoticed. "The doorways are no longer working."

"What!" exclaimed Emily. "What do you mean, 'not working'?"

"As we were walking down the hallways, checking for spider signs, we heard clanks and clicks from the doors near us. We reluctantly decided to open a door with an innocuous insignia; a beach, backed by tropical plants, and no animals. However, the door would not open. The handle would not turn." Garran's wooden face betrayed no emotion, but his voice was tinged with concern.

"We tried several other doors after that," added Ima. "None of them would open."

"Sullivan!" Emily drew out his name, simultaneously inflecting it with blame and a charge to act.

"I don't know." Ben raised his arms in helplessness. "Poppie, do you know what's happening?"

"Pop, pop," came the pixie's response.

Ben thought she even looked confused. Maybe her fluttering was a bit jittery. That could not be a good sign, either.

"It's obviously something to do with the power going out," Ben said. "And I think we know where the power is coming from."

"The basement!" said Calliope, in triumph. She was not in the least discouraged by this new predicament.

"The basement," said Ben.

"The basement?" echoed Emily. "All of us?"

"Unless you want to stay here. Waiting for who knows how long.

Not knowing what's going on," said Ben in resignation. "I think it's best if we all stick together."

"Me too," said Calliope. That earned her a disapproving look from her dad.

"I want to stay together, too, mom," said Stephanie. "I don't want to be in the dark, just us."

Emily sighed. "Me either, honey. All right, Sullivan. Let's go."

Ben had a sinking suspicion that his dinner date was now in question.

****

Nigel watched his son and granddaughter's feet disappear into the tube. Nothing to do but wait now. Fifteen minutes and it would be his turn. He gave Spot a quick scrub under the chin, then took some time to wander around a little more. He was very interested in the Cookers. Mostly, he was interested in how to turn one off, should he ever be trapped by one. From what he could see, there were no external buttons, or knobs, or switches. Just neatly folded pipes, and two antennae-looking things on top. Maybe breaking off the antennae would sever communication and render the thing inert, but Nigel had his doubts. Still, it was something.

"Nigel Sullivan," Sonam called out. "Something is happening."

"Is the elevator back?" Nigel asked.

The sprites, however, were not looking at the elevator corner. They were looking down the opposite wall, along the rows of mainframes.

"Not the elevator. The machines in this room. They appear to be shutting down," said the willowy sprite.

Nigel did not see any difference in the metal contraptions nearest him. In fact, the entire row along the closest wall looked normal; vacuum tubes glowing, all gears moving, and other parts whistling and whining and clicking at usual levels.

"Down there," Sonam pointed to the far end. "That far row has gone dark. And quiet."

Nigel gazed far down the huge room, but could not tell what was going on at this distance.

"A second row has gone still, two rows closer," added Kunga.

"Let's check it out." Nigel began walking across the cavernous room.

He could see it now. Not just two rows, but several end units had gone quiet. Nigel peered down an isle. The boxes closest to him were still working, but the gears on the fourth one in had stopped. The lights in its vacuum tubes faded, then went out. The boxes on either side of that one quickly followed. All around, now, Nigel could see the strange machines winding down.

"What in the world is going on, now?" he mused aloud.

"That is unknown, Nigel Sullivan," said Sonam. "But I do not think it is a good thing."

As if to underscore Sonam's point, the yellow tinged lighting faded, and was replaced by red.

"Well, that's certainly not a good thing," Nigel said. "On Earth, red always means danger. And the fact that this place changed from normal light to red light as things are shutting down, suggests red means the same here. Let's hope we don't hear alarms go off next. That usually follows red lighting, and alarms are a sure sign something bad is about to happen. Catastrophic, even, when you're inside a power plant."

They all waited quietly, half expecting a siren. Nigel held his breath in anticipation. No alarm came. It actually got quieter as more of the mainframes shut down. Soon, the only machines working were far down at the other end of the cavern. Nigel could just make out their glowing lights and hear their soft whines.

"Things seem to have reached some kind of end state," said Nigel.

"I don't see any more changes."

"Aye, it be very quiet now," whispered Tormad. The place did seem to warrant caution and stealth.

"Maybe we should return and check the elevator," suggested Sonam. "Perhaps it has returned."

They resumed their places around the elevator. Nigel even pointed his light straight up the shaft, but he saw no platform, no movement. Spot was at his feet, also looking up.

"I can't tell if anything is coming down, or if this thing has gone dead as well," he commented to the sprites.

"From what the females told us, and the two examples we have seen, the elevator should have returned some time ago," said Kunga. "It seems logical that the device has stopped working, as well. Which would mean, we are on our own."

"Oh, man," sighed Nigel. "Two thousand stairs."

"It be right easy," said Tormad. "One step after another. Be thankful it's no on the side o' a mountain, with a wind blowin' ya dis way 'n dat. An' hail rainin' down like small hammers."

"Right. It's all sunshine and lollipops," mumbled Nigel. He looked down at Spot. "Ok, boy. Let's go find Ben."

The remaining team members headed for the stairs.

—22—

When One Door Closes

S omeone is ascending below us," whispered Ima.

She and Garran were always a level ahead of the rest, but they had paused at their latest; level 41, if Ben was keeping the correct count. He could check with Stephanie. She always had the right count.

"Friend or foe?" asked Emily.

"We believe," said Garran with a touch of mirth in his voice, "it is at least Ben's father and Tormad. One voice seems to be complaining about the climb, and the other is complaining about the complaining."

Ben chuckled. "That sounds like them, all right. They are not going to be happy about going back down to the basement, either."

"Maybe they know what's going on," said Calliope.

"Either way, let's save them a couple of levels and hustle down to them," suggested Emily.

They intercepted the ascending group on level 36. After stories were exchanged, everyone agreed that all clues pointed to a problem with the power, and the power started in the basement. So, the caravan did an about-face and headed down.

They reached the basement, with its red glow still in effect, and most mechanicals still powered down. All but the four mainframes closest to the tunnel leading back to the power room were dark.

"Why do you suppose these are still running?" Emily had sidled up next to Ben to ask quietly. They had all slipped into a library-whisper and soft-footed sneaking manner.

"My guess," he leaned in to whisper back, and caught the scent of coconut in her hair, "is that this place is running on backup power. So only necessary systems are kept running. Those four mainframes—if that's what they even are—are necessary for keeping something else running."

"Backup power? But there are hundreds of generators down that hall. How could they all have failed at once?"

"I don't know. Let's go see."

Ben led the group into the dark tunnel. Each human had revived a headlamp or flashlight, so the walkway was polka-dotted with beams swaying this way and that. Calliope found it rather spooky, and exciting. She looked around at the others. Their group was quite large now. It was comforting, having all of her friends and family around her. Stephanie by her side, probably counting the number of steps from one end of the hallway to the other. Her dad, head down and whispering something to Ms. LaPointe. Did he just sniff her hair? Gross, dad! Grandpa was trucking along, looking younger than Calliope had seen him in years, every once in a while reaching down to pet Spot. Maybe grandpa should get a dog. Or a puma. And Spot seemed to enjoy having multiple people giving him attention. Even the sprites were starting to interact with the blinx.

Ima was up front, with Garran at her side, of course. That sprite was for sure in love with Ima. And why not? She was so cool. Graceful, and deadly, and very pretty for a tree.

She glanced back to see Tormad stalking along. He acted all gruff and surly, but those were always the ones in stories that looked out for everyone else. The caretaker of the group. The solid force nothing could shake. His eyes watched all around, and up to the ceiling, then behind to check on Sonam and Kunga. The mother lion, keeping an eye on her cubs. Calliope snorted softly to herself. The old evergreen would not appreciate that image.

And then there were Sonam and Kunga. Always so relaxed, and peaceful. Their willow dreads bouncing along like jellyfish swimming through the air. As always, they were heads together, probably talking philosophy or healing techniques, or maybe their newest passion: rock climbing.

She turned back around, very content to be with this crew. She wasn't sure she wanted this adventure to end. She surely did not want to run into any more spiders, or Slizeg, or Tree Lords, but she did like exploring this place. At least they were going to do a little more of that.

Garran and Ima were almost to the end. Did Garran just smell Ima's crown needles? Gross!

The group emerged from the tunnel to find the generator cavern lights at the same low-level red tone as the mainframe room. The sound level had dropped, too. Most of the generators had to have shut down. Some were still going, though. Ben could hear them distinctly below the platform.

As a group, they hustled over to the railing and looked down. Yes. Only the first generator of each row was running. Three generators out of hundreds. That couldn't be an accident. One generator down was a faulty wire. A dozen generators down, or an entire row, was a cascade failure problem; and bad architecture, to be sure. But hundreds of generators down, while the first three are still up? No, that suggested a plan. A reset maybe? A maintenance period?

"Poppie," Ben addressed their guide, "is there a control panel or maintenance display panel or something that could give us a clue as to what is going on?"

"Pop," said Poppie.

She flew to the nearest stair and zig-zagged down. The rest of the group followed, a few steps behind. At the bottom, they realized the true scope of the generators. Five times taller than any of them, and the size of a small house, they were massive metal contraptions. Their humming was the dull roar of a few dozen bowling balls rolling down an alley.

Poppie flew deeper underneath the platform from which they had just descended from. Back in the darkness, small points of light arranged in a circle intimated some sort of monitoring station. She flew straight toward them, then hovered. As Ben and the group approached, their headlamps pulled back the veil of black to reveal a C-shaped bank of computers from the 1950's NASA Mission Control room. No. Ben corrected himself. Not NASA. This was more like the control room for the Three Mile Island nuclear power plant. It was not painted the same mint green, but the top panel was jam-packed with lights and gauges and gears and switches and wires and maybe some buttons. It was a mess, and definitely not made to be monitored by humans. But possibly perfect for the steampunk robot snowman sitting in the center of the C, plugged in at its belly, waving four arms at Poppie, and not looking too happy to have visitors.

Poppie had her antennae up, electrical sparks flying between them. She did not look happy, either.

"I think they're arguing," said Stephanie.

"I think you're right," said Emily.

"He's quite the copper operator," said Ben. "Look at all those arms. He fits right in the command console, too. There's even a little indentation in the floor for him, so he doesn't roll around."

Ben was leaning over the control panel, peeking around. Custodian 452 spun his torso section in Ben's direction, momentarily pausing his argument with Poppie to wave three nickel plated arms at the human.

"Ok, ok. I'm backing off." Ben hopped back from the control panel.

"I don't see any red lights, or blinking things, or warning signals of any kind." He looked up at Poppie. "Poppie, if I may interrupt.

Do you know if he purposely shut down the generators?"

"Pop," came her quick response.

"He did? Was there a malfunction?"

"Pop, pop."

"Good. Can he turn them back on?"

"Pop, pop, pop."

"That's a maybe, dad," said Calliope.

"Hmm. So, let's assume he turned them off for a reason. Does it have anything to do with the spiders?"

"Pop, pop, pop."

"Another maybe," Stephanie offered.

"Does it have anything to do with us?" chipped in Emily.

"Pop, pop, pop."

"Well, that's not good," said Nigel.

"Is he performing maintenance?" asked Ben.

"Pop."

"Good. Will he turn the power back on when maintenance is done?" asked Emily.

"Pop, pop."

"No?! Why not?" Emily's frustration came through.

"It has to be a yes or no question, mom."

"Poppie, ask him if all of the spiders are gone from The City." Ben wanted to at least establish their safety.

Poppie threw some sparks. The copper snowman threw a few sparks of his own. It seemed the sparse copper coils on his head were antennae, just like Poppies. Just curly, and haphazardly placed.

After a brief exchange, Poppie turned back to the group and gave a "Pop."

"Oh, thank goodness," exhaled Stephanie.

"Great," continued Ben. "Would you please ask him if he could just turn on the doorway to our home, and the doorway to the Sprite's home?"

Poppie relayed the question, then the response. "Pop, pop."

A collective groan puffed from the group.

"It's probably an all-or-nothing setup," said Nigel. "He probably has to turn them all on, or all off."

"Pop," agreed Poppie.

"What about helping with maintenance," suggested Ben. "Can we help him with whatever maintenance he has to do?"

"Pop, pop," came the relayed answer.

Ben was out of questions. He was not sure what else they could do but wait. The rest of the group agreed; nothing to do but wait for The City to reboot itself. That led to more muttering, more wandering, and a little exploring.

Poppie kept up her somewhat heated conversation, but it looked like the control room's occupant had calmed down a bit. Ben got the impression that if the copper robot could cross his arms and put a nose up in the air, it would. He seemed to not approve of others in his area. If anyone got too close to his precious table of gizmos and gadgets, he made *shooing* motions in their direction, and emitted a few beeps and squeaks.

He reminded Ben of old man Dabrowski on the corner lot, always yelling at people to "Get off my lawn!" Grumpy and surly, but relatively harmless. He shared this with Calliope and Stephanie—frequent targets of Mr. Dabrowski's attitude—and they both laughed in agreement, immediately affixing the moniker to the robot; he was now Mr. Copper Dabrowski. The girls said it had a nice rhythm. They repeated it over and over, faster and faster for the next few minutes, until Emily politely told them they were getting on her nerves.

Once the joking had run its course, the group spread out in rough pairs. Stephanie and Calliope stuck around Poppie and Mr. Dabrowski. Sonam and Kunga were examining the closest working generator, fascinated by its many working parts. Ima and Garran explored further down the generator room, securing the perimeter, even traveling back upstairs and over to the mainframe room to make sure nothing had changed.

Tormad stuck with Ben and Nigel, who were discussing food and water rationing. They were thinking Poppie might know the closest Garden room to the basement. Ben and Nigel were not looking forward to a diet of plums, but the clean water would be necessary for everyone in the group.

Emily was reluctant to wander far from the girls, so she chose to see what other surprises this control area had to offer. She found an alcove around the corner with over two dozen wonky adjustable tubes that were dripping some thick blackish goop. Gross. She moved along. The walls were bare. Metal, like everywhere else in this godforsaken place, but lacking in any sort of decoration. No etchings, no filigree, no embossings. Plain, plain, plain. And boring. But that was a good thing. She liked boring when it came to The City.

But wait. Why was that section of wall bumped out further than the rest? Emily walked carefully over to the anomaly. The edge of one wall panel was definitely offset. In fact, the entire panel was angled, like it was falling off the wall it was attached to. Hesitantly, she pushed on it. It moved back into place, then bounced out again. She switched tactics and pulled gently. It swung towards her, easily.

"Uh, Sullivans!" she called out. "I think I found a door. And it seems to lead outside."

This caught the attention of the entire team. Even Poppie stopped her conversation with Mr. Dabrowski and flittered over.

Emily was not wrong. What appeared to have been a normal wall panel—well, normal for this place—was actually a four inch thick steel door. It had no handles, no visible locking bolts, no signs saying "exit" or "this way out." It was secret. Covert, one might suggest. But open. And it opened to actual daylight, and a view of the city streets, and the strange buildings Emily and the girls had seen from the penthouse observatory.

"Wow," said Calliope.

"No," said Emily. "I know what you are all thinking. And we should *not* go out there."

"Poppie," Ben addressed the pixie, but did not take his eyes off the scene outside the doorway, "will Mr. Dabrowski be finished with his maintenance anytime soon?"

"Pop, pop."

"Would it be ok for us to go out and look around out there?" he asked.

Poppie took a few seconds to answer, "pop." Her pause did not give Emily much confidence.

Ben looked around at the others. No one offered up an opinion.

"Dad, what do you think?" Ben asked Nigel.

Nigel thought for a minute. "Well, we're going to need food and water. There might be someplace out there with more than plums. And if we have the time, I think it would be worthwhile trying to learn as much as we can about this place."

"Anyone else object? Besides Emily?"

No one did. Ben turned to Emily and gave her a questioning, pleading look, one eyebrow raised, head slightly cocked.

"Ugh, fine! But don't say I didn't warn all of you. This is going to blow up in our faces somehow. You mark my words."

"Noted," Ben said. "Ok, gang. Let's see what we can find out about this world."

"Well, dad," Calliope smiled up at her father, "here we go on another adventure."

"Here we go, kiddo," said Ben. "Here we go."

"Yippie," mumbled Emily with disdain, just loud enough for the group to hear.

Stephanie put her arm through her mom's.

"I got you mom. We'll be fine."

Before they left, Calliope called out to the copper robot. "Bye Mr. Copper Dabrowski! We'll be back soon!" She gave a wave.

Resuming their reconnaissance positions, the team exited Generator Room 1 for the open air spaces of a crazy new world.

****

Custodian 452 could not believe the impertinence of the monitoring and reporting drone. For starters, it said it had a name: Poppie. A name! Of course she had a name. It was Monitoring and Reporting Drone 128. Custodian 452 would even grant it the nickname of MRD-128. But "Poppie?" That was illogical. It provided no description of its purpose.

Second of all, it said it was a "she." What was a she? It was an it. And it/she was calling Custodian 452 a "him." What was a him? It/she said his attitude was "unemotional, inflexible, and inconsiderate. Surely, Custodian 452 was a him." To which Custodian 452 replied that he required more data in order to have a more logical conversation with this unit. It/she was clearly malfunctioning.

However, it/she had mentioned that the biological units just wanted to go back to their respective planets. And that they had offered to help with maintenance duties in order to expedite their exodus. Custodian 452 was more than willing to expedite their departure. Unfortunately, he had already called for the Tactical Engineer, and *that* unit would expedite their removal with extreme prejudice and absolute certainty.

Custodian 452 dismissed Monitoring and Reporting Drone 128, letting it know the conversation was ended and they should both return to their duties. It/he was disappointed, however, when MRD-128 let the biological units exit from Generator Room 1 through the egress panel and into the greater compound. With an almost-sigh, wind-down-groan of his root planetary gearbox, Custodian 452 plugged back into the communications panel and sent new directions to the Tactical Engineer: the biological units had escaped from the Planetary Bridge Terminal and were now on the loose. Acquire and expire.

He unplugged and returned to his maintenance checks of the generators; 430 calibrations, taking 25.0125 centichrons each, per generator. It would take some time to complete them all. And until his tasks were discharged, he would not get his S22L mist bath. Unfortunate.

At least that gave the Tactical Engineer some time to execute his duties. Nothing could restart until cleansing was finalized. The sooner the biological units were removed and all traces expunged, the better.

With as much of a haughty attitude as a custodial unit could offer, 452 extended appendage 14 and plugged into port 60, thereby engaging the calibration algorithm and beginning his accumulation and evaluation of statistical feedback from generator 001. It was some consolation to Custodian 452 that he did find statistical processing relaxing. Perhaps this shutdown was not all bad.

Epilogue

In Building 1860, Maintenance Sub Annex, Slot 9, Tactical Engineer 5513 powered back to life. Its internal titanium gears squeaked and stuck, but begrudgingly moved, engaging mechanisms that had slept for centuries. Copper arteries carried much needed lubricants from a central pump and reservoir, throughout TE5513's frame to alleviate the friction. In its main operations module—a globe section sitting atop an extendable tube, riding above its chassis—TE5513's processing center sparked into consciousness. Boot commands, etched eons ago into flawless crystalline carbon cubes, began to execute.

> Startup procedures...
> Core system checks...
> Map of compound 27...
> Map of adjacent compound 486...
> Map of adjacent compound 551...
> Wireframe diagrams for buildings 000001 through 501970...
> Machine schematics 0000001 through 8232762...
> Service duty list...
> Extermination protocols...
> Weapons checks...

Despite age, all systems were nominal.

Coiled copper wires, sprouting haphazardly around the outside rim of its operations module bounced lazily as the globe rotated left, then right. The coils sent query signals out to the Directorate, then switched to receive mode, awaiting commands. Almost immediately, instructions were received, and TE5513 acknowledged.

Its control globe bobbled a bit as one of three chunky legs stepped heavily forward, moving the blocky, pear-shaped trunk from its port in Slip 9. TE5513 took a moment to direct lubricant into joints of all appendages. The next step, second leg, was a deliberate exercise.

> Raise leg 2, top joint, 45 degrees...
> Balance...
> Raise leg 2, second joint, 45 degrees...
> Lower leg 2, second joint, 20 degrees...
> Rotate three-pronged landing pad...
> Reset three-pronged landing pad...
> Push forward with lower appendage three...
> Obtain optimal floor contact with all three prongs of landing pad 2...
> Step complete...
> Maneuverability within acceptable parameters...
> Commence command execution...

TE5513 lurched from Slot 9, its gyroscopic navigational systems performing calibrations and improvements with each shank's descending *thunk*. By the time it reached the eastern egress of Building 1860, Maintenance Sub Annex, TE5513 was skittering along efficiently and quietly. Silicone cushioned landing pads absorbed the weight of TE5513's considerable bulk as it moved to methodically carry out its orders.

> Navigate to Planetary Bridge Terminal, Generator Room 1...
> Inspect control chamber for incursion...
> Sanitize all biological contaminants...

The End

Of Silk and Fang

A Sullivan Chronicles Adventure